Silent
Hearts

ALSO BY GWEN FLORIO

Under the Shadows
Reservations
Disgraced
Dakota
Montana

Silent Hearts

A NOVEL

GWEN FLORIO

ATRIA BOOKS

New York   London   Toronto   Sydney   New Delhi

ATRIA
BOOKS

An Imprint of Simon & Schuster, Inc.
1230 Avenue of the Americas
New York, NY 10020

First Atria Books hardcover edition July 2018

ATRIA BOOKS and colophon are trademarks of Simon & Schuster, Inc.

For information about special discounts for bulk purchases, please contact Simon & Schuster Special Sales at 1-866-506-1949 or business@simonandschuster.com.

The Simon & Schuster Speakers Bureau can bring authors to your live event. For more information or to book an event, contact the Simon & Schuster Speakers Bureau at 1-866-248-3049 or visit our website at www.simonspeakers.com.

Interior design by Amy Trombat

Manufactured in the United States of America

10 9 8 7 6 5 4 3 2 1

Library of Congress Cataloging-in-Publication Data

Names: Florio, Gwen, [date] – author.
Title: Silent hearts / Gwen Florio.
Description: First Atria Books hardcover edition. | New York : Atria Books, 2018.
Identifiers: LCCN 2017057630 (print) | LCCN 2018000966 (ebook) | ISBN 9781501181948 (ebook) | ISBN 9781501181924 (hardback) | ISBN 9781501181931 (paperback)
Subjects: | BISAC: FICTION / Literary. | FICTION / Contemporary Women. | FICTION / Cultural Heritage.
Classification: LCC PS3606.L664 (ebook) | LCC PS3606.L664 S55 2018 (print) | DDC 813/.6—dc23
LC record available at https://lccn.loc.gov/2017057630

ISBN 978-1-5011-8192-4
ISBN 978-1-5011-8194-8 (ebook)

For Scott
and for Razia

One

Each day she remained unmarried, Farida Basra played At Least.

She turned to the game as she waited for her bus on a street lined with high, bougainvillea-adorned stucco walls that shielded the homes of Islamabad's wealthy from the envious and resentful. A woman squatted knees to chin beside her, scraping at the filthy pavement with her broom of twigs. Her skin was nearly black from long hours in the sun. Farida drew forward her *dupatta*, the filmy shawl-like scarf that covered her chest and shoulders. She reminded herself to be thankful.

I may be poor, but at least I'm not a street sweeper.

She stepped back as a family approached on a motorbike. A graybeard husband drove while his young wife clung to him from behind with one arm, cradling an infant with the other. An older child sat in front of the husband, a younger behind the wife. Dust boiled in their wake.

I may still be unmarried, but at least I'm not bound to a man old enough to be my father.

She nodded to a group of schoolgirls in their blue uniforms and white head scarves, and directed the game toward them. *No matter what happens to you, at least your education will protect you*—that was the mantra her

1

father had taught her. He was a professor whose own professor father had made the mistake of opposing Partition from India and spent the rest of his life in unwilling atonement, opportunities snatched away, income and status dwindling apace.

"But he gave me an education, and I have given you the same," Latif Basra would tell his daughters. "It is how this family will work its way back to its rightful place. I have done my best. Now it is up to your sons." At which Farida and her sister, Alia, would study the floor, saving their rebellious responses for whispered nighttime conversations in their bedroom.

Farida let the dupatta slide back to her shoulders and held her head higher, mentally commanding the schoolgirls to see in her what she saw in herself—a professional woman, heading home from her job as an interpreter in the commercial Blue Zone, her satchel stuffed with important papers, her brain buzzing with phrases in English, German, French. Men, her own countrymen and even some foreigners, might disparage her skills and regard her work as little more than a front for prostitution. But those were old attitudes, fast being discarded in Pakistan's cities, if not the countryside. No longer, as she told her parents nightly and to no avail, did a woman need a husband. Not in the year 2001, when so many things were possible for women.

The girls rounded a corner, laughter floating behind them like the trailing ends of their head scarves. Farida tamped down envy. Old enough for some independence, still too young for the pressure of marriage, the girls had one another. Alia had departed the household for her own marriage, one that so far had produced only daughters, leaving Farida alone with her parents' dwindling expectations.

She braced herself for another evening involving a strained conversation over indifferent food prepared by a cook who also doubled as a housekeeper. Most of Farida's inadequate salary went to her parents for household expenses and helped maintain a toehold on the fringes of respectability, even if that proximity had yet to result in a marriage for her.

Her father and mother were too polite to remind Farida of how quickly she had taken to the unimagined freedoms she'd found when the family lived in England several years earlier. She was still paying for it. The fact that her work as an interpreter required constant contact with foreigners did not help her case. Despite her beauty, her parents had not been able to arrange a match with an appropriate civil servant, a teacher, or even a shopkeeper. According to her parents, these groups were the only ones who could accept her level of education along with the faint tarnish to her reputation from the time abroad. It clung to her like a cloying perfume, even after all these years. She had faced a dwindling procession of awkward second cousins and middle-aged widowers, men with strands of oily hair combed over shiny pates, men whose bellies strained at the waists of wrinkled shirts, men whose thick fingers were none too clean, men who nonetheless frowned at her with the same suspicion and aversion with which she viewed them.

By now, despite her mother's attempts to persuade her otherwise, Farida knew there was no man she could ever imagine herself loving.

Even as her potential suitors drifted away—marrying other girls less beautiful, perhaps, but also less questionable—so did her friends, into arranged marriages of their own, quickly followed by the requisite production of children. Their paths diverged, and she instead hid behind her work.

Farida shouldered her way from the bus and pushed open the gate to the pounded-dirt courtyard. What should she expect from her parents tonight? The silence, her parents retreating after dinner into the solace of books and music? Or more badgering?

"Farida!" Her father burst out of the front door, arms spread wide. He folded her into an embrace, an intimacy he'd not permitted himself since she was a child.

She extricated herself with relief and suspicion, the latter ascendant as she took in his appearance. "Is that a new suit?"

He stepped back and turned in a circle, inviting her admiration for the summer-weight worsted, cut expertly to disguise his sagging stomach and spreading bum. "What do you think of your papa now?"

"What happened to the old one?" A rusty black embarrassment, gone threadbare in the elbows and knees.

He waved a dismissive hand. "Gone." Sold, no doubt, to a rag merchant.

Farida's mother appeared in the doorway. She raised her arm in greeting. Wide gold bangles, newly bought, rang against one another, their hopeful notes at odds with her stricken expression. "Your father has a surprise."

Which was how Farida discovered that for the bride price of some twenty-two-carat jewelry, a knockoff designer suit, and almost certainly a newly fattened bank account, Latif Basra had betrothed his remaining daughter to the illiterate son of an Afghan strongman.

"It will be a disaster."

Alia, summoned by simultaneous phone calls from her mother and her sister, stood over Farida as she sobbed facedown on her childhood bed. Alia was one of the few women in Islamabad with a driver's license, and she used it whenever she could, which was rarely. It was after dark, dangerous for a woman to be on the road. For her to be here was a measure of her alarm.

Hearing her sister's words, Farida sat up and reached for the bookshelves, pulling out volumes at random and flinging them across the room.

"What use will I have for these now?" She raised her voice so that her father, cringing in his study, could hear. She took her gauzy dupatta between her hands and tore at it. "What use have I for this? He'll hide me away in a *burqa*."

She thrust at her sister a leather-bound copy of *Alice's Adventures in Wonderland*, its title stamped in gilt. "And this! He gave me a special edition of my favorite book, to bring to my life with a man who cannot read, not even his own language, let alone English. And these *hideous* bangles." She stripped them from her wrist and threw them at the wall, yelling at her hidden father, "Take these and sell them. Buy yourself another suit!"

Alia kicked the bangles aside and wrestled her younger sister back onto the bed, releasing her only when Farida fell silent. "Stop. It's done. You must decide how you're going to deal with this."

Farida sucked in oxygen. Strands of hair clung to her damp face. Alia smoothed them back and spoke with her usual pragmatism. "Something like this was inevitable. You were never going to be permitted spinsterhood. Not with this." She slid her hand to Farida's chin and turned her sister toward the large mirror across the room. Even red and swollen as a pomegranate, Farida's features—the large eyes beneath swooping brows, the imperious arch of cheekbone and nose, the full lips offset by the darling chin—commanded attention. Alia shrugged at her own reflection. "Who knew that my looks would turn out to be my best advantage?"

Farida leaned against her sister, averting her gaze from the mirror. Where her own features were sharply cut, Alia's doughy flesh was mottled and pitted, the result of adolescent acne. The same small chin that so perfectly balanced Farida's generous mouth was a liability for Alia, nearly disappearing into the plump folds of her neck. Their father had been unable to find a wealthy man for Alia. Instead, he reacted with humiliating gratitude when she suggested to him that most unlikely and unusual of circumstances: a love match. Alia's husband, Rehman Khan, was no less homely than she, albeit small and scrawny where she was large.

"Is he a grown man, or still a boy?" their mother had wondered after meeting him. "Will she be his wife or his mother?"

But like Alia, Rehman was a student of philosophy, and Farida, each time she visited them, was struck anew by their smiling, whispered conversations, more like talk between women friends than husband and wife. The two lived quietly, their lives centered on their studies and their three small girls.

Farida shuddered. She had once recoiled from the prospect of such subdued domesticity. She long assumed a similar match for herself, albeit lacking, of course, the luxury of love. There would have been nightly dinners with his parents and weekend visits to her own family, those gatherings featuring tiresome eyebrow-arching gossip about the people they would inevitably know in common. Now, facing this new, terrifying reality, she yearned for that old scenario of limitations.

Alia retrieved *Alice* from the floor and handed it to her.

Farida clutched it to her chest. "If only I could be like the Cheshire Cat and disappear. If we'd stayed in London, this never would have happened."

Again, Alia splashed her with the icy bath of reality. "If we'd stayed in London, Papa would have gone bankrupt."

Far from being the shortcut to success that Latif Basra had imagined, the family's move to London—where he'd wangled an instructor's position at what turned out to be a second-rate college—involved a succession of increasingly dingy flats, even as his debts piled higher.

"In a way, I suppose you saved him," Alia mused. "Although who would choose that way?"

"Stop." Farida didn't need another reminder that her own behavior had precipitated their hasty return. Those previous suitors, the ones she'd so casually rejected. How could she not have foreseen this inevitable end to her relentless faultfinding? Her parents had done her the favor of seeking out men who, if not wealthy, were at least from their own circle. She'd left her parents no choice but to opt for money. And they, perhaps wisely, had spoken for her this time. To oppose this decision would be to bring shame beyond anything she'd heaped upon them in England.

"You always wanted excitement—new things, different cultures." A filament of anger glowed within Alia's words. Farida realized now how deeply her implied criticism of Alia's life had cut her sister. "Now you will have them."

Two

Gul was twenty-three. War or no war, he was well past the usual age to have a bride chosen for him. Nonetheless, he had balked at his father's choice.

"Punjabi! She will be short. And black-black."

Gul himself was Pashtun, tall and pale, and proud of both. Although the family had fled Afghanistan eight years earlier, Gul knew his father viewed their time in Pakistan as temporary. Nur Muhammed resettled their family as close to home as possible, in Peshawar, not an hour from the border with Afghanistan. Now his father had chosen for him a bride from the Punjab, the very heart of Pakistan. It made no sense.

Nur Muhammed ignored his outburst. "A good family. Educated. College."

Gul set down his tea so hard that some of it sloshed onto the carpet. The scent of cardamom wafted from the wool fibers. A servant crept forward on his knees and blotted at the spot with a towel. Nur Muhammed waved him away.

"College," Gul repeated. He tried to imagine this girl, this dark, ill-mannered girl who most likely resembled the young women he saw whenever he had traveled with his father from Peshawar to business meetings in Pakistan's capital city. He had stared at them, both fascinated and repelled by the way they let their dupattas slip from their heads. The sheer shawls hung about their shoulders, ends teasing the small of their backs. Theirs were nearly the only female faces he had ever seen apart from those of his mother, sister, and aunties. As a boy, of course, he watched the unveiled Kuchi women as the nomad caravans passed on the outskirts of Jalalabad, but his mother always pulled him inside when the Kuchi were about. They were thieves, she had told him, and he was too young then to realize that his mother had worried more about what the Kuchi women might offer than what they could take away.

In Islamabad, unescorted girls clustered outside the restaurants and stores lining the modern capital's broad boulevards, so different from Peshawar's warren of dusty alleyways. The young women in their garments of shimmering embroidered silk were a far cry from those dimly remembered barefoot nomads. Diamond studs winked in their earlobes and noses. Gold banded their wrists. Scarlet stained their lips, and sweeping lines of kohl rimmed their eyes. They stared boldly back at Gul, tittering at the way he followed his father, his plain beige *kameez* flapping at his knees, rubber sandals slapping the sidewalks. Young men his own age lingered nearby, looking arrogant in European-cut suits or blue jeans, and *Amriki*-style sneakers of blinding white, puffy leather. Gul wondered how Americans walked in such footwear without tripping over their own feet.

The boys and girls stood separately, eyeing one another, voices raised, each group's conversation meant to be heard by the other. "They shame their families," Nur Muhammed had once said.

Gul retrieved his tea and sipped. It was cold. "She will be difficult to control. She will shame us."

His father kinked an eyebrow, and Gul realized his mistake. "If you cannot control her," said Nur Muhammed, "then the disgrace will be on you." There was no need to mention Gul's cousin Rashid, whose wife was seen speaking to a male neighbor. Rashid heard the rumors but foolishly refused to believe them until the gossip became so widespread that he had no recourse but to act. He confronted his wife during a family gathering, snatching from her hand the knife she was using to slice the lamb into cubes for the *korma*, slashing at her in front of the horrified women keeping her company in the kitchen. The women shrieked and wept as Rashid's wife staggered moaning toward the door, but they nonetheless blocked her escape, lest the disgrace become even more public than it already was.

Rashid had no choice, of course, but a bit of the cuckold lingered about him after that, and his new wife was nowhere near so beautiful as his first, older and a widow besides, a safer choice, but not one in which a man could take pride.

Gul thought of Rashid and the docile-but-ugly new wife, and his nostrils flared above his dark mustache. There would be no second-best wife for him. "Tell me about the family." His father nodded approval. This was the important thing.

Gul settled back against the cushions, but within moments, he jerked upright. He had expected to hear that the family was wealthy, one of his father's business connections, maybe one who would bring in a side business that he could run.

But no, his father explained. The family had connections, but they had nothing to do with trade. "They are educated," he said again. "They know people."

Gul felt stupid. What good was it to know academics? He himself could barely read or write, his schooling having been so often interrupted.

Again, silence. His father preferred that he work things out for himself rather than ask questions. "The more you ask, the more you reveal," Nur Muhammed liked to say. "The more you listen, the more you know." His father had listened well throughout his lifetime, well enough to know that when the Russian army limped bleeding out of Afghanistan and when the *mujahideen* split into murderous squabbling factions, it was time to reestablish his business and his family across the border in Pakistan. Once resettled in Peshawar, he deftly threaded his way through the web of spies and smugglers and found fortunes to be made in the troubles happening on the other side of the Khyber Pass.

His father motioned to the servant, who crawled to them with a fresh cup of green tea. Gul sipped at it. "They know people," Gul said finally, repeating his father's words. His father was always finding ways to widen his network.

"*Ho*," his father said. He dipped his chin toward his chest, his full gray beard, tinged fashionably orange with henna, brushing his woolen waistcoat. He balanced his cup in his good right hand, the four fingers of the left sliced away years earlier by shrapnel during the civil war after the Russians' retreat. "At the university, her father knows many influential people. Foreigners."

"Does her father speak English?" Gul asked.

"The entire family," his father answered. "They lived in London for some years, I believe. And they speak German and French, too, as well as Urdu, Dari, and even Pashto. Which is even more helpful to us, here." Approval crept into his voice.

"Ah." A tray of almonds and raisins appeared at Gul's elbow, and he scooped up a handful and munched them. Most of the vineyards on the Shomali Plain north of Kabul had been destroyed, first by the Russians and then by the infighting between local factions. But some still produced the green grapes that made the plump golden raisins so sweet. His father willingly paid extra to import them. It was a small weakness, one easily exploited by Nur Muhammed's trading partners—or so they thought. Gul knew his father let them overcharge him. They might think they'd taken advantage of him, his father said, but this small matter would cause them to drop their guard in larger, more important dealings.

"As I have said, they are no longer wealthy. The father's family opposed Partition," Nur Muhammed said. "He teaches some courses at the university, but because of his background, he will never be full faculty. This presents difficulties, financial difficulties." He filled his mouth with raisins and chewed noisily. "You understand that this is a man accustomed to fine things, who wants his own family to have those things. To get them, he works as an interpreter and allows his children to do so, also."

"Who do they work for?"

"Embassies. Journalists. NGOs. Amriki corporations."

"Wait." Gul talked past his father as the thought occurred to him. "The daughters, too?"

His father's mouth twisted. "The family is considered very advanced."

"But she will not work after—" Gul stopped. The thought of marriage still seemed so unreal that he could not speak the word aloud.

Nur Muhammed's eyes flashed a warning. "She will work if we need it." Gul thought of the shame, even as his father continued. "Allowances will be made."

Already, Gul disliked this girl and her American connections, useful though her family surely would be. She would be more than just difficult to control. She would be impossible.

"Her father has been working for some time now for an Amriki corporation that wants the oil. You know the oil I mean." Gul did. A pipeline across Afghanistan would be the most efficient way to transport oil from the north to Pakistan and the waiting tankers at the port in Karachi—a lucrative investment, if only peace could be guaranteed. But that meant dealing with the Taliban, as well as the various groups struggling to overthrow them.

Gul had watched as his father's once-prosperous smuggling network—chiefly opium, depending upon the severity of occasional, half-hearted crackdowns—grew more difficult every year to manage from afar, although still providing a comfortable living. If Nur Muhammed could attach himself to this family, with its links to the oil corporations, it might ease his quest for more cordial dealings with the Taliban—or whoever replaced them. And Gul, through his new wife, was to be Nur Muhammed's entrée into that world. He had longed for the day his father would bring him fully into the business. But like this?

Nur Muhammed spoke again. "At first, the girl's father was very much against this match. I had to work many months. There were sacrifices. Many sacrifices." Gul wondered how large the bride price had been.

"He said she would not want to leave her family. She would not want to come to Peshawar to live with us. A 'dusty frontier town,' I believe her father called it. She would not want to marry an uneducated Pashtun."

Gul stiffened.

Nur Muhammed stopped for another handful of raisins, and when he resumed speaking, his voice had lost some of its harsh tone. "She will be homesick. You will be a cooperative husband. You will bring her often to see her family. You will go with them to visit all of their old friends. She will be happy that you do this for her. She will try to bring you deeper into her own world. You will go. You will become part of it. For her—and for us."

Gul nodded even as he wondered what life would be like with such a wife, one who had spent so much time among the British and maybe even the Amriki. *Their* women were said to presume themselves to be men's equal. Islamabad had its contingent of expats, and Gul had seen their women striding beside their husbands—or maybe even men not their husbands—heads uncovered, voices abrupt, laughing immodestly or sometimes even arguing. Women who confronted their men, demanded things of them. How did these men tolerate such humiliation?

No matter how much his father needed this girl's connections, he vowed he would never become that sort of man.

Three

By eight that night, two hours after she'd expected her husband home, Liv Stoellner had worn a visible track in the living room rug, pacing, pacing, each step bringing her perilously closer to becoming a cliché.

Headlights swept the street outside. Muted sunlight filled the sky, the harsh glare of summer softening as darkness intruded, the street already in deep shadow. Surely that was Martin. Liv reached for the door, the knob cool beneath her fingers. Fine lines threaded its porcelain, the knob an original that, along with the warm cherry woodwork throughout, had drawn Liv to the house over the self-righteous Colonials dominating the neighborhood. Their bungalow, with its deep front porch, its dormer frankly admitting to the tucked-in nature of the second floor, cheered her with its reminder of her Midwest girlhood, when things—and people— weren't quite so . . . *striving*. Like Martin.

She backed away from the door, forced herself into one of the wing-back chairs, propped her feet on a footstool—so casual!—and picked up a book. Martin's dissertation on the end table sought the attention of the rare visitor. She opened to a page of maps. India, Pakistan, Afghanistan, Iran, borders drawn and redrawn, shaded areas indicating various factions depending upon the decade, the century. Martin had just been rejected—again—for a federal grant to travel back to the region, which was considered such a key strategic area when he'd started his career that his adviser had steered him toward it.

"Forget academia," the man had said. "Get yourself one of those sweet State Department jobs, regular raises, great benefits, retire after twenty years." But by the time Martin had worked his way to a doctorate, the U.S. government had already turned its attention away from Afghanistan, and Martin's sporadic attempts to get the funding that would allow him to update the book went nowhere. His dissatisfaction was a vibrating hum in the background of their marriage, one Liv strove to drown out with encouraging words about the next grant application, and the one after that.

The door sighed open. Liv turned a page with exaggerated slowness, took a breath, and worked on her voice.

"Martin?"

"Liv." A purposeful bustling at the door as he untied his shoes and kicked them off, and removed the lightweight blazer he insisted upon wearing, even though the college relaxed its standards during summer sessions. He padded across the rug and brushed her cheek with a kiss.

She breathed in. No cigarettes. Or booze. Or anything musky, damp, and dangerous. Martin just smelled like himself: soap, a hint of sweat, and in a nod to tradition she found endearing, Old Spice. She jerked her head back—she was pissed, after all—but he'd already pulled away, oblivious of her inner turmoil. In the fading light, she saw him as he'd been when they first met, the lanky frame, the extravagant curls. Morning sunshine would reveal the curls gone gray and steel-wool coarse, the fold of flesh beneath his neck, the unavoidable paunch. The voice, though, that hadn't changed, still pitched low, intimate.

"What's up?"

Dinner's in the fridge. Why didn't you call? Where have you been? Who have you been with? Or was it *With whom have you been?* It didn't matter. She wouldn't say it. Would not play the shrew.

"Who's Mandy?" *Hello, shrew.*

Give him credit. No rearing back in bafflement, hands raised, mouth agape. No exaggerated "What?" or "Mandy who?"

Martin tilted his head, knitted his brow. "Mandy Tarkio?"

Was that it? Liv hadn't caught the last name of the girl standing on the step, hip cocked, manila envelope in hand. Liv had just gotten home from work, hadn't had time to loosen her shirt, unhook her bra, trade skirt for shorts and shoes for sandals.

"Is Professor Stoellner here?"

Not one of the scary girls, slouching in Martin's office chair, cropped T-shirts riding up over hard tanned torsos, their lazy up-and-down inspections taking in Liv's longish skirts and boxy blazers. She'd endured their condescending smiles, the incredulous laughter that followed as she closed the door behind her on her way out. She always felt she had nothing to fear from those girls, who commanded plenty of attention from boys their own age. It was the needy ones, the ones just shy of pretty, she had to watch out for. Like this one.

The girl had sandy hair carelessly pulled back, a lot of it still hanging about her unremarkable face. Watery blue eyes, a crooked front tooth. A little pudge of flesh peeking between shirt and shorts. Strong legs, though. Field hockey, maybe. Or softball. Girls all played sports now.

"He's at school." Liv's tone dropped the temperature of a sultry day by a good ten degrees. No need for that cool drink now. "Did you try his office?"

"I did? But he wasn't there? And my paper's due?"

Tell them, Liv had often begged her husband, not to talk in questions. They came to her in the college library, these students, looking for help with their research. "About this Bede guy? A monk?"

"The Venerable Bede. Seventh-century Northumbria," Liv would say, in much the same way she'd just frosted Mandy. The girl lingered on the step, sweat beading a full upper lip, shiny with some sort of gloss.

"Why didn't you just email it to him?"

Mandy twirled a tendril around her finger, her eyes looking everywhere except at Liv. "My stupid computer's down." She thrust the envelope toward Liv. "Would you give this to him? And tell him I was here?"

"He'll know that, won't he, when he gets this." No question mark on Liv's end.

An uncertain laugh. "You're funny?"

Liv passed the envelope, damnably sealed, to Martin, who remained standing. "*Mandy* dropped off her paper. She said her computer wasn't working and that she couldn't find you on campus." Even though Mandy could simply have emailed the paper from one of the library computers. Or slid the envelope under Martin's closed office door.

He tore open the envelope, eased a paper-clipped sheaf partway out, and nodded. "Hers is the last one in. Par for the course." He shook the paper back down into the envelope.

Liv held out her hand. A test.

He handed her the envelope. Test passed.

"The Effects of Five Years of Taliban Rule on Afghanistan," she read. She grudgingly revised her opinion of Mandy upward. The girl was smart enough to play to Martin's main expertise: Central Asian history and politics. "Will it be any good?"

Martin shrugged. "These days, I just pray that their papers are in English and they didn't plagiarize. That alone gets a C. If she did anything resembling real research, I'll bump her grade up. But I'm not holding my breath. Wonder why she didn't just leave it at the office?"

Exactly the right thing to say. Liv set the envelope aside. She worked her jaw, clenched since her encounter with Mandy, and rolled her shoulders, unkinking the tension there. She reminded herself that she had it better than many faculty wives. They were an occupational hazard, these girls, hopped up on hormones and hope, still young enough to mistake pomposity for stature, craving for caring.

She should know. She'd been one of them. Except she'd married her professor, a rare enough occurrence that earned her the occasional raised eyebrow—suspicious from the women, assessing from the men. These days, there were rules against such things. Which didn't stop them from happening.

Liv considered herself impervious, her wedding band a shield of sorts, proof that her union with Martin was the exception to the rule. That, and the fact that his specialty was sufficiently obscure to attract the dullest of students, the ones who waited too late to sign up for their electives and found themselves consigned to Martin's class. Maybe that's how Mandy had ended up there.

"I can nuke our dinner," Liv said finally. "It'll only take a minute. I picked up something from the Thai place."

"You waited for me? You didn't have to do that. Come here."

So he summoned her, and so she went, turning her face to him for a real kiss this time.

She forgot to ask why he was late.

Midnight. Liv slumbered beside him, her breathing low and even. She'd fallen asleep almost immediately after their lovemaking. Martin had been smart enough to take her straight to bed, to hell with the Thai takeout.

His stomach gurgled. He eased out from beneath her arm. Waited. Assured himself of her unchanged breathing.

He stole from bed and eased downstairs to the kitchen and extracted a white cardboard container from the fridge. He examined the contents with relief. Liv occasionally tried to nudge him toward her own choices, fiery with chilies, but tonight she'd gone with his reliably bland favorite, pad Thai.

He grabbed a fork and walked naked down the hall to his office. He leaned over his desk, scooped up a forkful of noodles, and switched on his computer. Blue light filled the room, along with a welcome chime, too loud in the hushed house. He swallowed the rice noodles without chewing, hit Mute, and clicked on his email account.

Not the one from the college, his in-box cluttered with reminders of endless faculty meetings, nor his personal account, the one whose password he shared with Liv, even as she told him hers, a bit of nonsense he'd immediately forgotten. He sometimes went days without checking that one. But these days he often hurried back to his office between classes to check historyguy@hotmail.com.

Tonight, he had mail.

"You didn't tell me she was pretty."

The sum total of the message. Only one possible response.

"Nowhere near as pretty as you." Send.

He sat, the chair warming beneath him, and ate his way through half of the pad Thai as he waited for a response to blink onto the screen. Well. Mandy was probably asleep, too. His fingers hovered over the keyboard. He'd had another note in mind, a severe one about propriety and boundaries and for God's sake, are you crazy?

But he could hardly deliver that message now, not given the flirtatious one he'd just sent. Besides, he knew how Mandy would respond, pale eyes darkening in wounded protest: "But we haven't done anything wrong."

And they hadn't. Just office appointments where the conversations quickly veered off topic. One moment stayed with him. Her hand with its bitten nails, offering a mock-formal shake as she rose to leave after one of those early visits and her shocked laugh as he took it and lifted it to his lips. Heart knocking against his chest with the boldness of it all—despite his calculation that, with a girl like Mandy, he was probably safe. Though even with the safe girls he'd never dared it. Not since Liv. "They'll forgive you one," a colleague had said early on. "Make it good. Otherwise, learn how to say no."

He'd made it good, all the way to the altar, and without the push of incipient scandal, either. Marriage, he'd quickly and correctly ascertained, would be the only way to keep someone like Liv, even as over the years he'd come to realize that what he'd initially seen as an arousing insolence was just her natural reserve, the teasing half-smile merely shyness. The thrill of challenge was long gone; natural enough in a marriage nearing two decades, he told himself. And he knew Liv well enough now not

18

to take her seeming complacency with their settled life for granted. But sometimes it frustrated him.

Goddamn. He'd been stuck in this place forever, done his research, published his papers and his book, kept his nose clean, and what had it gotten him? Another grant application shitcanned. Time for some *yes* in his life. And this was but a dalliance, nothing more, a welcome reminder that the loins could still tingle, the step could still spring. Still, it could have gone wrong. A complaint to the dean, a warning. Publicity—the worst-case scenario.

Instead, he heard Mandy's laugh, followed a half second later by his own—of relief. She freed her hand and pressed her own mouth to the spot where his lips had been but seconds before.

So they continued their occasional, ostensibly accidental meetings. They exchanged notes. Martin had set up this new email account just for them, mumbling something about it being more reliable than the college email system.

"Sorry I was late to class today. I couldn't find anything clean to wear this morning and I know you didn't want me coming in naked."

His response: "Try me."

But she hadn't. Yet. With Mandy, everything was *yet*.

He unmuted the computer, awaiting the mail alert. Nothing.

He wondered, not for the first time, if he should get a cell phone, a second one. She'd given him her number, more than once. But he'd never called her and he didn't want her calling him, even on a hidden phone, leaving a trail that, even if *yet* never came, could too easily be misinterpreted.

He stared at the glowing screen, willing the chime.

Though he counted to a hundred, it didn't come. He turned off the computer and plodded through the kitchen to drop the take-out container in the sink, tiptoed up the stairs, and fell into bed with his back to Liv, who in the morning would shake her head in bewilderment over the discarded carton of perfectly good pad Thai.

Four

Her bare arms were the first thing Gul noticed about his bride.

The scandalous short sleeves of her crimson-and-gold wedding finery revealed soft flesh the color of milky chai, swirled with the cinnamon-red *mehndi* designs spiraling up from her palms to her knobby, childlike wrists. If he shifted his vision, he could follow the line of her forearm, burdened by engraved gold bangles, up past the crook of elbow to the tender place just above it. Unnerved by the sight, he caught his breath and jerked in his seat, ruining the wedding photograph.

His uncle, posing with them, leaned close. "Save the looking for later," he chortled into Gul's ear. Loud enough, apparently, for Farida to hear. Gul felt the heat of embarrassment rising from her. So, despite the exposed arms, she was modest after all. Good.

Gul's uncle rose from his seat and made way for another of the hundreds of guests waiting to pose with them. Gul slid his eyes back toward Farida, this time reminding himself to look at the face he'd seen only momentarily when the mirror was held before them during the ceremony. He glimpsed large, downcast eyes, sharply angled cheekbones above a generous mouth, a dainty pointed chin.

The photographer raised his hand and Gul wrenched his gaze forward for the obligatory flash and resulting blindness. It was only mid-afternoon, and already his head ached from the late-summer sultriness and the unfamiliar weight of his white satin turban with its showy cockade. The next guest, one of Farida's chattering cousins, another embarrassment in short sleeves, climbed the steps to the dais where the couple sat above their guests. She took Farida's hand and imposed a somber expression on her features with difficulty, falling into giggles as soon as the picture was done. Gul noted, again with approval, that Farida maintained her composure as mandated, impassive throughout the several hours of photography.

They left the tent well past midnight, Farida walking beside him, clutching a copy of the Holy Quran as the guests tossed rose petals, which fell like gentle, fragrant raindrops about them. Only then did she begin to weep.

Tears slid down her cheeks as they were driven to the mansion Gul's father had rented for just this occasion, on this night strung roof-to-doorstep with twinkling ceremonial lights. She cried again after they were ushered into the bedroom, where streamers draped a tall canopied bed with more rose petals scattered across the coverlet.

Gul, aware of the noisy crowd of relatives waiting just outside the door for the deed to be done, could not bring himself to the task at hand. Her breasts were a shock, and he stroked them in wonder as the commotion on the other side of the door grew louder. But it was her arms, finally, that undid him, the memory of the way she had displayed them for everyone to see. He circled her wrists with thumb and forefinger and slid his hands up her arms and squeezed so tightly that she cried out. He rolled on top of her, thinking with satisfaction as she sobbed hard beneath him that never again would she display those milky, beguiling arms for anyone but him, her husband.

THE GRAND TRUNK ROAD, SEPTEMBER 2001

The Toyota taking Farida from Islamabad to her new home in Peshawar slid through streets shrouded with early-morning haze. Farida ignored her husband sitting beside her and dug her fingernails into her palms, trying to follow her sister's advice.

"You will become hard," Alia had told her the night before their departure. "On the outside, you will appear tender. You will be like the most delectable of peaches. You will hide the stone within. You will do what they say." She put her fingers to the corners of Farida's mouth and urged them upward. "A smile will be your mask. It will protect these." She raised her fingers to Farida's forehead and tapped it. "Your head." She lowered her hand and let it rest on her sister's chest. "Your heart. These will stay the same."

"Who will know what is in them?" If Farida expected sympathy from Alia during those final moments together, she was wrong.

"You waste too much time feeling sorry for yourself, when instead you should be thinking about practical things. In Peshawar, you will come to know their servants. You will decide which ones you can trust—or bribe. Take this." She thrust a roll of rupees toward Farida. "Hide it somewhere. Hide it for as long as you can."

Farida looked at her, confused. Gul's family was wealthy.

"If you ever need anything, if there is a real emergency," Alia said, "you send for me. Use this if you need to. If you still have it."

Farida's hand shook as she folded the money in her palm. The past few weeks since the wedding had been bad enough, but she had spent them within the familiar environs of Islamabad. Despite her family's time in Britain, and their travels through Europe, she had never been to the northern part of her own country, on the border with Afghanistan. "Those people," her father would say, "they are barbarians. They still stone women to death, chop off the hands of thieves. They are not modern, the way we are."

"Pay attention!"

Farida reeled from a slap. Tears, suppressed since her wedding day, burst free.

Alia raised her hand again.

Farida caught her breath, dragged a silk-sheathed arm across her face, and straightened.

Alia nodded approval. "You are cold," she hissed. "You are hard. You are strong. This begins now."

Gul shifted beside her. "I am ice," Farida whispered. "I am stone." She trained her gaze forward, registering sights familiar and comforting: the four soaring minarets of the Shah Faisal mosque, the still-shuttered storefronts of Aabpara Market, the gentle green backdrop of the Margalla Hills. The car swung northwest toward Peshawar on part of the old Grand Trunk Road that linked Kabul and Calcutta.

Gul's father rode in front with the driver. Gul's mother and siblings had returned to Peshawar immediately after the wedding. Farida had not seen them since. She wore a new ensemble made especially for this day, with long sleeves and in muted colors, in deference to the more restricted life she imagined she would lead now. Still, it was of the richest material she could find, heavy silk of an appropriately dull green, but with a glinting golden undertone and intricate embroidery about the sleeves, neck, and hem. Instead of draping her dupatta at her throat, she wound it loosely around her head, securing it at the top with a hairpin so that it would not slip. Distracted as she was, she had still noticed Gul's look of approval when she emerged from the house to the waiting car.

Despite her resolve not to cry, her eyes stung as the car climbed the hills on the outskirts of the city and ascended the heights of the Potohar Plateau. All views of Islamabad vanished and, with them, everything she'd taken for granted. Family, friends, her job, safety. Farida's eyes and throat burned. She suppressed a cough.

Gul noticed. "It's bad today, isn't it?"

"Yes." She clasped her hands in her lap, studying the henna patterns there, vines and flowers and whimsical dots that took Alia hours to apply. Its beauty would fade, much like the memory of her old life.

Dense smoke wrapped the car. Other vehicles loomed beside them, then vanished into the haze. The murk briefly cleared, and she saw the brickmakers' tall conical kilns beside the road, discarded tires stacked beside them, black smoke pouring from their mouths.

"Why do they burn tires instead of wood? The smoke is so thick."

"The rubber is cheaper, and it burns hotter. The hotter the fire, the better the bricks."

An acrid scent permeated the car. She drew her dupatta up over her nose and mouth. "It's like nuclear winter. They shouldn't allow it. It must make people sick."

"Not any people who count." Gul's eyes were as cold as his words.

"What do you mean?" She lowered her voice to match his and glanced toward the front seat. Nur Muhammed reclined with his head against the seat, eyes closed. "That old jackal," Alia had said of Farida's new father-in-law. "You watch out for him. He is the one who has control. Not your husband." Farida decided Nur Muhammed was not asleep.

"The refugees work there." Then Farida understood. Pashtuns from Afghanistan, he meant. Like him, but lacking Nur Muhammed's wealth. Sometimes, on their way to various translating jobs at the embassies, Alia and Farida would pass the bus station, bordered by one-room mud hovels where the refugees lived with their chickens and bullocks, the latter treading phlegmatically through the streams of sewage running down the narrow alleyways dividing the homes. Afghan children would swarm their taxi, thumping on its windows, jabbering their pleas for money. Farida flinched at the memory.

They passed through the valley, leaving the kilns behind. The sun climbed higher, and traffic increased on the road, a mélange of buses, horse-drawn *tongas*, donkeys hauling carts piled high with new bricks, and swirls of cyclists and pedestrians. The driver wove his way through them so expertly that the sedan's quick feints and swerves left Farida slightly nauseous.

The car slowed through the crush of marketgoers in Taxila, and again as they passed the brick military barracks at the Cadet College in Hasan

Aabdal. The road curved sinuously, then straightened and gave way to a high, wide plain. Farida had dozed but woke when the car slowed. Gul put his hand on her arm. She resisted an urge to jerk away.

"I thought you would want to see this." The driver pulled over at Attock and stopped the car at the edge of a bluff overlooking a river. Gul motioned Farida to join him outside. Across the road, the stone walls of an old Mughal fort rose high above the riverbank.

She tried to look impressed. But Gul directed her attention to the river—two rivers, really. "The Indus"—he pointed to the one at their feet—"and the Kabul." He indicated the branch that ran into the Indus. The pale blue-green waters of the former caught the sunlight and refracted it to broken prisms shimmering in the mist. But the Kabul! A brown surge, more mud than water, shouldered its way into the dancing Indus, refusing to commingle, unspooling downriver in truculent curls. Across the river, the land rose sharply into hills that funneled the wind through the river valley. It tore past, snatching at Farida's dupatta.

Gul stood with his hands behind his back. "This is the real border with Afghanistan. Not the Khyber Pass. When you cross this river, you should consider yourself already there. And act accordingly." He brought his hands forward to show her a flat packet wrapped in cloth and tied in colorful string. "A gift for you."

She held out her hand. Another gust caught her dupatta, whipping the ends from her shoulders. She caught at them and held them tight at her throat. "Please. You open it."

He bent his head so that she could not see his face while he worked at the knots. He unfolded the cloth and she caught a glimpse of shimmery accordion-pleated silk the color of the Indus. He shook it out. Its folds billowed in the wind.

The sun was hot, but Farida grew cold. "A burqa."

He stepped closer.

She leaned away. He raised his arms high, holding the garment.

Farida slid the dupatta from her head. Her hair lashed free in the wind. Then the burqa settled around her. Everything grew dark and quiet.

Gul made some adjustments, and she could see again, badly, through the screen before her eyes.

Moments before, her gaze had taken in the sweep of the Indus Valley, the impregnable walls of the Mughal fort, the highlands rising smoky in the distant haze. Now her view was limited to the few inches before her. Her husband's face loomed, checkerboarded by the shadows of the screen.

"I know," he said.

She grimaced at the compassion in his voice. "You don't."

"*You* don't. This is better. This is safer."

"Safer?" She heard the impermissible rebellion in her words. "Safer than what? You are with me. Your father is with me. You're taking me to your home and shutting me up with the women. What possible danger can there be?"

She had raised her voice. Gul lowered his.

"You know nothing of the world and its dangers. You call me ignorant—no, don't deny it, I know how you think of me." She turned away, but still his words struck her. "You are the ignorant one. You are angry now, but you will learn. You will thank me. This is better. On this point, you must believe me."

The voluminous folds of the burqa flapped about Farida, and she gathered them in one hand. She took a step, stumbled, then righted herself. "I will never thank you for this."

Five

Peshawar appeared before Farida in a palette of brown and beige, with none of the lush greenery softening the concrete boxes that passed for architecture in Islamabad.

The car entered the mazelike center of the Old Town, where wooden homes with shuttered windows and elaborate carved balconies leaned over the narrow streets. Farida peered through the grille of her burqa, studying the faces so different from those of Islamabad's Punjabi population. She felt as though she had traveled to another country. In Islamabad, men were as likely to wear Western-style suits as tunics. Here, they wore local dress, topped with woolen waistcoats or heavy fringed shawls. A few men in black turbans, their kohl-ringed eyes strangely feminine above their beards, stalked hand in hand, and Farida recognized these from news accounts as followers of Afghanistan's ruthless Taliban movement.

There were far more tongas and donkey carts than in Islamabad, all of them competing for inadequate street space with impertinent three-wheeled motorized rickshaws that dashed, beeping wildly, among the cars and carts.

She gasped at a realization. Gul and Nur Muhammed turned to her.

"I thought I saw something," she said, and was relieved when Nur Muhammed resumed his conversation with the driver. Actually, it was what she hadn't seen: women. There were hardly any on the streets, and the few she had seen were swathed in burqas like her own, most of them the same sky-blue, but some green and even a few white, impractical in this land of churning dust.

But when Nur Muhammed bade the driver to stop outside a sweet-meats shop, she discovered that they were across the street from a cinema, its walls adorned with larger-than-life murals of bare-faced women, their generous hips and breasts outlined by clinging fabric. With Nur Muhammed safely out of the car for a few moments, she murmured a question to Gul about the contrast between the veiled women on the streets and the fleshy display of the murals.

He laughed indulgently.

"Yes, the cinemas are scandalous," he said. "The mullahs are always trying to shut them down. The murals are a way of showing what the movies are about."

Farida nodded. The men in the murals, their belts bristling with guns and knives, stood in attitudes of either threat or protection to the women. She thought of the genteel British costume dramas, with their ladylike yet spirited heroines, the only films that her father had let the family watch in London's cinemas. He didn't realize that Farida and Alia connived to slip away with their friends to other, far more interesting, features. She examined the murals more closely. Despite their sensuality, the women exuded helplessness.

"Aren't there any women heroes?" she asked.

"Don't be ridiculous," he said. "Ah, here is my father."

Nur Muhammed returned to the car with a white box wrapped in string, the scent of fresh pastries filling the car, and made a great show of directing the driver through streets the man obviously knew quite well. Khaki-uniformed members of the Frontier Corps were everywhere, even in the wide, quiet avenues of the old British cantonment, watching passersby with suspicious eyes.

Gul explained their presence. "The Khyber Pass is very near. Many Afghan people try to enter Pakistan illegally."

In the front seat, Nur Muhammed barked a laugh. "Try?" he said. "They succeed. These troops"—he lifted his chin toward one of the trucks—"are just for show, to please the Amriki who make a big stupid fuss about everything. Taliban this, Taliban that. As if the Taliban are a problem to anyone but themselves."

Farida tried to make her voice timid and questioning. "Surely so many Afghan people would not need to come to Pakistan if the Taliban were not a problem?"

Even through the screen of her burqa, she could see the displeasure that crossed Nur Muhammed's face. But he said nothing. Only after they had passed several more blocks, into wealthier neighborhoods where plane trees shaded wide boulevards, did she realize that his silence was his response. It was as though she no longer existed. So this is how it would be; she was invisible. For a moment, she was perversely grateful for the way the burqa disguised her distress.

She chided herself, remembering stories of brides beaten, stabbed, set afire. Silence, really, was an occasion for gratitude. At Gul's whispered "Hayatabad," announcing her new neighborhood, they rolled up before a rambling stucco villa whose verandas and arches enticed the rare cooling breeze. Here, at last, was the color she'd craved. Scarlet hibiscus nearly obscured its walls, drooping among well-watered bougainvillea vines thick with purple blossoms. She caught the scent of jasmine. Gul held the door for her.

"Home." Gul bowed, his courtesy nearly disarming her. "It is my home, and now it is yours, too."

Farida peered toward the front door, where Nur Muhammed waited. No, it was his home. She was merely a guest here, and Gul was little better. Even though the burqa severely curtailed her ability to walk, she tossed her head and lifted her chin high as she followed her husband and father-in-law into this new life.

Gul's mother, Maryam, a stout, handsome woman, greeted them at the door. She grasped Farida's elbow and ushered her into the house, simultaneously praising and scolding her for wearing the burqa.

"Ah, I see my son has turned you into a proper Pashtun," she said in broken yet confident Urdu. "Good, good. But you need not wear that here among family. What must you think of us?" She tugged the burqa back from Farida's face as they entered another room. Farida was vaguely aware that Gul and Nur Muhammed had disappeared to a separate part of the house. Her more immediate concern, as she smoothed her hair into place, was the crowd of women seated on the floor. They stared in silence, the tea before them forgotten. Even in the extended families of the Punjab, there were not so many aunties as had gathered in this one small room.

Maryam gave the burqa a final yank and tossed it into a corner. Farida saw a heap of accordion-pleated blue and wondered how she would ever distinguish her own from all the others. But the thought passed quickly as the women scrambled up and surrounded her, fingering the bangles on her wrists and commenting upon their number and weight, touching their fingertips to the tiered earrings that swung from her lobes, bunching the silk of her kameez in their hands and exclaiming at its softness. One woman put her nose to Farida's neck and sniffed at her perfume.

"It's French," said Farida. The word ran around the room, becoming two syllables on its journey. "Fer-*enz*."

All the while, Maryam stood by beaming, full of pride. She gave an order and the women fell back, resuming their seats on the floor, except for one, barely out of her teens, who remained standing next to Farida. Farida belatedly recognized her as Gul's younger sister Bibi. Gul had bought gifts for his whole family on their honeymoon trip to the old hill station of Murree, but he bought more for Bibi and her children than anyone else.

"We forget ourselves," Bibi said. "She has had a long drive."

Maryam clapped a hand to her face, then called toward the rear of the room. Servants appeared, bearing trays of food and more tea. The mass of women shifted to make a space for Farida, and a somewhat larger one for the food, which was placed on a piece of oilcloth, still stiff and new. Farida was accustomed to occasionally sitting on the floor while she ate. Still, in Islamabad, at least in the houses this large, many of the families had adopted the British custom of tables and chairs, as well as silverware. The women on either side of her began urging dishes upon her, scraping great heaps from the passing trays onto her plate until it was piled so high Farida wasn't sure how she'd manage to eat without spilling the whole business. The women dipped their right hands into the food, conveying it to their mouths so expertly that not a grain of rice went astray. Farida scooped up a handful of *pilaf*, only to lose most of it down the front of her kameez.

Beside her, Bibi spoke in quiet, careful Urdu. "Like this." She shaped rice into a ball with her fingertips and popped it into her mouth. Farida folded her fingers around a bit of rice. It crumbled against her palm. She glanced around to see if anyone noticed her incompetence. But the arrival of food seemed to have distracted the others from her presence. They stripped bits of lamb from meaty ribs with strong teeth, biting down on the bones to suck the marrow. Delicate hands, with fingernails polished in bright colors, glistened with grease. Purplish lipstick blurred onto chins. The air thickened with the mingled odors of spices and sweat. Her father's words came back to her. "Those people, they are barbarians."

Panic bubbled within her. She pressed her hand to the faint bruise on her cheek left by Alia's slap until the pain made her flinch. She inhaled deeply and dipped her fingers into the rice on her plate, surprised at the satisfaction she felt upon forming it into a passable ball. But she soon stopped trying to eat everything that was given her, though her hosts mercilessly plied her with more, and then still more, until even her loose *shalwar* strained tightly around her waist. As the hours dragged on, she hoped for a respite but, if anything, the gathering grew more animated as harsh electric light replaced the daylight fading from the high windows.

"I cannot," she protested as several *gulab jamun*, fried balls of spiced powdered milk, dripping with syrup, were placed on a new plate before her.

"Just eat a few." Bibi glared. "Maybe you eat like this every day. Maybe it is nothing for you to turn away food."

Farida had thought she might make a friend of the young woman but feared she had been too optimistic. "No, of course not."

"But you push food away." Bibi shoveled some *kulche badami* from her own plate onto Farida's.

Farida put a weary hand to the cardamom-flavored almond cookies. A commotion outside the room saved her.

People ran, shouted. Tinny voices blared from a television. The door opened. Gul stood silhouetted. Women turned their faces away and pulled their dupattas over their heads.

"Mother. Bibi. Farida. All of you. Come quickly."

The women moved, chattering through several hallways and into the main sitting room. There, they fell silent before a television so loud that its sound was distorted. Farida could not make out the words. The others seemed to grasp the situation before she did.

"*Aiee*," someone next to her whispered. "There will be big trouble now for sure."

Farida dodged from side to side, trying to see around people. Finally, she stood on her toes. The screen showed an urban skyline, plumes of smoke, two tall buildings. The view shifted. An airplane soared across the screen. Fire flashed orange from one of the buildings. Then, new scenes: the buildings again, smoke boiling up white and the towers disappearing, first one, then the other.

A collective gasp arose from the aunties.

Farida looked about. Bibi stood beside her, watching her rather than the television.

"Don't you understand?"

Farida shook her head. "What is it?"

"Amrika. It has been attacked. Some people—mujahideen, I think—bombed them."

Others whispered their horror as the towers fell again and again. All except for Nur Muhammed and, she realized, Gul. She looked toward Maryam, who eyed the men even more closely than she. Nur Muhammed said something to his son. Gul's face went dark with emotion.

Farida sidled through the crowd until she stood behind her husband. "What is happening?"

She saw the assessment in his gaze and willed herself to stay calm.

"We are leaving Peshawar."

"Oh." She tried to disguise the emotion she felt. Surely, she would have gotten used to it, but she could not deny the relief flooding through her at the thought of returning to Islamabad and her family. Already, she was thinking of how Alia would laugh at her tales of the voracious aunties. She remembered that Gul's father had ended the lease on the villa that the family had rented for the wedding. "Where will we stay now? Perhaps near my parents?"

Gul waited a long moment before he spoke again. "We are not going to Islamabad."

Farida stepped back. "No."

"Yes. We are going to Afghanistan. To Kabul. The Taliban are strong, but the Amriki are stronger. There will be a power struggle. My father will want to align himself with the winners. To do so, he must be there, talk with people, see things for himself."

"No." Already, she knew it was hopeless. "You are from the south, from Jalalabad. You told me so yourself. You have never lived in Kabul. What do you know of it? How will we survive?"

"What do *you* know? We lived in Kabul just before we left for Pakistan." His words ran beneath the hubbub in the room. "You must never speak of that time. Not to me, not to my family. But now we must go there again. And quickly, to reestablish ourselves before the Amriki come. Look there." He gestured toward the screen, where yet again, planes swooped and buildings fell.

"Do you really think they will let this go unpunished?"

Six

Liv rose late and unsettled.

She blamed scheduling—Martin taught afternoon classes on Tuesdays and she was working from home while shepherding a particularly demanding project—along with the torpor of a September morning. After fifteen years in the Philadelphia suburbs, the cloaking dampness of the heat still surprised Liv, who had never stopped missing the searing but mercifully brief season in her native Minnesota. It was a little past nine. Coffee. She needed coffee.

She poured herself a bowl of a cereal so lacking in taste that it made her believe its claim of healthfulness and, through force of habit, turned on the television. She muted the sound, mindful of Martin, who was still sleeping. The coffeemaker, set up the night before, hissed and burbled to fragrant life. She set the cereal aside, filled her mug, and welcomed functionality back into her synapses. Steam wreathed her face. Sweat pricked her hairline. She turned to the television.

A red banner at the bottom of the screen announced BREAKING NEWS. The anchor leaned toward the camera. Deep furrows plowed his forehead. Liv, her vision still sleep-blurred, squinted over the rim of her mug. The scene switched to a video of inky smoke pluming from a gashed sky-scraper. The words on the banner came into focus.

The mug slipped from Liv's fingers and shattered against the tile. Coffee scalded her bare feet. She registered the fact of the pain, of the jagged bits of porcelain, of the need to step carefully. Too late. She tracked blood down the hallway to the bedroom, grabbed at Martin, and shook him.

"What the hell, Liv?" He sat up. "Are you all right? What happened to your foot?"

"Come. Now. Something's wrong. Not with me. Maybe with air traffic control." She fled back down the hall.

The breached hull of the Pentagon filled the screen. Martin, safe in slippers, kicked mug shards aside and folded her in his arms. "Nothing's wrong with air traffic control."

"We're under attack."

Liv fielded the shrilling phone: the dean's office, calling once to cancel classes, then again to announce a faculty meeting the following day. Both sets of parents: "No, we can't see anything from here. New York is ninety miles away from Philadelphia. You know that." One of Liv's colleagues at the college library said a fellow researcher was attending a conference at Columbia. "Unless she's playing hooky, it's fine. It's at the other end of the island. Yes, really."

It rang and rang and rang. Someone's cousin had been on one of the planes. Someone else's son worked in one of the towers. Liv sought to submerge her dread beneath the effort of maintaining the same firm, detached voice she used with students who asked for last-minute help on their research papers.

"Liv, God." A friend's voice wobbled through the line. A birdlike object soared the length of the television screen. "Some of those people in the towers. They're just showing it now. Do you see? Oh, Jesus God, there's another." Someone else flew from a tower window. Liv's stomach heaved. She eased the telephone cord from the jack.

With the phone's clamor stilled, the newscasters' sepulchral voices echoed in the room. Late-morning sounds came separately through the open window. Their neighbor, unbelievably, was cutting his grass. The lawn mower, after a teeth-grinding time, clattered unevenly to a halt. Bumblebees droned heavily in the hollyhocks. A black-and-white dog lay in a patch of sidewalk shade, panting in noisy damp gusts.

Martin sat in a chair pulled close to the television, his bare knees nearly touching it. Like Liv, he hadn't dressed and was wearing only his boxers and a light summer robe. He tapped at his laptop, glancing from its screen to the television. Liv stood and kneaded her fist against the stiffness in her hip. "Turn it off. I'll get us some ice water and fix a cold plate." She took an uneven step and put a hand on his shoulder.

He dug a knuckle against bloodshot eyes. Graying stubble patched his cheeks. "I just got an alert from one of my listservs. Massoud is dead."

Liv tried to remember Massoud among the panoply of one-named characters in the obscure Central Asian countries comprising Martin's specialty. When he'd chosen the field, it seemed a sure thing, the world in a lather over the Soviet invasion of Afghanistan.

Martin's star flared bright and brief, illuminating conferences, speaking invitations, even a trip to Pakistan to interview Afghan refugees, all with the heady expectation of a better position at a university. But that unspoken promise vanished once the Soviets pulled out of Afghanistan. Martin found himself relegated to a quaint niche, unable to move beyond the suburban college where fierce battles over a dwindling endowment meant he'd never been able to return to the countries of his focus. One of those places had surely spawned this man, this "Massoud"? Liv prompted.

"A Northern Alliance commander in Afghanistan. The Lion, they called him. The Taliban feared him like no other. He's in here." He picked up the book from the end table. "Don't you remember?"

Liv kept her counsel. Of course she'd read his dissertation—she'd helped with the research, after all—but retained nothing but the sense of gratitude she'd felt upon reaching the end.

"He was assassinated two days ago. You know what this means, don't you?"

Liv waited for him to tell her.

"I have a better idea. Hand me the telephone. I need to call the newspaper and tell them what's going on."

On the screen, the towers yet again performed their slow-motion tumble into the boil of dust and debris. "Do you think they don't know?" At his look, she plugged the phone back in.

Martin's words trailed her into the kitchen. "Put me through to the newsroom. Yes, I know they're busy. This is about the attack." He wandered to the kitchen's entrance. Liv felt his eyes upon her as she pulled cold cuts from the refrigerator and arranged them on a plate, slicing a tomato atop them. She opened the freezer and stood a moment in the rush of cool air before dumping ice cubes with a clatter into tall glasses.

"Liv, for God's sake. Yes? Good. I'll wait."

Liv dropped a final cube into a glass and slammed the freezer door.

"This is Martin Stoellner—Dr. Stoellner—from the college. We spoke some months back about my presentation on tribal unrest along the Pakistani border. No. You didn't do a story then. No, I'm not calling about that now. Actually, in a sense, I am. You're writing about these attacks? Then write this: Afghanistan is involved."

Liv swung to face him.

"A *mujahid* commander named Massoud, an enemy of the Taliban, was assassinated there two days ago—never mind, this will mean nothing to you. Just forget that nonsense they're spouting on TV about homegrown terrorists. This was no McVeigh.

"This is *jihad*."

Seven

Farida started at the sound of a car moving along the hushed street. It was nearly four in the morning.

The same night that Nur Muhammed announced the family's departure from Peshawar, Farida slipped away. She tore out the title page to *Alice's Adventures in Wonderland* and scrawled a note, in English, to Alia.

"Please, if you value my life, you must come for me. They are taking me to that terrible country. Alia, I will surely die there." She folded the paper and palmed it to a servant, along with a good portion of the rupees Alia had given her.

"This must go now. Tonight." The stupid girl stared. Farida grabbed her shoulders and shook them. "Go! Run!"

The girl pulled away, brushing at her clothing as though Farida had dirtied it. "You are lucky I don't tell them of this." She took the note and the money nonetheless, slouching away at something considerably slower than a run. Farida spent the rest of the night in tense and solitary wakefulness, grateful that Gul was with the men in their quarters, discussing plans for the journey.

Now Farida made a despairing calculation. Three hours for someone to drive the note to Islamabad. Three back. She'd sent the girl into the night after ten. It was impossible that Alia would come to her so quickly. Unless—her heart leapt at the possibility—Alia had arranged for someone in Peshawar to help, someone local, who would know how to deal with these people.

Farida dressed, her hands shaking. Yes, the car had stopped in front of the house. Yes, that was the front door. Yes, those were footsteps.

She cast about for an excuse to Gul's family if they intercepted her. Something about a family emergency, maybe. She wondered if they would try to stop her, whether there would be violence. She squared her shoulders. She hoped Alia had sent more than one person. And money. A lot of money.

The footsteps stopped before her room. A knock sounded.

Farida forced herself to open the door slowly, trying to arrange her features into a neutral expression.

Maryam stood before her.

"Good. You're dressed. Come quickly. We must leave now. There's very little time."

"But—" Farida clutched the doorjamb for support. "But I heard a car."

"Yes. It's waiting for us." Maryam snapped an order to a servant bustling past, then looked into the room. "We can send for your things later. They'll store well here."

"Store?" Dozens of silk shalwar kameez folded within sheets of tissue paper filled Farida's trunks, stacked shoulder-high against one wall. Two were devoted solely to trays of shoes; slippers, really, flimsy things dyed to match the colors of the robes she'd wear with them. Smaller boxes within the trunks held her jewelry—the engraved gold bangles, the seed-pearl necklaces, the swaying jeweled teardrops for her earlobes, and the tiny sparkling studs for her nose. Soft squares of felt wrapped the cut-glass bottles of perfume, and there were even a few Western-style outfits from her days in London that she had tucked beneath everything else, mainly because she could not bear to admit to herself that she would likely never wear blue jeans again.

Maryam thrust Farida's new burqa toward her. "Put this on. They're waiting for us in the car. Take what you can bring in a small bag."

Farida reached into one of the trunks, feeling about for some underthings. Her hand bumped a familiar shape, emerging with a favorite bottle of perfume, and a dupatta to wrap it against breaking. The mutilated copy of *Alice* sat on the bedside table. She stuffed it into her bag. Maryam clasped her hand so hard Farida almost cried out, and jerked her toward the car.

Farida cast a final glance down the darkened street, but there was no other car, no one sent by Alia, no one at all to save her from being kidnapped—was there any other word for it?—into that wild land.

Maryam nearly dragged her the last few feet and shoved her into the car where Gul and Nur Muhammed waited. "We must get to the border before daylight." Farida seized at a last, forlorn hope. How would they get into Afghanistan? Guards would stop them. She was sure she'd heard someone say, in the confusion of the previous evening, that the border between Pakistan and Afghanistan closed within hours of the attacks, but the taut silence within the car warned her against posing questions. It was hard to see through the burqa's screen, and besides, it was dark. Still, Farida could see there were more doughboy-helmeted troops on the streets than usual.

The car quickly left the city and the soldiers behind, speeding through the countryside over roads increasingly rough. The headlights picked out large groups of young men walking in the opposite direction, toward the city, carrying signs and swinging what looked like children from the ends of ropes. The signs were in Urdu and English. BUSH IS DOG said one. CRUSH AMRIKA read another.

Farida dared a question. "Who are these people?"

"They are coming to town for the demonstrations. You see what they carry? Those things that look like large dolls? Those are George Bush and Tony Blair. They will burn them today," Gul said.

Farida sucked in her breath and tried to concentrate on keeping her balance as the car bounced and rattled onward, its occupants jostling against one another. It had been decided that only Nur Muhammed and Maryam, Gul and Farida would make the trip. Bibi, with a new baby, and her family would join them when safety had been established. Despite the discomfort of the ride, the others dozed.

They awoke when the car turned off the road and bumped across a field that climbed steeply toward a grove of plane trees, their pale, peeling trunks ghostly in the wavering lines of the headlights. The car stopped among the trees, well screened from the road below. Farida lingered in the car after the others left.

Again, Maryam pulled at her. "Hurry. *Hurry.*" The car backed away, carrying with it Farida's last hopes of escape.

A man waited in the deeper dark beneath the trees. Beside him, a burro dozed. Gul took the rope from the man's hand. He tugged at it and, after a brief back-and-forth, the burro took a single step forward. "This is for you," Gul said.

Farida found herself giving grudging thanks for the burqa's disguising abilities. At this moment, she realized, no one would be able to see the utter stupidity of her expression. Was it a pet? She stretched a timid hand toward its nose. It turned its head away as if bored.

"Please," Gul said. "Get on. We must be quick. It is for you to ride."

"But no one else is riding."

"The others are used to walking. You are not. The way will be rough. It will take some time." Gul urged the burro still closer to Farida. It lifted its tail and deposited a pile that sat moist and steaming in the chill morning air. Within her covering, Farida felt free to make a face.

"If everyone else walks, I must walk, too. The burro can carry our things."

Maryam stepped in. "If she wants to walk, fine. But if she falls behind, she rides."

"I will not fall behind." No one gave any indication of having heard. Nur Muhammed vanished into the shreds of morning mist. Maryam followed with long, smooth strides despite her limited vision. The folds of her burqa billowed and receded, giving her the appearance of a blue, heavily breathing apparition.

Gul turned to his wife. "Let's go, then."

Farida stepped onto a trail that she couldn't really see.

She had not yet mastered the art of walking within the burqa, using her feet to sense obstacles. Sharp pebbles bit into the thin soles of her fashionable slippers. She tried walking on the sides of her feet to avoid the pain but twisted an ankle so severely that she stepped normally despite the blisters she felt rising on her heels. She had divided her remaining rupees from Alia into two packets, tucking one into the toe of each shoe, and now they rubbed against her skin.

"Fifteen minutes," she told herself. She could stand it that long. Besides, wherever they were going could not possibly take more than that. But fifteen minutes passed, and then another fifteen, and after an hour and a half, Farida's feet blazed as though she had thrust them into the glowing remnants of a cooking fire. The path angled upward, and soon her lungs seared in agony. The others labored ahead of her, breathing audibly, but if anything, moving more briskly than before. Farida credited the excitement of their return to their homeland. She tried to stifle her own gasps. Sweat drenched her forehead. Salty rivulets stung her eyes. She squinted toward the blue mass that represented Maryam and willed herself to think of nothing but following close behind. She was aware of someone beside her but did not dare turn her head to look.

"Are you all right? Do you need to ride?" It was Gul, falling back to walk with her.

"Yes. And, no." Farida did not trust herself to utter more than single syllables. Still, she needed to know something.

"What"—she drew a breath that she prayed would not come out as a gasp—"are we doing?"

"The border is closed, as you know." Farida had just enough energy to be annoyed at the fact that he didn't even sound winded. "So we are crossing it here."

"Where"—breath—"is here?"

"This is one of the routes my father uses for his . . . his business.

The Afridi people along here know us. We will be allowed to pass undisturbed." Gul had never told Farida exactly what Nur Muhammed did. Her own father had been evasive on the topic, saying only, "a businessman, very successful." She thought she was beginning to understand.

"Don't worry." Gul's voice sounded far away. The sun was up. Heat radiated from jagged rocks that reared high above them but provided little shade. "Not much longer now. A few more hours, maybe. Cars will wait for us in a safe place."

Hours? Farida was more inclined to believe him than before. *Hours?*

With each step, pain radiated from her feet into her hips and the base of her spine. She concentrated on becoming accustomed to it. Just when she thought she had succeeded, a different sensation made itself apparent in her feet, one of moisture. She moved her toes within her slippers, and the sensation spread. Her blisters had begun to burst. Within the next half hour, as her shoes ground her stockings into the raw wet patches on her feet, Farida realized that nothing she had felt before even qualified as pain. She bit her lips, trying to distract herself, but left off when she tasted blood.

She began counting her steps.

When I get to one hundred, we'll be at the cars, she reassured herself.

Then two hundred. Five hundred. One thousand. Maryam was a blue smear ahead, Gul an occasional voice at her side. She had no idea what he said. She was too busy counting, concentrating on the rhythm of it, a new number each time she moved her right leg forward. They headed downhill, and the momentary relief when the fire in her lungs eased was replaced with a whole new aspect of suffering as her toes jammed repeatedly against her shoes.

Farida breathed and counted, stepped and counted. Sweat soaked her shalwar kameez, dried, and soaked it again. Farida counted. Her stiffened shalwar scraped her soft skin. Farida counted. She breathed openmouthed, no longer caring whether anyone heard her. Farida counted. She moved on wooden legs, shoving first one rigid limb and then the other ahead of her, rocking sideways with each awkward step. Farida counted.

A new awareness nudged its way into her consciousness, someone grabbing at her. She wrenched herself away, trying to whisper her count aloud through thick and cottony lips so that she would not lose her place in the numbers.

"Farida. Farida." Gul.

"Where does she think she's going?" Maryam this time. "The car is waiting for us."

"Farida. Stop." Gul stood before her, grasping her elbows. Her legs collapsed. He lifted her, bearing her weight. "Lean on me," he whispered. "It's only a few steps."

As he helped her toward the car, her dangling feet barely brushing the ground, Farida registered a dim surprise at his words. She saw a vehicle before her, and then she was in it, Gul sitting between her and his mother.

"We will go only to Jalalabad today," he murmured. "We'll rest there with family a few days, maybe longer, then on to Kabul." He raised his voice for the benefit of the others. "I think you will find it very beautiful. The Hindu Kush, so high, their peaks so white—you will wonder that you ever found the Margalla Hills remarkable."

He kept up in that manner for a while, chatting about sights they passed, as though she could see them, as though she were even capable of looking. Every so often, Maryam or Nur Muhammed chimed in, pointing out things they remembered. They rode not in the comfortable sedan that had borne them around Islamabad and Peshawar but in a sturdy Russian jeep whose design gave no thought to comfort but was able to withstand the cruel beating administered by the rock-strewn unpaved road over which they traveled. Gul casually guided Farida's hand to a bar over her head.

"Hold on to this," he said beneath his breath. "If you brace yourself against it, it won't be so bad." And so she clung, concentrating on keeping her fingers wrapped around the bar as fiercely as she had counted her steps earlier. At some point, she became aware that the jouncing had stopped, that the jeep rolled along on smooth pavement. Later still, the sides of the road seemed to be closing in on them, and she realized that it was lined with houses.

Gul pried her hand from the bar, whispering, "Jalalabad."

Eight

Martin's face, smeary with ink, peered at Liv from newspaper boxes around town. His voice poured from the radio.

"The myth of the Afghan as a tough, hardened fighter who will keep a multibillion-dollar fighting force at bay is just that: a myth. If we go to war, and I use the term loosely, against Afghanistan, it will be a matter of days, not weeks and certainly not months."

There were precious few specialists on Afghanistan, and those with the best credentials were so besieged that Martin found himself in immediate and ongoing demand from local reporters willing to overlook the fact that he'd never actually been there. The interviews for the moldering dissertation he'd done on Afghan refugees, parts of which he'd used for an op-ed that ran days after the attacks, had all been done at refugee camps within Pakistan.

Martin had the habitual slump of the tall man, and the years had padded a stomach that pulled him farther forward. But now he threw his shoulders back and moved once again with the confidence that reminded Liv of the rangy, loose-limbed teaching assistant who'd courted her, against the rules, two decades earlier. Accustomed to obscurity ever since, she found herself once again aglow in reflected light.

Her own project was set aside as the college library tried to cope with a rush of students and professors alike researching papers and articles on terrorism, Islam, and countries with a Muslim population.

"Talk with Mrs. Stoellner," became the library's mantra. "She'll know how to help you. Her husband, you know. Did you see him on TV last night?"

At first Liv, who worked in the silence and solitude of near anonymity, didn't like it. Then she did, cultivating an air of crisp efficiency as the weeks passed after the attacks, one that fell just short of annoyance at yet another interruption, and woe to the students who approached her unprepared. The attention went beyond the professional. Invitations to dinner parties and other events abounded, including one from the endowment-minded college president, who seated Martin between potential donors and prompted him to spin his secondhand tales of Afghanistan.

Liv, inevitably at the far end of the table, found herself flanked by one of Martin's history department colleagues and a stranger dressed in varying hues of gray. His jacket was gray tweed; his shirt, gray cotton; tie, gray silk; and even—she peeked when she bent to retrieve a dropped napkin—shoes of soft gray leather. Silvery hair and a fussy, clipped mustache completed the effect.

The meal featured the same generic chicken dish that seemed to make its appearance at all the lower-level faculty events. The wine was better, though. The history professor next to Liv maintained a sullen silence throughout much of it, probably unhappy at being relegated to the company of spouses. The Gray Man sat so still that it would have unnerved Liv, had it not allowed her to catch bits of Martin's conversation.

"And then Mahmoud said—"

"Yes, whole families, babies and all, shot by the Taliban. The faces of the survivors—my God. You never forget that sort of thing."

The B-listers near Liv eavesdropped openly. Liv strove to play her own part. "My husband," she said to those around her. "It was so many years ago, but it haunts him still. He couldn't believe the way the world forgot about Afghanistan. He was so afraid something like this would happen." After all, she told herself, B-listers had rich friends, too.

She caught Martin's eye and suppressed a smile at his nod of approval. Early in their marriage, her status as a student and his as an instructor still at the forefront, she'd preened in his company, electrified by the proximity to the sort of ambition she'd never permitted herself, raised as she was to see such naked aspiration as unbecoming. His raw hunger—for her, and for the rest of his life; to move up and out of the small Midwestern college where they met; to establish himself as an expert in regions across the world—awoke in her a sense of possibility both disturbing and thrilling. Then, her friends had reacted with simultaneous disapproval and envy. Now pride bloomed anew within her.

"I suppose he'll go back there now."

It was Martin's fellow professor, his features pinched with the same restless, fretful expression that, until recently, her husband had so often worn. She searched her memory for a name. "Ambitious," Martin had said. "Wait until he figures out that this place is the express elevator to oblivion." Jake. That was it. Jake on the Make, Martin called him, for his relentless pursuit of prestige and lissome teaching assistants alike.

"Go back?" Liv asked Jake.

"Over there. To Afghanistan. Well, not *there*—"

"More wine?" Liv interrupted him, before he could blab to the whole table about the limitations of Martin's earlier work. Jake's glass was nearly full. Still, she reached for the bottle.

He waved it away. "I should think he'd want to see things firsthand. For a change." He raised his voice. "Martin!"

Conversation stopped. Silver clinked against china as someone set down a fork. Liv tried to look a warning toward Martin, but his face was open, unsuspecting, as Jake pulled the pin on his verbal grenade and lobbed it.

"Maybe it's time for you to actually go to Afghanistan. Put your mouth where your money is."

"Oh, dear," the Gray Man whispered.

Jake the Snake, Liv thought. She contemplated bringing her heel down on his instep. Spilling her wine into his lap. But Martin batted the grenade right back. Rather, he deflected it toward the president.

"I couldn't agree more. Think of the benefit to the college to have one of its professors on scene. Maybe we could work out an exchange with the University of Kabul. They'll need books, materials. We could lead the way."

The president offered a tight smile. Liv's grin to Jake showed no such restraint.

"Right," Jake muttered. "Like he'd go to a war zone. Like any of us would."

"Oh, he would," Liv said, secure in the knowledge that no matter what the president might say in public, he'd never invest that sort of money. "Martin would go there tomorrow if he had the opportunity."

"Interesting. Are you sure?" A new voice at her elbow.

She'd forgotten about the Gray Man. "Of course," she lied. "Why not?"

He spoke so softly she had to lean toward him to catch his words. "I'm sure every single person at this table, even our enthusiastic young colleague here, could think of a dozen very good reasons why not."

The more Jake glowered, the more expansive Liv became. "But those people aren't my husband."

"No." The man blotted his mustache with his napkin, startlingly white against all that gray. "Most assuredly they are not. And what about you?"

"What about me?" Liv returned her attention to the chicken, which had not improved during the interlude. She took a rubbery bite and chewed and chewed.

The Gray Man waited until she'd swallowed. "Would you, too, be willing to go to Afghanistan? To accompany your husband should he find himself with the opportunity?"

The chicken lodged somewhere in Liv's throat. She ducked her head and coughed. When she raised her eyes, Jake stared a renewed challenge her way. She met his gaze as she answered the Gray Man.

"Martin would go at the first opportunity. And given the chance, I'd go with him."

Nine

The jeeps that had brought them out of the mountains to Jalalabad skirted the edge of town and headed into the countryside, pulling up before a compound with the high mud walls of a fortress.

Men with Kalashnikovs paced before a gate. Bandoliers crossed their chests. Dark eyes flashed a warning beneath elaborately wound turbans. Despite her exhaustion, Farida straightened at the sight of the guards. The men stood aside and waved them through, bowing toward Nur Muhammed as the first jeep passed.

In the confusion of their arrival, it was not so noticeable that Farida needed help getting out of the car. As before, Gul half carried her in a semblance of walking toward the door. She stopped at the pile of shoes beside it. Her own, she knew, would not be easily kicked away. Gul removed his and urged her onward.

"I can't," she said, grateful that Maryam was in animated conversation with a crowd that Farida could only assume included more aunties. Was there no end to Gul's relatives? "My shoes. They are stuck."

"Stuck?"

"Please, if you can just get me to a place where we can be alone, I'll show you. I am so sorry." She knew it would hardly make a good first impression for her to go trooping through this strange house in her filthy footgear.

"Stoop a little."

She obeyed so that the hem of her burqa covered the offensive shoes. Yet another use for this garment, she thought as Gul hustled her down a hallway and into a room. Where, finally, Farida sank to a thick carpet and lifted the burqa away from her face.

"Show me."

She raised one of her legs. He took her ankle in his hand and turned it, stopping when she flinched.

"*Aah-cha*. Wait here. I will be back shortly. I will see to it that no one disturbs you." Farida closed her eyes, afraid to see what had caused his dismay. She heard tremendous commotion in other parts of the house. Maryam's voice rose above the others, already giving orders. Gul returned bearing a basin of water and some rags. He took both her feet, shoes and all, and thrust them into the water. "Keep them there." He disappeared, coming back with another basin of clean water. "I am afraid that this will hurt."

Farida braced herself as he worked at her sopping shoe. The fire returned to her feet, so hot that she feared the water might boil up around them. Her shoes finally came free, but then there was the matter of her stockings.

"Excuse me. But could you please . . ." He looked away.

Farida was fascinated to see him blush, especially given how energetically he took her body every night. But except for that first night, she realized now, he had never really looked at her, and even then only briefly. She tried not to smile as she hiked up her shalwar and rolled her stockings down to her ankles. Gul took over, tugging at the stockings as gently as he could, but the skin tore away with them and by the time he was finished, tears slid down Farida's face. She blinked them away. Gul stared at her feet. Farida took a breath, then studied the damage.

She thought of meat hanging in the markets, bloody and raw. She remembered, wistfully and very briefly, brightly painted toenails, a bewitching tracery of mehndi all the way up her ankles to her calves. And then she pushed such thoughts away. "What shall we do? They cannot see me like this."

"You are ill." His voice was firm, decisive. Again, Farida was grateful for his instinctive understanding of her dilemma. "Possibly," he added, his voice lighter, mischievous, "you are pregnant." His expression became hopeful.

Farida coughed.

"So early in the pregnancy, the walk today cannot have been good for you," he continued in his bantering tone. "You must rest. You will spend much of the next few days in bed, your feet covered where no one can see them. When you need to get up, I will help you. I am, as you know, a very cooperative husband. But when I cannot help you, you must walk as though there is no pain. I'm sorry, but it will be only a few steps. I think you can do this."

Farida thought of the thousands of steps she'd walked that day. She lifted her chin. "I know I can do it."

"I will go to the chemist and get some salve. Really, in a few days, you will feel much better."

He was so solicitous that Farida feared she would cry again. "Thank you," she whispered.

"I don't suppose . . ." he said, and stopped, his confidence abruptly gone.

"What?"

"That maybe you are indeed pregnant?"

Farida shrugged. Her breath came short at the thought of pregnancy, nearly inevitable, just one more thing that would cement the impossibility of escape. She fought an urge to flee the room, the house, to run on her broken feet back over the mountains to safety. "If I'm not, I'm sure I will be soon."

It seemed to mollify him.

He came to her that evening, and the next, and the next with a pot of salve made of pine tar and mutton fat. He closed the door behind him and sat on the floor, and she pulled up the hems of her shalwar as he thumbed some of the salve into his palm and chatted with her as it warmed and softened in his hand.

The first few times, they were awkward, their conversations stilted, unsure of how to be alone together in ways that went beyond physical intimacy. But soon Farida spoke with him nearly as easily and freely as she had with her sister.

"And how is my mother taking the news of your pregnancy?" Even by the light of the oil lamp, Farida could see the playfulness in his eyes.

"*Oof.*" She smiled back. "You have no idea."

"I think I do. But tell me, anyway." He put his hand, sticky with salve, against the sole of her foot, holding it there until the pain eased. She forced herself to relax, grateful for his willingness to touch the dirtiest, most shameful part of her body.

He stroked her feet in widening circles as Farida told him how Maryam led a coterie of aunties into her room, where they surrounded her sleeping mat, alternately cosseting her with sweets and other delicacies, and pelting her with questions. In her parents' home, Farida had been painfully aware that she was viewed as a problem. Now she found herself enjoying this sudden warm bath of approval.

"They want to know everything. How long had it been since—you know." Farida hesitated, unsure if Gul did know, wondering how much any man in this place knew about the workings of women's bodies. But he nodded as though he were familiar with such things, so she continued. They wanted to know if her stomach was upset. They wanted to know if the discomfort was high in her stomach, which would mean she was carrying a boy, or low, and therefore a girl. When Farida assured them it was high—"a gnawing pain, right under my ribs"—it spurred a collective intake of breath and a high-pitched burst of exclamations.

Her skin was examined for its color, and she was made to open her eyes wide so that they could peer at the whites and ensure themselves of their clarity. "Stick out your tongue," Maryam ordered, and Farida, puzzled, obeyed. Maryam nodded in approval.

Farida imitated her, tucking her chin, and frowning in concentration, and she wondered aloud to Gul if she would ever find out what information her tongue had yielded.

By this time, Gul was laughing so hard that Farida forgot the pain in her feet. "You look just like her."

And he looked like no one in his family at this moment. Farida had yet to see any of them in a lighthearted lapse. Now here was Gul, his head thrown back, his face relaxed, his mouth soft and loose. His lips were nearly as full as a woman's. Only the severe planes of his features, the wiry curls of his beard, saved him from girlish prettiness. Gul's laughter subsided and he opened his eyes, and Farida looked quickly away, hoping he hadn't caught her staring.

He broke the silence first. "Here. I have something of yours." He held out a sheaf of crisp new rupees.

"I don't understand."

"There was money in your shoes."

Farida searched for a plausible explanation to stave off the anger she expected. There was, after all, no reason for a wife to have money of her own.

Gul's next words were calm. "It was destroyed. I couldn't tell how much it was. I hope this is enough." He laid the money on the floor beside her and left the room.

⬤

They developed a routine: the bedside visits from Maryam and the aunties by day, and the private time with Gul in the evening, which continued even after her feet had healed.

The women, as far as she could tell, almost never left the compound, although they spent the cooler morning and evening hours in its pleasant courtyards, working and gossiping in the shade of fragrant orange trees, slender poplars, and palms whose fronds rattled in the hot wind. Bibi's family arrived near the end of September, when the poplars dropped leaves that piled up like gold coins against the compound's earthen walls. Farida's workmanlike Pashto improved quickly in her time among the women, who leavened their incessant advice with humorous references to their own days as young brides. Farida felt herself drawn to this female world far more welcoming than that of Islamabad's educated women, where a corrosive competitiveness seethed just below the lacquered surface of any gathering.

The aunties showed her how to knead dough for *naan*, or helped her to crop a toddler's hair close to her head—"It will grow in so long and thick and beautiful that when you see this girl in a few years, you won't recognize her"—or showed her how to walk in her burqa, back and forth across the compound until she learned to look ahead through the screen, rather than down. They also spoke knowledgeably about the goings-on in the city and beyond. Farida was surprised to find them so well-informed, recalling with shame her father's dismissal of Afghans as uneducated barbarians.

"How do you know so much if you cannot go out?" she whispered to Maryam one day for fear of giving offense. But Maryam repeated Farida's words for all to hear, sparking a chorus of agreement about how men were foolish to think their women were incapable of weaving together the threads of overheard information into a tapestry as edifying as any newspaper—which, as Maryam acknowledged, rolling her eyes, none of them could read, anyway. "They think they keep us in ignorance."

Farida detected the bitter undercurrent in the laughter that rippled through the room. She folded a bit of warm dough in her hands, then stretched it. In her head, she composed letters to Alia about her observations. Oh, how her sister would laugh at the image of Farida in a burqa, or baking bread, or chasing barefoot children around the courtyard. But she abandoned those imagined efforts. Alia's amusement would turn to anger at the thought of her sister in such circumstances, and Farida could not summon the words to explain the increasing tug of this new life. Besides, with the closed borders and the Amriki expected to bring war soon, there was little likelihood that a letter would reach Alia. She had overheard Nur Muhammed telling Gul that even the smugglers' routes were blocked. She felt a pang of guilt when she thought of the worry her earlier note likely caused Alia but then reminded herself that, given the servant's defiance, that message had almost certainly never left the girl's grubby hands.

In the evenings, she questioned Gul more closely about the events outside the compound, collecting news to present to the aunties.

"The people are very angry. There are demonstrations almost every day. The police are building fortifications of sandbags at the major intersections," he said.

"Because of the demonstrations?" The thought of such large and unruly crowds frightened her, but stirred her also, after the stultifying tranquillity within the compound.

"No, the police just tear-gas the demonstrators and beat them with canes. It's because of the war."

"What war?" Farida sat up, her feet forgotten.

"It's said Amrika will attack any day. They are wild to get Osama. But I think they will not take him."

"Are we in danger here?" Farida had never been to America, but she well remembered Britain, with its casual abundance of wealth and technology. She imagined America would be the same way, only more so.

"I think they will go first to Kabul. That's why my father lingers in Jalalabad. Are you afraid?"

Farida lied and said no.

"Even if you are, no one will know. You should hear what the aunties say about you." Gul's eyes shone with pride.

"And what is that?"

"They were sure the walk across the border would finish you. Even with the burro, my mother told everyone that you would not make it,

that you would have to turn back. She wanted to leave you in Pakistan."
Farida was glad he so rarely looked at her. Otherwise, he'd be able to tell
how she wished she'd been able to do just that. But Gul was still talking.
"They say that you are a real Pashtun woman. Very brave, like us, and
strong, too, walking all that way. This trip was much more difficult than
when my family left Afghanistan."

Farida held her breath. Gul never talked about his past. She faked
a yawn. "You never talk about that time. What was that trip like?" She
closed her eyes as though dozing. He tensed beside her. She slitted her
eyes. His brows met in a single line. His chin jutted. His eyes, fixed upon
some point above her head, blazed.

"It is good you came with us," he said finally, his voice clipped. "You
would not have been happy in a soft place like Pakistan."

Farida thought of flush toilets, real beds with smooth sheets—she
would have preferred even a rope *charpoy* over her sleeping mat—of dining with proper utensils rather than scooping up greasy morsels with her
bare hand. "No," she said, hurrying to agree with him before he noticed
her reticence, "I do not like soft places."

"Sometimes soft is good. Your feet," he said by way of explanation,
changing the subject so thoroughly that Farida gave up any thoughts of
discovering details of her husband's youth. "They're healing well. The new
skin came in quickly."

Indeed, Farida realized that it no longer hurt for him to rub in the
salve, which he continued to do, long past the need for it. He worked his
thumbs against her soles, stroking them from her toes to her heels, the
movement so hypnotic that Farida found herself nearly asleep. She came
awake when she realized that his touch had changed, that his hands had
moved higher, reaching tentatively toward her calves.

"That feels good," she encouraged, and he massaged her with more
certainty, working out the kinks. His hands moved above her knees to her
thighs. He stopped rubbing and began to stroke them lightly, letting his
fingertips trail a little higher each time.

"Oh," said Farida, and then again, "oh."

Later, when she remembered how hurriedly she shoved down the waist of her shalwar, kicking at the baggy pants, the more quickly to bare her body for him, she would flush with the embarrassment of her boldness. But that thought was always followed by the intoxicating memory of how he had fallen upon her, as hungrily as ever, but more tenderly than before, whispering "beautiful Farida, sweet love"—and how she had pulled him hard to her, sharing his hunger, moaning so urgently that he covered her mouth, first with his hand, and then his lips, so that their shared pleasure was all the more intense for its silence.

———

Gul lay wakeful, his heart yearning backward, his agony a fresh wound. It had taken years before it scabbed over, grew scar tissue that toughened with time and even faded. But Farida's innocent question—"You never talk about that time. What was that trip like?"—landed upon that old injury like a blow, and now it throbbed anew with each beat of his heart, waves of pain pulsing through him.

There'd been no hike across the mountains, belongings piled high upon a burro, when his family had fled Kabul those many years before. They'd made the journey in the comfort of cars, the way smoothed by Nur Muhammed's generous dispensation of cash at each checkpoint, with each mile leaving the raging civil war farther behind, speeding toward the safety of Pakistan.

What was that trip like? It was the journey that had forever taken him away from Khurshid.

Ten

Martin didn't immediately recognize the diffident, nondescript man outside his office.

The wardrobe, more than the name, jogged his memory. He held the door wide at the man's further identification as the head of a newly formed nongovernmental organization to aid Afghan women. He wondered why that fact hadn't been divulged at the faculty dinner some weeks earlier. Maybe he'd forgotten. No, he'd have taken care to remember something like that.

As before, the man was all in gray, although this time he wore a cashmere sweater rather than a blazer. His hair was such an even shade of pewter that Martin, before he focused fully on what the man was saying, wondered if he dyed it. Martin asked him to repeat himself.

"We're building our staff. The job—deputy director—is yours to reject."

Martin gestured toward the chairs in front of his desk. "Perhaps we should sit down."

Yes, it would be a hardship, the man went on as he sat, and the organization was prepared to compensate him handsomely for the inconvenience. "This will change your career. You'll find our confidentiality clause quite workable. No reason at all you can't write a new book while honoring our need for some discretion. And it goes without saying you'll be offered a post at a major university upon your return. You'll have your pick, most likely."

The grant he'd sought would have taken him overseas for a matter of weeks. The Gray Man was talking years. Martin groaned. Everything he'd wanted, a glittering prize, held just out of reach by—

"What about my wife?"

"Best to let me handle that end of it. Spouses are the most difficult part of the equation. We have years of experience. I'll come to your house this evening."

Williams. That was his name. Clayton Williams. As forgettable as the rest of him.

They agreed on seven p.m.

Martin, brain ablaze with the unexpected gift of *future*, switched on his computer and outlined a farewell email to his colleagues and students, each gracious phrase designed to inspire envy.

He hoped they'd keep his account active for at least a few weeks after he left. He'd want to send another email, attaching a photo of himself at the Khyber Pass, standing where so many conquerors had trod throughout the centuries. The reporters who called him always cut him off when he flexed the muscles of historical perspective. And those requests for interviews, most with the smaller suburban newspapers and lesser radio stations that ringed Philadelphia, were already dwindling.

Martin thought of the exposure this new job would give him, maybe a regular rotation as a talking head on CNN and the Sunday morning shows, the voice of authority patched in from location by satellite phone, his portentous words jittery with static and odd electronic pauses.

He took a breath. For far too many years, he'd spent his time despairing in his cramped office. No more. He turned from the computer and wrestled the high casement window open. Unseasonably warm air poured in like syrup. Papers on his desk curled as the humidity hit them. He stuck his head out the window.

Two students tossed a Frisbee on the Oval, their throws desultory, wobbly. A young woman lounging in the grass directed good-natured mockery their way. They were too far away for Martin to see their faces, but he could imagine them, all good bones and straight teeth and clear skin over high and rattlingly empty foreheads. The college attracted the stupid scions of the rich-but-not-rich-enough-for-the-Ivies. They populated his classes unwillingly, the more alert playing games on their laptops, the rest outright sleeping through his lectures. In all his years there, not a single student had expressed a desire to follow Martin's course of study.

He'd never understood why Liv loved the college so, despite the flaws he often pointed out—the bricks too bright, the columns too narrow, the ivy too sparse, a parody of better-known institutions that fooled only those who didn't know they should have aimed higher. He even hated the goddamned Oval, subject of so many posters and cards, its towering fringe of trees saved from Dutch elm disease by an amount of money that would have funded Martin's department into the next millennium. Supposedly the Oval was a metaphor. For what, he'd never quite understood. That was Liv's department. She nattered on about ovals and eggs and life and possibilities hatched, but all he saw was a racetrack, something with horses, maybe, or better yet, greyhounds, endlessly chasing a rabbit they'd never catch. Except now Martin had the rabbit in his jaws, a hot burst of blood down his throat.

He looked past the Frisbee-tossing dullards and thought of young men wielding weapons instead of plastic discs, fighting for their freedom instead of scheming new ways to avoid class. Of female students whose very presence on campus marked an unimaginable courage. Of scorching winds that blew change. And he would be part of that change. Finally, a reward for all those years persisting when others retrained their focus to China, the Middle East, areas more reliably in the news and thus apparently deemed worthier of research grants. He'd continued to publish papers in increasingly obscure journals, had polished his rusting Urdu in the privacy of his office, seeking out bewildered exchange students for practice.

Now his deep knowledge, so rare among Westerners, would pay off, allowing him to slide into the roiling ferment of Afghan society with nary a splash, winning him the sort of respect that would demand at least a hearing, if not immediate acquiescence for Face the Future's mission. He'd balked at first—the plight of women had been nearly hopeless before the Taliban and would likely improve only incrementally after they were routed. Then Clayton Williams had explained there was more.

He closed the window and turned off the computer.

It was time to tell Liv.

The doorbell summoned Liv from the kitchen.

Not again. Apparently her chilly reception a few months earlier had done nothing to discourage Mandy. Although it might be another one. The students had just taken their midterms. The nervous ones would get progressively twitchier as the semester unspooled. Inappropriate behavior abounded.

"Wait." Martin brushed past her. "I'll get it."

He returned with neither gossiping neighbor nor importuning student. Liv remembered him, a little, from the dinner. His name, Clayton Williams, entered her brain and left again. The Gray Man, that's what stuck. She didn't remember Martin speaking with him that night. But Clayton Williams seemed to know her husband entirely too well. Within a few minutes Liv understood why.

She sat, staring. Martin pushed a scotch into her hand. She didn't like scotch. "You're going where? For how long?"

The ice clattered in her glass. Liv braced her wrist against the arm of the chair to stop her hand from shaking.

"It's a two-year appointment. Minimum. We'll need that long to get things up and running. After that, we can decide whether we want to stay on."

Liv tipped the glass against her lips and let the whiskey burn down her throat. "We?"

In the silence, the Gray Man watched.

"A moment, please." Liv ushered him into the den and waited until the door closed behind him.

"Martin." Her voice caught. He stood at her grandmother's heavy oak sideboard. It was too large for the living room, but it had been a wedding gift from her parents. Indeed, their wedding photo sat atop it, two tall, smiling strangers within an ornate silver frame. Martin's hair was untidy then just as it was now, his tie askew, his shirt working its way free of the cummerbund. As always, he drew attention away from Liv, with her high-necked dress, her careful makeup, her waist-length hair lacquered into smooth golden loops atop her head.

Liv tilted her glass and watched the ice settle into a new configuration. "This organization? It's connected to the government?"

"You heard the man. It's an NGO. Nongovernmental organization." Not exactly a denial. "Liv," he pleaded. "I can't pass up an opportunity like this. It won't happen again. You know that."

What about my job? She took a swallow of scotch, tightening her throat lest the words escape. A futile effort.

"But that's the good part! You'll be able to work with me. If anything, your skills will be more valuable than mine. We'll need to collect as much information as we can about the place."

Their eyes met. Liv saw something shaded in his. "Information? For whom?"

"It's not like that. It's an organization for women's rights."

"Then why that confidentiality clause? Nonprofits keep their books open. It's a requirement." Another quick swallow of scotch warmed rather than seared.

"This benefits you, too. You'll finally get the recognition you've always deserved. Your name as a coauthor. Well, at least in the credits."

Another nonanswer. But: coauthor. Something swelled within Liv. She touched her fingertips to her temples. "And if I stay?" Pushing the question past the constriction in her throat.

"Liv." Not a plea this time.

She thought of Mandy, bold enough to show up at the house. What else had she dared? She wondered about the kinds of young women who might work for NGOs. Resourceful. Adventurous. Heedless of convention. Two years at least, Martin had said.

She forced herself to recall the man's name. These things would be important now. "Call Mr. Williams back in." She waited for him to settle himself in the wingback chair, another legacy from her grandmother. He nestled birdlike within its sheltering contours, watching her with unblinking eyes.

"I understand there would be a role for me?" she asked.

"Quite right. And not just your research abilities, which, as your husband has led me to understand, are considerable. For a job in this region, a married man is essential, but a married couple would be far more acceptable. Your husband wouldn't be allowed in a private home, but you'd be able to talk to women directly. The combination of your work and that of your husband—you two make good partners. As I told your husband earlier, it's rare to find a couple so evenly matched in their skills, and with a strong marriage besides. Isn't that right"—he paused, looking at Martin—"History Guy?"

Martin choked on his scotch, a fit of coughing so prolonged that Liv rose, hand lifted to pound on his back. But he waved Liv away and spoke quickly. "We're both so excited about this opportunity. I've wanted to go back for so long now."

"And I've never been." Liv tried to tamp down a growing sense of panic. She splashed more whiskey into everyone's glasses. "I've heard so much about it from Martin. Would we be based in Islamabad? Are the refugee camps close by?"

The two men took an interest in their drinks.

"We'll do our orientation in Islamabad," Martin said.

Liv started. She looked to the other man.

"Oh, no," she said. "No."

"Oh, yes. Our organization benefits Afghan women. We've had to work out of Pakistan for years. But now, although we'll keep a small satellite office in Islamabad, we'll move our headquarters to Kabul."

"How? The Taliban shut the whole country down even tighter after 9/11."

The Gray Man bestowed a smile upon Liv so wholly unexpected that she started, spilling some of her scotch. He spoke to Martin. "You see? The fact that she knows that—it's exactly the sort of detail-oriented approach we're looking for." He turned back to Liv. "We don't expect the Taliban to stay in power much longer. As soon as they've been defeated, we'll begin the move. The office should be ready for you in just a few months. We'll have plenty of time for orientation. It's ideal. And once you're there, it will be quite safe. As in Islamabad, our compound in Kabul will be guarded."

"Kabul." Along with everyone else in the library, Liv had been called upon to do her share of research about the place since the attacks. She thought of tanks, turbaned soldiers. Makeshift bombs, mountain hideouts. Women in burqas. Stonings, beheadings.

Compound, he'd said. Guarded. Liv's chest tightened. "Will we be on our own? Or will there be others with us? Other Americans?" Her head ached from the scotch. She remembered why she didn't like it.

"There's a small contingent of Americans who've been there throughout. One can reasonably expect their numbers to grow exponentially now." He attempted a laugh. "But, no, in Kabul your staff will be all local. The more bridges we build with the Afghan people, the better. In fact, we discourage contact with the other NGOs, beyond what is absolutely necessary for information sharing. That sort of independence will build credibility with the Afghans. To an extent, you'll be largely on your own." He ignored Martin and spoke directly to Liv in creamy, irresistible phrases. "We feel quite lucky to have happened upon someone with your husband's expertise, and your own, of course, and with such a strong personal foundation as well."

Liv tried to remember the last time she'd seen Martin looking so purposeful, expectant. Kabul. "*Cobble*, yes?" She pronounced it as they had.

"Yes," Martin breathed.

"Ka*bool* sounds so much more exotic," she said pointlessly. It was time for an answer.

Partners, the Gray Man had said.

"I suppose," she said, "if I'm going to live there, I'd better make sure to say it right."

Eleven

AFGHANISTAN, 1993

"You must not speak of that time," Gul had told Farida about his family's earlier move to Kabul.

Wishing he could banish memory as easily as speech, could erase the events launched by his father's momentous announcement eight years earlier, amid the civil war that began in Jalalabad after the Russians finally fled Afghanistan. The Taliban, with the weaponry they'd acquired from both the Soviets and Americans, and egged on by the Pakistani mujahideen seeking to topple the government, had turned the eastern Afghanistan city into a war zone, which devastated civilian life—and Nur Muhammed's business.

Opportunity beckoned in the capital, where the government finally had collapsed under a prolonged assault by briefly united factions, his father said. Or so Gul surmised. He'd been drowsing after dinner, lying against his father, the rumble of Nur Muhammed's voice soothing him toward full sleep. He heard the word "Kabul." Nur Muhammed had just returned from yet another visit to the capital, so frequent that Maryam often griped that he spent more time there than at home.

A long pause followed. Moments later, Gul's cushion vanished as Nur

Muhammed leapt to his feet. Gul's head bounced hard against the carpet. A teacup hit the wall behind them.

"No!" Maryam screamed.

Gul had never heard his mother refuse his father anything. The oil lamp on the floor sputtered. Maryam's face moved in and out of shadow. Gul couldn't tell if she was more frightened by what his father had said, or by her own defiant reply.

Nur Muhammed, surprising his son as much as his wife, turned his back and left the room, his restraint more unsettling than a blow. He paused in the doorway and spoke with finality over his shoulder. "My business is there now. There is no reason to remain in Jalalabad."

Maryam sank to the floor. Gul crept across the carpet. She raised her face and he saw the fear in it, fear of the unknown in the outside world. Her plump cheeks were wet. "Kabul," she whispered, and tightened her grip on her son. Gul held his breath. In his whole life, he had never traveled beyond the outskirts of Jalalabad.

Nur Muhammed hired two cars to shuttle his family from Jalalabad to Kabul.

Gul had just turned fourteen, and his father now spoke to him of manly concerns—the significance of appearances and of actions to back up those appearances. Yes, he told Gul, the cost of the cars was high. But it was important that their new neighbors know them as people of worth, not the common refugees who had been arriving in the city by truckload for years.

Maryam, sitting in the second car with the children, her burqa wrapped tightly around her ample form, saw little of her surroundings. But Gul pressed his face to the window, jostling for position with Bibi, eager for the occasional lull in traffic, when the great clouds of dust briefly parted, revealing war's detritus: burnt-out cars, skeletal tanks already cannibalized of their metal plates, and the occasional rocket crater in the dirt track that had once been the main highway from Kabul east through Jalalabad across the Khyber Pass and into Pakistan. Even with the windows cranked so tightly shut that the car's occupants broiled, a fine layer of dust soon coated its interior. It settled on Gul's face, forming muddy tracks in the sweat that trickled into his eyes and blurred his vision.

The car labored as it climbed out of the wide river plain that surrounded Jalalabad. The driver sped through the notoriously bandit-ridden Tang-i-Gharu gorge. Several times, the car careened perilously close to the edge of the road, and Gul averted his eyes from the sight of the Kabul River rushing in a shining silver fury over hungry rocks far below.

It was dusk when they finally entered the outskirts of Kabul. The lowering light revealed houses clinging to craggy slopes. The ride smoothed, the car coasting on pavement. Gul hazarded a turn of the window handle and was rewarded with a rush of cool, reviving air. Maryam sighed and held the burqa's damp folds away from her. Bibi stirred in her sleep.

The car turned a corner and the mountains vanished behind the tallest buildings Gul had ever seen. A man sputtered past on a motorbike, swerving to avoid the car. He shouted something rude, his words lost in the noise. The car slowed almost to a halt in the bewildering maze of traffic. Maryam forgot that she needed relief from the heat and sank lower in the seat, barking at Gul to raise the window again. He pretended he didn't hear her. The car crept past a long, low mosque with a broad, deserted plaza, then a stadium with bullet-scarred walls. They crossed a bridge over the wide riverbed, the water only a filthy trickle. Merchants, packing up their wares at the end of the day, thronged its banks.

The cars stopped. Nur Muhammed got out of the first car and approached with small, quick steps. His expression, usually so impassive, was oddly eager. He tapped on the window. Maryam turned her head away.

"This is Macroyan," he said. "We will live here until I find a suitable house."

Rows of stained concrete buildings, five, six stories high, rose before them. Gul let his head flop backward, trying to take in their height. Narrow windows slashed the rough gray walls. Clothing hung from them, fluttering in a smoky breeze. The air smelled of fried onions and coal dust. His eyes watered. He lowered his gaze and saw small balconies beneath the windows. Stovepipes protruded above the balcony walls. A line of women toting plastic containers waited at a well. Children ran among them, barefoot despite the increasing evening chill.

One glanced in Gul's direction and saw the family and its two cars. All of the children, on a signal Gul somehow missed, drew close together and approached at a trot.

An older boy with bad skin shoved his way to the front of the group and reached for one of Maryam's bundles. Nur Muhammed's foot moved in a blur, and the boy lay on the hard earth, his friends jeering all around him. Nur Muhammed gestured for the drivers to pick up the bundles. With Nur Muhammed leading the way, they set off, Maryam shepherding Gul's two little brothers before her, Gul bringing up the rear.

A blow stung the back of his head. Something else hit the ground near him. He turned and sidestepped fast. A stone narrowly missed his face.

The boy was on his feet again, another rock readied in his hand. He smiled, and it was not pleasant.

"Welcome to Macroyan," he said.

Jalalabad was a horizontal city of sprawling warrens of mud or cinderblock homes. Only the wealthiest had two-story villas, their flat roofs barely visible behind high concrete walls. Or they lived like Gul's family, in countryside compounds, collections of low buildings within fortresslike mud walls thirty feet thick and twenty high.

Homes in Kabul strained toward the sky. People lived stacked atop one another like chickens in the cages at the market. Nur Muhammed hurried them through the courtyard created by Macroyan's surrounding towers and into one building so quickly that Gul barely had time to take it all in.

Nur Muhammed urged them faster past knots of feral youths. Garbage and chunks of concrete littered a dank stairwell, lit only by the fading evening light leaking through broken windows. People shoved past them, carrying water that slopped over its containers and spilled onto the steps, adding to the hazards underfoot. Maryam reached for a railing, but it had been torn away. She called to Nur Muhammed to help her, but he was already a flight above them, brushing at his clothes as he climbed. Gul moved to his mother's side, and she leaned on him, wheezing at the unaccustomed exertion.

Nur Muhammed stopped at the fourth floor, so abruptly that the younger children stumbled into him. He seemed barely to notice, preoccupied as he was with shaking the last of the road dust from his clothes and running his fingers through his beard, newly brightened with henna. He pulled a handful of candied anise seeds from the pouch beneath his tunic and chewed, sweetening breath made sour by the long journey. "This is good, yes? High enough for safety, low enough for an easy walk."

Maryam labored up the last steps, hiking up her burqa so as not to trip. "Easy? We've climbed into the clouds. Where is this place?"

Nur Muhammed jutted his chin toward a door down the hallway. Despite his haste into the building, he lingered, still straightening his clothing and smoothing his hair. Maryam waited a few steps behind him. Safe within the empty hallway, she pushed the folds of her burqa away from her face. The wavering call to evening prayer sounded faintly above the din within the building.

"Take us in," she said. "You'll want to pray."

Before they could reach the doorway, it was flung open. A girl stepped into the hallway, her face alight. She said something in Dari, and moved toward Nur Muhammed, smiling tilt-headed at him through lowered lashes. His features softened in a way that Gul had never seen. Gul thought his father looked foolish. Maryam stiffened beside him. She made a noise in her throat. Nur Muhammed remembered himself and shouted to all of them to get inside, that it was time for prayers and that he needed tea after the journey. Touching his head to a hastily unrolled prayer rug, Gul slid his gaze sideways toward the girl, who busied herself in an alcove. She was young, maybe a year or two older than Gul, slender, with the narrow face of a Tajik. She wore a brightly flowered velveteen dress over white pantaloons with cutwork hems. A white scarf inadequately covered her hair, which was pulled into a braid thick as his forearm. Gul muttered his prayers quickly, aware of his mother's harsh breathing somewhere behind him. He had not finished praying when Nur Muhammed stood and addressed his wife.

"This is Khurshid. She will help you with things."

Khurshid was already pouring tea. Good smells wafted from the alcove. Khurshid spread an oilcloth on the floor. She ducked into the alcove and came back with plates heaped high with *sabzi challow.*

"Sit," Nur Muhammed urged into the strained silence. The girl returned a last time with a bowl of water and a towel, and the family passed it silently, dipping their fingers into the bowl and blotting them on the towel. Bibi fidgeted beside Gul. Finally, she could contain herself no longer. "Is this Khurshid's house?"

"It is our flat for now. It was her father's. He is a good friend to Gulbuddin." He named the leader of one of the factions so busily destroying the city.

"Where is her father now? Why does he not live here? Where are her brothers and sisters?" Bibi was Nur Muhammed's favorite and thus able to get away with the sort of rude interrogation that would have earned Gul a rebuke, or worse.

"He has difficulties." Gul knew then that those difficulties were financial. "I helped him by renting this flat. And——" He said something then to the girl in Dari too rapid for Gul to follow. She blushed and smiled.

"How long will we live here? When will we go home?"

"As long as it takes me to conduct my business here. Finish your dinner."

They ate the rest of the meal in silence. The mutton in the challow was of a quality that had not been available in Jalalabad for some time, rich and fatty, and Gul rolled it around in his mouth, savoring the way it filmed his tongue with meaty flavor. Khurshid had also prepared *aushak*, Gul's favorite, and when she noticed how he enjoyed the dumplings of pungent green onions, wrapped in tissue-thin dough, slick with meat sauce and yogurt, she slipped an extra one onto his plate.

"Too much mint." Maryam pushed hers aside. But Gul stuffed handfuls into his mouth until Bibi made fun of the sheen coating his lips. Khurshid did not eat but sat unspeaking behind Nur Muhammed. When he had finished, she moved about the room, retrieving the plates and carrying them onto the balcony. Gul heard water splashing as she washed them.

The silence in the room thickened. Even Gul's rambunctious brothers had stilled. Gul eased a hand up to scratch his face and peered through a screen of fingers at his father, seemingly engrossed in studying the carpet's geometric pattern, and then at his mother, her eyes narrowed and jaw set.

"Well?" she asked.

"She will help you." Nur Muhammed did not look up from the carpet, whose garnet fibers bespoke its origins in Mazar-i-Sharif.

"Then she is a servant."

"Enough!" Nur Muhammed stood and crossed the small room, leaning low over Maryam, putting his face next to hers. "She is my wife."

The sharp intake of breath Gul heard was his own. For one more moment, Maryam sat stonelike, staring at her husband. In the next, she simply collapsed into herself. The sounds from the balcony stopped.

"Bibi, take care of your mother. Bring her some water."

As if on cue, Khurshid stepped back into the room and handed Bibi a full cup. Bibi took the cup, holding it in her fingertips as if it were dirty, then flung it into Khurshid's face. The girl gasped, and began to sob. Nur Muhammed grabbed Bibi's arm and spun her around, slapping her so hard that she reeled backward, crying out as she stumbled over her mother's prone form. On the floor, Maryam stirred, opened her eyes, and saw Khurshid dripping above her and Bibi keening beside her. She sat up and howled toward the ceiling. Gul was sure it could be heard halfway across Kabul.

Caution and laughter warred briefly within him. Looking at Nur Muhammed's face, he let the former win. Nur Muhammed stood silent within the din, letting all of them see the disgust on his face. Maryam wailed louder.

Nur Muhammed turned his back on her. "Come!" Khurshid stumbled toward him, the tears running unchecked down her face. He led her through a curtain that screened another room. Before he let the curtain fall, Gul glimpsed sleeping mats on the floor. His mother beat her breast and tore at her clothes. The little children, frightened by the commotion, crept sniveling to Gul's side. He wanted to put his hands to his ears but was mindful of what remained of his dignity as the oldest. So he sat, waiting for the storm to subside, unable to prevent himself from hearing, in the pauses when Maryam caught her breath, the noises coming from the other room, more ostentatious than those he had ever heard in their home in Jalalabad: soft rustling sounds, quickening harsh breaths and then, from Nur Muhammed, a long, deep groan, followed after a pause by a low chuckle that was his father's declaration of triumph and, therefore, satisfaction.

Twelve

The heavy metal can rocked in Liv's hand. Gasoline splashed onto her fingers and sluiced across the generator, some going into the generator's tank, but far too much onto the parking lot's macadam. The scent, sharp and accusing, rose in the icy air.

The instructor sucked in her breath. "You'll need to do better than that. Gas is too precious to waste."

Liv set the can on the ground and waved her hand, trying to dry it. She didn't want to wipe it on her clothes, and the instructor—Kirstie Davidson, entirely too cheerful a name for the humorless martinet assigned to prepare her for every aspect of life in Afghanistan—offered neither suggestions nor a towel.

Wind whipped around the corner of the featureless office building where her training took place. A bland sign proclaimed Security Systems Inc. Mall cops, Liv might have thought, had she ever noticed it among the hundreds of low-slung office parks necklacing Philadelphia. But many of the instructors were former Special Ops types who'd found it far more lucrative—not to mention safer—to train aid workers and journalists on their way to what they euphemistically called "conflict zones."

81

Liv glared at the recalcitrant generator. Not for the first time, she resented the fact that Martin had gone ahead of her to Pakistan for his own, more detailed, orientation. She'd meet him in Islamabad in February, and together they'd spend more time acclimating before finally settling in Kabul. By which time, she hoped, it would be spring.

A plastic shopping bag wrapped itself around her ankle. She kicked it away. The generator exercise would take only a few minutes, but had to be done outdoors, beneath the low and angry sky. Liv shivered, despite having shrugged into her parka on the way out. Davidson, her light trench coat flapping unbuttoned, appeared damnably unaffected.

"Again."

Liv hefted the can, steadied it with a hand against the bottom, and successfully directed a gurgling stream into the tank. She set the can aside, screwed the top back on the tank, and reached for the switch.

"Wait!"

Liv figured every single person within a fifty-yard radius stopped whatever they were doing at the sound of Davidson's bark.

"Have you checked the oil level?"

Gasoline fumes bent and distorted the air above the boxy metal contraption before them. The letters spelling out OIL wavered. Liv extracted the tiny dipstick and extended it for Davidson's approval, the viscous coating of oil appropriately between the "add" and "full" lines.

She replaced it. Her fingers, already turning blue, hovered over the switch. She wished she'd worn gloves.

"Wait!"

Liv mentally ran through the steps in the instruction manual she'd studied the night before. They'd seemed so clear.

"Air filter." Davidson heaved up an immense sigh.

Liv wiggled it from its compartment. It looked clean.

"They won't look like that in Afghanistan," Davidson warned. "The air is full of crap there. You'll need to replace them at twice, three times the recommended rate. Don't forget. Oh, and this nice shiny machine you're dealing with here? Things get beat up fast there. You won't see these pretty little labels, everything obvious. You should be able to start this thing in the dark. Even though . . . what?"

Liv knew this one.

"I will never take my headlamp off. Not even in the daytime."

"Because?"

"Because the sun goes down fast. Because you never know where you might be. Because plans change, and change again," she chanted. "You might think you're going to spend all day in the office, and then you have to go out for fieldwork, and if you're out there when the sun goes down—"

Davidson held up her hand. "Fine, fine. Just loop it around your neck during the day. After a while, you'll forget it's there. And what else?"

Liv knew this one, too. "And even if you've got your headlamp, don't ever get caught outside when the sun goes down." She bit her lip. No use repeating all of the things that could happen to anyone who did.

"Yeah. Think of that headlamp as a talisman. If you've got it on, nothing will happen."

Talisman? Such a whimsical idea from the no-nonsense Davidson. A wriggle of trepidation, persistent no matter how many times she squelched it, reasserted itself. But the whole idea of orientation was to allay such concerns. To be prepared for every eventuality and worst possible outcome. Hence, the growing stack of files on Liv's computer, labeled "land mines," "booby traps," "kidnapping," "disease."

At night, she drifted off to a panoply of dire images. Three rocks, splashed with red paint. Or three twists of dried grass. Three crossed sticks—all symbols that indicated a minefield. Davidson, for once not shouting: "Here, we usually think of three as a lucky number. In Afghanistan it is, too. Three can save your life."

Not everything carried a warning sign. A gleaming wire, thin as a hair, that led to an explosive. A door left invitingly ajar. Push it open, and trigger a bomb. And then? More instructions. Plastic to seal a sucking chest wound. ("Always carry baggies. Handy to hold toilet paper and wet wipes—you'll always want to carry some—and for first aid, too.") Never pull out a piece of shrapnel embedded in flesh. Never push intestines back in.

She'd vaguely titled her largest file "daily life." That's where the generator came in. And more.

"Are you on the pill?" Davidson demanded early on.

Liv, too startled for speech, shook her head.

"Then go on it."

"But . . ." Early in their marriage, when Martin's work had taken him to the refugee camps in Pakistan, and he'd assumed there'd be more of the same, he'd persuaded Liv that a family would complicate such a lifestyle, a career. A vasectomy followed. Oh, how she'd wanted to please him then. Something that, apparently, hadn't changed.

"Either that," Davidson said, her voice characteristically too loud, "or bring two years' worth of tampons with you. Because you won't find them in Afghanistan."

"I don't understand." Liv glanced around. They'd been walking through an office at the time, the cubicles largely populated by men, all suddenly bent over their work with reddened ears. Liv knew exactly how they felt.

"Take a regular pill every day of the month. Skip the week's worth of dummy pills. That way you won't get your period. Trust me, it's easier."

Liv revised her initial impression of Davidson's age downward. What was the woman's story?

"Were you in the military?" she'd asked once, only to be answered with a terse no.

Now Davidson pointed to the generator. "Okay."

Liv flipped the switch to On and the generator came to life, a chugging, stinking precursor to her new existence.

Day by day, the training changed her view of the world.

That car, idling in front of the student union. She gave it a wide berth. The clump of trash, overflowing its container. What might it conceal? A too-wide smile from a passing youth. She hurried to put distance between them. And, all around, the professors, staff, students, oblivious of the dangers the universe was capable of holding. Situations, she reminded herself, she now knew how to deal with.

In a parking lot, two students fumbled to connect jumper cables to their car batteries.

"Let me." Liv approached, took the cables without waiting for an answer, and clipped positive to positive, negative to negative, the second negative to a strut. She resisted an impulse to dust off her hands—too dramatic—and waved away their stammering thanks. That very morning, she'd learned to fasten tiny alligator clips to her own car's battery to power a laptop. The generator now purred to life in response to her ministrations.

Likewise, she'd become accustomed to the surprising heft of a Beretta M9, the metal warming in her hand. The kick when she pulled the trigger, learning to steady herself against it. "Under no circumstances will you carry one of these. Ever." Davidson's voice lowered, denoting an intensity unusual even for her. "This is a little popgun compared to what will be all around you. But it's a necessary skill. Because God forbid you should ever find yourself in the sort of situation where you have to grab one, use it. Sort of like always having a headlamp." Liv braced herself, steadied her breathing, squeezed. A hole opened in the chest of the paper target.

"Good." A first from Davidson. Liv didn't insult her by smiling.

In all her years at the university, Liv's skills had amounted to click-clacking away at a keyboard, finding things in the ether, her hardwon discoveries printed out and handed over to others. Now she knew how to *do* things. For herself. She touched a hand to her pocket, where a sheaf of baggies slipped and slid against one another. Because you never knew. She'd save the headlamp for Afghanistan. But it was ready, nestled within her purse, its hard practicality bumping up against the frivolity of lip gloss, a little-used compact.

Her fellow researchers at the library daily peppered her with questions. Aren't you scared? Can't you just stay here?

No and no. Delivered with a briskness meant to imply "of course not." And, increasingly truthfully, despite these ominous training sessions, "I wouldn't want to."

Liv, long accustomed to life in the background shadows, at first had shied away from the sudden spotlight. But its glare came from professors, too, even administrators. "I would never. You're so brave."

She found herself preening, a sensation as satisfying as it was unfamiliar. Never in her life had she been called brave. Never had there been a reason. Her work at the library now mocked her with its frivolity.

"What's my topic?" A student hovered at the counter, repeating the question she'd snapped at him in her best Kirstie Davidson imitation. The student took a step back. "Could damage from the bubonic plague have been diminished?"

Who cares? A little late for the hundred fifty million victims, no? Why not work on something that could actually help people suffering now? As she herself would be doing in a few short weeks.

Liv had resisted such responses. So far. "Give me your email address. I'll send you some sources. You'll have to take it from there yourself."

She looked at her calendar with its inked countdown of days left to departure. Only a week now until she was free of the students and their meaningless requests for help with papers that would be moldering in a landfill within weeks of being turned in. She was sick of their thanklessness, ready for real life and maybe a little goddamn gratitude, too. She smiled inwardly. Maybe this new self was the kind of person who'd curse aloud.

Movement at the edge of her vision. Another student. Another *goddamn* student.

"Excuse me? I have a paper due and I wonder if you can help me?"

Liv pulled her head out of Afghanistan and tried to focus on this latest annoyance.

Recognition flashed across the girl's face. "Mrs. Stoellner?"

Mandy. She looked different in the winter, small inside her puffy coat, face pale, lips chapped. She hefted a book bag onto the library's long counter. "I had your husband for one of my history classes?"

I had your husband. Unfortunate phrasing, that.

Liv swung in her chair to face the girl. Stood to take advantage of the height she usually considered ungainly. "So that's not the class you need help with. Unless you're turning in your paper late again."

Mandy's brow creased, then smoothed. "Oh. You're being funny again? How is Professor Stoellner?"

"He's seven thousand miles away." An impossible distance that suddenly seemed just right.

"I never got to congratulate him. I tried to email him but it got bounced back? Could you give me his new email address?"

"I don't think they have email set up at his new office yet," Liv lied. "But I'll be happy to tell him for you." *Like hell I would.*

Mandy chewed her flaking lips. Her pale eyes watered. "That won't be necessary."

Liv folded her arms across her chest and waited. "Your paper?"

Mandy dragged the book bag back across the counter. "Never mind. I'll do it myself."

She trudged away. Liv wondered what the attraction had been. She tried to imagine Mandy fumbling with the generator. Or at the gun range, her arm drooping with the weight of the sidearm. Someone like Mandy would miss the signs denoting a land mine, would almost certainly push open the door that led to the booby trap. Would forget the headlamp.

Liv turned back to her computer, to the dwindling stack of tasks awaiting her attention in her final week at the college, giving them half her attention, the other half focused on the fact that in just a few days, she'd present Martin with this new self, one that would erase any memories of a girl like Mandy.

Thirteen

Farida slept in deep oblivion, savoring the warmth of her husband's body curled around her, his bare skin silky against her own. On this night, she had whispered to him that the charade had become real, that there would, indeed, be a baby. She smiled as she slid into her dreams.

She woke screaming.

The earth beneath them rumbled and shook, the walls swayed. Crockery fell and shattered in the kitchen. Voices rose, sounded more annoyed than frightened.

The rumbling stopped. Then another crash, so loud the floor quivered.

Farida shrieked again. She feared the ceiling would collapse. She curled into a ball, folding her knees against her belly.

"Shhhh. It's all right."

"Is it an earthquake? Shouldn't we go outside?" She tried to recall what she'd read about earthquakes. Outside, or under a doorway? She couldn't remember. She struggled from Gul's grip, feeling about for her clothing.

"Not an earthquake." His voice was tense, with an edge to it that reminded her of Nur Muhammed.

"Then what?"

"The Amriki have come. They are bombing us."

Farida made as if to leap from the sleeping mat. Gul restrained her.

"Let me go!" Her breath came fast. "Hurry. We have to get out."

"*Inshallah*, we will be fine here."

Even in her panic, Farida noticed the resignation in his tone. The house shuddered with a new explosion. "How are we fine?"

"They are far away. In the mountains."

"But it sounds as though they're next door."

"Yes," said Gul, in that same flat manner. "That's how bombs sound." Farida collected herself enough to realize that for this family, bombs were nothing new. She let herself relax, just a little, against him.

"Where are they?"

Gul listened to the next blast and named a nearby area.

"It sounds as though they're hitting Tora Bora. That's where the mujahideen are. They won't get them, though."

Farida tried to still her breathing and lay beside him, listening. The rest of the house quieted. She wondered if people had actually gone back to sleep. She turned her face into her husband's chest and breathed in his scent, seeking reassurance from his calm presence.

"Why won't they get them?"

"They are deep beneath the peaks of the Spin Ghar. The mujahideen have tunnels in those mountains that they have worked on for years. They used them against the Russians. They would come up from the tunnels and attack, and then melt back into the earth. It is like a city under the Spin Ghar, electricity, everything. They live better beneath the earth than some people do on its surface."

Farida thought of the villages they had passed on their way to Jalalabad. Even in her stupor that day, she had noticed their poverty, whole families pouring from ramshackle homes to watch their jeeps pass, everyone barefoot and impressively dirty. But they looked like solid citizens in comparison to the ragged and filthy inhabitants of the Kuchi encampments they'd also seen, where unveiled women stared at them from the openings of their goat-hair tents.

"The people!" she gasped now.

"What people?"

"The people who live in the mountains. The bombs—oh, what will they do about the bombs?"

"They will do the same thing they did when the Russians came."

Of course. How stupid of her to forget. These people had years of experience with all types of attack. Surely, they had developed ways to deal with them.

Gul spoke again, his voice harsh in the darkness. "They will do what they have always done," he repeated. "They will die."

"But—"

"They will die." He fell away and lay rigid beside her. "First, I hated the Russians. Now I hate the Amriki. They will kill the people just like the Russians did, and then, just like the Russians, they will leave."

Farida imagined a burst of metal and flame against mud hovels, shrapnel shredding the walls of a tent. She thought of people whose only experience with an airplane was the death that exploded from its belly. She wondered what kind of country would kill so many innocents in the name of tracking down just one man.

She reached for her husband's hand and laced her fingers with his. "I, too," she said, her words low and urgent as a vow of love. "I hate the Amriki."

———

The bombing runs continued well past midnight. Gul whispered reassurances and stroked Farida's hair, easing her into a fitful sleep that at last put a halt to her questions. She had tried to distract herself from the explosions by asking about the shellings of his childhood, inflicted first by the Russians, then by his own people during the ruinous civil war that followed the Russians' exit.

His uninformative response—he told her only that his family had left

Afghanistan because of the fighting—prompted nervous jests as she tried to cover the sound of faraway blasts with words.

"You must have been"—Gul swore beneath his breath as she calculated—"just becoming a young man." She thought of her own wrenching leave-taking. Sympathy swelled her heart. "How difficult it must have been to abandon everything you knew."

Finally, she fell asleep. But Gul lay awake till dawn, tormented by the long-buried memories aroused by her questions.

KABUL, 1993

Nur Muhammed, ever averse to strife, spent as little time as possible in the Macroyan flat after his clumsy announcement that he had taken Khurshid as a second wife.

He filled his days calling on different factional leaders, sounding them out, assessing them all, committing to none, trying to determine where the best opportunities lay. During his rare hours at home, the family settled into an uneasy armistice. Maryam treated him with exaggerated respect, rushing to prepare his tea before he left each day, handing him a freshly laundered tunic and a woolen waistcoat brushed free of lint.

Khurshid lingered in the sleeping alcove until Nur Muhammed left. Maryam stormed into it—she herself slept in the main room, with the children—and flung aside curtains drawn against the chill, sniffing the musky air like a feral dog about to devour some small, unfortunate creature.

"Up!" she bellowed, as Khurshid cowered on the sleeping mats. "It is late and we are hungry."

It was not unusual for Maryam to reach down, wrap her hand in Khurshid's long, shining hair, and drag her into the main room, releasing her with a flourish, sending Khurshid staggering toward the kitchen alcove.

The children, lolling sleepily on their own mats, giggled. Bibi hissed through her grin, enjoying Khurshid's discomfort. Only Gul was silent.

His own recent introduction to humiliation by the boys of Macroyan, and their unerring aim with the shards of concrete littering the buildings' courtyards, made him feel sorry for Khurshid, who was, after all, so close to his own age.

Most mornings, after Khurshid finished preparing breakfast for the family and washing the dishes, she did the day's laundry, making several trips to the communal well in the courtyard and laboriously hauling water up the stairs. She heated it on the coal-burning *bukhari* stove on the balcony, and Gul watched her covertly as she stirred the mass of heavy cloth in the steaming pot with a stick, then plunged her arms in up to the elbows, working in the harsh soap with her hands, which grew rough and reddened in the chilly air. As soon as she had finished, it was time for the midday meal and then the cleanup, by which time Khurshid's shoulders sagged and her head drooped from exhaustion. Maryam, too, was always sleepy then. She would make a great show of rolling out her mat and reclining upon it, reciting the day's marketing list in a bored tone.

As much as Maryam liked to choose her own food, she refused to venture into this strange, cold city, her discomfort increased by the fact that few women in Kabul wore the burqa and instead bared their faces beneath carelessly wrapped scarves.

"People will think we are ignorant," Nur Muhammed would say, but once he was out of earshot, Maryam would remind the children that it was better to be thought ignorant than indecent. So it was up to Khurshid to take herself and her naked face off to the market.

"Gul," she would mumble, just before she dropped off to sleep, "go with your father's whore. Make sure she speaks to no one and that the merchants don't cheat her. Don't let her spend all our money."

Maryam deemed the markets near Macroyan too expensive. Instead, on her new neighbors' recommendations, she insisted that Khurshid shop at the bazaars on the outskirts of town. Sometimes, depending on traffic, the jolting bus ride could take as long as an hour, and Gul, from his position near the front of the bus, could see that Khurshid, held upright by the press of women in the rear, used the opportunity to sleep.

Gul, too, found relief in the long ride. It was crowded and hot and impossibly tedious, but at least on the bus he was safe from Fahim, a tall boy who ruled over Macroyan's swarms of dirty children. With schools closed and mothers who, like Maryam, were coping badly at best with their dislocated lives, the children ran wild. Nur Muhammed's pains to establish his family's importance had been for naught. Everyone in Macroyan had been someone where they lived before. The old Soviet towers were packed with former civil servants and businessmen and professors, the latter easily recognized in the courtyard by the stacks of books on the ground before them.

"Books in German, books in French, cheap for you," one man urged as Gul and Khurshid rushed past every afternoon, even as another wheedled, "Mathematics, chemistry. Educate yourselves."

In fact, the only thing that set Gul's family apart was that they were Pashtun in an overwhelmingly Tajik area. In Macroyan, only the Hazara, with their tilted eyes and their strange Shi'a ways, were more distrusted than the Pashtun. Unless Gul was accompanying Khurshid to the bazaar, or making a rare trip with Nur Muhammed, he remained indoors, something more easily accomplished than he expected. Here, his mother proved an unwitting ally, insisting that Khurshid make several wearying trips each day to the well, a job that might otherwise have fallen to Gul, as the strongest. But staying in the flat was only marginally worse than going outdoors and risking the torments of Fahim. At least, though, if he saw Fahim about, he could make a dash for safety. Indoors, there was no escape from Maryam's misery. His mother had quickly made friends with the women in their building, some of whom also had had to confront the indignity of new, young wives in their husband's beds, and so shared a heartache that trumped ethnicity.

For hours each day, their pitched voices lifted and sank in litanies of pain, the rhythm breaking only long enough for Maryam to order Khurshid to bring more tea, more almonds, more of her husband's favorite raisins. Finally, Khurshid complained to Nur Muhammed, or so Gul had surmised from what he could hear on the other side of the curtain.

Nur Muhammed's voice rose. He worked hard all day, he pointed out to Khurshid, and when he came home, all he wanted was peace—"not squabbling women." Besides, he continued as Maryam smirked beside Gul, Maryam had enough to do all day with taking care of the children. "It's not as though," he said, his tone sounding a threat, "you have any children yet."

The next morning, after Nur Muhammed left, Maryam managed to stumble into Khurshid as she was carrying fresh tea, causing Khurshid to falter and lose her grasp on the pot, which spilled its steaming contents onto the bare ankle peeking coyly from beneath her pantaloons.

"*Aiiii.*" Tears trembled in Khurshid's eyes. She bent over the ankle, lifting the pantaloons to inspect a patch of skin already bubbling an angry scarlet. Gul stared speechless at the exposed curve of calf.

Maryam glanced toward Khurshid and pushed herself up from where she had landed, but softly, on the floor. "I'm sorry," she said, "but I am so very tired. People were complaining last night, keeping me from my sleep. People should not complain. Here, let me help you up." She righted herself, then took Khurshid's upper arm, pinching it and hauling the girl so close that their faces nearly touched. "People shouldn't complain," Maryam repeated, then released Khurshid. She looked at the ankle. "That's ugly. What a shame. It might get infected. It will rot and stink. No one will want to be near you."

That very evening, Nur Muhammed, taking one look at Khurshid's reddened eyes, her swollen, puffy features, and her sullen bearing, snapped at her to sleep in the main room with the children, and indicated, with a jerk of his head, that Maryam should share the bedroom with him.

This time, it was Khurshid's turn to cry herself to sleep, although Gul noticed that she did so in near silence, only an occasional sniffle and shudder from beneath her blankets giving her away. In the next room, Maryam and Nur Muhammed sat up laughing and chatting, their lantern providing a line of light below the doorway that flickered late into the evening. In its dim glow, Gul could see Khurshid's eyes fixed upon it. When Khurshid shared the room with Nur Muhammed, there was never any talking, at least not that Gul could tell, just the noises that left him restless and shifting uncomfortably on his mat until he fell into a sleep from which he awoke wet and ashamed. He wondered if Khurshid continued to stare toward the door when the light was finally extinguished, or if she pulled her blanket tight over her head to drown out the soft, rhythmic sounds that, until recently, she herself had caused.

———————

Khurshid became so listless that Gul feared for her.

At the market, she turned her head away and so did not see when the vendor laid his thumb boldly on the scale containing the raisins. She said nothing when the baker snagged the pieces of naan hanging from the rusty hook above his stall where the bread had dried stiff in the sun and acquired a powdery coating of street dust, and she shrugged when Gul pointed out the indifferent cut of lamb from the butcher. Maryam, he knew, would have put her nose to the meat, then made such a show of gagging and retching that the butcher would have thrown in another quarter kilo for free. Khurshid, her burn still healing, limped as they left the butcher's stall, and Gul offered to carry the package for her. She handed it to him without a word.

"I have a little extra money," he said. "We could take a taxi home."

"Your mother will be angry." Khurshid spoke in a whisper.

"I'll tell her we took the bus."

"She'll count the money. She'll know."

Gul thought a moment. "I'll tell her that I did the shopping today."

Some hair escaped from beneath Khurshid's scarf. She tucked it back in, too fast for Gul to memorize its bewitching curl. "She'll never believe that."

"I'll tell her I did it because I thought you were too stupid."

A smile rewarded him. "That, she'll believe!"

Gul laughed. Khurshid joined in.

"*Hssst!*" An older man glared at them. Their conduct was unseemly. Khurshid quickly assumed a more serious expression, but Gul caught the mirth in her sideways glance, and he choked as he struggled to contain his own merriment.

"Why," he asked when they were in the taxi, "do you not wear the burqa?"

She gazed out the window, willing him to look with her. Although some of the women they passed were shrouded in blue, most opted for simple scarves, leaving their faces bare to varying degrees. Gul was used to Jalalabad, where the only women who showed their faces in public were the Kuchi, and he well knew his mother's opinion of them. But Kabul was different, and the daily parade of pretty girls was one of his favorite things about the city.

"My family thinks—" She paused and blushed.

"What do they think?"

"That only people who are . . . that only people from the countryside wear the burqa."

He considered her meaning. "Only people who are uneducated." He took her silence for assent. He voiced the question that had nagged at him ever since he first saw Khurshid.

"Why did you marry my father, then?" He whispered, so the cab-driver would not hear over the cacophony of street noise.

"They made me."

"Did you not want to?" He had heard, of course, of people who balked at their parents' choice, and had heard also of the dire consequences that resulted.

Khurshid's lips twisted. "Oh, I wanted to. I listened to him every time he visited my father. He said such interesting things. And he was so kind. *Then.*"

Gul could have told her that Nur Muhammed was always kind when he wanted something, but he decided that she had probably figured that out. Besides, it was already the longest conversation he had had with a woman not his relative. He sneaked quick glances at her

face, at the smudges of exhaustion beneath her eyes, the hollows beneath her cheekbones. Her lips were cracked and dry. Still, he thought
her beautiful. He ordered the taxi to stop a block from Macroyan so
that no one would see them arriving in such style. When she stepped
from the car, the pain in her ankle made her stumble, and she grabbed
his arm and leaned against him. Her hair smelled of almond oil. Gul
inhaled, then pulled away in confusion. But Khurshid held fast, shaking. She paused on the street, staring toward Macroyan's forbidding
towers. Gul was aware of the impropriety of the moment, but he, too,
lingered, excited by her nearness. He told himself he was taking the
opportunity to scan the area for signs of Fahim, but nothing registered
except his own regret when Khurshid exhaled and dropped his arm,
setting off toward Macroyan with firm and resolute steps despite her
injury.

They crossed the space between apartment blocks without trouble,
finding it unusually empty. Then Gul saw why. People clustered around
a taxi at the far end of the block, whose driver scurried into their building and reemerged moments later carrying a bundle and followed by
Maryam, berating him with every step, much to the amusement of the
crowd. She turned upon Gul as soon as she saw him.

"You. Help him. Quickly, quickly. Your father has found a new place
to live." She shifted her scowl to Khurshid. "There is no room for you in
the taxi. You take the bus."

Khurshid trembled anew. "But where am I going? Which bus shall I
take?"

Maryam laughed. "You were smart enough to figure out how to catch
my husband. Now figure out where we're going. Maybe you'll find us.
Maybe you'll get lost on the way." She climbed into the taxi, gathering the
little children to her. "Come. Quickly," she said to Gul.

He ran into the building, where the driver lifted the last of their bundles. He pushed a handful of afghanis at the man and found out their new
address. He gave him some more money, and the man called to a nearby

boy and whispered in his ear. The boy left at a trot, and the man assured Gul that a taxi would come in a few moments for Khurshid.

By the way he looked at Khurshid, Gul knew he wished he were driving her himself. Gul chastised him with a curse, and the man recovered, hefting the bundles into the car. Gul squeezed onto the seat next to his mother and willed himself not to turn and look back at Khurshid standing alone in the courtyard, pulling her scarf across her face as Fahim appeared from behind one of the buildings and glided toward her, his gang of younger boys in tow. A cab passed them, heading toward the courtyard as they pulled away, and Gul let his breath out in relief. The driver caught his gaze in the mirror and nodded.

Neither of them looked at Maryam, who had regained her old, regal posture as they left her husband's new wife behind.

Fourteen

Martin awoke hungover. He inched one hand across the sheet—slowly, slowly, no sudden moves, and fumbled for the phone.

"Bring me my special breakfast." He replaced the receiver with a groan of relief at the thought of the silver coffeepot, filled with real coffee. Shortly after his arrival in Islamabad, he'd gone into the kitchen to show Marriott staff how to make it to his specifications, despite their protests that they were quite accustomed to meeting the needs of foreigners. When his breakfast arrived, he dosed the coffee from the flask he kept in his nightstand, then lifted the dome from the plate, revealing not eggs but a stack of steaming towels that Martin draped over his chest and face, raising them occasionally to sip the coffee.

Eventually, he'd slip the aspirin, thoughtfully placed on the saucer, into his mouth and wait for the combination of caffeine and whiskey, steam and medication, to work their magic on his aching body. It was necessary after another round of the house parties that seemingly defined Islamabad's expat community. In his time at the Marriott, Martin had become a generous tipper. Consequently, his mornings were far more bearable, allowing him to put off, at least until he ventured out, the creeping trepidation that had plagued him since his arrival in Pakistan.

He'd expected to meet with Clayton Williams in Islamabad. Instead, a rotating cast of brush-cut young Americans and Britons worked to get him up to speed on every aspect of the political and military situation in Afghanistan, a level of detail down to the satellite phone contacts of various warlords. "A consulting group" was the terse answer when he'd asked if they were military. "We prepare organizations like yours." Their set faces, their clipped responses, warned him against asking exactly what they meant by *like yours.*

Afghanistan's cities had fallen quickly to the Americans, but pockets of fierce resistance remained. The Taliban retreated, but not even the most clueless of the foreign aid workers pouring into the country would believe they'd surrendered, with near daily reports of skirmishes in the outlying regions.

These days, though, such information lived in the back pages of newspapers, tucked among paragraph-long reports of bus plunges and ferry sinkings. Front-page real estate was reserved for the stories that implied everything was better with the arrival of the Americans: photos of children flying kites, people watching television, and girls going back to school—many of them teenagers sitting shyly among girls half their age, catching up on the five years of ignorance mandated by the Taliban.

About the girls. Martin ventured a query. Because surely, they were his main focus?

"Mrs. Khan handles that aspect of things," said Boy Wonder No. 1 (Martin had given up trying to keep track of his trainers' names), a six-footer who stood eye to eye with Martin and outweighed him by a good forty pounds of muscle. The younger man jutted his rocklike jaw at the lone woman in the room. She appeared dumpy even in the generous drape of her silk tunic. "She'll work mostly with your wife."

Was Martin imagining the sneering tone? He could hear Liv, as clearly as though she stood at his elbow, supplying the same sort of sotto voce commentary she often employed at faculty events: "Never mind about that. It's women's work. Nothing important. Now let's go back to comparing missile size."

Indeed, Boy Wonder No. 1 tapped a key that brought images of a startling array of weaponry onto the screen. "You'll need to be able to recognize these on sight. Don't worry. After a while, it's like knowing Fords from Chevys."

Martin wrenched his attention away from Mrs. Khan and back to the implements of death, reminding himself that he'd known what he was getting into when he took the job. The trick would be reassuring Liv, once she figured out the extras involved. Which she would—she was quick like that. How many times had she worked Mandy's name into "casual" conversation before he'd left?

Boy Wonder No. 1 placed a meaty forefinger to the touch pad, switching the screen to a display of sidearms. "The men yesterday. Were they carrying?"

Martin shrugged. Embarrassment flowed hot through his veins. Of course everyone would have heard about the incident yesterday. Just the sight of him—the raw scrape on his nose and chin, the swollen flesh shading from purple to yellow beneath his eyes—provoked whispers in his wake. He'd just hoped no one would mention it to his face.

His first trip to Pakistan, so very long ago, had been tightly controlled, with Martin and the other graduate students ushered into conference rooms to interview groups of carefully chosen Afghan refugees, their message artfully scripted to elicit more U.S. aid.

In this new venture, he hungered to strike out on his own, to slip away from the watchful eye of Pervaiz, the hovering functionary who headed Face the Future's Islamabad operation and who daily, in a thousand small ways, let Martin know that the appreciation he'd expected in response to his familiarity with the region and its customs would never come.

The previous day, a Friday, confident in his workmanlike Urdu and eager for a respite from Pervaiz, Martin had ventured from Face the Future's office during the languid hours after lunch and hailed a cab for Aabpara Market. He planned to shop away from the upscale stores in the Blue Zone, where too many of the offerings resembled the sorts of things he could buy back home.

But in his haste to flee before Pervaiz noticed his absence, he forgot to set a price with the cabbie ahead of time. When they arrived at the market and Martin held out a perfectly reasonable number of rupees, the driver pulled a wounded expression.

"Well, then, how much do you want?"

"As you wish." The man gave the standard reply, except that in this case, Martin knew it to mean "more than what you're holding in your hand."

Martin doubled his original amount and flung it at the man. "Take this and buy your mother a new dupatta, to hide the face she's been showing everyone on the street." He slammed the cab's door behind him and stalked toward the market, knowing Pervaiz would hear about this before his return. It had taken Martin about five minutes in Islamabad to realize that the gossip network linking the cabbies was nearly as fast as, and often more accurate than, the internet.

But his discomfort eased in the alleyways of Aabpara, as satisfyingly exotic as he'd hoped. He followed the smell of scorched fabric and found a man pressing clothing with a heavy iron containing glowing coals. He walked faster past a butcher's stall, where blood congealed on the skinny goat carcasses swaying from the rafters, flies beginning to collect on the meat in the day's increasing heat. The goats' severed heads sat on a waist-high counter, eyes open, their odd horizontal pupils still glistening.

A man in the shop called as Martin passed. He turned. The man held a cleaver high and let it fall. The two halves of a goat's head stood upright a moment, then wobbled and fell away from the blade. The man smirked at Martin and wiped the cleaver on the front of his spattered apron.

Martin looked away. His gaze fell on a far more pleasurable sight: a pair of young wives, muslin bags looped over their arms, doing their daily marketing. At Face the Future, under the watchful eye of Pervaiz, he dared not give more than a cursory glance at the local women. But here he was free to take in their beauty in sidelong glimpses. So tiny and quick compared with Liv; modest, too, in contrast to the college students back home whose outspoken feminism kept him on edge, made him dread the unwary remark that had seen so many of his colleagues castigated.

He'd long ago trained himself to stare past a girl's ear as she spoke, or maybe at the part in her hair, anything to avoid looking at her bare shoulders, the breasts outlined by a stretchy tube top. Now he saw only women's faces, and barely those, but it was all so alluring. Gleaming bangles drew the eye to fragile wrists, rings to tiny hands and their balletic gestures. Dupattas invariably slipped just so, revealing heavy earrings swinging from shell-like lobes, brushing slender, graceful necks. Eyes flashed dark within their bold definitions of kohl, reddened lips pouted promisingly. And those layers and layers of fabric, practically demanding him to imagine the marvels beneath, making him wonder what he'd ever seen in poor Mandy, flushed and sweaty in her jogbra and shorts.

"*Hssst!*" A passing man scowled. He'd stared too long. Martin hurried around a corner, slowing when he came to a shop selling DVDs and Bollywood-style posters. The movies were bootleg, no doubt.

He shuffled through the wares, stepping deeper into the store, realizing only belatedly that the Bollywood images gave way to a reverential display of placards, postcards, and buttons emblazoned with images of Osama bin Laden. Martin stared at the aquiline, heavy-lidded visage, the aristocratic features so at odds with the utilitarian Kalashnikov balanced in the elegant, long-fingered hands. A shelf displayed magazines, one of them showing a giant black boot propelling a hapless, monkey-faced President Bush into oblivion. Martin heard a footfall and looked to see a man beside him.

The man tilted his chin toward the magazine. "George Boosh is dog." He looked at Martin. "Amriki?"

"Canadian."

Martin feared his expression revealed the lie. He backed away, forcing himself not to look over his shoulder as he left the store and turned yet another corner. By the time he realized he was off the main street and couldn't easily find his way back, he'd attracted a crowd of children whose proximity made him anxious about his wallet, bulky and prominent in his hip pocket. But, surrounded as he was, there was no way to transfer it to his front pocket, where he could casually keep a hand on it. He finally resorted to slipping into a rare enclosed store and closing the door against the children. He found himself face-to-face with a merchant who, before Martin could protest, clapped his hands and ordered tea and bade Martin sit on a low stool, the better to view his wares.

All around Martin, wooden dowels held stacks of bangles. "These, I think, will be very beautiful for your wife." The merchant lifted a stack of rose-hued glass bracelets and fanned them out, Slinky-style, on a bit of dark felt.

Martin quaffed his tea, thinking to leave, but at a gesture from the merchant, a boy slipped from behind a curtain and refilled his cup. Martin groaned. He shook his head at the display and tried to invest the Urdu word for thanks with a sense of finality.

"*Shukriya.*" He rose, still holding the teacup.

"But of course. These are for every day. You want to buy her something special." He reached below a counter and came out with a handful of thin gold circles that seemed, to Martin's eyes, too dainty to slide over Liv's large American hands.

"I think that these will not fit." Martin spoke in slow and careful Urdu, but the man professed not to understand. More bracelets of gold, heavier and correspondingly more expensive, appeared.

The merchant half rose from his stool and whispered a price to Martin. "Special for you. In dollars only."

"Ah." Martin sighed his regrets. He had very little American money with him, having already changed most of his into Pakistani rupees. He pulled out his wallet, now safely in his front pocket, and showed the man his only greenback, a five.

The man recoiled. His eyes blazed the insult back at Martin. He swept the bracelets back onto their dowels with a tinkling noise and slammed the cabinet shut. He stood and held the store door open. "In our country, we value our women. We show them the respect of the best jewelry we can afford."

Martin had thought to offer the man the money for some of the cheaper bracelets, a present for Liv upon her arrival, but it seemed as though that wouldn't do. He backed through the door, apologizing profusely in both Urdu and English, wondering exactly what he'd done wrong. The children clustered just outside the door seemed to have divined the shopkeeper's attitude, because when Martin asked them how to get back to the main road where he could call a cab, they jeered at him and danced just out of his reach, loudly calling into question the honor of his mother, his sisters, his wife. They bent low and wiggled their asses at him, berating his own supposed penchant for buggery, attracting the attention of other merchants and their customers, who looked on the impudent boys with varying degrees of amusement and disapproval.

Martin walked faster and faster, but the boys drew close. Their fingers snatched at his sleeves, fumbled about his pockets. Martin pushed at them, glancing around for help, but the merchants and shoppers who only moments before had provided such an attentive audience had vanished, leaving him alone in a deserted alley with his pint-size assailants. When he swung at the boys before him, more moved in from behind. He whirled to face them, but still others swarmed close. Just as he reached for his wallet, thinking in his desperation to give it to them, anything to make them go away, the boys fell back.

Three men in business suits rounded the corner, grunting at the boys in Urdu too low and rapid for Martin to catch. The boys turned as one and fled, stumbling into one another in their haste.

One of the men bent his slender torso in a half bow toward Martin. "Please accept our apologies. These boys have no respect. They are not of good families." He spoke in the crisp, British-accented English of the well educated. His tailored slacks broke just so over polished Italian loafers.

The two men behind him were burlier, their suits rumpled, ill fitting, as if borrowed for the day. One moved to Martin's side and took his elbow, his fingers mashing flesh against bone.

"Come," said the first man, who appeared to be in charge. "We will take you to safety."

Martin had no choice but to follow.

As they had at the sight of the boys, shoppers melted into stores as the quartet approached, glancing over their shoulders with wide eyes before doors and shutters closed with decisive clicks behind them, the humming alleyways falling eerily silent.

"Where are we going?" Because surely they were heading deeper into the market. Martin tried again. "I'm staying at the Marriott."

The man in the lead lengthened his stride. "Thank you," Martin called to him. "I very much appreciate your help. If you can take me to a street where I can hail a cab, I can get myself back."

"Shut up, Amriki," the one holding his elbow growled, jerking him nearly off his feet.

Martin felt a brief, desperate pang for the boys, who had wanted merely to rob him. In their weeks apart, he and Liv had exchanged emails about their various trainings. "Your beige man," he'd signed off once, in reference to the instructions on how to behave if kidnapped. "Be beige. Call no attention to yourself. No eye contact. No speaking unless spoken to."

Now Martin desperately wanted to call attention to himself, to shout out to the people in the shops, to beg for mercy from his escorts. But speech was impossible, moving as they were at very nearly a run. Martin's heart slammed his ribs, breath coming in gasps, and a singular vow roiled his brain: *Get me out of this and I swear I will obey Pervaiz to the letter.* They turned corner after corner after corner in that terrifying deserted maze, surely the only place in all of Islamabad devoid of people—until a final turn brought them face-to-face with Pervaiz and a phalanx of uniformed men.

Martin's captors flung him to the ground and fled. No way to catch himself, to prevent his face from bashing concrete. He pushed himself up and tilted his head back. He put his hand to his nose. It came away coated with blood. The men with Pervaiz dropped their guns to their sides.

Martin's Urdu fled. "Make them go after them! They're getting away!"

"No," Pervaiz corrected him. "*You* are getting away. And you are lucky to do so. Let us leave before you cause further trouble." He handed Martin a handkerchief.

Martin held it to his nose, watching above its snowy folds as the trio strolled off, blending in with the shoppers emerging from the stores.

"Hey." Boy Wonder No. 1 snapped his fingers in Martin's face. "Where'd you go? You can't afford not to know this stuff. Did they check you out for a concussion yesterday?"

"No. No need." Other than the swollen nose and accompanying shiners, the worst injuries had been to his pride—and, he feared, his credibility. He'd known that Fridays could be tense—the mullahs saved their fieriest exhortations, increasingly anti-American these days, for the Friday midday prayers, and demonstrations frequently followed—but had chosen to ignore the fact that the Red Mosque, Islamabad's most militant, was only a few hundred yards from Aabpara.

"Listen." The Boy Wonder snapped his fingers again, the crack disconcertingly loud. "You've had your bad thing. And if you're lucky, that's the worst it will ever get. Those guys, they were amateurs, playing at being bad, probably all worked up from the weekly sermon. The real baddies never would have done it like that. In fact, I can't remember the last time we had a successful kidnapping. But here's the good part. You've been in the shit. Or gotten a whiff of it, at least. Now you know what it's like. It won't ever scare you like that again."

I've been in the shit. Martin rolled the phrase around in his brain, trying to acquire a mental swagger. But his gut won out, queasy with the fear, imbuing him with a keen new appreciation for the next screen that flashed a display of handheld missile launchers, with their innocuous resemblance to plumbing fixtures. His stomach settled. If he ever found himself in the shit again, his side had things like this at hand.

He took a breath, narrowed his eyes, and focused. "Left to right," he said. "Strela—NATO name Gremlin. Redeye. Fagot—NATO name Spigot. And, of course, Stinger."

"Stinger." The Boy Wonder underscored the word. "If you learn nothing else, learn that one. You hear about one, see one, you let us know right away. I mean, that very minute. Whatever you're doing, you stop, walk away, find a secure place, get us on the satphone."

"Us?"

His youthful instructor struck a key with a pinkie the size of Martin's thumb. The screen went black. "That's tomorrow's lesson."

Fifteen

JALALABAD, JANUARY 2002

Farida reclined in the beautician's chair for the ministrations that would maintain her appearance to Maryam's exacting standards.

The women were preparing for the six-month birthday of Bibi's second child, an occasion made more momentous by the fact that this baby, unlike the first, was a boy. So, for the first time since their arrival in Jalalabad, Farida, Maryam, and Bibi left the compound and traveled into the city to have their hair washed and arranged, their eyebrows threaded, and makeup applied. As much as Farida looked forward to the party, she was more excited about the outing. Not that she could see much through the burqa's grille. But she'd been so long confined that ordinary sights—the noisy, stacked-high crates of live chickens, the scarlet splash of roses affixed to the hood of a wedding-bound car, even the ominous rumbling from a passing Amriki military vehicle—thrilled her by virtue of variety. To be sure, Jalalabad lacked the sophistication of the smart streets in Islamabad's Blue Zone and diplomatic area, or even Peshawar's modern neighborhood of Hayatabad, where Gul's family had lived before returning to Afghanistan. But still, it was a city, full of people other than those with whom she lived.

Farida, hungry for more insights into her new world, had hoped the beauty shop would be crowded, serving up delicious morsels of gossip along with the inevitable tea and sweetmeats. But Nur Muhammed had demanded, and paid handsomely for, a private visit for the women of his household.

A thread slid across Farida's eyebrow. The beautician rolled a row of hairs between its cotton strands and clenched the end of the thread between her teeth. "Now."

Farida braced herself.

The woman jerked her head back. A line of fine dark hairs whispered free. Farida winced. It had been far too long since she'd tended to her appearance.

"You'll probably want to do this more often in Kabul." The hot towels covering Maryam's face to open her pores for her own threading muffled her voice but failed to disguise the censure it held. "No doubt you'll show your face at that job."

The move to Kabul was imminent. And through Nur Muhammed's mysterious channels, work there had been procured for Farida, although its exact nature remained murky. Maryam's dismay was anything but. The previous night, after Gul fell into the deep sleep of satisfaction beside her, Farida pressed her ear to the wall to catch the snatches of conversation from Maryam's room next door.

"She will shame us all!"

"I will declare it acceptable."

And the king has spoken.

"But she is—"

Farida held her breath. She was still early in her pregnancy, far too soon for the rest of the household, especially the men, to be told of it. Anything could happen. And even if the pregnancy proceeded without complications, Maryam had a point, albeit unspoken. Farida's pregnancy, camouflaged by her loose garments, would likely remain undetected upon their arrival in Kabul a few weeks hence, but that would change quickly. What then?

"She is what?"

But Maryam, for all her bluster, apparently had reached the limits of challenging her husband's authority. She tried another tack. "You know what happens to women like her in Kabul. Women who show their face. Don't tell me you've forgotten about *her*."

The slap echoed so loud that Farida fell away from the wall. She glanced at Gul, but he slumbered on.

"You are never to speak of that!"

At the shop, the beautician nodded toward the raised spot on Maryam's cheek, shiny and purple as the miniature eggplants in the market. "Some special makeup here, I think," she murmured. "Nothing will show. I'll teach you how to apply it." Farida wondered at the extent of her experience disguising the marks of men.

Until this day, Maryam had not mentioned the job to Farida or anyone else. Bad enough that the aunties knew Farida had worked before her marriage, a subject of endless questions and judgments.

Wasn't it difficult to type in a burqa? Oh, she didn't wear one? Shocked expressions all around.

"But I had my dupatta." Farida made a motion across her face, neglecting to mention that she'd merely draped her dupatta over her chest and shoulders, leaving her entire head exposed.

Eyebrows arched high, conveying the inadequacy of her answer. So the men with whom she worked—she did work with men, yes?—could see her face? And her father approved of such a place? Didn't the men take liberties?

"Yes. And no." How to explain that her father more than approved, even if his support for his daughters' careers was more rooted in financial need than feminism. As for liberties, Farida thought it best not to mention the occasional sotto voce dinner invitations, the approving remarks about her appearance, the impermissible hands to a shoulder or forearm that plagued her days. If a seemingly innocuous question had provoked a slap, what would happen if Maryam presented Nur Muhammed with such damning information? Now she sought to reassure her mother-in-law, and herself as well.

"Kabul is still some weeks away, yes? Things could change. Maybe there will be no job for me after all. *Aiiee.*" The beautician put the thread aside and wielded a tweezer, catching stray hairs.

"He will not change. And I will not try to make him." Maryam's warning was clear.

The beautician dipped a cloth in cold water and laid it across Farida's brows. Pleasure overcame discomfort as the woman massaged almond oil into Farida's scalp. Farida forced her attention back to the matter at hand, and others, too. Bibi was across the room, a manicurist tending to her nails. This was the first time Farida had been alone with her mother-in-law since her wedding. She didn't know when such an opportunity might come again.

"You've lived in Kabul before."

The folded towels stirred as Maryam nodded. Steam gathered in clouds above her chair. Water ran in slow drips down the wall behind her.

"What was that like?"

The beautician removed the cloth from Farida's brows. "Much better," she said. "The redness is almost gone. Oh, I missed one." The tweezer probed the delicate skin near Farida's eye.

Maryam expelled a forceful breath. "You must not ask. Not me, not anyone. It is bad enough that you have no sense of shame. Do not be stupid also."

"Now," the beautician said. The stubborn hair let go its hold.

Farida gasped, grateful for the pain that lent credence to her response, more grateful still that Maryam could not see her expression. And a few minutes later, as the beautician lifted the hot cloth from her mother-in-law's face, Farida wisely pretended not to see the tears leaking from Maryam's eyes, just as she had ignored the glimpse of a similar telltale moisture before Gul turned away when she'd asked about their previous life in Kabul.

The women swept back into the compound in a haze of perfume and excitement, the exhilaration of their brush with the outside world permeating the household. Gul knew from experience that it would take days for the daily routine to resume its somnolent pace, for the voices to tumble from their high, twittering chatter to the languid lower registers.

The aunties clutched one another's arms, eager to share what they'd gleaned from their hairdressers. Women's talk. Gul, drawn to a doorway by their arrival, started to turn away. Then turned back. Something was amiss.

Maryam stood to one side of the group, Farida to the other, each holding herself stiff, neither joining the conversation that would run on through the evening meal and well past midnight.

Gul started toward his wife, then reconsidered. Respect demanded attention be paid first to his mother. He eased to her side, as though he were merely passing through the room, and whispered, "Has something happened?"

His mother spoke so quietly only he could hear, the anger in her words nonetheless distinct, unmistakable. "Your wife. She asks too many questions. She should not poke her nose into other people's affairs." The command was clear. He was to convey the message to Farida and would be held responsible for future transgressions.

And yet, asking after other people's affairs was exactly what Nur Muhammed wanted Farida to do. As sorry as Gul felt for himself in that moment, he felt even worse for his wife, caught between competing demands. Even so, his mother was the most forthright of women. What could Farida have asked to provoke such a response? He could think of only one thing.

KABUL, 1993

Even the belated reappearance of Khurshid couldn't dampen Maryam's pleasure in the new house Nur Muhammed found during that first sojourn in Kabul, and Gul let himself hope that these more spacious quarters would ease the family's tensions.

The house was near the university and belonged to a professor who had the dual qualities that over the years would make Nur Muhammed return again and again to educators to achieve his goals. Because so many academics had traveled abroad, they had the foreign contacts and information about other countries that Nur Muhammed found useful. They also were more naïve, and thus more easily manipulated, than the leaders of the constantly shifting government and tribal factions also cultivated by Nur Muhammed. Those latter, however, proved their worth in helping him decide on the family's new location, tipping him off as to where the next round of skirmishes might take place.

Given the instability of the situation and the uncertain loyalties of those involved, it was inevitable that at some point Nur Muhammed would get bad information. But his folly was not immediately apparent. It was springtime, and the scent of roses scraggly and neglected, but blooming nonetheless, perfumed the courtyard of the new house in the neighborhood that Nur Muhammed had been assured was safe.

"It's good, yes?" he said to Maryam. She looked away, unwilling to show pleasure in any move short of a return to Jalalabad. But Gul saw his mother's approval in the way she swept her gaze across the thick walls that would ensure a cool, hushed interior. The house was set well back from the street, a luxury in the crowded city. And besides, there was that garden. Inside the house, all was dark, the windows shuttered. Maryam walked into the courtyard, flipped the front of her burqa away from her face, and lifted it to the sun. Strands in her dark hair glinted auburn. Her strong features, lately crabbed with worry, relaxed. It wasn't a smile, but it was the closest Gul had seen in quite some time, and that night, Nur Muhammed shared her room again while Khurshid nursed her blistered ankle.

When Gul awoke, his father was gone, and his mother moved about slowly, sleepily, arranging their possessions in this new space so much larger than the flat. When Maryam first saw the house, she imagined luxurious furnishings within, but was disappointed to find it bare of nearly everything but outlines in the dust that showed where things once stood.

"Looters," Nur Muhammed said. Gul thought he knew what had

really happened. He could imagine Nur Muhammed arranging the sale of the professor's possessions, pocketing the proceeds, and then professing ignorance when the home's owner returned. There was a civil war, Nur Muhammed would say. No one, and nothing, was safe. Ignoring Maryam's brief dissatisfaction, Gul and Bibi ran from one empty room to the next, choking on the dust stirred up by their passage. Only a large old cabinet, too unwieldy and ugly for quick sale, remained in a back room, and Gul impatiently opened its doors and banged them shut again, disappointed to find it empty.

"Gul." His mother's voice sounded sharp behind him. Gul sighed. He wanted to keep exploring. Bibi slid away as Maryam approached. Gul awaited his mother's instructions, but she forgot him, intrigued by the cabinet, which stood taller than either of them. Maryam opened it and inspected the emptiness within. She started to close the door, then stopped and yanked it open again. She peered inside and rapped at the back of the cabinet. It echoed hollowly. Maryam ran probing hands across it. She gave a push, and the wooden panel swung open into a darkened space beyond. She crawled into it and emerged empty-handed. Whatever precious goods had been hidden there were long gone.

She pulled the makeshift door shut and closed the cabinet's outer door. She grabbed Gul's upper arms and drew him toward her. He had grown so quickly in the last year that she had to stand on tiptoe to be at eye level with him. "Say nothing of this. Not to Bibi, not anyone." She pinched him and shoved him ahead of her out of the room and toward the courtyard.

"Khurshid!" Maryam's voice lost no time in regaining its old peremptory tone. Gul looked up and saw the girl's face peering between a slit in the shutters that covered an upstairs window. Maryam stood over a pump, working a handle that shrieked from long disuse. Brownish water trickled, then gushed in rusty coughs. Maryam lifted the handle and let it fall once more. She stuck her hands beneath the fast-clearing stream and raised them dripping to her face. A circle of damp widened around her feet.

"Khurshid!" Maryam bellowed. "Come and wash the clothes."

That night, Gul lay with his arm flung across his eyes, inhaling the fresh scent of clothing cleaner than Khurshid had ever been able to get it in Macroyan's sooty air. There, with too-large families crammed into too-small flats, the nights had been punctuated by greasy cooking smells, heavy footfalls, and arguments, with their occasional slaps and shrieks. Here, even the sporadic nighttime gunfire seemed quieter, its crackling muffled by the thick carpets Maryam had brought from Jalalabad and finally was able to unroll to their full size. For the first time in months, Gul slept without waking until the quavering wail of the daybreak call to prayer from the neighborhood mosque.

Many of their new neighbors were like them, essentially squatting in houses that had been deserted. From his prone position in the next room, as close to the doorway as he could get without being detected, he heard the women talk. "You shouldn't have come here," one of them said. "We're leaving. You should, too."

Maryam busied herself with the tea. Gul knew it pleased her to be able to serve it in such a gracious setting, to send the children off to another room rather than have them always underfoot, leaning up against her, tugging at her, demanding her full attention no matter how busy she was, when by rights she should have been surrounded by the female relatives who would have shared in their care.

"We can't leave. My husband just went away again. We have to wait for him to come home."

"When will that be?"

Maryam slurped her tea. "I don't know. Weeks, maybe."

The neighbor started. "That's too long. Anything could happen in that time. You should come with us."

"Without my husband, that is impossible."

Gul heard the regret in her voice. But he was glad. He liked this new house.

The neighbors left the next day, their possessions piled high on a clumsy wooden cart. Gul remembered the tension of the trip from Jalalabad, the car's weaving feints through the gorge. He imagined this small, slow-moving group trundling toward the bandits there, wondered if they would make it even that far. Still, many people remained in the neighborhood, and they coached the new arrivals on the best ways to manage.

That other family, they told Maryam, had been too afraid. Yes, the factions were shooting at one another across the neighborhood, but each side was equipped with powerful weapons, and for once, this was an advantage. The artillery pilfered from the Amriki shot high and true, whistling above the rooftops at nightfall and wreaking damage on the surrounding hillsides, but leaving the houses below unscathed. During a large part of each day, Maryam was assured, the two sides took time to rest and reconnoiter. Then it was safe to shop and go about one's business. Everyone made sure to be back inside by late afternoon, before the evening skirmishes that began with bursts of gunfire here and there, building to a few hours of shelling. Really, one could live an almost normal life.

———

At first, Maryam spent her days huddled indoors, much as she had at Macroyan, muttering curses directed at Nur Muhammed, wherever he had gone off to this time.

But day after day passed free of her dire predictions, and she began to venture from the house. The roses bloomed anew beneath her ministrations, and she sent Gul and Khurshid to scour the markets in search of seeds for the fruits and vegetables she craved, the tiny eggplants and rich pumpkins and sweet melons that would let her—rather, Khurshid, following her exacting instructions—serve the foods that reminded her of home.

When Gul managed to escape his mother's endless list of chores, he cautiously approached other youngsters living there. Maybe because they weren't crammed together here the way they had been at Macroyan, they seemed more inclined to friendliness. Each day, Gul and his new companions ran from their homes to inspect the previous night's damage. Their own streets lay largely unscathed, but the outskirts of the neighborhood crumbled a little more every day. Gul and his friends always waited a few days after a house was hit, until the dead were buried and the crowds of wailing relatives had dispersed, before creeping like cats through the gaping holes in the shattered walls to see what they could find. No matter how thoroughly a family packed before it fled or its home was destroyed, a few things always remained—an unbroken plate, a shoe or, best of all, if the dead were children, an abandoned toy. Sometimes, thrillingly, there were the intangibles that bespoke destruction, dark splashes of dried blood, the long tracks gouged by shrapnel across a mud wall, and once, in an otherwise anonymous heap of rubble, bits of bone and flesh quickly mummifying in Kabul's dry heat.

"Don't touch it!" Amer, like Gul, was Pashtun. "It's unclean."

Gul jerked back, but the others joined him, crouching low over his find, studying it, agreeing finally that it was part of a heel.

"He shows his foot to the Tajiks," Amer whispered to Gul in approval, and the two of them yelled with laughter and scrambled back down the heap of sun-baked mud bricks in search of more useful gleanings. Some of those things—a bent spoon, a hair ornament, a discarded shirt—could be sold from the street corners, and Gul savored the feel of creased afghanis growing soft and moist in clenched fingers. Most often, he and Amer spent their earnings on sweets, but sometimes they played at being men like their fathers. They lounged on the pavement and ordered tea from the chai boys, swatting at youngsters barely smaller than themselves if they did not come quickly enough with their tin trays on which balanced tiny steaming glasses in filigreed holders.

They tilted their glasses, the tea made the way they liked it, a sludge of sugar at the bottom, and congratulated themselves on being born into families brave enough to stay in Kabul and take advantage of all this wondrous city had to offer.

The silence in the street should have alerted him. But after another successful day of scavenging, Gul was so distracted by the folds of cash bumping against his belly in the pouch beneath his kameez that he noticed nothing.

"Tonight," Amer had whispered to him as they parted, "I will come to your gate and whistle. There is a house in the Ashiqan-o-Arifan District. With women. We will go there."

His thoughts a disjointed haze of pleasurable images, Gul came to his own street and ambled its deserted length. At the far end, a woman howled. Gul cocked his head and listened a moment, then relaxed as the words became clear.

"Meena. Meena. Meena. Oh, my Meena."

It was a neighbor, whose simpleminded daughter was always wandering off. Gul guessed the little girl had gone again, and that this time, one of the many awful fates that people were forever predicting for her—crushed by a bus, kidnapped by Kuchis, used by soldiers for their own immoral purposes and then thrown aside—had finally happened.

Only as he approached his own courtyard, and saw the gate swinging open, did it occur to him that more might be amiss than the demise of one unfortunate girl. The hairs on the back of his neck prickled as he gazed back upon the silent street. He stepped through the gate. The icy press of a bayonet against his throat stopped him in midstride. Gul swallowed convulsively, his Adam's apple bumping against the triangular blade. He slid his gaze down its length, following the barrel of the Kalashnikov, and met the grinning gaze of a Tajik mujahid.

He said something Gul didn't understand, then switched to badly accented Pashto. "The man of the house finally arrives to protect his family. But where are his women?" He edged the bayonet upward. He and the others wore *pakols* instead of turbans, the flat brown woolen caps sitting like pieces of naan atop their heads. Gul stretched his chin high, only his eyes moving, his gaze roaming the courtyard. The little boys sat sniveling before the house. His mother and Bibi were nowhere to be seen. He thought of Meena down the street, younger even than Bibi. What had these men done to her? Gul remembered the cupboard, the cavity behind it. He heard noises within the house and began to tremble. A soldier appeared in the doorway, a rolled carpet over his shoulder. He tossed it into the courtyard, atop a pile of the family's belongings, then disappeared back into the house.

Gul began to pray, forcing his lips not to move. Khurshid did not know about the cupboard, he remembered. Where had she hidden?

The creak of the gate, the feminine gasp that followed, told him that she had not hidden at all. The bayonet was gone as the fighter who had been holding him flung the gun aside and bolted past, grabbing Khurshid as she dropped her packets from the market and whirled to run. Gul thought to snatch the gun, then stopped as the soldier's shout brought several men running from the house. The man holding Khurshid stooped to retrieve his gun, then used it to shepherd Gul and Khurshid before him.

Khurshid clutched Gul's arm for support. He remembered the day when she had done that before, after she had burned her ankle. He thought with shame of his own arousal then. Now he felt only terror. Men surrounded them, all in bits of uniform, a cap here, a camouflage jacket there. Only one had the complete ensemble, a thickset man whose heavy green trousers were tucked into black lace-up boots like those the Russians had worn against the Afghan winters. His legs swung wide in an exaggerated swagger as he approached the center of the circle where Khurshid clung to Gul.

He put his face close to Khurshid's and jerked his chin toward Gul. "Your brother?"

Khurshid's "no" was barely audible.

The commander smiled, his tongue protruding between his teeth. "This is not your husband. He is too young. But he is not your son. He is too old. Where is your husband?"

Khurshid did not answer. Her teeth chattered. Her grip on Gul's arm tightened, her nails digging deep through the rough material of his kameez.

The man's small eyes were bloodshot, and Gul smelled liquor on his breath. He must have found Nur Muhammed's vodka, the one Russian import to which Gul's father had never objected. The man raised his hand, flecked brown with what Gul realized must be dried blood, to Khurshid's face. She flinched as he ran his fingers across her cheek. The man glanced at Gul and smiled wolfishly.

"Pashtun, no?" he said. "And your women are supposed to be so modest. But not this one. She shows her face for all to see. What am I to think of this?"

Gul found his voice. "She's Tajik," he said, and forced himself to add, "like you."

The man's hand slammed against Gul's face, knocking him free of Khurshid's grip. Khurshid swayed, then righted herself. Gul's knees buckled. He drew himself upward with difficulty and braced for another blow. But the man had turned his attention back to Khurshid. He reached for the scarf covering her head and pulled it away, laughing as she tried to draw it back. He slapped at her arms until she dropped them by her sides. He held out his hand and barked a command. One of his men extended a Kalashnikov. The commander twisted the bayonet into the folds of cloth at Khurshid's throat, then with a practiced movement, brought the weapon swiftly downward, torn fabric falling free in its wake. Khurshid squeezed her eyes shut and groaned. Gul heard the collective intake of male breath from the circle around him and looked with the others at Khurshid's pale breasts, so startling in the sunlight, a thin line of blood trickling between them. The commander shouted to his men. They jumped with alacrity to hold her down as she shrieked to Gul for the help he could not give.

"You will thank me," Gul told his bride years later, on the day he presented her with a burqa. "This is better. On this point, you must believe me."

Sixteen

ISLAMABAD, FEBRUARY 2002

Liv had been awake for nearly thirty hours by the time the plane's wheels smacked the runway in Islamabad, bounced once, then caught and held. Exhaustion sandpapered her throat. Her joints complained.

The plane slowed. Liv took a ragged breath. Kirstie Davidson's brisk practicality had banished her initial stereotypes of mobs rampaging through narrow streets, brandishing placards of the crumbling towers, calling down death upon America and its leaders. Now those uneasy images rushed to the forefront.

Liv peered around the turbaned man beside her, trying to see if the streets of Islamabad—actually, she reminded herself, the airport was in the adjoining city of Rawalpindi—were seething at that very moment. The man stood, blocking the window, and motioned for her to leave her seat. The plane still taxied, but people banged at the overhead bins, catching the cascading luggage. Liv found herself in the aisle, clutching her purse to her chest as passengers pushed toward the front of the plane with no regard for order. Her hair, lank after so many hours beneath the flowered silk square she'd purchased at Gatwick when she realized hers was the only uncovered head in the waiting area, escaped its careful twist and hung about her face. She ran her tongue across her teeth, furred with sleep, and inhaled the rank odor of sweat. She couldn't tell whether it was her own, or the general miasma of the crowd carrying her along toward the jetway.

She forgot her self-consciousness over her appearance in the scramble to claim her luggage from the baggage carousel and the struggle to answer the questions put to her in nearly incomprehensible English from a bored customs official. With a belated show of effort, he stamped her passport so hard that the counter shook, and handed it back.

Outside, warmth and humanity surged toward her. Hands tugged at her sleeves. Faces pushed so close that they blurred.

"Taxi, miss? Taxi?" Someone reached for her luggage cart, and she tried to jerk it away. The man kept his grip on the handle. "You will come with me. Finest taxi in Islamabad." Dirt mapped his face. His left eye leaked an oily fluid. Liv tried to recall the rudimentary Urdu that Martin had insisted she learn. Surely there were words to make him go away. Another man stepped to her side and in a single swift motion wrenched her tormentor's wrist so hard he let go of the cart. This man was young and clean and wore a Western-style blazer over a plaid rayon shirt whose tails hung out over his herringbone pants. Liv wondered if Martin had sent him, and decided, as the man took her elbow and began to propel her forward, steering the cart with his other hand, that he had. The man spoke in commanding Urdu and people fell away as they moved toward the far side of the open-air terminal, whose concrete walls framed rectangles of sunlight blazing so brightly that Liv could make out only the vaguest outlines of the cars and buildings beyond. The humidity was ferocious and the noise pressed against her, and Liv feared she would faint. A sound cut through the uproar, over and over, her name, shouted by a tall, sweating white man at the rear of the crowd.

Martin.

"Where were you going with him?" Her husband's first words to Liv after such a long time apart were anxious, harsh.

He advanced, speaking Urdu, upon the man pushing her baggage cart, who hesitated only a moment before releasing his grip and melting back into the throng. Martin stopped a few feet away, not touching her.

"He meant to rob you, I'm sure of it. If not here, then in the taxi. Do you have all your bags? What were you thinking?"

"I thought you sent him." Liv looked at the cart. "He didn't take anything."

"Never go alone with anyone here. Especially a man. My God, Liv. If you can't handle Pakistan, what will we do in Afghanistan?"

She forgot her new self, that woman who could run a generator, nail a bull's-eye, patch a sucking chest wound with plastic wrap. She'd held herself rigid throughout the hours-long flights, the layovers in run-down sections of terminals where whole families simply curled up on the floor and slept next to possessions that strained rope-bound cardboard boxes rather than smart roller bags, where English was such a rarity that her head snapped sideways when she heard it, so keenly did she crave familiarity.

The brittle self-control she'd imposed upon liftoff from Kennedy shattered. She began to cry. She ducked her head and covered her face, aware that she was attracting stares. She felt Martin's arms around her.

"Liv, Liv. I didn't mean to snap. But when I saw you going off with him—I was afraid I wouldn't get to you in time to save you."

"Save me?" Liv gulped back another sob. "From what? Surely he wouldn't rob me in front of all these people."

"You have no idea." He rubbed at his face, as though to ease some soreness there, and led her to a waiting car. A Pakistani man, this one also in a suit, but well cut, with a starched and pressed white shirt beneath, sat at the wheel. Martin introduced him as Pervaiz, and put Liv in the back, then walked around and climbed into the front. He reached back across the seat, clasping her hand in both his own. The driver flinched and Martin quickly pulled away.

"I'm sorry." His face and neck, normally a hearty pink, had gone a dull, patchy red. "I know it's strange now, but you'll get used to it. In a few weeks, it will all seem normal." He spoke to the driver. "We won't go back to the office now. Tell them I won't be in for the rest of the day."

Her first day here and he had planned to work? Liv checked the words before she spoke, unsure of how much English the driver understood. Besides, Martin had already turned his back on her. She studied his profile, looking for signs of change during their time apart. Frosty air blasted from the dashboard vents, and his face gradually resumed its normal high color. His hair, an unruly thatch, flopped across his forehead. He still wore it too long, something she'd found mannered even when they were younger. Now they were both graying, their bodies thickening, the changes coming so gradually that Liv sometimes stopped in surprise before her mirror. She felt herself receding, her disappointments masked by smooth new layers of flesh. It was easier for Martin. He'd always tended toward pudginess, with soft features that hinted, inaccurately, at an eager, puppyish affability. The extra weight suited him somehow, squared his face and gave him a solid heft that at home could seem awkward, but here—or so it had seemed to Liv as he'd led her through the crowd—gave him a sense of authority and certainty that was new to her.

She rested her head against the car window. Office parks populated by stained concrete buildings marked Islamabad's outskirts. Goats grazed on the lawns. She'd left behind Philadelphia's leaden skies that met crusts of dirty snow in an unending monotone landscape. Here, soft air heralded spring. Flowers provided dizzying splashes of color across the patchy grass. Cyclists and pedestrians crowded the sides of the highway. Buses sputtered past them, so jammed that people crouched on the roofs and swung from the doors, clinging to invisible handholds within, women's robes flashing vividly as cars whipped past. A truck labored beside them, painted in complex, swirling hues, clinking chains swinging from its undercarriage. An intricately carved wooden prow heaped with sacks of grain extended over its cab, the entire vehicle so top-heavy that Liv held her breath as the highway took a sharp turn. They came upon a man leading a camel, its knobbed legs swinging wide with each deliberate step. Liv stared as they passed, and the camel, loose lipped and lecherous, blinked its yellow satyr's eyes at her before another turn hid it from view.

Something reverberated within Liv, the tap of a felt-wrapped hammer on a piano string. She took a deep breath, then another, filling her lungs with the cooling air within the car. Her parents had flown to Philadelphia to see her off. As the airport shuttle waited in the driveway, her mother cupped Liv's face between her hands softened with decades of faithful application of Jergens. Her faded eyes, once as blue as Liv's, searched her daughter's face. "You can always come back. With him, or without him. You don't need to do this."

"Yes." Liv echoed the vow she'd taken so many years earlier. "I do."

She folded her arms against the chill of the air-conditioning and thought of the word that had sustained her throughout the trip.

Partners.

———

The Marriott, where they'd live while making final preparations to leave for Face the Future's office in Kabul, was the most secure place in Islamabad after the embassies, Martin told her.

The car halted before soaring wrought-iron gates flanked by a pair of Uzi-toting guards. A third uniformed man circled the car, sweeping beneath it with a mirror at the end of a long pole. "Bomb check," Martin said. Liv blanched at his matter-of-fact tone.

The guard waved them forward, and the car coasted beneath an arched portico. Men ran to the car, surrounding it. Liv, still shaken from the scene at the airport, slid toward the middle of the seat, but they kept their distance, flinging open the car doors and trunk, whisking her luggage away, beckoning her into a cavernous lobby. The crowd within rivaled that at the airport, but the Marriott's noisy occupants were Westerners, most of them dressed in wrinkled cargo pants and many-pocketed vests as though preparing for a hike, despite the opulent setting. Liv tilted her head back and squinted into the shimmering lights of starburst chandeliers. Instinctively, she moved out from beneath them. She surveyed the raffish mob and looked a question at Martin.

"The press." His lip curled. "I hear they arrived about a minute after the towers went down and they've been here ever since. It's sort of a staging area here for the ones going in and out of Afghanistan. They've taken all the rooms and driven the prices through the roof."

"If they took all the rooms, how is it that we're staying here?"

Martin permitted himself a smile. "We outbid them."

At her elbow, Pervaiz coughed. Liv had forgotten he was there.

He and Martin exchanged glances. "Because it's an American chain, they gave us quite a discount when they heard about our humanitarian mission," Martin added. He steered Liv toward the elevator, comically small given the outsize proportions of the lobby. There was a complicated dispersal of tips outside a half-open door, and finally he closed the door behind them on a room whose improbable dimensions were softened by overstuffed furniture piled high with embroidered cushions. "You'll want a bath." He led her to a room that reminded her of a smaller version of the lobby, all gleaming marble and bright lights. A screen shielded one corner, and Liv peeped around it to see a tub with its commodious ledge holding a store display's worth of posh scented soaps and lotions and shampoos, and stacked high with plush towels.

"Oh, Martin." The weariness of the trip caught up with her. She sat down, harder than she had intended, on the edge, sending a couple of the little bottles rattling into the tub's depths.

Martin leaned past her and picked them up, then twisted the taps. He took her wrist and held it beneath the stream. Steam billowed into the room that, like everything else in the hotel, was air-conditioned to the point of discomfort.

"Too hot?"

"Perfect." She shrugged out of her wrinkled blazer and unbuttoned her blouse.

Martin's voice came from a distance. "I'll leave you alone now." The door closed behind him. She lowered herself into near-scalding water to her chin, then held her breath and sank deeper. Her hair, finally free, rose and floated about her face. At home it was her nightly ritual to linger in a bath, soaking away the day's frustrations. She thought of Martin waiting for her on the sprawling bed, and hastily scrubbed at herself, vowing a longer sojourn later. She wrapped herself twice in one of the huge towels and tiptoed, her skin still rosy and damp, into the other room, heart knocking hard in anticipation. But Martin slept, snoring lightly, and when Liv let the towel fall and slipped into bed, he only rolled away from her into a deeper slumber as his wife lay beside him, wondering what other changes were in store.

An hour later, Liv found herself still jittery and awake, with the keen alertness of resentment combined with overexhaustion.

A computer printout sat atop the nightstand. She reached for it, careful not to rustle the paper and disturb Martin. It detailed a summary of Martin's charges so far. The room cost nearly three hundred dollars a night. The bill, according to the receipt in her hand, was paid weekly, with no mention of a discount.

She calculated the total cost, an exercise that finally nudged her toward sleep, even as she puzzled over how a small, fledgling organization like Face the Future could afford to throw around that kind of money.

Seventeen

Only one thing distracted Gul from his beguiling evenings with his new wife: the gatherings organized by Nur Muhammed, trying to knit together old cohorts with new as he shored up his smuggling operations in Jalalabad and prepared to expand his reach into Kabul.

The men met in a small building at the far end of the compound, their conversations as hushed and terse as the landscape beyond the compound's high mud walls. Warmth nudged the days, but winter returned at night, the cold pouncing. A few flakes of snow swept past the window, borne by a moaning wind that forced its way around the window frame and beneath the door, searching out the room's inhabitants with icy fingers. Two oil lanterns provided wavering light. A servant prepared the *sandali*, stoking a pit with coal, setting a frame atop it, and covering it with thick blankets. The men sat around the pit, their feet beneath the blankets. The scent of charred wool permeated the room. Gul hugged his knees to his chest and wrapped his striped woolen shawl more tightly around himself as the servant returned with the meal.

The men spoke little while they ate. Nur Muhammed tore chunks of naan and dipped them into the pilaf, shoveling bits of lamb and rice into his mouth so quickly that his hand blurred between bowl and mouth. Later, though, over tea and sweet *firni*, he leaned forward and the other men angled in close, talking in hoarse whispers even though the women were far from earshot. Gul leaned against his father, barely daring to breathe.

"This is worse than when the Russians left," Nur Muhammed said. "Not so much fighting now, but when it comes—just wait. The Taliban are regrouping."

"The factions will fight among themselves. They always do," another man said.

"Eventually, yes. But together, they can cause a lot of trouble in the meantime. The routes could close."

There was a collective intake of breath. Opium supported them all, but if they could not get their harvest through the mountainous territory to markets as far away as Uzbekistan, there was nothing to fall back on.

"I have been thinking," his father said. "We continue to grow opium. We sell it, we don't sell it, no matter."

Gul narrowed his eyes, taking in the incomprehension on the faces of the other men, relatives all and close ones at that, uncles and a few cousins, older ones. This was the part he loved, the part where his father confused everyone, then brought them inexorably to understanding.

"We will take the money we still have," his father continued. "We will invest in another crop."

"There is no other crop," one of Gul's uncles spat. "Pakistan has them all, the maize, the oranges. They take our water"—the others glowered at this reference to Pakistan's dams that captured precious water from the Kabul River—"and they sell their produce back to us for cheaper than we could grow it here."

Nur Muhammed ignored him. "For this crop, the routes will stay open, no matter who has the upper hand."

"What is this magical product?" said the uncle, not bothering to conceal his skepticism.

Nur Muhammed took another spoonful of firni, and Gul licked his lips, imagining the velvety coolness of the rice custard sliding down his throat. His mother made it the way Nur Muhammed liked, topped with crushed pistachios and his precious raisins. Nur Muhammed reached behind him. Something metal and cold slid past him. Nur Muhammed held his Kalashnikov briefly aloft, then placed it reverently in the center of the oilcloth that protected the carpet from the various dinner dishes.

"This." He laid his hand on the gun's curved steel stock, shiny from frequent contact with his shoulder. "Everyone will need more soon. And not just these, but RPGs, Oerlikons, Stingers. Especially Stingers." The men nodded at strange names long ago grown familiar. "I have already made arrangements to collect as many as we can from any source that has them. The Amriki want them back and will pay dearly. And our own people want them even more. We will supply."

He stared each man in the eye to make sure everyone understood.

"From now on, we will grow guns."

Gul lingered with his father in the outbuilding as the others left and the servant cleared the dishes and banked the sandali. Gul lifted the lanterns and started to follow the servant from the room, but Nur Muhammed called him back. The lanterns swung in his hand as he turned. Shadows leapt and shuddered.

"There is another thing. Your wife."

Pride warred with apprehension. Gul had noted his father's approving expression on the rare occasions Nur Muhammed encountered Farida at work with the other women in the household. It was as his father had said. He himself had been a cooperative husband. And Farida had rewarded his patience by becoming a most pleasing wife.

"We leave soon for Kabul. You know that a position for her has been secured there. She will begin as soon as we arrive."

"But—" Farida had forbidden him to mention her pregnancy, and

Gul didn't know if Maryam had said anything. Still, Gul was sure that when it became apparent, Nur Muhammed would release her from her responsibility.

His father waited.

"It is nothing." Gul set the lanterns on the floor and wrapped his shawl around his head. With the sandali extinguished, the cold reestablished dominance.

"She must bring us information. I have a list of questions. You will put these to her. She will take them to the Amriki and bring the answers to you. And you will bring them to me." He rattled off a list, his breath puffing visibly in the lanterns' unsteady light.

Gul's chest seized as though he'd gulped a lungful of the frigid air. "These questions—they will know why she's asking. This could cause trouble for us."

Nur Muhammed threw his head back and laughed and laughed.

"That is not the remotest possibility. No one remembers anything a woman says or does."

Still laughing, he took the lanterns and strode into the night, leaving his son to find his way back to the main house by the indifferent light of the stars.

Eighteen

Her first night in Pakistan found Liv at a party. Martin told her their hosts worked at the Dutch embassy, although Liv, still jet-lagged despite her nap, never did figure out exactly what they did there.

The man was dark-suited and charming in a professional sort of way, all hand kisses and "my dears." His wife glittered in a bright off-the-shoulder frock that made Liv, who'd packed a black dress with long sleeves and a full, calf-length skirt for just such occasions, feel dowdy, at least until she met Mrs. Khan, a lumpy woman who worked with Martin at Face the Future. As far as Liv could tell, Mrs. Khan was the only Pakistani guest in a room full of junior staffers from the various embassies and NGOs and corporations, and even a few journalists. Mrs. Khan seemed to know everyone in the room, pulling people aside at times for intimate and, from their expressions, serious conversations. As people began drinking with more purpose, though, Mrs. Khan withdrew to a corner of the room, watching with dark, calculating eyes.

These private parties, Martin told Liv, were the only places they could drink in Islamabad outside the few "foreigners' clubs" in the larger hotels such as the Marriott. The foodstuffs passing on trays borne by white-coated men were of the same sort that Liv had eaten at innumerable wedding receptions and college functions back home, generic hors d'oeuvres and bland entrées in pale, viscous sauces.

"You did not enjoy the food."

It was not a question. Mrs. Khan approached Liv after the dessert, another anemic and inoffensive concoction, was cleared away. Martin was in one corner by the sideboard that held the liquor, methodically getting smashed with a banker and a couple of young women who worked for the United Nations. This, too, was new to Liv. At the college, ever conscious of the presence of someone he wanted to impress, Martin tended to sip wine or the occasional beer. Now he upended a bottle over his glass so carelessly that the liquor splashed onto his hand.

"Excuse me," Liv said to Mrs. Khan. She made her way to her husband. "This isn't exactly what I expected."

"You wanted camels and a tent?" Martin took her hand and Liv curled her fingers around his. After only a few hours in this new place, she was already beginning to crave the casual public affection she'd taken for granted at home. "You should enjoy this while you can. None of this, just having a glass of wine with dinner, women and men socializing together, this"—he raised their clasped hands—"will be possible once we go to Kabul. Eat, drink, and all that, for soon—"

"Martin, *komm bitte her*," a woman commanded him. She cradled an armful of sweating brown bottles. Apparently, German beer had been procured. Martin shrugged, laughing. He dropped Liv's hand and backed away.

Liv found Mrs. Khan at her elbow. She tried to remember their conversation. "The food," Mrs. Khan prompted.

"I thought it would be different."

"Different in what way, please?" Mrs. Khan spoke precise, British-accented English.

"Oh, I don't know." A single glass of wine had made her feel fuzzy and uncertain. "We're here, after all. Not in New York or London or Amsterdam. Shouldn't we be eating something else?"

"Something local, maybe?"

"Yes. I'm in another country, but it doesn't feel that way." It had struck her, midway through the evening, that despite the variety of accents swirling around her—the partygoers comprised a dozen different nationalities, yet they conversed mostly in English, with varying degrees of competence—she'd attended far too many tedious faculty parties that were not really so different from this one. She looked around at the other women in the room. Like their hostess, they wore dresses that would have seemed abbreviated at home. In Islamabad, Liv worried that their clothing was downright indecent. "I was told I shouldn't dress like that here."

"What do you mean?" Mrs. Khan asked. "All the women here except you are dressed like that. And me, of course." Her laugh, a surprise after her severe expression, was enchanting.

"Everything I read, everyone I talked to, said this was such a conservative place."

Mrs. Khan laughed again, not so prettily this time. "It is very conservative. But the people at this party aren't really in this country. They stay in their own little compounds. They socialize only with one another. To whom would they give offense?"

"I'm sorry. I haven't even been here a full day. I don't know what I'm talking about."

"Your dress is much more appropriate," Mrs. Khan reassured her. "People here will appreciate that more than you know."

Liv ducked her head to hide her inordinate gratitude for the compliment. She studied Mrs. Khan's attire, a richly embroidered silk version of the tunic outfit that most of the locals seemed to wear. "What you're wearing—what is it called?"

"This is our shalwar kameez." She bent her knee in a curtsey so the voluminous drape of the pants billowed. "Shalwar." She lifted her arms, displaying the graceful lines of the tunic, which easily disguised her plumpness. "Kameez, like the French *chemise*."

"It's beautiful."

"It's also very comfortable. Much more so, I think, than that." She cut her eyes toward their hostess, whose dress featured a bodice that dipped dangerously south.

"Do foreign women ever wear the shalwar kameez?" Liv pronounced the words carefully, mentally adding them to her small vocabulary list. Mrs. Khan was probably the plainest woman in the room, but Liv thought she was by far the most attractively dressed. Before she could enlighten Liv further, Martin came up behind them. He wrapped an arm around Liv and reached with his other for Mrs. Khan. She side-stepped him.

"My favorite employee." His voice was loud in Liv's ear.

"We've been colleagues for so little time, and already I'm your favorite?" Liv noticed the way the woman emphasized words. *Colleagues.*

"Employee," Martin had said. Liv blushed at her husband's slight, but Mrs. Khan continued speaking as Martin hugged Liv closer.

"I've been getting acquainted with your wife. I hope you'll let me begin her orientation tomorrow."

"Mrs. Khan will be a good teacher for you," he told Liv. "She knows everything about Afghanistan. She takes a personal interest in the place. Her sister is there."

"Oh?"

"It's a sore subject," Martin said. "It has to do with an unfortunate marriage." He laughed again. His hair flopped over his eyes. Liv eased away from his grip. She was tired again, as drained as she'd been earlier in the day.

"I think maybe we'd better go home." She smiled an apology at Mrs. Khan. "Jet lag."

Mrs. Khan looked pointedly at Martin, who, freed from his anchor, listed. "I think that's best." She put a hand on Liv's arm. Her nails, filed to perfect ovals, were a deep shade of coral. "Tomorrow we'll get started, *inshallah.*"

In the taxi, Martin slumped against her, eyes shut, mouth open. Liv caught their driver's gaze in the rearview mirror and recoiled from the fury she saw there.

"The Marriott," she said.

"Of course, the Marriott." He made a spitting noise and started the car.

The bedside phone buzzed far too early the next morning. Martin snored through a likely hangover. Liv held the receiver to her ear.

"I am in the lobby. The driver is outside. I could of course drive us myself, but for what we are doing today, it is better to preserve appearances. You have a covering for your hair?"

Liv remembered Mrs. Khan, the orientation they'd scheduled. "Yes," she said, thinking of the scarf she'd bought at Gatwick.

"Fetch it and come along. Quickly, now. It's going to be a long day."

Mrs. Khan looked none too pleased when Liv emerged in the lobby fifteen minutes later, the flowered scarf barely covering her damp hair. A headache that Liv recognized as lack of coffee—the cart in the lobby featured only tea—creased her forehead.

"This will never do. We will stop at a tailor's on the way."

"A tailor?" Liv looked down at her clothes, a beige linen blazer over a blouse buttoned to the neck, and a calf-length skirt, opaque hose, and low-heeled pumps. Mrs. Khan wore another shalwar kameez, a comfortable cotton one in dark tones.

"Where we're going, those shoes will be destroyed in five minutes. Haven't you got something sturdier? And maybe some slacks, to hide your ankles? Please, go and change. I'll tell the driver to wait." By the time they left the hotel, it was nearly ten. Martin was just beginning to wake when Liv finally left the room, this time in slim dark pants whose fresh creases, hastily pressed by the ever-hovering Marriott staff, looked incongruous over sneakers.

Mrs. Khan pursed her lips when she saw the new getup but said nothing. Not far from the Marriott, she directed the driver to pull over in front of one of the hulking concrete towers with the cavelike openings on their lower floors. Liv followed her up pitted cement steps into a dark hallway and turned into a small room so stacked with bolts of cloth that there was barely space for Liv and Mrs. Khan, along with the proprietor, a tape measure hanging over his shoulders. He waved his hand, and moments later, tea appeared, two cups on a pressed tin tray borne by a boy of no more than eight. Liv sipped the tepid liquid, wondering if the water had been boiled. She tried to ignore thoughts of the microbes swimming in it, and tried even harder to ignore her longing for coffee.

Mrs. Khan finished her tea in two gulps. She spoke a few words to the man, who moved in front of Liv, grasping her elbow, lifting her arms high and measuring their length, as well as the distance between her shoulders. Finally, to Liv's mortification, he wrapped the tape around the fullness of her breasts and then hips, somehow managing not to touch her body. Mrs. Khan, meanwhile, hauled bolts down from where they leaned against the wall, holding coordinating colors against one another. She stared critically at Liv, considering her for some time, then banged two bolts of deep blue, one with a tiny geometric print, another with a larger coordinating pattern, onto the narrow counter.

Mrs. Khan pulled the scarf from Liv's head. "With your hair and your eyes, these, I think," she said. Liv's hair, long and fine, only a few threads of silver woven through its shining gold, was the one feature about which she remained vain. Even the proprietor, who had been careful not to look directly at Liv's face, stopped and stared.

Mrs. Khan said something to the man. He chose a third bolt of blue, this one thin and filmy, pale as a summer sky, and cut off a six-foot section. He mounted a ladder in one corner of the room and handed the cloth up to someone. Liv heard a rhythmic thumping noise and a whir. She craned her neck and saw, in a dark cubbyhole above them too cramped to allow even someone as short as Mrs. Khan to stand up straight, a man hunched over an old treadle sewing machine. Within moments, the cloth came back with its cut edges neatly hemmed.

Mrs. Khan took the cloth and draped it over Liv's head. She wound one end beneath Liv's throat and let it trail over her shoulder and down her back, then did the same with the other. It formed a sort of wimple beneath her chin and across her chest, an extra layer of cloth, light though it was, covering her breasts. "This is your dupatta. In Islamabad, in the Blue Zone where people are more sophisticated," she said with a twist of her lips, "you do not need to wear it over your head. But for where we are going today, it is necessary to cover your hair, if for no other reason than as a sign of respect. And you should always wear one, even if it's not over your hair. Pay close attention to the women you see here. See how they arrange their dupattas. And the young women, oh, la! You will see how very much can be said with the simple drape of cloth. Besides, I think your husband will like this, too. He is cooperative?"

"Excuse me?"

"He doesn't mind you starting work today without him?"

"I didn't ask him."

Mrs. Khan adjusted her own scarf more firmly. "I will never understand your Western marriages. We will return for your shalwar kameez tomorrow."

Back in the car, Mrs. Khan played tour guide. "Now we are leaving the Blue Zone." She explained that this was the district of foreign businesses, NGO offices, and smart shops. As far as Liv could tell, "smart" merely consisted of storefronts where whitewash covered the moisture stains that darkened the concrete buildings elsewhere in the city. Otherwise, the shops looked as small and mean as those she'd seen on the ride into town from the airport. But she wasn't about to say as much to Mrs. Khan, who was in the process of burdening her with more information and an onslaught of initials.

"Pakistan plays host to three and a half million Afghan DPs," she told Liv as the driver maneuvered the car through a seemingly impenetrable wall of traffic. "About a third of its people left the country during the war with the Soviets and then the civil war. Still more left after the Taliban took control. Most of them came here. The idea is that they'll all go back to Afghanistan now that you Americans have brought them peace." Liv noticed yet again

143

how she emphasized certain words, in a sarcasm bordering on insolence. *You Americans. Peace.* "Here in Pakistan, Face the Future works to resettle them back across the border. Your job in Kabul, as you know, is to devise training programs for these women with neither education nor skills."

She handed Liv a fat binder. "You will find everything I'm telling you in here."

Liv opened Face the Future's report, its cover featuring photos of Afghan refugees, the children nearly winsome in their wide-eyed, high-cheekboned proximity to starvation. She flipped through it, searching for the terms Mrs. Khan threw around with such familiarity. "You've already lost me. DPs? And, the report mentions IDP?"

"Displaced persons. Internally displaced persons."

Liv was remembering her World War II history, textbooks with grainy black-and-white photos of families trudging along muddy roads, each person toting his or her belongings in a single suitcase, walking beside vehicles piled high with furniture.

Mrs. Khan dispelled those images. "They arrive with nothing. Only the clothing they are wearing. You must imagine this. Not a pan for cooking, nor a pot for tea. No rugs for their floors, no sleeping mats. No blankets. Here it is not so bad, but in Peshawar and along the Frontier, it is higher, colder. You can freeze to death there, and people do. The women have too many children, and are too malnourished to nurse their babies. Their breasts are shriveled flaps upon their chests. So they give the babies water, and none of the water is clean, you understand. Or they wet their babies' lips with a bit of tea they beg from someone. This keeps the babies alive longer than you might think possible. An aid packet here or there, from the UN or maybe a group like ours, strings them along for a few months. But the babies die eventually. You'll see."

Martin had mentioned that Mrs. Khan's sister lived in Afghanistan. "What does your sister do there? Is she an aid worker?"

As she had the previous evening, Mrs. Khan shook her head in a way that brooked no further questions. The car stopped before a warren of tented stalls fronted by makeshift wooden counters piled high with produce. Even from inside the car, Liv could hear the flies buzzing in clumps above the mounds of wilted greens and discolored melons.

"This is Sabzi Mandi, the vegetable market." Mrs. Khan pointed across the street. "And that, a *katchi abadi*—you would call it a slum, I think—is our destination. Today, here in Islamabad, even though we are far from the border, you will begin to see Afghanistan."

———

Acres of one-room mud houses roofed over with bits of board nearly obliterated the low, rolling landscape. The odor of rot filled the air.

Liv stepped out of the car. A clot of children surrounded her. She beamed at them. Their fingers wormed into her pockets. "Hey! Stop that!"

The driver yelled. The children scattered, but not very far. Mrs. Khan called to them, and they crept back, eyeing the driver. She held a few folded blue rupees toward them, then pulled her hand back and dangled the money high, speaking in what sounded like a different language, more guttural than Urdu. "I told them that if we are permitted to walk here undisturbed, that if we come back and our car is exactly as we have left it, these rupees shall be theirs. But if there is the least bit of trouble, there will be no money, and besides, I shall send the police to search for the opium that I know is sold here, and then no one who lives here shall have a full belly tonight. Not that anyone will, anyway."

She began to pick her way along a muddy, trash-strewn alley between two rows of houses. Liv walked behind her, trying not to step in the thin stream of raw sewage that trickled down the center of the alley. She pulled her dupatta across her nose and mouth against the stench. Already, she was beginning to appreciate this strange new garment.

The children trailed them, providing a shouting accompaniment to their progress. They trod barefoot through the sewage, leaving damp footprints on the hard-packed ground of the alley. Liv trained her eyes forward, where she could see fast-moving wisps of blue, women in burqas darting into doorways as they approached.

Once again, Liv felt the frisson that had stirred within her upon her arrival. Research here, she realized, would not be a bloodless matter of clicking through websites. Another feeling sneaked in, despite her attempts to push it away. Martin had interviewed his share of Afghan refugees, but Liv knew that the circumstances had been carefully controlled, with hand-picked subjects bused to antiseptic conference rooms far from the squalor in which they lived. Liv allowed herself a moment of self-congratulation as she imagined telling him what she'd braved so soon after her arrival.

Mrs. Khan stopped before a gateway shielded by a tattered bit of cloth, and called out. A dirty hand clutched the cloth from within and moved it slowly aside. A man stood there, and Mrs. Khan spoke to him in that new language. Pashto, Liv concluded. She and Martin were to study it in Afghanistan. The man stood aside as they entered a small courtyard. Skinny chickens fled squawking at their approach. They halted outside another door, this one without even the benefit of a cloth across it, and Mrs. Khan kicked off her shoes. Liv bent to untie her sneakers and tried not to think about what her socks would touch. They ducked through the low doorway and into a dark room whose single small window, a hole in the mud wall, let in barely enough light for Liv to distinguish a thin woman lying on a straw mat atop the dirt floor.

Mrs. Khan stooped and whispered to her. Liv crouched in awkward imitation of Mrs. Khan's effortless pose. Her knees screamed in protest. The woman struggled to sit up, but Mrs. Khan urged her back down. An infant lay beside her, its papery skin wrapped tight around a prominent skull.

Liv's hand flew to her mouth, pressing back the rising gorge. She hadn't expected to see death on her first outing. "Oh, no . . ."

The baby blinked, a corpse come to life. Liv fell back, hands scrabbling blindly at the dirt floor as she struggled to right herself.

Mrs. Khan waited until she had regained her composure. "This is one of the babies of which I spoke." Mrs. Khan reached beneath her kameez and withdrew a packet, unwrapping it to show a bag of rice, a wad of tea leaves wrapped in cheesecloth, and a tin of what Liv would later realize was UN-distributed baby formula. "Maybe this will keep it alive a little longer." Mrs. Khan spoke again to the woman, who obediently opened her mouth wide. She peered down the woman's throat. "It is still very infected."

She pulled a pouch from beneath her kameez and laid it beside the woman, speaking softly to her in Pashto. "Antibiotic pills," she explained to Liv. "And some for the pain. I told her she must take them herself, and not sell them."

The husband loomed in the doorway. Even in the dim light, Liv could see his glance, quick and avid, toward the pills. Mrs. Khan spoke sharply to him. "I told him that if his wife is not better when I return, I will know he stole her pills, and that I will report him."

She turned away. "Come," she said to Liv. "I'll show you more babies."

Liv found herself so grateful to leave the dark, despairing room that the reek permeating the katchi abadi no longer bothered her. "That woman. Was she starving?"

"No. She is sick. Her family was supposed to be resettled back to Afghanistan last week, but she suddenly fell ill. I think she took some sort of poison, a little bleach, maybe, so she wouldn't have to leave. More likely, her husband fed it to her. She would not have been able to refuse him. But nobody in their right mind would want to go back to what these people know they will face in Afghanistan." Her voice rose as she spoke, and she stopped and took a breath.

"At any rate, other than the babies, people here generally don't starve. They get just enough to keep them alive, but not enough to keep them healthy. They get tuberculosis, or cholera. Or the men sleep with prostitutes and bring home venereal diseases to their wives, which weaken them so that they catch other diseases. You pile one disease on top of another, and you realize that even if you dispense antibiotics, the people will sell the pills to buy food, and so the accumulation of problems finally kills them. It takes years, though. These Afghan women will surprise you. Things that would kill an ordinary person, not just a Westerner, but even a person here, they can survive. That's one thing I've learned working at Face the Future."

"How long have you been with Face the Future? Have you worked for similar organizations before?"

"Here, only recently. As to before, I've worked as an interpreter for all manner of groups, some like this, others not. But these Afghan people have been coming to Pakistan for the whole of my life. You can't help but know about these things. Of course, since coming to Face the Future, I've learned so much more. And besides . . ."

"Besides?"

Mrs. Khan shook her head, cutting off her questions.

They stopped. The alley ended, giving on to a broad field of trampled earth. Children ran about, anchoring crude kites that dipped and swirled in a sky hazy with woodsmoke. Liv laughed in a mixture of pleasure and relief. "So things aren't entirely hopeless after all."

"You think not?" Mrs. Khan's tone, previously pleasant and informative, turned bleak. Her next words came as though driven by some inner compulsion. "Look closely at this place."

The field stretched into the distance, so big that even the hordes of children playing there could dash about without fear of running into one another. Liv had not seen so much open space since her arrival within the crowded confines of Islamabad. The children wore filthy beige shalwar kameez, but the kites above them were made of bright bits of paper, and below, on the ground, green cloth pennants fluttered from tall, spindly sticks poking out of the hard-packed earth, giving everything a festive air. Liv looked again at the sticks, many of them surrounded by mounds of rocks.

"Oh, no. Those are—"

"Graves. This is the cemetery for the katchi abadi. I would imagine the majority of these hold children."

Liv shrank from the bitterness in her voice. But she didn't know where to look as the children pounded across the graves of their brothers and sisters, their cousins and friends. Behind her, Mrs. Khan continued speaking.

"In just a couple of weeks, you'll be in Afghanistan, working, as you people say, for its future." *Future.* "But its real future, its children, will remain here, beneath the earth. So what, really, do people like you"—*people like you*—"expect to accomplish there?"

"But that's why it's so important that we go!" Liv, too vehement, trying to persuade herself as well as Mrs. Khan. "We have money, resources. People like you"—she barely avoided the same sort of emphasis Mrs. Khan had just employed against her—"can show us where the worst problems are, help us figure out the best ways to relieve them."

Mrs. Khan's sigh went on and on. "Look well at what you see before you. You will think back on it with nostalgia. This small loss of life, these easy deaths due to mere sickness? It is nothing compared to what has been visited upon Kabul."

Liv took her arm and turned her away from the cemetery. "Then we must visit good things upon Kabul, yes?" Another inadequately disguised appeal to herself.

A hot wind swirled through the alleyways of the katchi abadi, stirring a noxious mix of dust and stink. Behind them, the flags above the graves snapped in the breeze. Mrs. Khan's voice was barely audible beneath the cacophony of wind and flags and shouting children. "I hope I've done the right thing."

Nineteen

At least Mrs. Khan alternated the disturbing with the practical.

"Today, you learn the most difficult lesson of all for you Westerners," she told Liv as they set out in the car another morning.

"Eating only with my right hand? I can do that." Liv came up with her own trick early, tucking her left hand, the one used for the bathroom in a region nearly entirely lacking in toilet paper, beneath her thigh during meals.

"You underestimate me. And overestimate yourself." The car stopped before a market. Mrs. Khan opened her door and gestured for Liv to follow. "Today, we bargain."

Within minutes, the burgeoning affection Liv felt for her demanding instructor had vanished.

"You shame me!" Mrs. Khan hissed as she dragged Liv away from a stall where Liv, charmed by the wooden models of the garish jingle trucks that made Islamabad's streets such a challenge, had acquiesced to the second, barely lower, price named by the proprietor. "It is not worth half that. Not one-quarter."

"But it's nothing." Liv would have paid twice the original amount and more. Which, she realized, the proprietor probably knew. And most likely resented. "I can't win this one," she told Mrs. Khan. "If I don't bargain, I hurt his pride, right? But he needs the money more than I. Which is worse?"

Mrs. Khan put a hand to Liv's back, its force just short of a punch, propelling her toward another stall, one displaying soft woolen paisley shawls. "Do you want to be respected? Try again. And remember, no matter what he tells you, these are not pashmina."

Whatever it was made of, there would be no shawl for Liv. No embroidered pillow covers. No knife for Martin, its silver—"hah, tin," Mrs. Khan interjected—handle carved into the shape of a snarling leopard, as she dragged Liv away after yet another incompetent attempt.

"Almost," Mrs. Khan allowed when Liv argued down the price of a *chapati* basket by two-thirds. Liv replaced it with reluctance, admiring its woven conical circles of red, green, and yellow, imagining it full of puffed circles of pan-fried bread.

"Useless," Mrs. Khan muttered when Liv departed the next stall with a pair of curled-toed slippers embroidered in metallic threads. At least, she finally allowed, the price was acceptable.

"I'll hang them on the wall. No one at home has anything like this." The slippers, the largest in the display, were far too small for Liv. "I like them." Mrs. Khan ignored such foolishness, caught up in her own examination of cookware.

"Oh!" Strips of wool, bright with tassels and pom-poms, caught Liv's eye. She made her way toward them, trying her best to fake disinterest.

"For camel." A man stood at her elbow. She waited as he assessed her ability to pay, weighing blond hair against local dress. He named a price. She spread her hands in regret. A lower price. She shook her head. He lifted one of the strips—Something functional, like reins? Or solely decorative? She had no idea but could see it hanging in a narrow hallway in her home in Pennsylvania—and tried to hand it to her. Her fingers twitched. She clasped her hands behind her and turned away. His shout—probably a lower price still, possibly even an acceptable one—was lost in the swirl of noise as she turned a corner.

Liv vowed to return another day, and then a day after that, both for the camel trappings and a basket. An armful of packages acquired in a single trip would make her more of a mark to rapacious merchants, Mrs. Khan had warned her. Still, she slowed before stacks of more woolen shawls. So what if they weren't pashmina? Kabul's mountain air would be cold at night. Why not go prepared?

"Liv!"

She whirled at the sound of running footsteps. Mrs. Khan stopped before her, breathing hard, one hand pressed to her side. "You must never do that!"

"Do what?" She hadn't said anything to the shawl merchant.

"Go off alone. It is not safe."

Liv glanced around. Mrs. Khan's rebuke, her own puzzled response, had attracted attention. People frowned, shook their heads. "Really? It seems fine."

"Come." Mrs. Khan led her away. "I think our lesson is done for today. You have learned something far more important than bargaining."

"What?"

"Never, never, go anywhere unaccompanied."

Liv walked a step behind Mrs. Khan so that her mentor would not see her roll her eyes. "I was in public, in a crowded place. No one hurt me or said anything to me. I felt perfectly safe. Please, tell me what I am missing."

"Never mind." Mrs. Khan's steps quickened. Liv hurried to keep up. "If you do as I say, *inshallah*, you will never find out."

Twenty

The car purred to a stop outside, the footsteps echoing in the hallway, Maryam gasping at her door. "They are here! Come quickly, come quickly."

Farida fought a slow smile. "Just a moment. I'm almost ready."

She closed the door behind Maryam, shutting out the turmoil ricocheting around the compound. Bibi and the other young wives bid tearful goodbyes. Maryam snapped orders, relayed along by shouting servants. Chickens flapped squawking from older children ordered to catch them; boys drove bleating sheep through the compound's gate on the way to the day's grazing, the animals' double pads of rear-end fat wobbling ridiculously.

Farida wanted to linger just a moment in the cool hush of the room where she'd learned to love her husband, to luxuriate in the difference between this moving day and the one before, when Maryam had dragged her from the Peshawar house to what she was certain would be her death in Afghanistan.

And instead, she had found—yes, she dared named it: happiness.

Not at all what she'd feared when she'd scrawled her panicky note to Alia. Another knock at the door. This momentous day allowed no

155

time for sentiment. Farida stood aside as servants entered to carry her trunks—they'd finally made their way to Jalalabad, contents miraculously almost intact—to the waiting vehicles. She would need her best clothing in Kabul, a realization that hovered at the edge of her contentment, the way a certain jaundiced flatness creeping across a luminous sky portended a storm.

Her smile dimmed. She remembered Alia's words, on the eve of yet another leave-taking, that of her wedding to a stranger.

"You always wanted excitement—new things, different cultures."

A sharp reminder of what that craving had cost her. And now she was to have those new things, to enter again—even if only for a few hours a day—that different culture. It was impossible to explain her own reluctance to Gul, her awareness of the damage such exposure could bring.

LONDON, 1996

She'd learned, oh, how she'd learned, the consequences of her early fascination with such openness during her family's years in Britain, when she had felt herself as bold and free as a foreigner.

Even though she and Alia attended a girls' school, there were plenty of opportunities to meet boys. She wrote to friends in Islamabad about how in this new life it was nothing to walk down the street with a certain boy, sit with him in a chip shop, steal quick kisses in an alley, and slip into a cinema with him on an afternoon when she and Alia were presumed to be rehearsing for a school play. She assured her friends that boys were just like their own brothers—awkward, annoying and, just when you were ready to give up on them, surprisingly sweet. Really, there was no reason to be so bloody stupid about the mingling of the sexes, she wrote, excited to scrawl the swear word she'd never dared to speak aloud.

But she remembered the confusion of those times, too, the trembling warm sensation that lingered for hours after the boy touched his lips to hers, the fear that her parents could look at her and tell what had transpired. Whenever the boy kissed her, Farida vowed never to let him do so again, but in short order she found herself yearning for the next time when, on the walk home after school, the two of them would drop behind the rest of the group and step into a doorway and he would pull her close. At first, the kisses had been quick and furtive, but they grew longer, and Farida let him part her lips with his tongue and press his body against hers. On the days that happened, she could barely breathe and took herself to her room immediately upon arriving home, pleading crushing amounts of homework in order to be alone with her thoughts.

Still, she was not prepared on the afternoon she once again skipped practice for the school play and went instead to the cinema, where the boy—a soft, shy-seeming youth given to easy blushes—guided her to the rear row of seats and proceeded after only a few minutes to drape his arm over her shoulders and ease his hand toward her breast.

"Stop that!" she hissed. He withdrew his hand and began kissing her in their old way, his tongue twining with hers, on and on, so that she got lost in the sensation and barely noticed that his hand had returned to her chest. She pushed it away again, but the third time she let it stay, a transgression so great that it seemed pointless to protest when he slid his hand beneath her blouse and inside her bra. She would not have believed the difference skin against skin made, and when he rolled her nipple in his thumb and forefinger, she crossed and recrossed her legs, hoping to contain the heat intensifying between them. But the boy must have known, because his hand went there next. She locked her thighs distractedly, telling herself that now was the moment to stop, but he was kissing her again and rubbing at the front of her panties, and really, as bad as this was, they were in a public place and she didn't have to worry about the worst thing, Farida told herself as she let her legs fall open. The movie was loud, car chases, buildings disappearing in thundering blasts. The noise enveloped them and her hips rose to meet his hand, moving in unison with it.

She refused to let herself think about that later, nor about the way he took her own hand and rubbed it against the front of his pants, nor of the sensation of power that rose within her as the boy moaned suddenly and writhed against the seat, drawing shushes from those in rows far ahead of them. When the lights came on, people turned back to look at them, smiling knowingly at her disheveled hair, her half-buttoned blouse and rucked-up skirt. She suddenly saw herself with her parents' eyes and began shaking so hard that the boy inquired solicitously whether she was cold and offered her his school blazer.

Afterward, back with their friends, the boy wrapped his arm around her waist and held her close to him as they walked, and the other girls cast questioning glances even as the boy's friends stared with frank, appraising eyes. She couldn't look at him, or any of them, without feeling hot waves of shame, and every time the boy so much as took her hand, it was all she could do not to snatch it away. At home, she washed her hand again and again, trying to rid it of the feel of the boy through his trousers. An unexpected hatred for him rose within her, and that night she fell into a fitful sleep with her hand clamped tight between her legs, guarding what she knew was already, except in the strictest sense, lost.

When her family returned in haste to Pakistan—inevitably, word reached her parents that their daughter was spending time alone with a British boy, a fine excuse to leave an increasingly unsatisfactory situation—it was a comfort to put the incident far behind her. Her jobs at the embassies and NGOs were usually of the lower-level sort, where she worked mostly with other women and foreign men who had been in the subcontinent long enough to have mastered the art of looking past the female employees as though they were so much furniture cluttering up the offices.

Farida knew that when her father betrothed her to Gul, he had harkened back to what little he knew of that long-ago time to justify handing her off to such an unsuitable mate.

On the morning after her wedding, as Gul slumbered satisfied beside her, she had gingerly lifted the heavy coverlet and scrutinized the sheets in the gray morning light, nearly weeping in gratitude at the coppery stain there. Her quivering shoulders wakened Gul and, mistaking relief for modesty, he praised her even as he eased himself atop her again, far more gently than the previous night. Farida, so cheered that everyone would soon know her for an honorable bride, responded with a thankful enthusiasm that had surprised them both.

Odd, she thought now, that the episode in that British cinema had, in its roundabout way, brought her to this man and this place. She pushed the memories down, not wanting to face the knowledge that in her new home, such an incident likely would have meant her own death as well as that of the boy. The important thing was her present happiness. Nothing, not even this pending job among the foreigners, must be allowed to interfere with that.

"Aren't you ready yet?" It was Maryam again, face flushed with the exertion of making sure every single thing about this move proceeded to her satisfaction. Well, Nur Muhammed's satisfaction.

"Just one more minute. I forgot something."

Farida thought it unlikely her previous note had reached Alia, but on the possibility it had, this might be her last best chance to communicate with her sister, to ease the despair that earlier note would have caused.

She dug some of her stash of tattered rupees from their hiding place in her undergarments, tore another page from *Alice*, and fashioned a halting follow-up. She chewed at the stub of the pencil she'd filched from the beauty shop. Then she wrote: "I know this will make no sense to you, but you must believe this. I have come to love him, more than I could have imagined possible. On pain of death, I could not leave him. Even more, I cannot leave his people. They are my people now. This place, strange as it may seem to you, has become my home."

She stopped. She read the simple phrases and saw them through Alia's eyes. Alia would find such sentiments preposterous. She would think that Gul had forced her to write them. Farida looked at this new note for a very long time. Then she tore it into tiny pieces and, as she followed Maryam to the waiting car, stepped into the cooking annex and slipped the shredded handful into the fire, staring into the burst of flame until it subsided into a few glowing threads.

Twenty-One

ISLAMABAD, APRIL 2002

After his near disaster in the market, Pervaiz treated Martin with exaggerated deference that bordered on insolence.

It didn't help that Liv, after some initial awkwardness, seemed with the help of Mrs. Khan to be taking to the place. Every day, she went off somewhere with Face the Future's office manager, her safety guaranteed by Mrs. Khan's presence, exploring the city or the surrounding countryside, forgoing the office altogether, arriving home each evening barely in time to change for the night's dinner party. On the advice of Mrs. Khan, she wore the local-style clothing during the day. Martin thought she looked absurd, towering over the smaller Punjabis in yards of patterned fabric, her blond hair shining incongruously beneath her sheer veil. But when he said as much, she shrugged him off with an unfamiliar assertiveness.

"Don't be silly. It makes things so much easier for me here. You'll see. Tomorrow, I'll show you."

The next day, she postponed her morning rounds with Mrs. Khan to accompany him to Face the Future's offices. But they didn't even have to go to the office for Liv to prove her point. When they emerged from the elevator into the lobby of the Marriott, Pervaiz waited. His normally severe expression softened when he spotted Liv, who that morning wore a buttery yellow silk shalwar kameez bordered with an olive-green geometric design. Rather than wrap the long scarf around her hair, she let it slide to her shoulders, and the ends floated behind her as she walked across the lobby, her steps smaller than usual, toward Pervaiz.

"Miss." Pervaiz leaned toward her in a bow. "You look so smart in local dress. Much more, if I may be allowed to say it, very much more beautiful."

Martin listened for the oily tone that seemed to accompany every sentence Pervaiz addressed to him, but he didn't hear it. Instead, the man rushed to hold the car door for Liv. As Martin slid in beside her, he caught the aroma of perfume, different from Liv's usual soap scent. Lipstick plumped her mouth, and her nails were lacquered in the same dark shade.

"What's all this? Aren't you a little overdone for morning?"

Liv seemed not to mind. "Mrs. Khan took me to the beauty shop yesterday." The car turned onto the broad boulevard that led into the heart of the Blue Zone. "I don't know if you noticed, but women here wear a lot more makeup than back home. They taught me how to do it."

Martin lied and said he hadn't noticed.

"It feels a little strange. But I want to fit in as much as I can. It makes things easier here. Don't you think so?"

Martin didn't know what to think. He tried to imagine himself padding about in the pajamalike getup that so many men wore, their bare feet flopping in sandals or loafers that could be easily kicked aside five times daily for prayers. He thought he would both look and feel ridiculous if he tried something like that. Maybe it was another lingering hangover, but Martin couldn't seem to stop needling her. "You've really had a change of heart."

"I'm still nervous. But I'm curious, too, especially after talking with so many of the refugees. I can't wait to see what Afghanistan itself is like."

Martin told himself he was imagining the reproach in her voice. He was responsible for the reports about the refugee camps, but the details that Liv related every evening when she got home were so repulsive—the

flies, the smells, the pervasive disease—that he decided it was more efficient to let her collect the information he later compiled. Still, he, too,
was eager to meet Afghan people on their own turf. Even though Face the
Future was set up to help Afghans, its Islamabad office was staffed mostly
by Punjabis, small, darting people who invariably made Martin feel overly
large and clumsy by comparison. The Pashtun refugees he remembered
from that long-ago trip had been tall and soft-spoken, with a dignified
reserve that he hoped would translate into an acknowledgment of his own
good intentions and that would prevent the sorts of vaguely challenging
responses he always seemed to receive from Mrs. Khan and Pervaiz.

He'd hoped to regain the approval of the latter by paying him handsomely, a bonus of sorts, for the trip to Kabul. Despite the warnings
against it, he wanted to travel overland, if for no other reason than to
drive to the far end of the Grand Trunk Road, a route whose evocative
name thrilled him, never mind its prosaic modern designation of N5. To
Martin, it would always be Sher Shah Suri's Great Road, Kipling's River of
Life, a device to use to give structure to the book already taking shape in
his mind. He'd planned that he and Liv would make the three-hour drive
to the border on the first day, stopping for the night in Peshawar, giving
themselves time to see something of that ancient frontier city. Despite his
experience in Aabpara, he even hoped to prowl its bazaars, provided that
Pervaiz agreed to accompany them for security.

If all went as Martin had planned, they'd cross the border into Afghanistan the next morning as the sun rose above the ramparts of the
Khyber Pass, a moment he'd anticipated ever since his arrival in Pakistan.

But when he pulled Pervaiz aside to mention his plan for driving to
Kabul, the man's reaction went beyond cheek to outright insubordina-
tion. "Absolutely not."

Martin stood silently, letting his objections—bandits, land mines, rov-
ing Taliban remnants, trigger-happy U.S. troops—wash over him. He allowed himself, one final time, to imagine the summit of the pass the way
he'd seen it for so long in his mind, the road behind them falling back toward civilization, the track ahead snaking into the wild rocky regions popu-

lated by centuries of turbaned warriors. Then, as though erasing a memory file, he banished the image. "But of course. It was foolish of me. We'll be happy to take the UN flight. What day? Sunday? That will be perfect."

He called to Liv, across the room with Mrs. Khan, the two of them sitting at a computer, doing something with a database. They'd missed the entire confrontation, for which Martin was grateful. "If you two have any more shopping to do, or one last trip to the beauty parlor, you'd better do it now. Liv, take another one of those baths you like so much. We leave in three days."

―――――――――

Martin saw the Khyber Pass from the air.

The drive would have been a disappointment, he told himself, face pressed to the prop plane's scratched window. The zigzagging road below was nothing more than a strip of darker gray in a landscape composed of various shades of dun. The Spin Ghar range, the mountains that formed the southern end of the Hindu Kush, were lower than he'd expected, and he wondered why these unimpressive peaks had become the stuff of legend. He reminded himself that it was not the mountains, but what they represented—the last barrier between the arid highlands of Central Asia and the infinite stretches of the subcontinent's rich, fertile lowlands and loamy cropland well watered by wide, slow-moving rivers.

No wonder the armies of Genghis Khan and all the other invaders who followed had been so bloodthirsty, Martin thought as he craned his neck, seeking a wider view of the brown, crumpled landscape through the inadequate window of the blue-and-white UN shuttle to Kabul. Coming from a land such as this, the sight of the water and greenery that bespoke the alien concept known as *ease* must have maddened them, made them crazy to have it for themselves.

Liv leaned past him. "It's so barren. How can anything live there?"

"If you believe the reports, half the Taliban live there somewhere.

Osama is probably looking up at our plane right now." Martin thought back to his glib commentaries, in which he'd so lightly dismissed the Taliban. Now, as the plane droned above their rumored stronghold, he wondered if he had discounted them too easily. He couldn't imagine so much as a woody shrub or a blade of tough mountain grass surviving in such a landscape, let alone the ragged remnants of an army. Yet the regular dispatches that showed up in Face the Future's secure mail bag told him the blank landscape below crawled with fighters and "entrepreneurs," as the warlords had so quickly re-named themselves when they returned with comical ease to their old habits of smuggling opium across arbitrarily drawn national borders. More than opium, Martin reminded himself. There were reports of weapons transports, as the strongmen hastened to round up old Soviet armaments and bartered enthusiastically for the American hardware so temptingly displayed by the U.S. troops who searched the country in their heavily armed convoys. Even without the cautionary briefings at Face the Future, Martin was well aware of what such munitions, so much more accurate than their workmanlike but outdated Soviet counterparts, could do in the wrong hands.

The sound of the plane's engines deepened. Liv rapped at the window. "There it is."

The blue-tinged mountains caught his attention first, thrusting above the haze of the city, as if floating against the pale sky, their peaks—higher and more jagged than the Spin Ghar—washed with white. He focused his attention downward with difficulty. The city rose to meet them. From above, it seemed orderly, neat grids cut by wide, angled boulevards, but as the plane drifted lower, Martin saw block after block of low mud homes interspersed with acres of bombed-out wasteland. Despite the mountain snow, Martin had been assured temperatures already were beginning to climb toward Kabul's searing summer.

He touched his hand to the front of his jacket and felt the crackle of paper in the breast pocket within. As he was leaving the Islamabad office, Mrs. Khan had thrust a sealed envelope into his hand. "I would normally have given this to your wife, but I fear things are different there. One woman giving printed material to another may be suspect, even now.

You must give this to your interpreter." Her voice caught. She turned and walked rapidly away.

Somehow, through the mysterious channels by which so many things seemed to be accomplished, Mrs. Khan had used her connections to arrange for her sister to work as the interpreter in Face the Future's Kabul office.

"We are an organization that works with women. We cannot approach them with male interpreters," Pervaiz explained. "We're lucky to have signed this woman. It's quite difficult to find an educated female there, especially one whose family is willing to let her work with foreigners."

The plane touched down before Martin was prepared for the jolt of being earthbound. Liv gathered her things. The runway ran through a graveyard of rusting aircraft, their metal skins pierced by shrapnel, nose cones shot away. The plane rolled up to a low concrete building, its walls bearing the long raking scars of automatic-weapons fire.

The Boy Wonders had stuffed his head with names, with numbers, with images of weapons, static on the screen, preparing him for everything but the devastation those weapons could cause.

"Good God," he said.

Liv stood, waiting for him.

Martin forced himself from his seat, fighting an urge to stay put until the plane taxied back down the runway, lifting itself out of this mad place and speeding back to the reassurance of Islamabad's tedious inefficiency. He motioned to the other passengers to go ahead of them. A refrain ran through his head: *What have I done, what have I done, what have I done?*

He must have spoken it aloud because Liv turned back to him. "You're about to find out."

———

"It is a most modern home."

Ismail, one of the local employees at Face the Future's Kabul office, showed Martin and Liv around their new home in the organization's compound. Martin thought that at least Ismail's appearance was reassuring, even if nothing else about Kabul was. The man was tall and lean, with a neat beard and a thatch of coarse black hair above expressive eyes, everything Martin had remembered of Pashtuns from those long-ago meetings. Kabul was higher, and correspondingly colder, than Islamabad, and Ismail wore a woolen waistcoat over his shalwar kameez. More than anything, he had a solemnity that Martin found refreshing after the garrulous criticism so freely offered by Pervaiz.

Ismail had coolly negotiated the drive from the airport into the center of town, making relaxed small talk as the car dodged a variety of vehicles and pedestrians that made the chaotic streets of Islamabad seem orderly in retrospect. As in Islamabad, the cars were British-style, with the steering wheel on the right, but the traffic lanes used the American system, or at least Martin thought they did. Actually, it seemed to him as if nobody made an effort to keep to the proper side of the road, and it cost him a great effort not to close his eyes against imminent disaster as Ismail whipped the car around the teetering overloaded buses, donkey carts, and bicycles carrying entire families, the women's blue burqas spreading like sails in the backwash of passing vehicles.

Face the Future's compound was in Wazir Akbar Khan, Kabul's best neighborhood, Ismail told them with a bit of a flourish. So Martin tried to hide his apprehension at the sight of the small cinder-block house, its stone floors bearing the streaks of an indifferent attempt at cleaning. Rolled-up rugs leaned against the walls.

"Western-style dining room." Ismail stood beside a wobbly table and chairs. He led them up a narrow staircase. "Real bed." A lumpy mattress topped a plywood frame. "View of courtyard." He pushed aside a sheer curtain that did little to deflect the blinding sunshine pouring through the dirty glass. Martin stepped to the window. The roof over the kitchen formed a balcony of sorts. Below lay a courtyard of bare earth bordered by a few anemic rosebushes, leaves white with dust.

"And finally," Ismail's voice rose in excitement, "real WC." He held open the door to a closet-size room that indeed featured a toilet, its bowl stained orange, beside the more traditional hole in the floor. A green plastic pitcher with a long spout sat beneath a faucet in the wall. Higher up the wall, directly above the faucet, was a rusty showerhead. There was no separate stall or even a curtain, just a drain in the floor. Martin thought longingly of the palatial bathroom at the Marriott.

"Well," he said into the silence. "This will be—"

Liv broke in. "This will be very fine."

She did not look directly at Ismail. Sometime before she'd left the plane, she'd tucked all of her hair beneath her dupatta and wound it around her neck so that it wrapped her face, nunlike, giving her eyes extra prominence.

"*Dera manana*, Ismail." She used the Pashto phrase for thanks. They had learned just a little of the language before leaving. Martin missed his facility with Urdu but knew it would be of little use in Kabul, where the main languages were Pashto and Dari and smatterings of Russian, a remnant of the Soviet invasion. Not for the first time, Martin regretted his failure to learn more than the basics of Pashto years earlier. But the country had been at war for so long that his college adviser had insisted that Urdu, Pakistan's main language, would be far more useful.

"I understand there is someone to teach us Pashto," he said to Ismail as his new employee led them from the house.

"The interpreter is coming here this morning to meet you. I believe you already know her connection in Islamabad."

"Yes. Mrs. Khan assured us she would be most helpful." He sighed inwardly, imagining another lumpish, bossy female. He'd never understood why Liv was so taken with Mrs. Khan. He dreaded spending hours cooped up learning Pashto with someone just like her.

"Ah," said Ismail. "Here they are now."

They?

The corrugated metal gates to Face the Future's compound swung open, revealing a couple chatting with the Kalashnikov-toting guards who flanked it. Rather, the man spoke. A woman stood silent behind him, draped in the ubiquitous blue burqa that had shrouded the few women Martin had seen on their ride into town from the airport. Ismail called to them. The man turned away from the guards and stalked toward them, the woman following more slowly behind. Martin wondered how she could see to walk at all, tangled as she was in all that fabric. The cement sidewalk bordering the courtyard was broken and uneven in spots, and Martin watched in fascination as the woman approached, placing her feet firmly on the level spots, even though she couldn't possibly have seen them. He noticed that she wore fashionable patent-leather pumps, filmed though they were with the dust that gave Kabul's air a fuzzy, filtered quality. She must have been able to see him staring, because she flicked her burqa in such a way that only the very tips of her shoes protruded from its narrow pleated folds.

"This is your interpreter," Ismail said. "She will teach you Pashto. I think you will find her very helpful."

"*A salaam alaikum.*" Martin held out his hand to the woman's husband, who like Ismail was very nearly Martin's height, and strongly built, but with a more guarded expression.

"*Ve alaikum salaam.*" The man touched his fingertips to Martin's. He glanced toward Liv, and it seemed to Martin that his expression softened at the sight of her attire. Liv made her *salaam* but kept her eyes fixed on the ground.

The man spoke to Ismail. "He says that his wife, like yours, is a very modest woman." Without waiting for a response, Ismail talked for some moments with the man, who fixed Martin with a skeptical, almost angry, gaze. "I told him," Ismail said, "that Face the Future is a program for the betterment of Afghan women. That within these walls, the strictest proprieties are observed. That here, no woman, most certainly not his wife, will ever be disrespected in any way."

Martin wondered what the husband might think if he knew more about Face the Future's stated agenda of better health care, education, and jobs for Afghan women—a job Clayton Williams reassured him superseded the other goals he'd been given—the unspoken assumption being that those things would help them become less dependent on their men. But the man strode back down the path without a word to his wife or anyone else. Martin noticed, though, that he raised his hand to brush his wife's elbow as he passed, and he also noticed how she leaned into that barest hint of a touch. But that seemed so unlikely he thought maybe he had imagined it.

They entered the small office building where they'd do most of their work during the two-year contract. The interpreter stood by in silence as Ismail made introductions. The permanent staff was small and all-male. The only women in the room besides Liv and the new interpreter were a couple of German girls on loan from another NGO, there to set up the record-keeping systems and databases, jobs that Martin planned to assign to Liv. They pulled Liv aside, leading her to a computer that looked to be a decade old. Watching them, Martin wished that Face the Future's administrators had not been so set on relying on locals. He understood the philosophy behind it, but even in Islamabad, whenever he came into contact with people from other NGOs, he was struck by the camaraderie of their staffers, the reassurance they obviously felt in working with their own countrymen amid such pervasive strangeness. The German girls laughed easily together as they showed Liv how the computers and other appliances in the office were hooked into jury-rigged extension cords that ribboned behind the desks and disappeared through a window, where a steady chugging and faint gasoline fumes announced the presence of a generator.

Martin rubbed his hands together after the introductions. He would hold a staff meeting at the end of the day, he told everyone, after he'd had time to look things over. In the meantime, since the tutor was present, he and Liv would start this and every day with a language lesson.

"Shall we go to my office?" He pointed to the walled-off space at one end of the room. "Liv will join us when she finishes with the computer."

The interpreter flinched visibly beneath her burqa.

Ismail stepped to Martin's side. "It would not be proper for her to be alone with you there. I will bring tea," he added, turning to the region's default handling of awkward situations.

"But to work out here will be impossible." The building's main room was small, with several conversations going on simultaneously. A clerk shouted into a satellite telephone in a mixture of Dari and Pashto, while another wrote a report laboriously on a manual typewriter, striking the keys with—so it seemed to Martin, long accustomed to the quiet clicking of a computer keyboard—unnecessary force. The German women conferred in their own language, then helped each other translate their instructions into English for Liv. The generator rattled beneath the window.

"You will just have to concentrate. Perhaps it will help you learn."

It took Martin a moment to realize that the low, melodic voice had come from within the burqa. The folds of blue cloth shifted in what to Martin seemed like impatience. "Shall we begin?" She moved toward an old Formica table that Ismail had hopefully identified as the "conference center" where one could speak with visitors. The front of the burqa briefly parted to enable her to lift a tote bag crammed with papers onto the table.

"Wait," said Martin. "I can't work if you're going to wear that. No one else here is covered," he added, aware that even to his own ears, he sounded petulant. The other women wore only light scarves, and Liv, as soon as Ismail had departed, loosened her own dupatta around her face.

"But of course. I think we must make a study of culture as well as our language. The burqa is for use in public only. At home, a woman does not have to fear seeing strange men. Her husband or her father would take great care to make sure such a thing never happened."

"In this office," Martin said, "we are not strangers. We are colleagues."

"Yes," the woman agreed. "There are gray areas, and the office is one." She slid the garment over her head in a single motion, draping it carefully over the back of a chair.

Martin exhaled slowly.

He'd thought her bulky, but attributed that girth to the packet she'd held beneath her burqa, now clasped to her midriff like a shield. This woman was as slender and graceful as one of the poplars bending so prettily before the harsh gusts scouring Face the Future's courtyard. Her hair, wound into an artful bun, was covered by a sheer white drape that set off the darkness of her wide eyes and the deep color she'd applied to her generous mouth.

"So very nice," Martin heard himself say, then hastily added, "to make your acquaintance."

He touched his hand to his jacket pocket, feeling the letter. He crossed his arms in front of his chest as if to hide it. The letter could wait.

"Perhaps," the woman said smoothly, sitting and gesturing that Martin should do the same, "we will begin with introductions. I will speak in Pashto and then in English.

"*Zema num Farida dai*. My name is Farida."

Twenty-Two

KABUL, APRIL 2002

The poverty that had so dismayed Liv in Islamabad seemed quaint compared to the desperation confronting her each day in Kabul.

Before, she'd pitied the burros that plodded beneath towering loads of bricks. In Kabul, men stacked the bricks into slings, hoisted them onto their own backs, and staggered down the street. Children barely older than toddlers collected burlap bags full of the brittle leaves that dropped from Kabul's scrawny trees, an activity that bewildered Liv until Farida commented that it was a pity it took so many sacks to sustain a fire long enough to cook a single meal.

"They cannot afford coal or even sticks," she said. The widows were the worst, drifting ghostly in cheap, tattered burqas, seemingly everywhere in the city racked by a quarter century's unceasing warfare, their wretched lives made even more hopeless when the Taliban arrived and forbade women to work. "After that, if they had no families to take care of them, they begged. Or the ones young enough sold themselves." Farida went hoarse with embarrassment as she explained the situation to Liv. "You understand, of course, that the punishment for prostitution is death. So if a woman displeased a client or, more likely, someone decided he didn't want to pay, or give her a bit of food, he could report her crime with no real fear of retribution to himself."

Liv thought of her life in the sheltered embrace of the college campus, first as a student, then a researcher and Martin's wife. Of the things in that universe that depended upon the whims of men. A door held open for her, or not. A date. A promotion. In this world, a woman's very life could turn on whether a man had had a bad day. "How do they stand it?"

Farida tapped Liv on her head, then her chest. "You play a role. You learn to lie. You turn these—your head, your heart—into stone, into ice."

But surely the years of poverty would grind stone into dust; the scorching glare of oppression would evaporate ice? Liv kept this thought to herself.

Farida ran her hand over her face as if wiping away a troubling memory and, her tone lighter, reminded Liv that the United Nations managed to alleviate the situation in a few cases by negotiating an agreement with the Taliban that permitted widows to work in United Nations–funded bakeries, as long as no men were present.

Liv and Farida were on their way to one of those bakeries. Martin had come out of his office to see them off, puffed with the false heartiness he assumed around Farida. "You ladies have fun," he almost shouted, his face reddening. "Stay safe." He held an envelope in one hand.

Jesus, Martin. Liv had dropped her guard when they'd left the college. Now a pretty woman in a veil turned him into a blushing schoolboy. "What's that?" She pointed to the letter he held.

He looked at it as though he'd forgotten what it was. The paper—thin, grayish, easily torn by a pen—was endemic throughout the region. "This? Something I wanted to show Farida."

Farida stood near the door, her burqa draped over an arm. She pulled it over her head and adjusted the grille over her eyes. "Now? The driver is already here. But I suppose we can ask him to wait."

Martin backed toward his office. "No. It's not important. Never mind." He slid the envelope into his shirt pocket. "Forget I said anything."

Liv reminded herself to ask Martin about the letter when she got home. But first, she'd have to survive the trip. She gripped the door handle to avoid being flung forward and back as the driver alternately hit the gas and stomped the brake, occasionally yanking hard at the wheel to avoid hitting something or someone. As usual, cars, trucks, scooters, and bicycles darted about with no discernible regard for orderly traffic flow. Horns blared nonstop, in a cascading series of notes so much more intimidating than the childish beep of cars destined for Western nations. The chaos eased only with the appearance of a dust-colored armored creation that looked like a jeep on steroids. It belonged to ISAF, the International Security Assistance Force purportedly keeping the peace in Afghanistan. Drivers, suddenly respectful, made way. Space appeared. Horns went silent. The vehicle lumbered past, antennas waving as though in greeting.

Farida cleared her throat. "This bakery. It is a replacement."

The ISAF vehicle swung wide around a corner and disappeared from view. Anarchy resumed. Liv realized she'd been holding her breath, only half listening as Farida explained that the original bakery had vanished some months earlier when an American bomb went astray of its target and landed instead in the warren of hovels across the wide boulevard from the airport, destroying several homes as well as the bakery.

"So the Amriki," said Liv—how quickly she had adopted the term— "killed the people they were trying to help."

"Yes. Your army did that." *Your army.* The fleeting emphasis of certain words, just short of sarcasm, reminded Liv of Farida's sister's mannerisms, and she suggested as much, adding that she thought it odd that she hadn't gotten even an email from Mrs. Khan since her arrival. But just as Mrs. Khan went silent whenever Liv probed about her mysterious sibling in Afghanistan, Farida now settled wordlessly into herself, not speaking again until they arrived at the blast crater.

They left the car and teetered at the edge, trying to ignore the press of people who, as word whipped through the alleyways that a foreigner was in their midst, jostled for a better view, threatening to send Liv and Farida toppling onto the litter of broken mud bricks below.

The attention, too, was strange for Liv. Although people had stared openly at her in Islamabad's poorer neighborhoods, she'd drawn barely a glance from the fashionable women focused on the enticing wares in the Blue Zone. But Afghanistan seemed so long cut off from the world by its wars and then the Taliban's restrictions that many of its people had gone years without seeing a foreigner on television—that being one of the many pleasures forbidden by the Taliban—or even in person.

"Their lives are the same, day after day after day. Their husbands are mujahideen, away fighting, so the women are left to fend for themselves."

"Mujahideen? Terrorists? Fighting who? Us?" Liv twisted back, looking toward the car parked at the alleyway's entrance, a distance that suddenly seemed too far.

No mistaking the derision in Farida's tone now. "You Amriki. Terrorists here, terrorists there, behind every rock, I think."

Liv thought it best to admit ignorance. "Please. Help me understand."

Farida's voice softened. "The mujahideen fight to protect their own— their family, their tribe, their country. Not like"—she glanced around, and whispered—"those crazy Taliban, working to tear down everything, dominate everyone, saying their way is the only way. And not like the true terrorists, seeking to destroy others." Her chin lifted. "We are proud of our mujahideen. They fight those Taliban trying to return. So we must help their families. All day long, these women scratch and scrape for food to feed their families. The only distractions have been bad things. Like that." Farida pointed to the pit yawning before them. "Our visit is entertainment for them. And you are the main attraction. Come. We will do our interviews indoors. That will limit the commotion."

They pushed their way toward the bakery. So many people had come that Liv could no longer see the crowd's borders, just a sea of burqas flowing through the tributaries of the alleyways, pooling before the bakery. Farida posted the driver in the doorway. "I told him to admit only women." Liv glanced back and saw a few men, pushing and shoving their shrouded wives into the restive throng.

The interior of the new bakery was dark and warm and comforting, and Liv admired the fast-moving ballet of dough shaped and formed and slapped onto long-handled paddles and thrust into a glowing mud-brick oven.

"They hope to make big sales today because of all the people who are waiting to talk to us," Farida said.

"Then we must be very thorough in our interviews. The longer we take, the more bread they will sell." Liv enjoyed such glimmers of complicity with Farida, whose initial reserve she'd found far more forbidding than Mrs. Khan's frankly overbearing manner. And there was the way Farida scurried away as soon as their work was done each day, nearly running toward the gate where her scowling husband waited.

"Poor thing," Martin said. "She's terrified of him. It's so obvious. That's why our work is necessary. The more we go among these women and show them there are other ways to live, the more quickly things will change here."

Our work. Liv had bristled. She was the one actually doing the face-to-face interviews, assignments so immediate and absorbing that she wondered how she'd ever found satisfaction just working at a computer. She didn't bother correcting Martin's impression of Farida's husband. With the composure that Liv had come to expect from local women when they discussed, if at all, their marriages, Farida rarely spoke of him. But when she did, she lingered over the words "my husband," lips curving upward almost inadvertently. Liv wondered how she herself looked when she mentioned Martin. She deliberately injected his name into the conversation, trying to smile as she did. But Farida's face became so severe that the attempt faltered. Besides, there was little time for frivolous talk.

Every day, she and Farida interviewed women and girls wherever they could find them: at the university, to which a handful of women had only recently returned, their studies in disarray after the five-year gap of Taliban rule; the orphanages, overwhelmingly populated by girls; and of course wherever there were widows. This bakery, for instance.

"*Dera manana*," Liv said to one of the women, accepting a piece of naan, making sure to take it in her right hand. She tore off a piece with her teeth and chewed exaggeratedly, patting her stomach. Tea materialized and she lifted a chipped cup to her lips. The bakers clustered around her with more bread. Liv protested, holding up her pen and pad. There was the usual list of questions. Name. Age. Family situation. How many people in the household. How many children. How many (Liv always hesitated here) other wives. Injuries. Illnesses. Abilities. Skills—the idea being to determine which programs might best serve them. Liv thought that the bakers, despite being widows, were better off than the married women. The bakers, at least, had salaries that allowed them to support themselves, albeit barely. But the married women were dependent upon their husbands for every need, and Liv's interviews made it clear that all too often, few of those needs were met.

Her interviews ranged beyond the obvious queries. There were other questions, too, ones that Martin had added.

"Ask them," he said, running his finger down a printed list, "about the situation in the neighborhood. With whom their neighbors sympathized during the civil war. During the Taliban rule, too. How did the neighborhood defend itself? Was there a local militia? Is there still?"

Liv thought the questions strange and said as much.

"You mean to tell me that you just walk in and right away start asking them personal questions about themselves?" Martin rebuked her. "Liv, that's rude, especially in this culture. If you ask them these other things, they'll see that you care about their lives. They'll relax, they'll open up to you. Trust me. I know what I'm talking about."

But he didn't. It was Liv who was out there, doing her job.

Impossible to say that, though, to Martin, who on the rare occasions that she countered his suggestions reminded her of his years of expertise. *From books! From reports! From an office within a guarded compound!* Liv wanted to shout at him, something she had never done at home and that would be even more unthinkable here, where women rarely spoke up in the presence of men. Besides, the few times she'd broached his questions, the women had gone silent and sullen as Farida translated the phrases so brusquely that Liv could only imagine her words held a command not to answer. But all she said to Martin was, "They seem to prefer talking about themselves."

Of course they did. Who else ever asked them about what they thought, what they felt? Her interviews often ranged far afield from her prescribed list, though never in the direction Martin sought. In the bakery, one listless wife with dark half-moons beneath her eyes and four children tumbling dangerously close to the oven surprised Liv by saying that she hadn't minded when her husband took a second wife. She spoke softly, staring at the floor, as Farida translated.

"In fact, she helped him find her. She saw a beautiful young girl around the neighborhood, still too young for the burqa, so that he could see her face, and she said to him, 'That one. She would be a good wife for you.'" Liv started and looked around the room at a girl, a little older than the rest, playing with the children. Liv had assumed she was a sibling or maybe a cousin. The woman, following her gaze, nodded confirmation as Farida continued, "Now he spends his nights with the new wife and this one can rest. Besides, the other wife helps with the children."

"But she's just a child herself!"

"No longer."

Liv looked again at the girl, at the swell of belly beneath her kameez. "How old is the husband?" She tried to keep her voice neutral. The woman and Farida consulted for some moments.

"This is his second family. His first family, his wife and all his children, were killed early in the civil conflict. He was a young man then. He married this one shortly before the Taliban came. Maybe he is about forty?"

"But that girl," Liv said, trying not to stare, "she can't be more than thirteen, fourteen."

"Yes."

"And he—with her—I mean, look at her."

Farida stopped translating, but the woman seemed to divine Liv's thoughts, and spoke for some moments. "Yes, the new wife cried very much at first. Every night, she would try to creep out of the house to get away from him. But now she is accustomed to her woman's role. And who knows?" Farida lifted an eyebrow as she translated, her voice taking on the sudden hardening of the other woman's tone. "Maybe someday this girl, too, will go in search of yet another wife to relieve her from her own burdens."

Liv looked up from her notes. "I never thought of it that way."

Twenty-Three

Martin hummed as he reviewed his paperwork, the same two lines, over and over again.

"O Tannenbaum, O Tannenbaum, mm hmmm hmmm . . ."

Liv sat across the room and thought about killing him. Or at the very least, finding him a new wife to share her burdens.

Stone, ice. Farida's advice had become a mantra. Liv forced her mind to the mundane, running down a checklist of delayed tasks.

"The letter," she said.

"Letter?"

"For Farida. You had one—well, you had something in an envelope you wanted to show her. What was it? Did you give it to her?"

"Oh. That. It's nothing."

Flicking away her query, just as he did when she asked him about his report, the big one he'd deliver in a few weeks at a meeting of administrators of some of the NGOs and a commander from ISAF, whose polyglot troops seemed to be everywhere in the center of Kabul and nowhere beyond that. Technically, Liv had contributed to the report. But when she asked yet again to see it, Martin demurred.

"O Livele, O Livele, all things in their good time," he warbled now, with Christmas still months away. He'd assured her that for him, no matter what words he sang, the tune would always be "Maryland, My Maryland," the state song of his birthplace. She assured him that she hated it. Yet now he was humming again. Eight notes, then seven.

Liv imagined guns, knives, bare knuckles. She ground her teeth. Lectured herself. This is what bothered her? She spent her days talking to women who routinely tolerated beatings, degradations, second and third wives, and still this silly song drove her to the traitorous thought: If they divorced, she would never have to hear O goddamn Tannenbaum again in her life. The pilaf she'd eaten for dinner churned in her stomach. She coughed.

"Oh, Livele, my Livele, do you need a drink of water?"

If there were a second wife, a younger, subordinate wife, Liv could give her a little push toward Martin and say, "He's all yours tonight. Him and his humming. For God's sake, teach him a new song, will you?" She remembered Martin's colleagues, their various affairs and remarriages, and wondered: All that juggling of wives and mistresses, was it really so different from this system of taking on younger wives as the early ones aged? Her thoughts wandered mutinously further afield, recalling those abandoned faculty wives and her own assumptions about the humiliation they must have felt. What if they weren't so much ashamed as relieved? Their husband's shortcomings and imperfections, revealed by long years of marriage, now some other woman's problem?

"Liv. Liv!"

She looked up and unclenched her hand. She'd been knuckling her fist against her forehead, could feel the mark that must be there.

"Are you all right?"

"Just tired." The evening call to prayer, broadcast from a nearby mosque, echoed around them. Martin thought it annoying, far too loud and distorted by a tinny sound system, but Liv loved the sinuous melody, and the way the city came to a sudden, hushed halt. "*Allahu akbar,*" her lips formed the words once, twice, three times, then a fourth. God is greater. "*Ashhadu an la ilaha illa Allah.*" Twice. There is no God but Allah.

Martin waited until the last juddering note died away. "Maybe you need a break from the fieldwork. Is that it?"

She blinked back sudden tears. "It's their lives," she said when she felt able to control her voice. "What's Face the Future actually doing with the information we're gathering? Are they going to help these women? They're starving."

———

Another day, another interview, another exhausted wife.

So beautiful, Liv had thought when she first met the women of Afghanistan, their features so fine, eyes so prominent, cheeks hollowed in a way that would be the envy of any American model. Which should have been her clue. But she remained oblivious, until the day a woman wrapped her fingers around Liv's upper arm, sucked in her breath in wonder, then let her hand coast to Liv's waist, where through the layers of cloth she squeezed a handful of excess flesh.

"*Wah*," she breathed, and said something that made the other women in the room lean in close.

Farida translated. "She says she, too, used to be beautiful like you. Nice"—with visible effort, she suppressed a grin—"and fat."

"Um, *dera manana*." Liv coughed her thanks, giving herself a moment to think about a world of plenty that viewed skeletal women as beautiful, and the world in which she now found herself, where a precious layer of fat bespoke unimaginable security.

"I like your food very much," she blurted out. "Obviously." She puffed her cheeks and patted her stomach, earning a round of laughter. "It is so different from what we eat in Amrika. Could you please tell me how you cook your evening meal?"

The woman dropped her hand, sat up a little straighter and, for the first time in the interview, spoke with authority. "You must go to the market and buy an onion, a tomato, a potato. At home you will have some oil and some rice, yes?"

"*Ho*." Liv nodded, grateful for the woman's broadly smiling reaction to even a single word of Pashto.

"You take a handful of rice and cook that first in your pot, and then you put it on the plate. Then you heat the oil in the pot and chop the onion, the tomato, and the potato and stir them in the oil until they are cooked. Then you eat that with the rice. You see? It is really so simple. If you can afford a bit of salt, of course, it will taste better."

Liv knew the woman was married with several children, despite her youth. A single tomato and potato would hardly suffice for that mob. "And," she said, her pen scratching fast on the paper, conscious of the other women pressing forward for their turn, "the meat? How do you prepare it?"

Farida translated the question very quietly, and there was a long silence afterward. Liv looked up. When the woman spoke, her lips barely moved.

"There is no meat," Farida said. "You have shamed her," she added, telling Liv what she already knew.

Liv apologized. "The shame is on me."

Farida did not disagree.

Martin left the house and crossed the courtyard toward Face the Future's office. One hundred forty-four steps. He'd counted.

The compound's blue gate stood exactly halfway between the two buildings. Beyond it, the streets of Kabul seethed with car horns and hoofbeats, the singsong calls of vendors, the shrieks of children, and below it all, an indefinable buzz that on his best days Martin took for hope, but on his worst he feared held something darker. A warning.

He stopped and looked toward the closed gate. He could see the guard's sandaled feet in the gap between the bottom of the gate and the ground. Maybe this would be the day he ventured beyond it. Oh, he'd been out—but nearly always within the confines of the car, accompanied by Ismail and one of the guards, on his visits to the other NGOs or the

UN. Sometimes he and Liv went to one of the restaurants frequented by foreigners, which guaranteed a contingent of aggressively armed guards, hired by a proprietor eager to protect the influx of Amriki dollars. Early on, he'd even forced himself to stroll along the relative safety of Chicken Street, whose antiques shops and galleries only tourists could afford. He shoved his hands into his pockets to still his trembling fingers and clamped his arms tight to his body to conceal the damp patches widening beneath them. He'd be fine, he told himself. After all, he'd been in the shit.

But even with Ismail on one side and the guard on the other, so close their arms sometimes brushed his, he couldn't shake the memory of that day in Aabpara Market. *Shut up, Amriki.* The rough hand on his elbow, the rush past the stalls whose shopkeepers turned away so as not to see.

"Let's go," he snapped at Ismail, who was steering him toward a display of conflict rugs, those prayer-rug–size floor coverings adorned with tanks and helicopters, beloved by journalists and aid workers as souvenirs.

"But—"

"Now." Just because he'd been in the shit didn't mean he wanted to chance it again. A child approached, palm up, mouth curved down. Eyes beseeching. "Mister, please."

Martin remembered the jeering swarm that had set upon him in Aabpara, the fingers in his pockets. Were the boy's cohorts waiting around a corner, betting on their ability to distract Ismail and the guard? Worse yet, what if the boy was a decoy, sent unknowing by an entrepreneurial father or uncle, someone more practiced in kidnapping than the trio in Aabpara?

"*Now.*"

But there was no escape the next day, when an officer from ISAF showed up without warning at Face the Future's door. The Boy Wonders had taught Martin all about matériel but neglected to throw in a session on military rank, so Martin had no way of deciphering the brass on the shoulders, the hardware on the chest, knowing only that it signaled Importance.

"Tea!" Martin shouted unnecessarily to Ismail, already assembling the cups and the tray. The lieutenant—major? captain?—cut his eyes toward Ismail. Martin got the message and waved Ismail away. The officer pulled out a flask, dosed the tea, and got down to business.

He established that Clayton Williams, Martin's stateside supervisor, was a mutual acquaintance. He established that it was ISAF's business not only to train Afghan troops but also to protect the interests of the United States. He established that the NGOs were invaluable partners in that enterprise.

"Anything I can do to help," Martin interjected. He tried not to gulp his tea, with its welcome enhancement.

"Your reports," the officer said, and Martin knew better than to ask how he'd seen them, "they could use more detail. So much information about families. About women. But nothing of what the men are up to." He eased the flask from his starched shirt pocket and raised an inquiring eyebrow—a test, maybe.

Martin thought he should decline a second splash. He pushed his cup forward, anyway. He'd dropped clumsy hints to Liv—"Ask them if their husbands have any way of protecting them"—but so far, she'd yet to mention as much as a Kalashnikov in any of the places she visited, let alone the more lethal hardware of such intense interest. The officer had said he knew Clayton Williams. But did that mean he knew everything?

"Yes, very little about the men," Martin said carefully. "After all, our job is to help the women."

The officer paused, holding the flask above Martin's cup. "Let's cut the bullshit."

Martin hitched his chair forward. A rebuke almost certainly awaited. He wasn't delivering the goods they wanted—and now he knew *they* included ISAF. But there'd be a certain relief in frank censure. He'd thought academia was all bullshit, but it was nothing like this world of opacity he'd entered upon landing in Pakistan and now, here, where every sentence carried indecipherable meaning, every action the risk of being misunderstood. Finally, someone who would talk straight.

"The women." Whiskey glugged into the half inch of tea left in Martin's cup. The officer made as though to pass over his own, but at the last minute his hand jerked, a few drops added. His hair was iron and his skin coppered by the sun, and his blue eyes had the hard stare of too many of the people Martin had met here. "Equal rights. In this place. Do you think that's possible?"

"Maybe not equal." Martin sipped at tepid liquid that nonetheless burned. "But better. We at least have to try."

The officer grimaced. "Oh, we'll build a few schools, invite the reporters in as soon as they open, and pray to God they don't come back a few weeks later to find the building bombed and the teachers killed and all the girls gone to who knows where. *Women.*"

He spat the word like a curse but looked more exhausted than angry. "Of all the insoluble problems in this place, we've got to solve the bigger ones first. Any information we can get helps. Any. And we need it yesterday. You understand?"

Martin understood. But as much as he pushed Liv to ask the questions he provided, her accounts remained frustratingly vague. A few days after the officer's visit, he called up Liv's most recent report on his computer, scanning past the usual details of too many children and too little food. His gaze snagged on a phrase.

"Husband absent."

Martin's fingers hovered over the keyboard. He thought of what he knew of Afghanistan, of what he'd learned since arriving. The NGO gossip network buzzed with news of insurgent activity, tidbits that could save a life if they meant a trip postponed, a route changed. What had he heard lately? Something about the border, beyond Kandahar, a place with a strange name. He closed his eyes until it came to him. The keys clattered as he typed by touch.

"Husband gone to Spin Boldak, along with other men from community. No word on return date."

He opened his eyes, checked for typos. And hit Send.

Twenty-Four

The blue metal gates to Face the Future's compound swung open.

Gul, watching from a half block away, shook Nur Muhammed awake. Together they peered through the smeared window of the ancient Lada they had borrowed from one of Nur Muhammed's employees. A white Toyota sedan pulled through the gates and nosed into traffic. Gul stepped on the accelerator, swerved to avoid a horse-drawn cart, and drew nearly even with the Toyota.

"*Hssst.* Not so close. They'll see us."

"What if they do? To them, we all look the same. Farida heard That Man say so." It still was an effort, even after so many months of marriage, to speak so familiarly of his wife to his father.

"But the driver."

"He is new. They fired the old one. He was Hazara, but the guard was Tajik and refused to work with him." Nur Muhammed nodded understanding. Only foreigners would be so stupid as to pair members of the two groups, one Sunni, the other Shi'a, enemies from the beginning of time.

"They go now to the United Nations," he told Nur Muhammed. "That Man prepares a packet of information that no one else sees, and he takes it himself to the UN."

"Maybe he should get the UN to give him one of its cars."

Face the Future's car was small and dented, more like most of the other vehicles on the street than the UN's shiny Land Cruisers that careened through Kabul, outsize antennas waving aggressively, scattering lesser vehicles in their paths. The Toyota Taliban, people called them. Griping about the United Nations was a favorite pastime, not only among Afghans but also by members of the smaller NGOs that lacked a worldwide cash flow.

"They have heat in the UN offices, even in deep winter," Gul said now, repeating some of the things that Farida had told him. "Only the finest carpets on their floors, carpets that mysteriously disappear when someone goes back to his own country. But new carpets always come. All of their offices have running water. And those European-style WCs."

"I never liked those. They are unclean. There is no way to wash afterward."

Gul himself had never seen such a toilet until his family moved to Pakistan, and then only in the hotels catering to foreigners. It confused him, the way one perched upon them and did one's business from a great height, and how afterward they roared and swirled with water, but that there was no separate water with which to adequately clean oneself, just paper. Farida had confided to him that the ones in France were much better, with a sprayer any civilized person would find a comfort.

"Hurry. That way," cried Nur Muhammed as the car made a turn. Gul sped up to catch it, making sure he was following the right vehicle. Kabul was full of white Toyotas. Nur Muhammed craned his neck, looking back toward the street they'd just left. "But the UN is there. Where are we going?"

Gul squinted down the long boulevard, through the ever-present haze of dust and smog that blurred the outlines of the bulky green trucks at the far end of the road. "He's not going to the UN after all. He's going to ISAF."

They waited two hours, Gul shifting to stay alert in the sweltering car, Nur Muhammed dozing beside him.

Gul lowered his own eyes, letting his mouth fall open slightly, feigning sleep as yet another military truck rattled through the gates, raising choking clouds of dust. Gul fought an urge to raise the window. Even with it lowered, the car was an oven. Through the open gate, he glimpsed men in drab uniforms moving purposefully about. The gate clanged shut, too late to block Gul's flash of envy at the plenty within—the soldiers' expensive boots, their matching uniforms, and their gleaming new weapons, not the ubiquitous Kalashnikovs, dull and pitted from years of abuse in the desert, seemingly carried by every male over the age of twelve in Afghanistan.

He jerked in his seat, yanked from true sleep by the clanking gate. Nur Muhammed's words reached him, insubstantial as smoke. "He comes now. Don't move."

Martin and a man in uniform approached the gate. They spoke, voices loud. The man in uniform shook Martin's hand, slapped him on the back, grinned, and said something in English.

Gul rolled the unfamiliar syllables in his mouth, memorizing them. He would ask Farida what they meant.

The men moved out of sight. A car started. A few moments later, it emerged through the gate. Again Gul followed, but it returned to Face the Future with no further stops.

Martin never went to the UN that day at all.

"*Gujabadi?*"

"Something like that." Gul had recited the ISAF officer's words to Martin in his head all day, burning the sounds into his brain. Now he whispered them in the dark, his lips to Farida's ear.

It was late, and they had already loved each other that evening. But Gul fought to stay awake afterward, not wanting to waste their private time together in sleep. The morning would come quickly enough, and with it the obligation to go their separate ways during the day, Gul with his father, Farida to her job at Face the Future, or more often than not these days, into the courtyard with Maryam and the aunties, who hovered ever closer, protective of her advancing pregnancy. The house was always crowded. This time, Nur Muhammed had not repeated his mistake of going to Kabul in isolation, but instead had persuaded several relatives, and all of their family members, especially the young men, to come with him from Jalalabad.

"*Gujabadi.*" Farida's earlobe brushed his mouth as she shook her head. "It doesn't sound like English. Say it again, slowly, please."

He did. She repeated it. "*Gu. Ja. Ba. Di.*"

"Not exactly. The last two faster, I think. The second, louder."

"*Gu. JA. Badi. Gu JA. Badi* . . . Oh!" She laughed, burrowing her head against his chest to muffle the sound.

"What? What is so funny?"

"I just figured it out. '*Good job, buddy.*'" She translated it for him. "Where did you hear that?"

"On Chicken Street," he lied.

"Ah. Well from now on, whenever one of Those People says those words, I shall think *gujabadi.*" A peal of laughter escaped.

"You make fun of me. You are not a respectful wife." He shrugged her away and turned his back, maintaining his mock anger just long enough for her to put her arms around him, pull him to her, comfort him with kisses, and more and more, until once again they lay sweat-slicked and smiling.

"Do you know who truly has no respect?" Farida whispered.

"Who?"

"That Man. He does not respect his wife."

"How does he disrespect her?" Gul shifted, solely for the pleasure of feeling their bare bodies slide against each other. He eased his hand over her hip to her belly, still moist, and ran his fingers across its taut, rounded surface. "Is my son asleep?"

"Almost. Here." She put her hand on his, guiding it to the fluttering within. "When I am as big as this house, will you still lie with me like this? Besides, how do you know that it's a boy?"

Gul ignored her and returned to his question. "Does he beat her?"

"The British and the Amriki, they don't beat their wives. No, they are cruel to their wives in a way that I think hurts worse than hitting." She rolled on her side and put her arms around his neck and told him how foreign men would talk about their wives right in front of them as though they weren't there. "They say the most awful things and then laugh as though it were a joke." She told him how Liv's eyes went dark with pain when Martin did this and how, even though Liv was a tall woman, she somehow became smaller and smaller as Martin spoke.

"What does he say?" Gul was nearly asleep. But his father would give him no rest in the morning if he did not bring new information, and the only way to get it was to talk first of things of no consequence. It was important that Farida be seen as useful, even if that meant continuing her odious work for the foreigners. He saw how his father looked at Farida, his gaze cold, assessing. Gul was sure he was recalling the crushing bride price that had gotten him what, exactly? Nothing made Nur Muhammed angrier than a bad bargain.

So Gul questioned Farida nightly and hoped to persuade his father of her continued worth. "Does he laugh at her? Is it because she is barren?" Liv and Martin's lack of children was the subject of endless speculation, especially considering that Martin had not divorced her and taken a new wife years ago, the only reasonable response to such circumstances.

"Nothing so terrible, at least not on the surface. He makes fun of how she likes to wear our local dress and eat our food. He says the lamb makes her fat. It's just the way he says it. I don't like it. Sometimes I think our way is good, with the men and women apart so much. A man can't talk about his wife then. To say such things, especially in front of another woman . . ." Her voice trailed off and her arms slackened their gentle hold.

He shifted again, forcing her to return to wakefulness. "Surely he doesn't spend all day making fun of his wife."

"No. He sits at his desk and writes reports. That's a fancy way of saying he doesn't do much. She goes around town with me, talking to women all day long, but he never seems to want to hear what she has to say."

Gul held his breath, then exhaled, trying to sound natural. "What are his reports about?"

Farida spoke slowly, with an edge of thoughtfulness to her voice. "History mostly. But not long-ago things. Recent times. He asks about it all the time. Who was aligned with whom when the Taliban were here. Where they stand now. The strength of their factions." She paused, speaking even more slowly. "Where they are headquartered. What weapons they are likely to have. He says it helps him to understand Afghanistan, why we are the way we are. I think it does help him understand, but I don't think it has anything to do with the women they say they are trying to help."

Good job, buddy.

"Gul? Gul. What's the matter?"

He didn't even have to lie. "Are you alone with him when he asks you these questions?"

"Of course not. That would be wrong."

Gul told himself he imagined the hesitation before her reply. He turned onto his stomach and feigned slumber. But he felt her next to him, as tense and awake as he.

Twenty-Five

Gul thought it was unfair that just as he was learning to take such delight in his wife, Nur Muhammed finally brought him fully into his work.

The next morning, an embarrassed servant shuffled and coughed outside the door until Gul emerged to the unwelcome news that Nur Muhammed again demanded his company on business, earlier than usual this time. Nur Muhammed had made several recent trips of some length, traveling not just beyond Kabul but also—as he told only Gul, brushing aside Maryam's anxious queries—out of the country, to Syria and once even to Saudi Arabia, returning tense and purposeful, though largely uncommunicative. He'd acquired a satellite phone and despite the exorbitant per-minute cost conducted long conversations almost nightly, out of earshot of the rest of the household, whose members grumbled about the phone's priority status on the generator.

They kept those thoughts to themselves, though, mindful of the sudden flow of luxuries into their midst, the prime cuts of lamb and goat available at every evening meal, thick new Baloch carpets that replaced ones threadbare from years of use, and—Maryam's pride—a washing machine imported from Turkey, one that required a generator recharge to get through an entire cycle, its rattle and shake so alarming that the neighborhood children shrieked and ran away.

In Kabul, Nur Muhammed's "business" involved meeting with certain factional leaders, many of them once bitter enemies but now increasingly willing to shed old hostilities to unite against the Amriki. The meetings took place all around the city, rarely in the same place two times in a row, never at the same time of day.

On this particular day, Nur Muhammed and his associates gathered in a small room behind a general store that belonged to a man in debt to Nur Muhammed. Normally, Nur Muhammed was ruthless in the collection of money, but this store owner had fought beside him against the Russians. Once, he saw the sun glinting on a telltale thread of wire protruding from a rocky trail and shoved Nur Muhammed aside just before he stepped on the mine, allowing him to escape with the loss of only those four fingers to a bit of shrapnel. So, while Nur Muhammed could not, for the sake of his own pride and that of his debtor, forget about the money his friend owed, he could accept the man's offer of a place to meet in secret.

They gathered in a windowless room behind the stall that sold palm-size packets of shampoo and other sundries. As it filled with men, the air became heavy with the odors of unwashed bodies and hair oil liberally applied. Their host fussed about them as they slurped tea. There was desultory talk of the weather, and inquiries after everyone's health, but the conversation quickly focused on the Amriki.

"They came here, they bombed us, they took over our cities. They chased the Taliban away, or think they did. They won. Why are they still here?" a Turkman in a wildly striped coat demanded.

"Oil, I think," offered another. "They hope still for a pipeline. If they provide the security, what do you think they will demand in return? Some of the oil? All of it?"

"They want to kill Muslims," offered yet a third, younger and more intemperate than most of Nur Muhammed's new allies.

As far as Gul could tell, this man was a former Talib who had merely shed his black turban and melted back into the general population as soon as the Amriki arrived. It was as Farida said: To the Amriki, all Afghan people looked alike, even though to Gul this man radiated the problematic stink of the fanatic.

"What do you think?" Nur Muhammed spoke to his son. "Do the Amriki want to kill us?"

Gul raised his tea to his lips, needing time to consider his answer. Clearly, Nur Muhammed was courting the young Talib, though for what reason Gul could not imagine. He lowered the cup and licked the moisture from his mustache. "I think they are disrespectful. I think they disdain our customs and are insolent with our women. I think they shoot their guns and drop their bombs and kill innocent people and then say it's all a big mistake. I don't think they want to kill us themselves. That would make them look bad." He took a deep breath. He hoped he was saying the right thing. He thought back to some things that Farida had told him, and continued with more confidence. "I think they want to make us angry, in many small ways, so that we fight among ourselves and kill each other. We'll do the job for them." He sat back, awaiting the reaction.

It came immediately. "*Ho!* That is exactly right!" The Talib leaned forward. His beard was ragged and thin, but long, even though most men had trimmed theirs as soon as the Taliban fled. The beard rose and fell as his chest heaved with excitement. His eyes burned and he stabbed at the air with his hand. Spittle dampened the corners of his mouth. Gul forced himself not to pull back, even as others in the room leaned closer as the Talib collected himself, then spoke again.

"We must strike back at them. We must drive them from this country, the same way we drove the Russians. A jab here, a poke there. A bruise, a cut. So slight that at first they don't notice how severely they are bleeding. Until, that is, they realize the very life is draining from them." From the back of the room came a low shout: "*Ho!* We have done it before. And the Amriki are softer than the Russians."

Gul thought that surely his father's clandestine trips were in the furtherance of something more than small guerrilla actions, the kind anyone with a Kalashnikov—and in Kabul, nearly every household had at least one—might carry out. On the other hand, if Nur Muhammed wanted to announce a more dramatic effort, he'd have done so. He'd always favored opacity, a quality that would serve him particularly well if indeed a larger plan were afoot.

"Yes," Gul said cautiously. "That is a good start." He cut a glance toward Nur Muhammed. His father's expression was impassive, but when his eyes met Gul's, the corners crinkled in an almost imperceptible sign of approval.

Nur Muhammed customarily conducted his business outside his home. So Gul was surprised one day not long after the meeting to come home and find his father entertaining the young Talib. His name was Hamidullah and he had, Nur Muhammed said vaguely, special talents.

Nur Muhammed changed the topic to inconsequential things as a manservant entered the room and placed an array of steaming platters upon the oilcloth. Gul saw aushak, Farida's new specialty. She worked extra hard at getting the dumplings just right after he had mentioned to her one night that they were his favorite. After that, she would ask him whether she had balanced the spices to his satisfaction. She fretted about the texture of the dough, worrying that it was tough, "like Bibi's," she added slyly. She began to play with subtle variations, so that he could always tell which were hers.

"It's the way you crimp them," he said to her in triumph one evening. "The pattern is different. And, of course, the taste is superior!" He muffled her delighted laughter beneath the blanket, lest the rest of the household hear and chide him for being one of those men too much under the influence of their wives.

The manservant passed a basin of warm water and a towel. Each man dipped his fingers and dried them, and then the meal, and the business, began. Nur Muhammed and Hamidullah discussed the continuing difficulties posed to their opium and arms deals by the presence of the Amriki.

"They are very much opposed to drugs," Hamidullah said, and even

Gul joined in the laughter that followed the jest. They all watched the pirated television shows from Amrika, depicting a country of addicts, its streets full of vacant-eyed men and women who prostituted themselves.

"It is the effect on the new business that troubles me," said Nur Muhammed. Hamidullah grunted vigorous agreement. He stuffed a dumpling in his mouth, and then another, chewing with his mouth open. Gul grimaced in annoyance. He could hear the muffled voices of women in other parts of the house, and knew—because Farida would not let him forget—the trouble to which they had gone to put such a lavish meal before this guest, who treated it as though it were a bit of rice and tough scraps of lamb from a humble street stall.

One night, Farida had thrust her hands before him. They were red and swollen, with patches of skin scraped raw. The polish on her nails was chipped, and the nails themselves were broken.

"You see what I do for you."

He was not sure whether she was truly angry, or teasing him again. "What do you mean?" Every time he thought he was beginning to understand her, she presented him with some new, baffling topic.

It turned out that she had not cooked, ever, before her marriage. "We had a cook. Not a good one, but still."

"So do we." Did they? He took it for granted that food would appear at mealtime, just as clothes were regularly laundered, the house cleaned, the courtyard swept. He wondered if she felt him less of a man for not providing her with some of the luxuries she'd known in her previous life. Yet he had seen her family's home, small and mean, its furniture worn and scratched and piled high with dusty old books that should have, in his opinion, been packed away. The bedchambers in the home that Nur Muhammed had procured in Kabul were simple, just carpets and sleeping mats, but the sitting rooms were crowded with overstuffed brocade sofas and shiny lacquered cabinets, with glass vases full of brightly colored silk roses everywhere. Her life, as far as he could tell, was easier now.

"Why are you cooking? And should you be doing that sort of work?"

"Oh, la. That." She took great pride in the fact that she was not sick, even a little, during her pregnancy. "But the cooking—I want to learn. Your mother and Bibi are quite accomplished." Even though it had been years since Maryam had had to prepare the family's meals, she still supervised them minutely and was known to push a servant aside so she could correct the seasoning herself. And Bibi had complained, when they were young, of the long hours Maryam forced her to put in at the kitchen. "I want to fit in," Farida said. "And of course I want to be a good wife to you. But it is so much work! You cannot imagine. You bend over and chop-chop-chop. Onions, carrots, squash. Your back hurts, your hand hurts from holding the knife so tightly, but still, chop-chop-chop. Did you ever wonder how your food gets to be in such little pieces?"

Gul didn't have to tell her that he never thought about it.

"You remember this the next time you men are sitting out there, drinking your tea and talk-talk-talking while we are working. And never a word from you, to show that you've noticed."

Gul felt foolish, letting a woman speak to him in such a way. Still, he had to admit the meals were delectable, and he realized that when he said something to Farida about this dish or that, she became even more attentive and affectionate. Now he watched in disgust as grains of rice dribbled from Hamidullah's mouth into his beard. Gul wondered again what Hamidullah was doing there. He supposed it had something to do with opium. The Taliban had, after all, financed much of their operations with drug money, and Nur Muhammed had profited quite handsomely even in his limited role as go-between.

"They want them all." Nur Muhammed's voice lowered ominously, and Gul jerked himself back to attention. Even Hamidullah closed his mouth.

"They won't get them," the man told Nur Muhammed. "They will never find them where we have them. They bombed Tora Bora. People were there. But not the missiles."

So they were talking about the Stingers. Gul began to understand. The Amriki had provided Stingers to the mujahideen when they were fighting the Russians. But when the Russians went crawling back to Moscow, and Amrika tried to round up unused matériel, much of it had vanished. The Amriki went away, probably reasoning that the country was too wrecked by its long war to make mischief with the Stingers. But now that Osama had asserted himself so very forcefully, they had returned—ignoring the fact that the troublesome man who had brought so much distress upon them had long ago fled to Pakistan—this time with bombs and planes and troops of their own. And they wanted the Stingers back.

"The Amriki must be made to leave," Nur Muhammed said. "This is not something we can endure."

"We are trying."

Gul thought of the attacks on the ISAF convoys, of the snipers whose bullets bounced harmlessly off the armored vests of the Amriki soldiers, of the crude roadside bombs that exploded harmlessly after the convoys had passed.

"They are not like the Russians." The food that Hamidullah had devoured so indiscriminately now seemed about to choke him. "They are too strong. The men, themselves, I think they are weak. But their equipment is very good."

Nur Muhammed spoke briefly and nostalgically of the notoriously shoddy Russian tanks and jeeps, of the helicopters whose blades faltered and then went silent, of the way they lurched and yawed through the thin mountain air onto the heaps of rock below. "But these new attacks are not working. And the Amriki are killing more of our people when they fire back. Too many women and children dead, and people will become angry with us instead of the Amriki." Again, as he had at the earlier meeting, Nur Muhammed looked to Gul. He didn't even bother posing the question this time. He just waited.

Gul strove for assurance, aware that this Talib was only a few years older than he. "I think that maybe we are attacking the wrong people. And that our actions lack ambition." His thoughts churned. Of course they were attacking the wrong people. That's why the actions had failed. He chewed a dumpling, trying to detect the dominant flavor in the subtle blend, so that he could comment to Farida. *Danrhya*, coriander. He swallowed, the velvety dumpling sliding with ease down his throat, and stifled a prideful smile. "It is as you said," he told Hamidullah, aware that it would be good to flatter the man. "The Amriki are weak. But when they are in their tanks and trucks, they are strong. You must hit them when they are away from their equipment. The loss of matériel matters little to them, compared to the loss of men."

"This is true. I have heard that their entire country stopped working after the killings by the airplanes."

"All this trouble over just one day." They had discussed the subject endlessly, but the wonder remained in Nur Muhammed's voice. It did not need to be said, but Gul said it, anyway.

"I would like to see what would happen if the Russians had attacked *them* for twenty-five years."

"If the Russians attacked them," Hamidullah took up the subject with relish, "and they did not have their strong tanks and their bombs. If they were like us. Barefoot villagers." His chest puffed with pride, his beard riding it like some sort of scrawny rodent.

Gul felt his father's eyes upon him, and he knew it was time to bring the talk back to the matter at hand. "Imagine what one attack here could accomplish."

"There is no place for such an attack. Even their places like the UN are very heavily guarded. And when they go out on the streets, the soldiers are with them."

Gul said nothing for a few moments. For years, he had watched his father use silence to his advantage. It made people nervous, Nur Muhammed often reminded Gul. Their minds began to race, and they frequently became so agitated that, when you spoke to them again, it was such a relief that they often seized upon your proposal as the only possible solution. "There are many places," Gul said, noticing that Hamidullah's tensed shoulders relaxed as he finally spoke, "that are not so heavily protected. Not every foreign organization has money for so many guards."

Hamidullah's body stiffened again. His resistance was palpable. "I know those places." He spoke around a mouthful of food. "They are unimportant. No one cares what happens to them."

This fellow was impossibly ignorant. Still, Gul kept his voice soft, another trick he had learned from Nur Muhammed. Shout, his father had told him, and everyone shouts back at you. Soon, there is so much noise that no one idea can be heard. But whisper, and everyone stops talking, the better to hear you. "To the foreigners, everyone is important."

Gul repeated what Farida had told him about the craziness in England, when the Irish were bombing the streets, people afraid to leave their homes. She had read, she told him, that in Amrika they so feared their own black citizens that schools and government buildings had guards at the entrances.

"You kill one of them, twenty will cry," he said. "Especially if that one is not a soldier. They will yell about unfairness, but they will also become afraid. It does not take much to make them run and hide." He followed the implicit rebuke with another nod to Hamidullah. "It is as you said earlier. We must jab at them. A little bit here and there, enough to put them on notice. Not just the Amriki, but the places they have influenced—the markets that sell alcohol. But soon, I think, a big action is necessary. Something to show them that we have the power to inflict true damage, so that they know it will not be worth their while to stay." He finished in a rush, enjoying the flush of success as Hamidullah chimed in with suggestions to accomplish his plan, targets where foreigners congregated—schools, the journalists' hotels, maybe one of the popular restaurants that they frequented, eating their odd tasteless foods, pizza and the like, provided by those establishments with an eye to bringing in crisp Amriki dollars.

Nur Muhammed interjected the necessary note of reality. "What does anyone gain by striking again at ISAF and not succeeding? Or at the UN? We cannot penetrate their defenses. Another failure gains us nothing. But hitting something smaller, as we have already discussed, would almost surely guarantee success."

Hamidullah's grimace smoothed as Nur Muhammed continued. "We are seeking a target. We have a possibility, one on which we have good intelligence. The fewer of you who know of it, the better. But first, we need the device. We will speak again next week."

———————

So it began.

Like Kabul's NGOs and other foreign organizations, Face the Future percolated with new reports daily.

One morning, the UN drivers went out to their gleaming SUVs and found all the tires slashed.

The next, an American colonel from ISAF stopped by his favorite store among the tourist haunts of Chicken Street, the one where the proprietor always pulled the bottle of vile Tajik vodka from beneath the counter as soon as he saw him coming. But on this day, the store's windows were boarded up, the interior darkened. Someone had splashed green paint in lacy script across the rough boards. The colonel's interpreter read it, his face darkening. "It says that this man sells liquor and therefore his business must not be patronized."

Farida told Liv that girls from the university, who had taken to striding around campus in bold blue jeans under their tunics, wearing only brief black scarves over their hair, were reminded so forcefully of the risks they took that they began keeping their burqas with them at all times, rather than shedding them in careless piles in the lobby of whatever building in which they had class that day. There was no question of leaving the campus with their faces uncovered.

And the day came when Martin burst through the office door, cursing, wiping his reddened face.

Liv jumped from her chair. "What happened?"

"One of those bastards hanging around the gate spit on me."

She sank back, wordlessly acknowledging this new fact of life. For her own part, she found herself staying indoors more and more, forgoing even the interviews with Afghan women that she had found so absorbing. "Maybe you had a point," she typed one night in an email to her mother. "Maybe it was a mistake to come here."

She sat in the dark, studying the glowing screen.

Then she moved her cursor to the end of the sentence and tapped Delete until the screen was blank.

Twenty-Six

Farida knew something of the men's plan, of course.

She found it simple to do her mending or to knead dough or other-wise occupy herself with some small task just behind the curtain that separated the women's quarters from the men's when Nur Muhammed held rare meetings in the house. Maryam was usually busy during these visits, supervising the preparation and serving of food. Bibi was always elsewhere, caring for her children and astutely avoiding Maryam in the process. Farida easily worked in relative solitude, alert to the conversations in the next room, the memory of Nur Muhammed's words fresh in her mind: *We are seeking a target. We have a possibility.*

Her salary from Face the Future, which disappeared weekly into the pouch beneath Nur Muhammed's kameez, was no doubt going to bol-ster his operation—as well as the information she passed to Gul, each pretending to the other that their conversations were merely casual. She ground the heels of her hands into the dough at the men's big talk, made possible only by her work. *Her work.* Always before—as an interpreter in Islamabad before her marriage, and even as a fixer of sorts for Liv—in a subordinate role. But now everything hinged upon her. Even Nur Muhammed acknowledged her presence, according her a brief, grave nod just minutes earlier as he passed on his way to the men's sitting room.

Her kneading stilled as the men's voices rose, each trying to outdo the other with suggestions that would guarantee glory. Bitter pride welled within Farida.

She was as much a fighter as all of them. Without her—a woman— those men had no plan.

It was the same with Martin and Liv, Martin taking credit for the information gleaned during Liv's excursions, while he compiled those reports of which he talked so much but revealed so few details. The longer she worked at Face the Future, the more Farida thought she knew exactly what Martin was up to. And when she was certain, that knowledge, too, would be handed off to Gul, details that would steer Nur Muhammed and his men toward a time when Martin would most likely be alone in the office.

Likewise, she fought the temptation to ask Liv for access to Face the Future's computers to send Alia a quick, reassuring email, despite the fact that early on, Martin had stressed that, for security purposes, only he and Liv were permitted to use them. The fewer people with whom she had connections these days, the safer they all would be. "I am stone," she reminded herself, turning to her sister's advice. "I am ice."

She resumed her homely task, digging her thumbnails into the dough's warm, yielding surface, patterning it with rows of quarter-moons, and imagined shards of metal scissoring the air, embedding themselves deep within Martin's plump, yeasty form. Her abdomen quivered with a series of swift kicks, almost as though her mujahid son were responding to her thoughts. Farida put her hand on her stomach.

"Soon, my sweet boy," she said.

"I have noticed something."

Farida kept her tone light, striving to sound casual, but not so much

that Gul dismissed her entirely. The men had discussed a number of possibilities but, as far as she knew, had yet to settle on a final target. She
needed Gul to pay attention to her words, and also for him to believe that
she herself had no idea of their import. They were in the market, a rare
trip outdoors for her these days. Even within the confines of her burqa,
Farida enjoyed the sensation of fresh air—relatively fresh, she reminded
herself, as she tasted the pervasive dust mingled with charcoal smoke and
dried dung and diesel fumes. Still, it was good to be out among people
who ignored her, unlike at home, where her pregnancy made her a constant focus of the women's attention, which, while pleasing, also could be
exhausting.

The aunties pleaded with her not to leave the house. Who knew what
could happen, with bombs going off around the city nearly every day and
the ISAF troops so jumpy they shot at anything that moved too quickly?
But she had learned something from her time among the women, after all.

"You are right, of course." She allowed her hand to linger over her
stomach. "But my husband insists I go with him, and honestly, I must
agree. No matter how clearly I tell him what I need, the man would come
home with all of the wrong things." She grimaced at the obvious incompetence of men, earning understanding laughter from the aunties.

Now she lingered before one booth and the next and then the next,
beseeching Gul to wander with her a bit longer. "It has been such a while
since I've been out, other than to go to my job at That Place. Please, I just
want to look at everything."

He obliged, leading between the aisles of waist-high tables presided
over by the spice vendors, their wares shaped into conical mounds, the
dull gold of turmeric placed for maximum effect between the scarlet peak
of red pepper and the olive-green of dried, crushed coriander. The vendor
measured a bit of pepper for another woman. Farida sneezed as the breeze
carried some of the grains toward her.

"Be careful." Gul hurried her away. "You'll hurt the baby, sneezing
like that."

"What are you now, one of the aunties? Shall we admit you to the women's rooms so that you can sit with us and gossip all day?" She laughed at the scowl that crossed his face.

He strode ahead of her, toward the fabric sellers' stalls. "What have you noticed?" he called back over his shoulder, reminding her of the conversation she had started.

She moved quickly to keep up with him, holding the burqa's edges together in front while lifting the hem, but not so much as to expose an ankle, or to give an unthinkable glimpse of calf. She had perfected the sliding gait that let her feel for the broken pavement.

Gul halted before a stall. Maryam had recently expressed such vocal admiration for a certain auntie's garments, that Farida knew—and now, Gul did, too, because Farida was sure to tell him—that her mother-in-law wanted some new clothing of her own. With Farida's help, Gul would buy the fabric and then pass it on to Nur Muhammed so that he could make a gift of it to Maryam. All around them, women in burqas zigzagged back and forth between the stalls like so many blue shuttlecocks, shopping in large groups for propriety. The fewer men who could overhear her conversation with Gul, the better, Farida reasoned. She would linger among the fabrics. She signaled to the seller that she wanted to look at several bolts from the back of the stall. As he went to fetch them, she spoke quickly. Nur Muhammed must see but a single target.

"I have noticed that there is only one guard at Face the Future these days."

Gul's expression did not change, but she sensed an alertness that had been absent from their casual banter a few moments earlier.

"And that guard," she continued, "is not armed."

Gul did not raise his head, addressing his words to the remnants of cloth on the table before them. "He has a gun. I have seen it myself."

"But the magazine is empty. I have heard the servants talking among themselves. They say Those People are trying to save money. That Those People think no one will attack a charity, anyway, so why bother to spend the money, especially with the staff stealing all the ammunition provided?"

The vendor, his face red with the exertion of carrying so much cloth even a few steps, returned and dumped the bolts on the table with a loud bang and explosion of dust. The women who had flowed toward the stall to examine Farida's choices, eager to comment upon them and offer advice, backed away, coughing beneath their burqas as the cloth ribboned across the table in a rainbow of hues.

"Aren't they afraid? Especially given all of the attacks on foreigners these days."

"They are too foolish to be afraid. They think that because they say they are helping the women of Afghanistan, the Afghan people will be too grateful to hurt them."

"And do they indeed help them? Send girls to school?"

As he spoke, Farida realized that she had never once heard him voice an opinion on the subject, even though voluble groups of schoolgirls, the younger ones wearing white head scarves, the teenagers in burqas, trooped past his family's gate every morning.

Even Bibi, who had attended school in Pakistan before her marriage, took an interest in her interrupted studies, asking Farida to help her learn English.

Farida introduced her to *Alice's Adventures in Wonderland*, albeit with unconventional results. "Brillig!" Bibi was apt to utter these days when something went wrong, even though Farida had tried to explain to her that the satisfyingly foreign-sounding word made no sense even to English speakers. Despite the sketchiness of her education, Bibi made rapid progress. She read with a stubby finger running under the lines of strange print in *Alice*—"left to right, Bibi, left to right," Farida corrected her tendency to revert to the right-to-left reading of Arabic script. But Bibi always got distracted by the drawings, not so much those of the fantastical creatures but of Alice herself, of her defiant scowl so much like Bibi's own.

"*Ah-lees*," she mouthed, finding the one whole word she knew on page after page. The name was strange to her, but a name was an easy thing to grasp. She struggled, though, with the concept of Wonderland. "A magical place, where people become bigger and smaller, or disappear altogether," Farida told her.

"A place like this." Bibi had yet to reconcile this new Afghanistan with the one so dimly remembered from her childhood.

Farida started to disagree, then thought of the book—of the incomprehensible rules confronting Alice at every turn, of the scramble for power, even the threat of beheadings. "Yes. Like this."

Farida thought Bibi's headway was an example of what could be accomplished, if only resources were devoted to the effort. But even though Martin and Liv talked and talked about just how much they cared about bettering women's lives, they had done little, as far as she could tell, to actually further the cause that brought them to Kabul.

"No," she told Gul finally. "Not a single widow is now working because of them. Not a single girl has received a scholarship to university. They don't even hire women to work for them."

"Except for you." He meant it as a rebuke, she knew.

"Except for me." Echoed with defiant pride.

In silence, they examined the assortment of fabric before them. Farida slid her fingers beneath a piece of silk and lifted it, seeking to distract him, admiring the easy drape, the shimmering silvery print across a background of deep royal blue. "This, I think."

He took it from her and held it to the dim light that leaked into the stall's interior. "Like the stars emerging in the evening sky," he said with a shy smile.

She turned, delighted, the moment's tension forgotten. "You are a poet."

He made no reply, but by his halfhearted argument with the vendor, barely an attempt at bargaining, Farida knew he enjoyed the compliment. "Your mother will be pleased," she said as the man began to wrap it for them.

"This is not for my mother. This one, maybe." He patted another bolt and called for the man to cut the appropriate length and wrap it, too, reminding him that a discount was in order because he was buying more than expected. "The blue is for you." His fingers brushed the small of her back.

She let his touch linger, and then she pulled away, murmuring that maybe they were done shopping for the day and should go home?

Quickly, yes? She knew that such talk, the words innocuous, the tone saying everything, both stirred and pleased him, and she wasn't sure which she enjoyed more—her easy sway over him, or the anticipatory thrill of her own surrender.

———

At night, as Gul slept with one hand on her belly, Farida lay awake, the baby tumbling slowly inside her. She thought of a kite soaring through the sky, all smooth motion, endlessly swooping and dipping. She wondered what it was like when a baby swam from the womb into the world, bumping up against hard dry surfaces from which it could not simply float away. She slid her hand beneath Gul's and pressed down, feeling for the sharp knob of elbow or knee.

This baby would be a new kind of mujahid. Not one who hid in the mountains, always half starved and underequipped, doomed to guerrilla exercises, lucky to survive into his twenties or even thirties with only the loss of a limb to a mine. No, her son—however she might tease Gul, she, too, willed the baby to be a boy—would use his mind to vanquish his foe. Those People.

At the thought of Liv, her features tightened in regret tinged with guilt. Try as she might, she could not consider Liv an enemy. She forced herself to relax. It was important, more now than ever, to present a placid surface. The stronger her discipline, the better her façade. Still . . . Martin. A tremor ran through her. The baby quieted, as though its tiny being focused with her on the important matter at hand. It was difficult to conceal her feelings about Martin.

———

"Farida."

That's how he summoned her—the disrespectful use of her name.

Not even lifting his head to look in her direction, although she saw his eyes following her when he thought she wasn't looking. The way he called her close to him, sliding documents to one side of his desk so that she was forced to lean over him in order to read them. And always, during these consultations, some sort of personal remark. It had started with her work—comments about her perfect English grammar, her typing skills, the depth of the information presented—but soon the tenor shifted.

"That is an especially attractive shalwar kameez."

"Thank you. My husband selected the fabric." She stressed the word "husband" and decided never to wear that particular shalwar kameez to work again. Later, she would not respond at all to such compliments, remaining silent until the topic returned to work. Still, when she least expected it—say, during a review of a nutrition program in one of Afghanistan's more troublesome provinces—he would lower his voice so that Liv, working at the computer across the room, could not hear.

"Why do you wear your dupatta here, Farida? You have such beautiful hair. Even Liv goes bare-headed in the office." Farida bowed her head, flushing in shame.

How dare he presume to speak so familiarly with her? She thought of what would happen among Gul's relatives if a man, a stranger—invited into their home, yes, but not a relative—had approached a woman to say anything at all to her, let alone so obviously lustful a remark. Farida contemplated with fierce enjoyment the mayhem that might follow such an insulting and imprudent action, even as she realized the impossibility of her fancy. No strange man in a Pashtun household would ever encounter any of the women. It was only within the odd arrangements of the foreigners that these things happened.

When she was done with this job, no matter how Nur Muhammed pushed, she would never again work for such people. Gul rarely asked about her family, her previous life in Pakistan, but even his few queries betrayed his fear that she would feel the tug of the worldly life from which he'd taken her. She hoped the vehemence of her desire to end her time at Face the Future would reassure him otherwise.

She stroked her stomach, feeling the waves within. Her son would not be the kind of man who would blame a woman for attracting a man's attentions. He would have his father's strength and courage, his mother's cleverness and compassion. He would outwit his enemies, his own and the family's.

But until he grew to manhood, she would have to outwit them for him. And she would start, she thought, with Martin.

"Why do they still need you?" Gul asked as he walked Farida to the gates of Face the Future a few days later. "You yourself said that Those People hardly leave the compound anymore, even to shop on Chicken Street."

"They are finishing their reports in preparation for one of their meetings with the other organizations. I help with the typing, and I check for the proper use of our languages. He speaks our languages, Urdu well and some Pashto, but makes mistakes when he writes it."

"Why do they need to learn our languages? Why don't they just stay home and speak their English among themselves?" He changed the subject. "Is the office very crowded?"

Farida tensed at what was surely not a casual question. "Sometimes. Tuesdays, they have a big meeting to plan the week's work. All of the staff must be there and usually people from other NGOs. This week's will be the largest yet, with some representatives from the UN. Those People are very nervous, wanting everything in order, so there is more work for me because of it."

She didn't have to pass him wrong information about Liv after all. As it turned out, Martin had insisted, over Liv's objections, that her presence at the meeting was unnecessary. For insurance, Farida planned to arrange a final outing with Liv that day, so that she would be far from the compound.

"Does ISAF accompany the UN?"

She recognized the studied disinterest as he posed the question. It was the same technique she often employed herself. She wondered for a moment whether either of them was fooling the other, and decided it didn't matter. "That Man has assured them there is no need. That we have our own security guard, who searches everyone entering the office. If you can call it a search. They make me hold open my bag"—she lifted the flimsy plastic bag she carried when she did her marketing—"and they pat down the men."

"Not the women?"

Farida affected shock. She did not tell him about her visits with Liv to the UN compound, which could afford the luxury of female guards to search women visitors. The women were notoriously thorough, lifting Farida's pregnancy-swollen breasts and feeling roughly beneath them, ordering her to stand with her legs apart and prodding so deeply at her crotch and between her buttocks that she had felt faint. Still, she had to laugh at the look on Liv's face after her own session, and the remark she made afterward to Farida: "Even my husband doesn't touch me like that!"

Farida chortled a moment later when Liv added, "If he did, maybe I would like him better."

So it was the same with all women, Farida thought, this habit of making sport of their husbands' foibles. She herself had had to invent some minor complaints about Gul, so as not to be conspicuously silent during the aunties' interminable recitals of their husbands' shortcomings.

Face the Future's guard never touched the women, she told Gul. And he barely searched the men. It seemed the organization had more to fear from those hired to protect it than the people who called at the offices. "They are looking for a new guard. This will be the third since they've arrived. The man who is here now, they caught stealing."

"What did he take?"

Farida shook her head in wonder. "Some towels. His wife has a new baby and they used the towels for blankets. These Amriki are so rich and so stingy at the same time. They have a shelf stacked with hand towels in the office WC, more than they need, and yet when two go missing, a man loses his job."

Gul sucked at his teeth in sympathy. "Is that him?" He and Farida had reached the gate and waited in the short line there. A young man in a patched waistcoat, weariness bruising the skin beneath his eyes, made

cursory work of checking people's parcels. A battered Chinese-copy Kalashnikov was slung across his back, its magazine clearly empty. When
Farida approached, he respectfully lowered his eyes.

"Your bag, please."

She dangled it before him with one hand, letting it gape open, using
her other hand to hold her burqa modestly together.

"Pass."

She bade her husband goodbye and walked into the compound. She
heard Gul's voice behind her. She turned and saw him speaking with the
guard. His hand flashed toward the man, and she saw the dull blue of
afghanis pass between them. The guard bowed low. It all happened so
quickly that she had no time to hear their conversation. But she was not
surprised at all the next day, when Gul left her at the gate, to see a new
guard, one whose erect posture, so different from the defeated demeanor
of his predecessor, instantly put her on alert.

He asked for her bag and she stiffened. She knew that voice. She
held out the bag. Unlike the previous guard, this man pawed insolently
through her papers, removing the string that neatly bound them, and
shuffling them into disorder. She sighed in exasperation. At the sound, he
straightened. Even though she knew he could not see her features through
her burqa, she merely peered sidelong at him.

"You may pass. Although I must advise you, for the good of your own
reputation, to return to your home. I have seen nothing but men pass
through these gates this morning, and now you go to work among them.
I see this with my own eyes, and yet I still cannot believe."

Farida snatched the bag away and hurried past him, into the compound,
his words ringing in her ears, in a voice that was its own introduction. It was
the Talib, the one with whom Gul and Nur Muhammed had been spending
so much time recently. Surely, his presence at Face the Future only boded
well for her plan. Still, she felt his eyes on her back as she hurried across the
courtyard, and cold fingers of apprehension traced her spine.

Twenty-Seven

"We will need a very brave mujahid."

The Talib's words dropped like large flat stones into a quiet pool. There were five men in the room—the Talib, Gul, Nur Muhammed, and two of his most trusted deputies—and Gul saw the words' meaning ripple toward them, and their visible resistance as it became clear. Nur Muhammed betrayed nothing, but Gul was sure he knew his father's thoughts and was relieved when one of the others voiced them.

"This thing that you speak of, it is not our way. The Arabs, yes. But not us. We stand and fight like men." This, from one of Nur Muhammed's oldest associates. He spoke with difficulty, his mouth contorting around the gabbling sentences. A Russian rocket had blown away his wife, his children, and much of his jaw. Below his nose, his face collapsed into his neck.

In ordinary times, it would have been nearly impossible for such a man, so difficult to look at, to find a woman. But the years of war had taken away so many men that this one found a new wife just months after his injury. And then, after the loss of his young second wife—who foolishly ventured unaccompanied from the house, only to encounter some bandits roaming Kabul—he promptly found yet a third wife, who obediently, even gratefully, spooned food into the flapping hole of his mouth every morning and evening, and wiped his ruined neck and unkempt beard clean afterward.

The others murmured agreement as he spoke. A couple threw pointed glances at the Talib, but he smiled glassily, apparently oblivious. Gul wondered, not for the first time, if he made use of the opium that helped finance Nur Muhammed's operations.

"Yes, yes, yes," the Talib said now. "We fought, in our rags, we chased the Russians and their tanks from our borders. And who remembers us? No one. The Amriki come and occupy our land and give us a pittance of their treasure, and the world forgets all about the poor, noble Afghan people. Who gets the attention now? Those who carry out the most dramatic acts. Our own efforts are pitiful. Our bombs fail to explode, our rockets go astray. If the world notices at all, it laughs at us. No, we must have our own spectacular act, one that cannot go wrong. And we must have someone willing to carry it out."

The Talib's interrogator persisted, doubling over with the effort of speech. "Fine words. But where will you find such a one here? Are you volunteering?"

The Talib hesitated just long enough for Gul to enjoy the moment. "I think none of us should be the one. We will be needed to plan follow-up actions."

The relief in the room was palpable, but so was the underlay of contempt. No one should suggest this sort of thing, Gul thought, unless willing to carry it out himself. Gul lifted his head, signaling his desire to speak. "It must be someone very courageous, someone whose loyalty is unquestioning. And maybe someone without a family, with little to lose." He took a breath, ready to continue, but was surprised when Nur Muhammed broke in.

"I know such a one. I will speak to him. In the meantime, we will proceed. Equipment is needed. When we meet next week, all of you will bring the items assigned to you. Remember, ball bearings are best, but they will be hard to find. Nails are also ideal, but any sort of scrap metal will do, the smaller and sharper the better."

The men around him laughed, prematurely white beards bobbing. If anything was plentiful in Kabul, it was shrapnel. Fragments of exploding shells and mines were embedded in walls and tree trunks and covered by the powdery layers of dust in the streets, ready to slice open the foot of the unwary child running around.

Nur Muhammed acknowledged the grim amusement in the room. "I think this will not be a problem."

———

Gul stood outside the small general store kept by Nur Muhammed's old friend. It appeared to be open, the goods removed from their nightly storage and arranged on the shelves that lined the side walls of the stall, not locked away behind the stout door that led to the back room where Nur Muhammed and his associates had met. Gul waited some moments. It was early, but already the street was busy.

Just a few doors away, a man sat on a stool, facing an ungainly box camera. The proprietor of the camera shop dove beneath a cloth and held up his hand to signal his subject not to move. A line of young men, dandified with kohl-rimmed eyes, oiled hair, and just-clipped beards, jostled impatiently to one side, awaiting their own turn before the lens.

The Taliban had banned photographs during their interminable reign, and now any man with a few extra afghanis was eager to possess his own portrait. The boldest among them would attempt to palm these from one friend to the next, eventually into the hands of a sympathetic sister who perhaps could find a way to show the photo to a particular young woman who somehow, through her musical voice or the long, tapered fingers holding her burqa closed, had captured the imagination of the man in question. But this was the most foolhardy sort of behavior. To be caught was to risk death at the hands of the girl's father and brothers, and to almost certainly guarantee it for the girl. Still, Gul looked at the men with a bit of nostalgia, remembering his own long-ago stirrings for the unattainable.

The morning was agreeably warm, the punishing heat of midday still hours off, and a young man might be forgiven for succumbing briefly to the fantasy that life, like the lengthening days of summer, had grown easier and more enticing.

Indeed, activities all along the street catered to that very notion. In front of one stall, boys industriously yanked the rivets from oilcans and hammered them into satellite dishes, their blows ringing in syncopated rhythm to the music from a radio blaring behind them. Both radio and television had, of course, been anathema to the Taliban, which also had forbidden the books now sold openly in stalls all over the city. So what if street urchins snatched a book or two from the stacks and darted away, intent next upon stealing the food that their mothers would cook that night over the fire fueled by those selfsame books? The freedom to touch a match to something once so emphatically forbidden was enough to make one giddy with a sense of possibility, especially with the too-recent knowledge that to have so much as held a book—no matter that one couldn't actually read it—during those dark years had risked, at best, a lashing from the stinging bamboo staffs or car antennas carried by the black-turbaned members of the much-despised and equally feared Ministry for the Propagation of Virtue and the Prevention of Vice.

Gul filled his lungs with air. His people had broken free of the Taliban and their impossible, impractical restrictions. Now they must cut the fetters in which the Amriki had so quickly wrapped them. The thought brought him back to the task at hand. There was still no sign of the proprietor. Gul coughed and shuffled his feet. He heard stirrings from behind the door and stepped back as it swung open and the owner emerged.

"*A salaam alaikum*, my young friend." The man pressed his hand to his chest and bowed, beaming, toward Gul.

"*Ve alaikum salaam*." Gul wondered at the difference in the man. He remembered him as sad-eyed and stooped, beset by the debt brought on by his need to care for his half-mad son. The boy, now a teenager, was as large and vigorous as his father once had been. But a few years earlier, in the same partisan attack that had killed the boy's mother, a piece of metal had pierced his skull and tunneled through to something vital in his brain. Now he wandered the neighborhood with a smudge pot, his sheer bulk and inarticulate cries frightening people into giving him a few afghanis. The worries involved in raising such a child had turned the father into a nervous shell of a man, and Gul always felt apologetic when he came by to collect the rent. But on this day, the man stepped briskly to the counter.

"What will it be? You have come to shop, yes? The rent is not due, I think." A shade of his old fearful expression crossed his face.

"No." Was that kohl widening his eyes? And what of the orange overlay of henna hiding the gray in his beard? "My father wishes to see you."

The man's smile vanished. A summons from Nur Muhammed was not necessarily good news. "When does he wish me to come? Now?" The man's gaze darted to the door behind him, and back to Gul.

"Tomorrow will be fine. Come to our home. Dine with us."

Gul knew what the man was thinking: That a meal with Nur Muhammed could not possibly mean trouble. Or could it? The merchant's obvious fearfulness made Gul uncomfortable, but what the man did next made him feel even more so.

"Here." He felt along the shelves of the shop, grabbing at worthless things. A packet of crisps. A faded plastic comb. "Take these with you. Gifts for your family."

"It is not necessary." Gul moved away so the man could not put the items in his hands. "We will be happy to see you tomorrow."

"Wait." The man removed the board that blocked access to the store's interior and put his hand on the door behind him. "Please. Come. There is something here that you must see. Something very special for the son of my oldest friend. Please." He opened the door and spoke some words to a person within.

Gul wanted to leave, but the animated conversation had drawn the attention of others on the street, and he did not wish to cause a scene. He stepped into the narrow stall and let the man usher him through the door, which he closed and barred behind him. Gul started to object, but was distracted by a rustling noise within the darkened room. A woman rose from a sleeping mat and gave an exaggerated shrug, the folds of her burqa falling like water about her as she stood before them, the green garment pooling at her feet.

————————

Gul's chest tightened.

He tried not to stare. She stood straight-backed and sturdy before them, head bowed, her long hair unbound, falling across her face so that he could not see her features. Although the burqa at her feet was of cheap cotton, green instead of the ubiquitous blue, the clothing she wore beneath it appeared clean, if somewhat worn.

"Very beautiful, yes?"

Gul didn't know how to respond. Had the man remarried? But no, no man would bring a stranger to his wife.

"I don't understand."

"She comes to see me. To—" The man made an obscene motion with his hands.

A whore? Gul fought to control his disgust. He glanced again at the woman. Although her face was still turned away, she held herself proudly. There was no hint of the cringing servility expected from someone of her lowly stature. He thought of the widows on the street, how they begged for money and, sotto voce, offered to make their gratitude known, for a few more afghanis, of course. They would lift their burqas to show faces hideous in their desperation. "I have a sister. A daughter. A virgin. She has saved herself for you."

"Yes," said the man, as though reading his thoughts. "This one is special. Look how she keeps herself tidy. She goes to the baths every time before she comes to see me." He leaned closer to Gul and spoke in a whisper. "She once had a husband, so there is no concern about defilement. And she cannot have children."

"Why do you tell me these things?" Gul tried to ignore the stirring within his loose shalwar. The woman stood so very near. A step, maybe two, would bring him close enough to touch her.

"Why, because!" The man's face glowed with goodwill. He gestured expansively. "I give her to you. To the son of my dearest friend. Today she is yours. For me, she has only a few moments, but for you, the whole day."

The woman gasped, and Gul looked openly at her. She stooped to gather up her burqa, lowering it quickly over her face, speaking in rapid Dari as she did so. The man replied, his commanding tone unmistakable. She turned her back on them and squared her shoulders, but otherwise made no move to leave.

"I will close the store. No one will bother you." The man left before Gul could say anything. Gul confronted the closed door. He hesitated, and looked over his shoulder at the woman, her back still turned. He had never been with a woman other than Farida. Still—a whore. He reached for the door.

Fabric whispered behind him.

He knew without looking that she had again removed the burqa. By the time he turned, she had stepped out of her shalwar. Strong calves flashed beneath the hem of her kameez. Still with her back to him, she raised her arms and pulled the garment over her head. She put her hands on her hips and tugged down her undergarments, then stood as she had before, straight and unmoving, her hair falling forward over her shoulders.

Gul thought of how Farida modestly slid off her clothing beneath the blankets when he came to her at night, and wriggled into it again before leaving the bed in the morning. He told himself it was not wrong just to look. He crossed the room and put a tentative hand on the woman's shoulder. She trembled, and he pressed his hand more firmly against her, as though calming a restive horse. He slid it down the length of her back, marveling at the smoothness of her skin. She must have been but a girl when she was married, he thought, to still be so young. He cupped her buttocks, and then, barely breathing, eased his hand between them. She obligingly moved her feet apart and stood motionless. All day, the man had said.

His couplings with Farida were hushed and hurried with family always in the adjoining rooms. He glanced over his shoulder toward the reassuring sight of the door's heavy planks. He pressed himself against the woman's back and brought his arms around her to put his hands on her breasts. They were small and high, unlike Farida's, now heavy with her pregnancy. There was a raised vertical line between her breasts, and he fingered the thin scar before dropping his hands to unfasten the drawstring of his pants. He lifted the long tail of his tunic, then rubbed himself against her again.

She sighed. "You will pay, yes?"

Gul's hands, which had returned to her breasts, stopped moving. "You are a gift." She was, after all, he reminded himself, a whore.

She thrust her hips backward, rubbing against him. A groan escaped him.

"Yes?" she whispered again. She reached back and took him in her hand and guided him between her legs so that he could feel the heat there. He thrust eagerly, but she pulled away a little.

"Yes? You will pay?"

"Yes," he almost shouted, tugging her down onto the sleeping mat, so roughly that she nearly fell, and he laughed because it didn't matter. His lovemaking with Farida had, of necessity, been slow and careful of late. The whore rolled onto her stomach and obligingly tilted her buttocks toward him, but he turned her over, pinning her shoulders against the mat, and mounted her hastily. She cried out and he thought it was another of her whore's tricks, but he didn't care, and he pushed himself hurriedly between her legs, frantic to enter her. But her body had gone rigid and she slapped and shoved at him, calling out, "Gul, wait, no!" and she shook her head so that her hair fell away from her face. She put her hands to his cheeks and tugged at him until he was forced to look at her, and even now, so many years later, with the ravages of war etched upon her features, he knew Khurshid.

Twenty-Eight

Liv paced Face the Future's sad courtyard twice daily to work off a diet of fatty lamb and the inertia as a result of being prohibited from venturing on foot beyond the compound.

"Courtyard" being a generous term for the dusty half block of pounded earth, the house at one end, the office at another, enclosed by a high stucco wall topped by glittering shards of glass. A few rosebushes withered beneath the unrelenting sun. At first, Liv had dutifully poured the dirty dishwater around their roots, but it seemed not to matter. Their leaves remained dull and brittle, their blooms wizened and short-lived, and eventually she gave up. She knew she should be thankful for the spacious quarters and the compound's location at the far edge of Wazir Akbar Khan, an upscale neighborhood in Kabul housing the presidential palace and most of the city's diplomatic quarters.

Still, she couldn't help noting the peeling paint, the suffocating dust, the unreliable electricity, the poisonous water. Philadelphia's worst neighborhoods had better conditions than Kabul's best, she often thought, even as she berated herself for her longing for first-world creature comforts. She undressed in haste at night, and showered beneath a tepid trickle just as quickly in the morning, to avoid the sight of her pale, soft belly, her widening thighs, the hair stubbling her calves. With the constant shortage of water, and the difficulty finding razor blades, it no longer made sense to shave her legs. She thought longingly of her tub at home, of her nightly soaks, of prodding the faucet with her toe to add more steaming water as the bath cooled.

She sweated through her shalwar kameez within moments of whatever ablutions she managed. These days, she went about in sturdy cotton garb in dull hues that survived even the most determined mishandling. The richly detailed silk sets the tailor had made for her in Islamabad stayed packed away, after one came back in tatters from a local laundry. Liv thought then of the women along the trash-strewn banks of the muddy ditch that was the Kabul River, draping sodden garments across boulders and pounding them with smaller rocks, and wondered if her favorite shalwar kameez had been given that same treatment. On her better days, she was able to laugh at the memory of having once considered the use of her washer and dryer a tiresome chore.

She made a final circuit of the compound's packed-earth courtyard, trying to banish thoughts of a time when she walked freely down a street in light summer clothing, her face exposed, welcoming a sun that warmed without searing. When velvety nights brought the soothing chirp of crickets and the gurgle of spring peepers, the occasional susurration of tires on pavement dampened by lawn sprinklers. Nightfall in Kabul was heralded by hot winds skating down off the mountains, flinging grit against the windows and distorting the rattle of the gunfire that began at dusk, even as the last wavering notes of the muezzin's final call to prayer hung in the air.

She tried to distract herself by writing home, short, cheery emails designed to reassure her mother, whose own notes barely concealed the panic beneath her stoicism. Each time she wrote, Liv sought to recapture the airy confidence with which she had arrived in Kabul. The trick, she thought, was to give a flavor of the place without letting too much reality intrude. Too often, she failed.

Just a week earlier, she'd begun an email she would never send. "The children are mischievous, darting between cars to get to you, their fingers in your pockets before you even know they're there. This morning, as we interviewed refugees who had returned home from Pakistan, we could not work until we paid a man with a Kalashnikov to keep them away from us. Imagine, pointing a semiautomatic weapon at a group of eight-year-olds." She paused, thinking that the sentence did not do justice to the surging mass of scab-faced children, their voracious cries, the way they clawed and fought to push closer to Liv and Farida. The man they'd hired waved the bayoneted gun at them, but they held their ground.

"We can't work like this. Let's go," Liv had said.

"We can't leave," Farida protested. "They know us now. They'll remember that they could make us leave. It will be even worse next time."

"There won't be a next time." The children's jeers echoed as they drove away. Farida pressed herself against the car door, as far away from Liv as possible. They traveled some blocks in this fashion, away from the refugee settlement and back among bombed-out, broken shells of buildings.

"Please," Liv tried. "Why are you so upset?"

Two more blocks rolled past. Liv mentally noted the booksellers in their stalls, the occasional flicker of a black-and-white television in a shop-window, and reminded herself that these things represented progress. Liv really didn't expect an answer from Farida, so was startled when she lifted her burqa away from her face so that Liv could see the anger in her eyes.

"You just walked away."

"You saw what it was like. We were never going to get through that crowd to talk to the mothers. We could accomplish nothing there."

"That's not why. It's because you're afraid."

"I think it's wise to be at least a little afraid, don't you? If we are cautious, nothing bad will happen."

"Nothing bad will happen to *you*."

"What do you mean?"

"Bad things will continue to happen to other people, just as they have always happened here." Farida's accent became even more clipped and British as her anger swelled. "But they can't leave. All those women you talked to? Whose stories you took down so importantly in your notebook and then put into your reports? Do you think those reports will change anything for them?"

"Not for them, maybe. But perhaps for other women in their situation."

"No. I am talking about these women, the very ones with whom we speak. The widows. We draw attention to them. Their neighbors see them talking to a foreigner. In a place like those refugee camps, that puts them above everyone else. People will assume we gave them money. If only they could get some of that money for themselves! What do you think happens to those women after we leave? Their houses, such as they are, are torn apart. And that's the good scenario. Men see us visiting without a male escort. Maybe they think us prostitutes. And if these women consort with us, what does that make them?"

"Stop! So many of those women are widows."

"Even better. Then it's not like defiling a virgin, or dishonoring a man's wife. And if a bad thing happens to them—if they are robbed, or worse—they can't leave. They have to stay, living among the people who did those things to them and will do to them again. You'll leave here someday. But they'll never escape."

"We will stay, too." Liv lifted her chin, mentally thrusting aside her own secret, growing desire to go home, preferably on the next plane. "Our contract with the NGO is for two years. We will honor it."

"Then the problem will continue. Because they know nothing of NGOs. The term is meaningless to them. All they know is foreigner, and foreigner means money. Always."

Liv's face grew hot. She thought of the way the children tore at one another over the pieces of candy she had foolishly handed out during her early visits to the refugees. They drew blood, scrabbling for stale gumdrops that left only a fleeting sensation of sweetness on the tongue. But it was a treat more exotic than they had ever known, and they were willing to gouge and punch and throw the smallest aside to get at it. Liv imagined adults doing the same thing to the exhausted, sagging widows she'd interviewed.

"Then why did you let me talk to them, if it was going to cause trouble for them later?" Liv had little time for her own accusation. Face the Future's compound loomed at the end of the street.

"Because I am no better than you," Farida said. She said something to the driver, and the car pulled to the curb and waited as she spoke. "I, too, was curious about them. They are my husband's people. I didn't realize, until recently, the danger we've put them in. I'm as much to blame as you. But I can't leave, either. I have to stay and live with the problems I've caused."

She slid her hand across the seat and folded Liv's fingers in her own. "I am sorry. Please try to understand that my anger is as much for myself as you." She took a breath. "Also, I think it better that, in the coming weeks, you and I work on our reports in the house. I have such a difficult time concentrating these days . . ." Farida never spoke openly of her pregnancy, but Liv nodded comprehension.

"That will be fine. I'll explain to Martin. As to the other— Oh, Farida. You'll leave, too. Surely, with all the issues here—the opium, the land mines, the—"

"The jihad." Farida spoke so quietly that Liv had to lean forward to catch the word.

She started to repeat it, but Farida put out a hand to stop her.

"What do you mean?"

"Surely you have noticed the . . . incidents. They will only increase. You remind me of my sister. You value safety above everything. I will stay here. She will remain in Islamabad. You will go back to Amrika. Like the Russians before you, like the British before them."

She reached across Liv to open the door, giving her no choice but to leave the cab, Farida sliding out behind her, joining her waiting husband and walking away, leaving Liv standing at the gate, cold despite the sun, unable to forget what she'd glimpsed before the blue cloth fell across Farida's face—a hint of the same smile that, far more openly, flashed across the face of the driver.

None of this, of course, went in Liv's missives home. Moments after writing about the troublesome children, she erased her initial sentences and began anew, mindful of the ease and confidence she strove to project.

"You should see the boys with their pots of incense," she typed. "They swing tin cans on the end of sticks. Fragrant herbs burn inside the cans. For a single bill—I can never remember how much afghanis are worth, but it takes nearly a brick of them just to make one dollar—they'll waft the smoke over you and thus ward away evil."

She sent that note without adding just how often she furtively summoned such boys. It would not do for her mother, or for anyone, to realize that her existence had become so improbable as to make the use of evil-banishing smoke seem reasonable. She was sure the boys laughed at her. The longer she and Martin remained in Afghanistan, the more she was sure everyone there was laughing at them. Even the war widows, who keened pitifully outside the *chaikhanas*, their dirt-stiffened burqas thrown back to reveal seamed cheeks caved in over missing teeth, turned loud and insolent if those dining in the teahouses refused to give them money.

Nor did she mention that she and Martin no longer went to the chaikhanas but limited themselves to the few restaurants in town catering to foreigners. Other outings, even more rare, took place within the gated, heavily guarded compounds of various aid organizations, or in the towering concrete mass of the Intercontinental Hotel, on a hill overlooking the city. There, a broken elevator required her to switch on her headlamp—giving silent thanks to Kirstie Davidson, martinet of that long-ago training, for her foresight—for the walk up several flights of a pitch-black stairwell. Still, the journalists who often threw the parties felt the additional safety of the upper floors was worth the inconvenience. A few weeks earlier, a low-aimed rocket had torn away a balcony and most of a corner room at the Intercontinental. The room, like much of the hotel, had been empty.

"But why dwell on all of that?" asked their host one night, an agreeable Swiss television reporter, who thrust cold beers into their hands as they arrived, compliments of the Australians from down the hall. One thing Afghanistan had taught Liv: Finding booze was only as problematic as finding the resident Australians. "Drink up. There's plenty where that came from. You should see their room. It's a regular pub."

Liv wondered why she and Martin were there. The parties they had attended in Islamabad had included a few journalists, but they were usually longtime foreign correspondents, adept at mingling with the embassy staffers and corporate executives. Martin had cautioned her to steer clear of them. This new fascination with journalists, most of them freelancers and new to Central Asia, baffled her. On this night, he left Liv—one of only three women at the party—alone almost immediately and huddled across the room with two young Italian reporters, their jeans low on slim hips, effortlessly handsome in the way of Italians, their looks enhanced by the same beards that looked so scruffy on Americans.

Liv sipped her beer and concentrated on the conversation among the others but found herself unable to follow the intricacies of the usual who-was-sleeping-with-whom NGO gossip, or the journalists' fast-paced chatter about which particular warlord seemed ascendant. Both groups traded news of the most recent foreign casualties: the two aid workers in Mazar-i-Sharif; the ISAF contingent that hit one of the few effectively constructed roadside bombs; the reporter shot on the street in Kandahar, not a single witness among the dozens of people on that same street.

With each telling, people focused on the fatal errors. The reporter was walking alone. The aid workers had visited rival factions in succession. Members of the second group had assumed they were spies, so caught them and slit their throats, tossing their bodies outside the compound of the warlord who led the first faction. As for the soldiers, well, everyone knew ISAF was a constant target.

"So if we don't walk alone, if we don't visit different factions, if we're not members of ISAF, then we're safe, right?" Liv said into a lull. There was a ripple of nervous laughter, then one of the Australians raised his beer. "Right! If we don't join ISAF, we're safe."

Someone turned up the volume on a boom box that a TV reporter must have brought into the country in one of the big equipment crates that now served as benches lining the room. Through the hubbub, Liv recognized Pink Floyd's *Dark Side of the Moon*. Perfect. She wandered away from the others and tucked herself into a corner, behind a stack of sound equipment. Cords snaked across the room to a generator on the balcony, awaiting the inevitable power outage. She heard a little scream and looked up to see one of the women mock-slapping a German aid worker. He laughed and pulled back, but when she turned away, he put his arm back around her and cupped her breast. This time, she just shrugged his hand aside, smiling.

The Italian reporters fidgeted, glancing toward the women, as Martin's questions persisted. "Better watch out, boys," Liv said. "The Germans are marching on your territory."

"How's that?" It was the Australian who'd made the ISAF crack. He stood before her, blocking any escape from her cubbyhole, holding out another beer.

Liv shook her head. "I'd better not. I'm not used to drinking anymore. I've only had one, and already I'm talking to myself."

He was a few years older than the others in the room, hair cut short, neat beard tinged gray. His denim shirt, while faded, looked freshly laundered and pressed, as were the quick-dry cargo pants that all the reporters wore. Liv looked him up and down and wondered how to make him go away. "You're very clean. That's quite a trick, in Kabul. What are you, a hotel reporter?"

It was the derogatory term for reporters who stayed in the luxury hotels inhabited by foreigners in third-world countries, doing most of their work by telephone, or from interviews in the lobby or restaurant. Well, the Intercontinental wasn't lavish—Liv had noticed the buckets of water beside the toilet, a sign of problematic plumbing—but it was Kabul's best. The man's raised brow slid back into place. His eyes were kind. "I'm sorry," Liv said. "That was rude. I'd like to blame it on the beer, but I don't think you'd buy that."

"I don't." He studied her so openly that Liv began to feel uncomfortable. In contrast to the increasing hilarity filling the rest of the room, his manner was markedly contained. Maybe it was because he didn't fidget. Most people spooked easy after a while in Kabul, she'd noticed.

"How long have you been here?" he asked.

She chose to misunderstand. "Only about an hour." She took the beer from him and held its cool metal skin against her forehead. He pried the can from her hand, popped the top, and gave it back to her.

"It works better if you drink it. How long have you been in Kabul? I'm Howard, by the way."

"Liv." She took a swallow of beer, savoring its cool bitterness, a change from the tepid, sugary Mirinda orangeades that inevitably appeared with her meals. "Just since April."

"Then you should know by now that very small things matter a great deal. Cleanliness, for instance. Neatness." He held out his arm, the motion forcing her to look at the knife crease along the sleeve. His cuffs were tightly rolled past his elbows, revealing muscled arms. His bulk was of the sturdy variety. She sneaked a look at Martin, at the sweaty blotch on his shirt that accentuated the slack paunch above his belt. "Beer matters, too. Especially cold."

"I noticed." Liv dragged her attention back to him. "How did you manage? I know for a fact that there's not a single cube of ice in Kabul, let alone a whole bag of the stuff."

His smile was so brief that Liv barely caught a glimpse of a broken front tooth. "When one has a generator and a refrigerator, then there is ice."

"A refrigerator!" Liv tried to remember the last time she'd seen one.

"Just a small one. You've got to get to Tajikistan some weekend. Those old Soviet republics are full of stuff from the black-market days. Of course, the place you really want to go is Dubai. It's just like shopping at home, only for twice the price. But stuff that good is wasted here. Go to Dushanbe in Tajikistan, get yourself a fridge, and leave it with your staff when you go home."

"How long have you been here?"

"Since October, back when you Yanks started bombing the place further into the Stone Age than it already was."

"But after September eleventh . . ." Liv stopped. She'd had this discussion too many times to want to hear the inevitable lecture about how the Taliban hadn't bombed the World Trade Center.

Howard gave an approving nod, the sort bestowed by a teacher upon a student who'd finally worked out the answer to a seemingly insoluble problem. He offered a bit of advice as her reward. "I leave every few weeks. You should, too. Don't think you're going to get used to it here. You won't. You just have to find ways to make it bearable."

"Bearable." Liv glanced again at Martin.

Howard followed her gaze. "Your husband?"

"Yes."

"He won't get anything from them, you know." His expression didn't change, but Liv bent toward him, as though he had urgently beckoned her near.

"What do you mean?"

"Those journalists. They've been here awhile. They're not some green freelancers who will talk too much to someone just because he's a Westerner, and at one of their own parties."

Liv waved her hand in front of her face, as though clearing away the room's cigarette fug would help her focus. "I don't understand."

"I mean, they know a spook when they see one." He leaned in, his body pushed tight against hers, so that anyone passing by would have thought it just another party come-on. He placed his lips against her ear, speaking fast. "They know it, and believe me, so does everyone he's ever talked to. Maybe not some of these newer reporters. But don't forget, they've got English-speaking interpreters listening in on every word, and those guys figured out early how to double-dip."

His beard scraped her cheek. "The interpreters take the money we're paying them and then turn around and sell what they hear from us to people here who are happy to pay a lot more. Half the bad actors in

Kabul, maybe more, know exactly what you're up to. Face the Future. That's a good one. See a Secret Agent, we call it. That fake-shabby little NGO is no cover at all. It just means you're not nearly as safe as you would be if your husband were working directly for the CIA, instead of this sort of nonsense."

"Bullshit. We're not working for the CIA." But she hesitated. Images clicked rapid-fire through her brain—the extravagant hotel bill in Islamabad, Martin's list of questions. His reports, his fucking reports.

Of course.

"Bullshit yourself. Now," he said, eyes flickering to something past him, "I'm going to kiss you to make this look good, and also because it's been too long since I've kissed a woman."

His tongue twisted inside her mouth. Liv sagged against him and he gripped her shoulders, holding her up. She reached and pulled his head even tighter to hers, kissing him back, hard.

"What's this, what's this?" Martin's voice rang loud and close.

"Sorry, mate." Liv noticed the exaggerated accent. "Your wife, of course. Don't know what got into me. Apologies all around." He bent at the waist, then straightened and backed away.

Liv looked at Martin, red-faced, breathing hard, a bit of beery foam cresting his thick lips, then at Howard. "Thank you," she mouthed.

"He just kissed you without any encouragement on your part?" Martin jerked her arm. "Come on. Let's get out of here."

Liv twisted in his grasp as he dragged her toward the door, looking back at Howard. Compassion washed his features, the look of someone who knew he'd made her face the truth about herself.

Liv tore a piece of paper from a legal pad, ran the point of her pencil down the middle, and wrote two headings at the top: "Reasons to Stay" and "Reasons to Go."

She looked over her shoulder. Martin was at work in the anteroom he'd claimed as his office.

"Stay" was easy. And not. She tried to imagine herself explaining the appeal of the words that stacked up so quickly on the page.

"People." The women who, no matter how poor or sick or merely exhausted, insisted upon preparing tea, pressing her hands between their rough ones, exclaiming at their softness. The children, despite their penchant for picking her pocket or fighting one another bloody to get at whatever treats she might distribute. She reminded herself that even the boys had gone years without the steadying effects of school, and the girls, most of them, had been effectively imprisoned indoors during the years of Taliban rule. And the men . . . here she had to dig deeper for sympathy. But so many lurched through Kabul's streets on crutches or in clumsy, hand-pedaled tricycles that served as wheelchairs, limbs blown off by land mines. She didn't know who had it worse—the younger ones, who'd spent their adult lives fighting in one conflict or another, or the older men, who remembered times of peace and relative prosperity.

"Bazaars." Their panoply of scent and color. The snaggletoothed man who gripped a thick piece of leather between his bare toes, knife flashing as he sawed away at it, carving out a sole. More slices of the knife yielded a vamp, a tongue, a toe cap, all of which he attached to the sole with a needle like a small spear and leather thread. When he saw Liv watching, he displayed the completed shoe with a flourish. Or the noisy row of tinsmith shops, where men hammered out teapots and trays, each stall's wares seemingly identical, but each with its own loyal clientele. Liv wondered if she'd ever be content with factory-made goods again.

"The land." At once so harsh and so achingly beautiful. Her eyes, which initially saw nothing but unending variations on beige, had learned to seek out color—the dust-coated green of the spindly trees that somehow clung to life along the city's boulevards, the scarlet splashes of the ubiquitous rosebushes, the sky like a canopy of sapphire silk.

And, finally: "Farida."

Just the other day, in the office, Farida had upended her bag in her search for the day's lesson. A leather-bound book slid out amid the papers, falling open upon the table to reveal a pen-and-ink illustration of a young girl with pale crimped hair, whose stiff garments exposed both arm and calf. The girl gazed curiously at the dark bottle in her hand, its large label commanding, "Drink."

"Alice!" Liv and Farida dove simultaneously for the book. Liv's hand reached it first. She bent her face to it, breathing in leather and paper and ink, the scent taking her back to long childhood hours in the crook of a willow tree, spent in the company of a girl whose curiosity led her to ever-stranger places, who did her best to adjust to incomprehensible circumstances, but who inevitably called stupidity what it was.

"Oh." Liv closed the book and caressed the cover. She blinked back tears, undone by the unexpected reminder of home. "This was my favorite book when I was a little girl."

Farida's hand, reaching for the book, fell to her side. She smiled. "Mine, too. Like nothing else I'd read. Those silly rhymes."

Liv closed her eyes and let the words come. "'You are old, Father William,' the young man said, 'and your hair has become very white,' um . . .'"

"'And yet you incessantly stand on your head,'" Farida prompted.

"'Do you think, at your age, it is right?'" they chorused together, laughing.

A sudden bond, something they shared that no one else around them understood, so that the next time an officious guard crowded too near as they passed through a checkpoint, Farida was able to relieve Liv's tension by whispering, "'There's a porpoise close behind us, and he's treading on my tail.'" Kindness and humor, the ingredients of friendship, something Liv had not dared to hope she'd find. Yet there it was.

Intangibles, all. But they nurtured a fierce and growing attachment. And then there was the matter of her work, the chance to help the women so desperately in need of it. If that, indeed, was their mission.

Liv moved her pencil to the next line and wrote a final word, letter by reluctant letter: "Failure."

Stay, or else she'd have to face them all, the colleagues who'd remember her casual dismissal of their skepticism. Her mother, her very silence a rebuke. Liv would find herself back in the library carrels, books at her elbow. Or, at her computer, scrolling through websites, compiling information to buttress theory instead of talking to people in person to collect facts. Which no one seemed to want to hear.

The pencil hovered over the paper. How to put in writing, even privately, the suspicions raised by the journalist at the party? Which, if she forced herself to admit it, had been there all along.

"Hey." Martin stepped from the anteroom. Liv crumpled the paper, slipped it into her pocket, and pulled a UN report toward her.

"Where's Farida?"

"We're doing most of our work in the house these days. Why do you ask?" As if she didn't know. Farida's presence in the office acted as a magnet for Martin's gaze, the pull nearly palpable. Liv had to bite her tongue against the sort of comments she once made about Mandy. But at least she knew there was no risk of Martin acting on his feelings. To do so would put both his and Farida's lives in danger. His crush, as Liv thought of it, would likely be forgotten the minute they left Afghanistan, if not long before.

She thought of the list in her pocket, the blank lines awaiting her verdict beneath "Reasons to Go."

"Martin."

He fell into the chair beside her desk and blew out his breath, his disappointment obvious. "What?"

"What if we were to leave early?"

Just like that, she had his full attention. "Are you crazy? We're only a few months in. I've barely begun my work. Our work."

"And what work is that, exactly? All this stuff we're collecting on women—we don't do anything with it. But what about the other information we're gathering? What are we—you—doing with that, Martin?" This was as close as she'd come to confronting him directly.

He slammed a hand onto the desk, sending a stack of papers cascading to the floor.

"Jesus, Liv. You sound like a broken record. We've been through this. We can't initiate any programs until we know what we're dealing with. Why is that so hard to get through your head?"

He rose and stalked back into his office. If there had been a door, Liv thought, he would have slammed it.

Liv collected the documents from the floor and rearranged them on her desk, squaring them with exaggerated care. She thought of Farida's bitter words in the car. She thought of the escalating attacks: How much longer would she be able to enjoy their outings, or even make them at all?

Furious sounds came from Martin's office, a keyboard clacking triple time. She slid her hand into her pocket and extracted a ring with its three lonely keys: house, desk drawer, and strongbox, nothing like the bulky set—house, library main door, office door, door and trunk for both cars, gym locker (rarely used), bike lock (ditto)—that had weighed down her purse in Philadelphia. She glanced over her shoulder, twisted a key in the drawer lock, extracted the strongbox and unlocked it, too. Stacks of crisp American hundred-dollar bills lined up within, Kabul's currency of choice for anyone but its current residents.

Martin's keyboard rattled away. Liv calculated, then filched a bill from the bottom of each stack, twenty in all. Two thousand should be more than enough for the cab ride to the airport and the UN shuttle to Islamabad, where she could catch the direct flight to Dubai, then London and finally home. She locked the box, replaced it in the drawer, and locked the drawer. She walked across the courtyard to the house, nodding to Ismail without looking directly at him, not so much out of courtesy but because she didn't want to know if his own gaze went straight to the rectangular packet in the pocket she'd insisted the tailor sew into her shalwar. Impossible—the shalwar was comfortably loose, and draped with the kameez besides.

Later in the house, safely alone, she retrieved a kitchen knife and carried it into the bedroom. She tugged her carry-on bag from beneath the bed, dislodging a cloud of dust as it banged the bed frame. She ran the knife down the satin lining, creating a three-inch slit along the seam, and deposited the cash, warm from her pocket.

She filled the suitcase with a day's worth of clothing—underwear, slacks, a blouse she hadn't worn in months, a few toiletries. Something she could change into in the airport in Dubai so she wouldn't look too out of place.

She kicked the bag back under the bed with a sense of satisfaction. There. If she had to leave in a hurry, she was ready.

Her pocket crackled as she turned to go. Had she missed a bill? No, it was just the list she'd started in the office, before Martin had interrupted her. He hadn't answered her question.

She carried the paper into the kitchen, smoothed it on the table, and again picked up a pencil.

Under "Reasons to Go" she wrote a single word, as unambiguous as the "Reasons to Stay" were vague:

Death.

Twenty-Nine

Gul and Khurshid sat side by side on the mat, Gul with his shalwar pulled up and drawn more tightly than necessary around his waist, Khurshid with her burqa wrapped around her like an inadequate blanket. As she spoke, the awareness of her bare skin beneath the burqa competed with her words for Gul's attention.

"I was sick for a long time after that day, as you know."

The soldiers had passed what felt like hours in the family's courtyard, as though unable to believe their good fortune in encountering a woman as comely as Khurshid. This was not the slow-witted daughter and her elderly mother from the home next door, to be perfunctorily raped and cast aside. Gul feared they would never leave.

But they were still soldiers, and when the commander finally called to them, they reluctantly assembled in the center of the courtyard. Some hoisted carpets, others toted cooking utensils. Even Bibi's little doll went with them, dangling incongruously from an outsize paw. The commander looked back at Khurshid, lying broken and bloodied in the dirt. He affixed the bayonet to his gun and placed the tip of the blade between her breasts.

"Make it quick," Gul prayed.

But the commander merely drew the bayonet from the middle of Khurshid's chest, lengthening the earlier cut, trailing a scarlet thread down her torso. "We should skin her, eh?" the commander said, lifting the gun. "And hang her carcass from the gate, like the sheep she is." The men laughed again, but they also looked impatient, burdened as they were, standing in the late-afternoon sun, with the unaccustomed effect of alcohol beginning to make itself felt. Some of them looked greenish, and as the commander waited for a response, one of the men leaned to the side and vomited. Even the commander appeared confused, as though he had forgotten why they were there. He walked to the gate, his men straggling through it behind him.

The two holding Gul let him go. He pitched forward onto the dirt, listening to their retreating footsteps. He assumed Khurshid was dead. She had not so much as twitched when the bayonet parted her skin as easily as a fingernail drawn down a peach.

It did not occur to him to look for his mother and Bibi. He would be grateful to them, later, for saying nothing about it, but he also knew they kept silent to disguise their own shame at the fact that after the attack of the soldiers, it was the women of Nur Muhammed's household who took things in hand.

———————

"But I did wake up," Khurshid reminded him.

"Yes." They sat in silence awhile longer, neither wishing to speak of what followed.

Nur Muhammed did not return for more than a week. Long enough for Maryam, marshaling resources that Gul had never suspected, to force herself unaccompanied into the streets of central Kabul, wheedling and browbeating passersby until she had begged enough afghanis to purchase a worn shalwar kameez and ragged burqa for Khurshid, a single pot and some limp vegetables, a chip of strong soap, and two thin blankets. Gul and Bibi huddled beneath one, the little children between them, while Maryam cradled Khurshid in her arms at night, soothing her with quiet clucking noises when Khurshid woke herself with raw, hoarse screams. Despite this nighttime tenderness, by day Maryam was as brusque as ever, wordlessly bathing Khurshid's unspeakable wounds every few hours, cleaning them of pus and scabs, ordering her to at least drink something.

After a few days, Khurshid could sit up and swallow a few sips of tea. After a few more, she let herself be pulled to her feet and took several hesitant steps before sagging against Maryam. Her once-lustrous hair drooped in brittle hanks about her bruised face. Not once since the soldiers left had she looked at Gul. She spent most of her time sitting in a corner, staring at the wall, her hands moving in the mindless tasks that Maryam gave her, using a shard of crockery to cut a potato Maryam had managed to procure, or scuttling across the floor on all fours, listlessly sweeping it with a leafy twig Maryam had broken from a tree in the park outside the presidential palace—one of the few places in the city that had not been stripped of its greenery.

Gul watched his mother watching Khurshid. Maryam pursed her lips, creased her brow, muttered darkly to herself. Once, she broke from such a reverie, turning to Gul so suddenly that he stepped back. "Maybe we should take her away. Before—"

"Take her where? Before what?" But he knew, or at least he knew what, if not where. Before Nur Muhammed got home and risked everyone's lives by avenging Khurshid's honor.

Gul did not want Khurshid to go away. He imagined the scene when Nur Muhammed arrived, his father's rage, his vows for vengeance. Gul wondered if his father would let him be part of that mission, and he passed long, fiercely satisfying moments imagining the hairy commander on the ground just as Khurshid had been, a bayonet pressed to his chest. Gul thought if he were to give that bayonet the merest shove, it would feel like slitting a sleeping mat—a bit of initial resistance and then the quick slide into the interior, slashing downward to enlarge the opening, the wholly enjoyable spill of the contents. He wanted to be the one to announce triumphantly to Khurshid that her tormentors had been dispatched, that she was avenged. She would look at him with her former shining gaze tinged with a new respect and appreciation.

So certain was he of this scenario that when Nur Muhammed returned, Gul missed the warning signs—the way Maryam hung back, her face set, her shoulders squared, rather than hurrying toward him with her usual commanding officiousness. Gul leapt to his feet when his father appeared in the broken doorway, long splinters still hanging from the frame.

"But what is this?" Nur Muhammed looked first at the doorframe, then scanned the dim interior. Gul took in the shock on his face as he saw what was there—or rather, what was no longer there. No rugs on the floor, no cabinet shelves neatly arranged with Maryam's cooking utensils, no sleeping mats rolled against the wall, folded blankets stacked just so atop them. Maryam stood motionless, Bibi behind her. The little children crowded the doorway to an anteroom, poised for retreat. Khurshid did not even rise upon Nur Muhammed's entrance. She sat in her corner, head lowered, rocking.

Nur Muhammed crossed the room, put his hand beneath her chin, and tilted her face upward. It was much improved, but Gul saw her as Nur Muhammed did—the swollen eyes, the lips cracked and crusted, the cheekbones yellowed with fading bruises.

Nur Muhammed forced her to her feet. "Who did this to her?" He looked accusingly at Maryam, then at Gul. "Well?"

"Soldiers came." Gul hoped it would suffice.

"And?"

"They took our things."

Nur Muhammed still clenched Khurshid's chin. He turned her face toward Gul. "How did this happen?"

"They beat her," Gul whispered.

"Only her?" Nur Muhammed looked at Maryam and Bibi, conspicuously unblemished.

"We hid." Bibi spoke up, then ducked back behind Maryam.

"Not her?" Ice frosted Nur Muhammed's words.

"She wasn't here," Bibi said.

Nur Muhammed's face was so awful that Gul felt compelled to help his sister. "She was at the market. And when she came home—" He stopped.

"They beat her." Nur Muhammed filled in the blank.

"Yes."

"And you did not protect her."

Gul thought he had known shame ever since the soldiers appeared at their gate, but he realized that was some earlier, lesser emotion compared to the crawling feeling inside him now.

"They had guns." Bibi spoke up.

"How do you know? You were hiding."

"It's true." Gul directed the words toward the floor.

"Do you think that when men with guns came to attack my family, I would stand aside? Do you think anyone would have hurt my family without killing me first?"

Gul could not even summon the strength to shake his head.

A rasping noise startled him. For a moment, he could not even place it as Khurshid's voice, so long had it been since he'd heard her speak. "They caught him and held him. There were many. He could do nothing to stop them."

There was a terrible, long silence. Gul prayed for an end to Nur Muhammed's interrogation. Maryam's lips moved. Bibi went ashen.

"Stop them from what?"

From beating her. But Gul's lips would not form the words.

"I am a soldier. I know the ways of soldiers. And you"—he let go of Khurshid's jaw and wiped his hand on his tunic—"going to market alone. Is this your custom, whenever I am away? To go out on your own and consort with men?"

"Gul goes with me," Khurshid said in her new strangled voice.

"But not that day?"

Gul tried to remember where he had been. He had slipped out of the house early to scavenge with his friend Amer. It seemed so long ago. He had not seen Amer since. His family had wisely disappeared as soon as the soldiers left. He did not know what had happened to the women of Amer's family. Maybe Amer had protected them, and died for doing so, the way he himself should have died protecting Khurshid.

Nur Muhammed said he knew the ways of soldiers. Gul wondered if it was from firsthand experience. His thoughts ran on unbearably as Nur Muhammed glowered at them all in turn. Just as he had convinced himself that his father could not possibly have done such things, Nur Muhammed put his hand to Khurshid's throat and grabbed a handful of her kameez, tearing the thin, worn cotton from neck to hem, revealing her breasts, bruised purple and yellow like fruit gone bad, and the still-red scar between them.

"Who did this?"

No one spoke.

"You let them touch you."

"They had guns," Khurshid whispered.

"You let them defile you." He slapped her.

Her head rocked back, but she held her stance. "They had guns," she said, louder. "They were many."

He slapped her again. "After everything I've done for you, you shamelessly give yourself away."

"They hurt me."

For days, Khurshid had crept around the house like a broken thing. Now she stood straight, her arms at her sides, not bothering to hold the rags of her clothing across her mutilated flesh, looking Nur Muhammed in the eye, keeping her gaze on him even as he struck her again.

"You bring dishonor to my home."

Slap.

"You shame my wife and daughter by your very presence."

Slap.

"Whore."

Fresh blood trickled from the corner of Khurshid's mouth. She stooped and felt behind her for her torn kameez. She pulled it around her and moved in halting steps toward the door. Gul made as if to help her, but Maryam crossed the room and held him back.

"Let her go." She raised her voice. "What will people say of your sister, a young unspoiled girl under the same roof with such a one?"

Something relaxed in Nur Muhammed's face at her words. Maryam kept talking. "Let the whore go back to the streets where she belongs. After she is gone, I will wash everything she touched. You will take tea now. Please, you must sit. I am sorry for the bare floor, but you must be tired. Tomorrow, we will get new things."

"Tomorrow," said Nur Muhammed, "we go to Pakistan."

"Yes," said Maryam. "I think that is best. Now, please. Sit. Bibi, your father is home. Make tea."

———

"Pakistan!" said Khurshid. "I wondered where you went. I came back, you know, but the house was empty. I wanted to thank your mother for her kindness to me. I have always wanted to go to Pakistan. There is no war there, I think."

"No." Gul thought that not even the annual bloody clashes between Sunni and Shi'a during each other's holidays, nor the interminable guerrilla attacks in Balochistan, between Pakistan and Iran and Afghanistan, by those determined to create a new Pashtun republic, qualified as war.

"It is very prosperous there, I have heard."

"Very." Gul could not bring himself to describe the markets, with their firm, ripe vegetables piled high in artfully arranged pyramids, the carts wafting spicy scents of kebabs and samosas and fresh-baked naan, the people riding in shiny new cars, not clumsy tongas pulled by bony horses with sores oozing wetly onto cracked leather harnesses.

He sensed Khurshid looking at him with new attention, taking in his clothing of heavy, tightly woven cotton, the new, knitted waistcoat, the sandals of leather rather than cheap rubber. She took his hand between her own, so that he could feel her calluses pressing against his smooth palm.

"Your father did well in Pakistan. He was good to me, you know."

Gul jerked in surprise.

"Yes, truly. He only did what he had to do. Any other man would have killed me. But he has found protectors for me. It's not enough, though. I cannot live with this man here, so of course there must be"—she raised her chin and spoke almost defiantly—"there must be others."

Gul found it difficult to look at her. Anger and shame churned within him. She was exactly as he'd first assumed when the shopkeeper had brought him into the room—a common whore. But his father, seemingly without a twinge of conscience, had put her in this position, likely even congratulating himself for his generosity.

Throughout his silence, Khurshid held his hand, and he was very conscious of her touch, of her nearness, of the burqa that had slipped down, revealing more of her creamy shoulders and part of her bare arms. "And you?" she asked. "What of your life?"

"I am married, just this past year. Soon she will have a child."

Khurshid drew circles on his palm with the tip of her forefinger. "Soon? So your wife is very large now?"

Gul could not speak.

Her finger moved lightly up his arm, beneath his sleeve. "You are a young man. That must be difficult for you." Her finger traced its way back down his arm to his wrist. She took his hand back in hers and brought it to her breast.

Gul groaned.

He closed his eyes as Khurshid lay back on the mat and pulled him atop her, sliding down his shalwar with practiced movements and guiding him to a pleasure more intense than anything he had ever experienced with Farida.

Gul came home in the evening, as he had for so many recently, in a foul temper. He stomped through the door, into the women's quarters, and slammed a stack of naan onto the oilcloth in front of Farida, and then left without so much as a word or a glance.

She felt the aunties' eyes upon her. Even though that sort of behavior was customary among men, she could not recall Gul treating her so indifferently, not when they were alone, and certainly not in front of others. In fact, his attentiveness had resulted in much sly teasing about the charms with which Farida had presumably bewitched him.

"They are like children when they are angry," one of the aunties said now, after an awkward silence. The others chimed in eagerly on the familiar subject of the unfathomable and inferior ways of men, their animated chatter giving Farida time to blink back the tears that stung her eyelids. One of the aunties leaned over and patted Farida's arm.

"He won't stay angry for long. After all, you are about to have his son." The comment sparked a new, albeit an equally familiar, round of conversation about Farida's child. Surely it would be a boy, they agreed, trying to cheer her. She smiled wanly at their good-hearted attempts, reminding herself of her fortune in finding such acceptance by Gul's family.

The aunties were full of stories about brides deemed unsuitable not just by their husbands but also by the women of the family—young wives who did not know their place, who sulked and did not show proper deference to their new mothers-in-law, who did not help about the house, and who, over time, fell victim to an uncommon number of household accidents. Razor-sharp knives mistakenly came down upon their fingers as they stood side by side with their husband's female relatives, chopping onions. Hot oil splattered from pans onto their arms and faces. Pots of boiling water tipped from the stove and splashed down their legs. In the worst cases, a defiant bride would just have time to register the fist between her shoulders before stumbling into the fire, her loose clothing a shimmering veil of flame. Some survived, but really, given the future faced by a scarred and crippled woman, such brides were considered lucky if they simply burned to death.

Farida thought of the life she had envisioned when her father married her off to Gul and wondered, if her husband had been a different sort of man, whether she, too, might have welcomed a fiery end compared to the slow agony of such a marriage. She saw them, sometimes, these wives. At family gatherings, there might be a woman sitting to the side, speaking just when spoken to, claiming only small bits of food for herself, her eyes downcast and dead.

"Poor Siddiqa. She has lost her face," an auntie said of one such woman at a recent wedding.

Farida looked at Siddiqa with new curiosity. Indeed, there was nothing of the play of emotion across her face that provided clues to personality. Farida could not tell if she were soft or stubborn, sober or silly. Still, the aunties' sympathy moved her. Usually, these broken women were presumed to have brought their fate upon themselves. But there was also an acknowledgment, rarely discussed, of the suffering that an uncooperative husband—one who beat his wife, and used her cruelly and insistently, even through her pregnancies, only to take a new young wife when she became exhausted and old before her time—could inflict upon a woman.

Farida knew she was fortunate to have a husband who treated her so gently, especially as her pregnancy entered its last phase. The aunties had warned her that relations with her husband could hurt the child, and had hinted that Gul, being a young man—"But they are like that at any age, no?"—would try to avail himself of her body, anyway. Farida, well acquainted with Gul's urgent need, nodded knowingly.

But he had begun to stay away, spending long afternoons out of the house and sleeping in another room at night. That was almost certainly the source of his testiness, she reassured herself. That, and the pressure of Nur Muhammed's plan.

That night, though, he came to their room. Farida, who had dozed off, heard the door open and moved heavily to one side of the sleeping mat to make room for him. But he stood motionless in the doorway, not turning on the light, even though she could tell by the way the generators had fallen silent that the electricity was on.

"Hamidullah spoke to me," he said without preamble.

"Hamidullah?" Farida remembered the young Talib who had been spending so much time at the house, and who had recently turned up as the new guard at Face the Future.

"He says you put your burqa aside when you are among Those People."

Farida sighed. This was not the encounter she hoped to have. "I work indoors. No strangers see me."

"That Man is there. And other men."

Farida did not reply. Martin and the others were like relatives, she wanted to say—the sort of relatives one did not much like, but familiar nonetheless. But then she thought of the men who visited Nur Muhammed on such a regular basis, Hamidullah among them, men she knew by their voices but whose faces she had never seen and who, if they were to look upon hers, risked a quick and ruthless end. Many had been friends with Nur Muhammed for decades, yet they had never met his wife or daughters.

Gul's stubborn silence awaited an explanation.

"It is impossible," she said. "I cannot do my work in a burqa. The filing, the writing. And to read—it strains my eyes if I wear it. I wear my dupatta, always. I'm sure Hamidullah told you that," she said, trying to keep the spite from her voice. Although the man would surely be useful for the plan she knew Nur Muhammed to be hatching, he was an intolerable busybody, the sort of man who, she thought, would cause a wife to lose her face.

"Why do you still go there?" Gul asked, ignoring her words. "You should not leave the house at all now. It is dangerous for you."

She strained to see his features in the darkness. He stood straight and still, an inky silhouette, pronouncing judgment upon her with each measured phrase.

He should know why. He needed the information she provides. Because his father demanded it. *Their plan—the one they think me ignorant of—will succeed because of me.* She sensed that to speak the truth aloud would only stoke his ire. Still, her own anger surged.

"If your father approves," she said, silkily placing the blame on Nur Muhammed, even as she reminded her husband of his powerlessness against his father's wishes, "I will gladly stay away from the Amriki. I would be happy never to see them again." She paused and tamped down the flare of rebellion, reminding herself that to voice such vexation was impermissible for a woman. "I'm sorry if I have given you cause for concern."

"My wife is not a whore," Gul snapped.

Farida recoiled from the ugly word. Hamidullah, she thought. She wanted to ask Gul to stay with her—even in this moment of discord, she missed his comforting warmth—but thought it might only offer more proof of her apparent wantonness. Besides, Gul left her no time to issue an invitation, but left as abruptly as he had come.

Thirty

It took weeks of pleading on Liv's part, but Farida finally succumbed to her desire to visit a real Afghan market, not just the tourist shops on Chicken Street.

Farida resisted at first, even enlisting Martin's help in protesting that it would be unseemly for a foreign woman to venture out unaccompanied. His vehemence shocked them both. "The markets are dangerous. I forbid it."

Farida saw Liv's back stiffen at the word "forbid," a flash of defiance, infectious. Her own shoulders tightened. Her chin lifted as the words slipped from her lips. "Dangerous? I myself shop in them all the time. And yet here I stand before you, having survived such a dangerous experience, day after day." She dared not look at Liv, fearful of seeing her lips twitch toward a smile, the sort of thing that could nudge them both into full-blown laughter.

"But you just said—" Martin was befuddled by her lightning change of opinion.

"Oh, la, we women. You know how we are. Like the wind, blowing this way and that. Come, Liv. Let us go before I change my mind again.

Mr. Stoellner"—with Liv, it was first names; Martin, never—"I promise to bring your wife back safely from our sojourn among the very dangerous vegetables and household goods."

She swept from the office, savoring her sense of power over Martin, conspiracy with Liv. For all the unexpected and growing warmth of her relations with Maryam and Bibi and the aunties, her time with Liv was something different, a harkening back to her bond with Alia, a match of wit and shared experience of the outside world.

Liv named a market to the startled driver. He turned to Farida for approval. The man's hesitation chased the smile from Liv's face. "You'd better tell him politely that I'm not kidding," Liv said. "I don't have the right Pashto words for that yet."

Farida lowered her burqa over her face and spoke the necessary phrases. The driver called to the guard and the gate swung open. A beggar in a green burqa slipped through. The guard shouted and reached for her, but Farida waved him away, pressing a few afghanis into the unfortunate's hand. The woman gasped as their fingers met.

"It is too much," she murmured after she recovered herself.

"It is not enough," Farida corrected her.

"Little mother, if I may be so bold," the woman ventured, her voice shaking.

"*Ho,*" Farida encouraged her.

"I would like to thank you by name."

"Farida. And yours?"

The woman shook her head so vigorously the accordion folds of her burqa swirled about her as she backed away, out into the tumult of the street.

"Farida! We're leaving."

Farida slid into the backseat beside Liv but twisted to look through the rear window as the car pulled away, remembering her old game of At Least.

Even in this country of privation, I live a life of ease. At least I am not a beggar woman, depending upon the unreliable kindness of foreigners.

She looked and looked as the car crawled through traffic, but the green burqa had vanished into the throng.

As soon as they arrived at one of Kabul's largest markets, Liv leapt from the car and headed for the warren of stalls, the driver and Farida scrambling to catch up, Farida taking her arm, the driver close behind.

"I'm so happy we're doing this," Liv said. In Islamabad, she'd found Aabpara wonderfully strange, with its jumble of narrow shops and vivid colors. Now, confronting this new bazaar, Aabpara's wide concrete walkways and shops in actual buildings seemed as decorous as a suburban shopping mall back in Philadelphia. Here, wooden shacks leaned against one another in the barest semblance of order. Dirt alleyways, narrow and crooked, divided the rows. Liv had heard of Kabul's main money market in the city's center, where it was said the equivalent of a million dollars changed hands daily. In this market, a lone moneylender—a sort of satellite office, maybe?—sat before bricks of blue afghanis, hands a blur, the bills snapping like playing cards within them as he counted them out.

"Stay with me," Farida commanded.

But Liv sensed Farida's own distraction, her head swiveling in its burqa as she peered this way and that. "Come see." She tugged at Liv, pulling her toward a garish display of toys, cheap plastic figurines and threadbare stuffed animals, their button eyes dangling, fur stiff with Kabul's inescapable dust. For a moment, Liv envied Farida's burqa, fearful her face betrayed her own aversion. She thought of the gifts she'd bought for friends' babies, Steiff bears from FAO Schwarz, stiff-backed and unsmiling, or the faux-primitive Scandinavian wooden toys painted in primary colors, and of how those friends might have reacted had she shown up with, say, the rayon-clad plastic doll within her crackling cellophane wrapper.

The proprietor immediately detected Farida's condition despite the burqa. By now, Liv had acquired enough Pashto to get the gist of his words.

"Something for your child. A boy, I am sure." The ultimate compliment.

He pushed toys to the front of the display. A screaming yellow dump truck, huge, bigger probably than a baby itself. A packet of the ubiquitous green plastic army men, something Liv might have seen in a Walmart at home. Liv imagined them in a baby's fist, his mouth, the inevitable choking. A collection of knockoff G.I. Joe–type soldiers. Most were white, but one sported a bushy mustache that obscured much of his face; a peaked green cap shaded the rest. Unrecognizable weapons—grenade launchers? something more vicious still?—rested in his jointed arms. Farida's sigh was light, nearly imperceptible. Her head turned toward a half dozen books barely visible beneath the other toys. Her hand, resting lightly on Liv's arm, jerked, even as she shook her head and murmured her apologies to the shopkeeper.

Liv composed the sentence in her head, and spoke. "I would like to buy a gift for my friend's child." She took a breath, summoning those long-ago lessons with Mrs. Khan, and launched, choosing first the truck, then something equally expensive looking, her voice growing loud, shrill as she berated the shopkeeper in her broken Pashto for the inadequacy of his goods, their unreasonably high prices. Finally, she picked up one of the books. Careless, disdainful.

"This, then. Although it is not adequate."

And it wasn't, its pages crudely stitched to the flimsy cardboard cover with coarse black thread, a justification for more arguing. Liv heard Farida chuckling beneath the burqa, before the man finally wrapped the sad excuse for a book in a bit of cloth and tied it with string, muttering darkly below his breath about Amriki who refused to spend their obvious riches.

Farida squeezed her arm. "I am as happy with your bargaining skills as I am with your gift. You do me honor on both counts. My son will start his life knowing the importance of education."

Liv forgot the need for reserve in public. She beamed a smile toward the burqa's grille. "It was fun!" All of their other outings had been so purposeful, the endless procession of oppressed women so discouraging. On this day, to wander among the stalls playing the tourist, especially one so unexpectedly adept at bargaining, came as such a relief that she fought a brief urge toward tears. How long had it been since she'd simply enjoyed herself?

She forced her attention to the market's wares. A man sold pomegranate juice from a device that cleverly pressed the garnet liquid from the seeds, then distilled it into glasses, where it glittered, cool and inviting, an antidote to the punishing sunlight. Liv smiled at another stall that offered conflict rugs at a fraction of the price demanded by the Chicken Street merchants. She wondered how Farida felt about them and turned to ask her, but Farida, too, had relaxed, enough to step away toward a stall selling baby clothes.

Liv wished they'd seen that first. She'd far rather have bought Farida a onesie. Assuming Afghan children even wore onesies. She couldn't see into the stall for the crowd of women around it. She moved back, giving them room.

Something jostled against her, and at first she thought that maybe a parcel had bumped her bottom. She edged away, but then she felt it again and realized with a shock that it was someone's hand, hurriedly searching. She yelped and pulled back, but a knot of men pressed in close, moving her in a mass around a corner into a dark, narrow opening between two stalls, out of the main flow of shoppers. They pinched and twisted her breasts, and cupped their hands roughly at her crotch and buttocks, fingers squirming insistently upward. The layers of cloth she wore seemed suddenly insubstantial.

"Farida!" she shouted into the low, gasping laughter all around her. She struck out at the men, but they caught her arms. A man rutted at her hip, his breath hot and moist against her cheek. Liv screamed again, and he ground harder against her. He grunted again, the sound different. Something solid crunched against bone. The man toppled back as the driver waded into the crowd, wielding a tire iron, Farida following. Invading fingers retreated. Hands loosened their grip on her arms and her wrists, fell away from her breasts, untangled themselves from her hair.

Liv looked back as Farida hustled her away from the mob. The men bent double, laughing at one of their own who lay on the ground, clutching his broken arm, his gaze boring through her in a mixture of triumph and contempt.

"Are you all right?" Martin demanded an hour later. "Did they hurt you?"

She sat curled into the corner of the unforgiving sofa, arms wrapped around herself, head turned away. Dirt smeared her kameez. Martin noticed she'd changed her shalwar, into a muddy orange pair that clashed with her lavender kameez. He went into the kitchen, put on water for tea, and tried to compose himself. He returned, looked again at the clean shalwar, and avoided asking the question directly.

"Did they just fondle you, or—?"

"No, Martin. I wasn't raped, if that's what you want to know. It was in public. It was over very quickly. It's what you said. They just grabbed at me. Not that there was anything *just* about it."

"I don't suppose we should go to the police."

"Why not? We should tell someone. Not the police, but ISAF, maybe. Somebody who would actually do something."

Martin imagined word of this getting back to his supervisors, as it surely would. Their instructions had been clear: "Do nothing that will draw attention." Although his supervisors were in Pakistan and Washington, they would surely hear by evening, the next morning at the latest, that Martin's blond wife was seen cavorting with men in a public place.

Liv put out a hand against the sofa's arm and pushed herself slowly to her feet. "You're not going to tell anyone, are you." It was more accusation than question.

"I think it's better that this not get out of hand. Do you really want people to know what happened to you?"

"Nothing just *happened*. Something was deliberately done to me." She moved stiffly toward the kitchen.

"Liv."

She didn't answer.

He tried again. "Do you need to see a doctor?"

The teapot shrieked.

He heard tea splashing into cups, and then her voice, faint but firm. "I want to go home."

"You know that's not possible."

From the kitchen came nothing at all.

———————

Liv lay at the edge of the bed that night, curled on her side, her back to him and her arms clutched across her chest, her breath catching occasionally. After an hour, Martin got up. He came back with a glass of water and some pills. "These will help you sleep."

He lay back down and listened to her breathing lengthen and deepen. She rolled onto her back and moaned, and turned again onto her side. He rose on one elbow and looked at her in the yellow light of the security lamp just outside the window. She was asleep. Beyond her, a new burqa hung from a nail driven into the wall. Farida had brought it late in the afternoon, knocking softly at the door and laying the bundle of blue fabric in his arms. "Tell her it's better," she said in response to his unasked question, and drifted away, lowering her own burqa back across her face as she did. He saw the shadow of her husband outside the gate. Martin had gotten so used to seeing Farida working unveiled in the Face the Future office that he'd forgotten she wore the burqa at all.

In the market, Liv told him, the men had put their hands on her behind, and touched her breasts. "They felt me up," was the phrase she used, with its reminder of innocent high-school fumblings. Back then, Martin had always stopped when a girl protested. But he wondered what it would be like in a place like this, where a woman alone and unveiled was presumed to welcome attention. Where the penalty would fall upon her for inviting, not the man for accepting an invitation so clearly offered.

He thought of what it might be like to encounter an unveiled Farida, not in the office where she was protected but in the market, parcels balanced against her swaying hips, her dark hair sliding across her face, so alluring that he understood the necessity of a covering. At such a sight, any man might be compelled to act—to come up behind her, to cup the fullness of her breasts with his hands and pull her against him with righteous impunity.

"I tried to get away, but I couldn't," Liv had said. "They held me too tightly."

In Martin's reverie, Farida struggled in his grip. He put his lips to her bare neck, bit her exposed earlobe. Her hair was fragrant against his face. He slid a hand down past her waist. His erection ached.

"I screamed," said Liv. "But they moved me where no one could see or hear me."

Farida would know better than to scream. She would consider herself lucky, he knew, to be pulled into a place where no one could witness the shame she had so boldly courted by revealing her face to men.

Liv groaned again in her sleep. Martin moved closer. He touched her bare thigh. She didn't move. Her breathing continued soft and regular.

"I went numb. I couldn't move. I tried to make my mind blank. I just wanted it to be over. But they wouldn't stop."

Of course they wouldn't. They couldn't. No man could. Martin imagined Farida still and submissive in his arms.

"A man pushed his hand . . . there." Liv had gestured vaguely behind her.

Farida would accept her fate. Martin thought of the pomegranates in their bins at the market, their taut skin, the sweet shock of the ruby interior. These sorts of things happen here all the time, he told himself. It's the way things are.

"Farida, Farida," he whispered, moving urgently between Liv's thighs, realizing only afterward that she was weeping in her sleep.

Thirty-One

Martin sat very still at his desk inside the cinder-block box that passed for the world headquarters of Face the Future, engaging in what he had come to think of as the Afghan national pastime—doing nothing for hours on end.

He'd already made the rounds of his contacts in the city. While Liv visited the women, Martin roamed among the dozens of NGOs whose offices populated Kabul and whose workers were happy for a chance to talk with another Westerner about the problems—so many problems!—they faced in this city where loyalties shifted and rearranged themselves like the crumbly soil underfoot. He made sure to tip their guards on the way out, thus ensuring clandestine meetings in chaikhanas, Ismail and his own guard just out of earshot but always close. He ate and drank as little as possible as they ranted about the injustices perpetrated upon them by members of clans and ethnic groups other than their own. He was now a regular at ISAF, where military careerists, grown-up Boy Wonders who'd stuck it out rather than opting for fat civilian paychecks, dropped the hearty we've-got-this-under-control front they maintained for the press and confided in him about flare-ups in the outlying provinces. These meetings always inspired a mixture of envy—at least these men got to act, as opposed to his own strictly defined role of observing and reporting—and relief. Because acting meant being in the shit.

But now he was alone. He assumed that the other Face the Future staffers had found ways of their own to spend an afternoon of indolence, at least until four o'clock, when someone would materialize at his elbow bearing the inevitable tray with teapot and cups. A rattling fan lifted a curtain of dust. Motes veiled the air, then sifted to the floor, only to be scooped up again as the fan rotated back with a clatter.

Martin studied the wall. Bright posters advertising Face the Future's mission in English, Dari, and Pashto covered the cracks and chips in the uneven concrete. Women and girls looked into the camera and smiled broadly as they crowded together on rough schoolroom benches, or bent with great determination over computer keyboards in offices much like the one in which he sat. The posters, Martin knew, bore no relation to reality, any more than they related to the contents of his locked desk drawers, crammed with fast-fattening files on arms stockpiles, the movements of different militias, and detailed notes on individual warlords. No longer did he need to pepper Liv's reports with falsehoods. Reality—gleaned with increasing ease from other NGO workers and some of the more inexperienced journalists—had quickly sufficed.

"But what of the training programs?" he'd emailed the director recently, trying to get a sense of just how closely Face the Future was to adhere to its ostensible mission.

"We can't design appropriate training until we know everything possible about the society we're dealing with," came the reply. "Better to spend months in preparation than inadvertently alienate people because of an imperfect understanding of conditions, especially the security conditions."

"What a crock," Liv snorted when he showed it to her. After which, he no longer shared the emails. The longer Martin was in-country, the more he agreed with the director's approach and that of his new ISAF acquaintances. Remnants of the Taliban were already regrouping, fire-bombing girls' schools and bullying village elders. Whenever Liv and Farida were away from the office, he turned to his own research, the ISAF officer's words echoing in his brain. *Any information we can get helps. And we need it yesterday.*

The fan, wobbling back through its arc, stopped halfway. The dust settled into a clump, its descent nearly audible in the sudden silence that signaled the daily intermittent loss of electricity. His shirt dampened within seconds. The summer sun grew fiercer by the day. With the fan quieted, the street noises—the creaking wheels of wooden carts, arrhythmic hoofbeats, and the incessant blaring of horns—asserted themselves. Martin wondered how people found the energy to move about in the pressing white glare of midday. He couldn't even summon the energy to step outside and start the generator.

He looked around the room to reassure himself that it was, indeed, empty, then slid open a desk drawer and pulled an envelope from beneath a file. It was wrinkled from the time it had spent in his jacket pocket, its cheap paper already yellowing, its flap long ago steamed open. He pulled the letter from the envelope and reread it, although he could have recited it from memory, so often during the last weeks had he read Mrs. Khan's words to her sister: "I have arranged it so that you will work for the same organization with which I work here. You must ask the Amriki couple to help you return home," Mrs. Khan had written in English, in flowing, confident script. "I cannot imagine what you must be enduring there. It makes me ill to think of you in that place."

Martin told himself yet again it was long past time to give Farida the letter. Even though she had no password allowing access to the office computers, at some point Farida would discover her sister was trying to contact her. But Martin was sure that if he showed Farida the letter, she would seek his help in leaving immediately. His guilt warred with despair at the thought of the office without Farida's enchanting presence, the tedium of days alone with the Afghan staff broken only by infrequent meetings with leaders of other equally dispirited NGOs. And, of course, there would still be Liv, with her increasingly pointed suspicions, her resentments, her clanging hurt silences, longer and more pronounced since the unfortunate incident in the market. She'd said she hadn't been raped, but the way she carried on these days—bracing a chair under the doorknob at night, flinching whenever Ismail or any of the male staff came near, eyes swollen with furtive tears—you'd think she had.

Just a little longer, he told himself. His imagination hurried agreeably along well-traveled paths. Let Farida get to know him better, expose her to the freedoms of a different sort of life. Then maybe she would want to bypass Pakistan altogether and go directly to the United States and, once there . . . well, anything could happen. He sensed movement and stuffed the letter back into the envelope, then tucked it beneath the file and closed the drawer. He picked up a pencil and twirled it, trying to look busy.

Liv stood in the doorway. "What's new?"

He shrugged, the movement exaggerating the discomfort of his sweat-soaked shirt. "It looks as though we've created a prison at Guantánamo. In Cuba," he added, in response to her blank look. "It's an old U.S. military base."

"We?"

"The government."

"Why is the government building a prison in Cuba? And what does that have to do with us?"

"It's for the terrorists." He caught her look. Liv was increasingly skeptical—vocally so, in a way that sometimes made things uncomfortable for Martin—of the seemingly indiscriminate sweeps that netted dozens of Afghans and labeled them all terrorists.

"Terrorists. You mean the mujahideen? People fighting for their country?"

Martin braced himself for one of her outbursts. But she contented herself by following up with a listless jab.

"What are you doing? Filing another one of your so-called humanitarian reports?"

"I'm not doing anything."

She went to her desk and punched at the keyboard. "Power off again?"

"Yes."

"What are you doing about it?"

"Nothing." He thought it was the only way he had appeared to adapt to Afghanistan. The national torpor had so seeped into his consciousness that these days it merely exasperated him. Whenever he went over to the old presidential palace, whose high-ceilinged rooms with their painted-over bullet scars and gouged parquet floors housed innumerable bureaucracies, the guards at the front gate routinely ignored him until they had finished watching the latest Bollywood music video on a generator-powered television, the grainy black-and-white screen full of young women with bare arms and bellies, shaking prodigious amounts of flesh. The guards leaned forward, openmouthed, as though they did not spend all day, every day, watching spectacles exactly like this one. Martin often thought, as he waited and waited in the heat, that a terrorist could have parked himself in front of them, planted a bomb at their feet, and smilingly triggered the detonator without the guards ever having known what hit them. It made him wonder if maybe the Taliban hadn't had a point, banning music and television as unacceptable distractions.

He could imagine Liv's disgust if he were ever to voice such a thought. She had dived into her make-work duties, combining anecdotes from the interviews with whatever statistics she could glean into memos that she emailed to the United Nations, and to various corporations and wealthy people back in the United States, seeking support for the NGO's work. Martin did not think it necessary to tell her that Face the Future's emails queued up for a batch transmission every twenty-four hours, and that he reviewed them all, editing her reports or deleting them entirely as he saw fit—along with the increasingly frantic incoming emails from Mrs. Khan. Liv's way of coping with the aftermath of her experience in the market was to keep busy, even though that left her preoccupied and even obsessed. But that was another thought he kept to himself.

"Listen to this." Liv brandished her most recent collection of outrageous statistics. It didn't matter that they were at their favorite restaurant, one of the few still deemed safe for foreigners.

It was across the street from the cinema that had been shut down by the Taliban but was now enjoying a brisk resurgence. She was the only woman in the main dining room, as was frequently the case. Afghan women, fully shrouded in their burqas, when they came with their husbands and children moved quickly through the dining room into a curtained space beyond for families.

"One in four children dies before the age of five. We're talking something similar to the scale of HIV in Central Africa. Except that we don't need expensive antiretrovirals to fix this. Just clean water, antibiotics, adequate nutrition—that's half the battle. How hard is that? Because at some point, these sorts of things are part of Face the Future's mission. Aren't they?"

Whenever Liv went on one of her rants, Martin thought of Farida, of how she moved with quiet efficiency around their small office, rarely speaking. Sometimes, she would stand silently at his side, waiting until he noticed her there, before bringing something to his attention. When she spoke, always in a murmur, she bent her head and gazed at some point on his desk. The rare occasions when her glance slid across his stayed in his memory.

He sometimes wondered whether Liv's manner had indeed changed, or whether she just seemed increasingly strident the longer he went without being around Western women. She waved computer printouts in her left hand. With her right, without looking, she scooped up bits of meat and rice in a torn piece of naan, nimbly bringing it to her mouth.

Martin pushed his own food around with a fork. "How do you get the antibiotics to them? Fill up a jeep with pills and drive out to the villages? Oh, wait. I forgot there's no road. And the trails are still mined."

"Maybe if ISAF took those damned trucks out of Kabul once in a while instead of tying up traffic here—"

Martin cut her off. "You know they're targets. It's bad enough for them in town. Do we have to go over all of this again?"

The waiter brought a salad, as he always did, even though Martin always asked him not to. During their first week in Kabul, he'd made the mistake of eating a kiwi—after first washing it in a bleach solution, then peeling it—an experience that despite his precautions brought home the inadequacies of Face the Future's little toilet.

"Honestly, Martin," Liv had said on the second day, handing two buckets through the bathroom door, one of warm, soapy water so that he could clean himself, the other to help the toilet flush, "just use the hole in the floor. That's what I do. Why not take advantage of a system that has worked for centuries?"

It infuriated him that Liv rarely got sick. She bit into a slice of *kharbooza*, the sugary white melon frequently served as dessert, its delicate color and flavor making cantaloupe and honeydew seem garish and cloying by comparison.

They sat at long tables that ran the length of the room, well away from another part of the dining area, where men lolled on carpets on a raised platform, reclining against cushions as they ate. The space beneath the platform was inadequately curtained. Boys squatted there, rinsing heads of lettuce at a streaming tap that Martin was sure spewed little better than raw sewage. Goats lurked and shat nearby, snatching at the lettuces before becoming meals themselves. Martin's stomach knotted. He always ordered his meat barbecued, reassured that it sat directly above the glowing coals in the braziers on the sidewalk just outside, where other boys waved rubber fans to coax the low flames that, Martin hoped, charred every last microbe. Two of the boys snared one of the goats and dragged it from beneath the platform and around behind the restaurant. It bleated and kicked within their grasp. Those awaiting their meals laughed in anticipation. The restaurant was famed for the freshness of its meat.

Martin felt another forceful tug in his gut. He hoped he wouldn't have to use the restaurant's latrine, with its ubiquitous green plastic pitcher beside the hole. He carried folded squares of toilet paper wherever he went. He looked away as Liv finished her last slice of melon, then ran her finger through the juice left on the plate.

"You don't have to eat like that, you know. They expect us to use these." He held up his fork. Her fingertips were stained red with the spices from the lamb. He hoped the melon had distracted her. It hadn't.

"We're not making one goddamned bit of difference here. I tell you these things, and you talk to me about how I eat. You, touching your food with your left hand, talk to me of etiquette."

"Christ, Liv." He dropped his fork. It thudded against the table's greasy plastic cloth. Around them, turbaned heads lifted again. Sometimes, the scrutiny he attracted whenever he was out in public made Martin feel as though he were on television. "I don't wipe my ass with my hand." Martin had no idea whether those around them understood English, and didn't really care. "So it's okay that I touch my food with it. Don't you think that to pretend to be anything other than who we are is to insult them? Or to invite trouble? You of all people should know that. You think of yourself as Farida's friend, but don't think she doesn't know she's just your pet."

Liv's eyes seemed pale and lost within their heavy outlines of kohl. Her hands fell to the table, her painted fingernails digging into the scarred wood. Her voice dropped to a whisper.

"Only a friend would do what she did for me. You know exactly what would have happened to me if it hadn't been for Farida."

Thirty-Two

Of course word of Liv's assault had gotten out. Embers of gossip smoldered among the shopkeepers and even the wives doing their shopping, catching flame with the drivers and cabbies, becoming puffs of noxious smoke that coiled through the bars of the gates guarding the NGOs and the ISAF compound. By then it was all so distorted that Martin believably smothered it with a roll of his eyes.

"Some people said something to her, that's all. It got blown way out of proportion. She wasn't even sure what they said—just the tone. You know how things are these days."

And they did know, chiming in with tales of far worse incidents, ones that quickly erased all talk of whatever had or hadn't happened in the bazaar, and to women, after all. Liv dropped—mostly—her foolish idea of notifying the authorities. Martin breathed easier. Life resumed, normalcy underscored by yet another daytime power failure that erased everything from his computer screen, leaving it a mocking blank.

"Goddamn it." It came out weary, more plea than curse.

Liv sat across the room, her back to him, bent over a report she was editing by hand. She did not turn, but merely lifted her pencil and waggled it accusingly. While even pens ran out of ink, she was fond of saying, a pencil never broke down. "Did you save it?"

He cursed again, more emphatically. Liv put pencil back to paper.

"When in Afghanistan," she said. She wrote most of her reports by hand now, later retyping them into the computer.

"That's your solution? To go back to the eighteenth century? That's the problem with this country. They're content to live like this."

Liv's back stiffened. "Maybe not content," she said. "Maybe they have more to worry about than your report."

It was always this way now. No matter how reasonable his complaint—really, was it too much to expect reliable electricity in a city of three million people?—Liv met it with a calm, exasperating acceptance.

He pushed back from the desk, chair scraping loudly across the concrete floor. "That's why nothing ever changes here. Everybody just shrugs and says, 'This is Afghanistan,' and so nothing ever gets fixed. And now you're doing it, too."

"Yes, Martin sahib." It was her new term for him, implying that he was some sort of condescending colonialist. There was a routine in these sharp exchanges. Martin criticized Afghanistan, Liv criticized Martin, in a back-and-forth of rising voices and well-placed barbs that led to another evening of tense silence, and a night where each kept to his or her side of the bed.

Bad enough that Liv said these things at all, but she hardly confined them to their home. On this day, Farida moved about the office, silent as usual, her face a lovely mask as Martin fumed about the failure of the generator. "How is it that we ran out of gasoline? I gave— What's the new one's name? The one who needs a bath. I gave him money just a couple of days ago. He probably pocketed it. Now I've lost all my work."

"I don't think it's Hamidullah's fault that ISAF bought up all the gas this week." Martin took Liv's easy recall of the new guard's name as the rebuke it was meant to be, and seethed at her showing such open disrespect before Farida.

"Is that true, Farida? Did ISAF take the gas?"

"I don't know why there is such a shortage of petrol." She stood before an open file drawer, addressing its contents.

"Thank you, Farida." He pitched his voice lower, as he always did when he spoke to her. He wanted her to notice how he appreciated her, but she never gave him any sort of acknowledgment, speaking to him in the same cool, impersonal tone she used with everyone except Liv.

Liv stood and stretched. "I'll go talk to Hamidullah about the gas, and then I'm going home. Everyone else here takes a midday break, and we should, too. It's too hot to work."

Farida grimaced. Martin thought he knew why: Hamidullah was markedly uncomfortable in Liv's unveiled presence, averting his eyes and scowling theatrically. Well, let her talk to him. For all her vaunted understanding of the poor, benighted Afghan people, she'd get nowhere.

The door closed behind her. Martin rested his head in his hands and rubbed his eyes, ever sore from the constant scrub of the dust in the air. He wanted nothing more than to go back to the house and read the three-week-old issue of *Time* magazine that had arrived in the mailbag on the morning's flight, but he did not relish the chill of Liv's presence. Taking a walk was out of the question; he would have to wait until the next day, at the combined meeting of NGO administrators and ISAF brass, to see if he could find a few people to accompany him on another outing to Chicken Street. Although he referred to all the merchants there as Ali Baba, he enjoyed the brief sensation of normalcy involved in a simple stroll.

A drawer closed. "I have finished the filing. Is there anything else you need?"

Martin crossed the floor to the file cabinet and pulled open the top drawer. He had never been alone in the office with her before and wanted to prolong the moment. He chose a file at random. Farida turned up the file behind it, marking its place. Martin opened the folder and found a report. "This one. I'm unclear about it. Maybe you could explain it to me?"

She glanced at the page and looked at him in bewilderment. She looked back at the page. "The Opium Rapid Assessment Survey for November?"

"Yes." Anything to keep her there, less than an arm's length away, her increasingly lush proportions evident even within the generous disguise of her kameez. "Remind me what the summary says."

Her gaze darted to the side, and she made as if to move past him, but he leaned toward her, just enough to check the impulse. She stepped back against the drawers and began to read, her voice unsteady. He stopped her after a few sentences. "You are feeling well? The baby?"

"Yes, yes, I am fine." But she didn't look fine. She gestured with a shaking hand toward a chair across the room. "Maybe I need to sit down."

Martin took her arm, thrilled to touch her. She tried to pull away, but he tightened his grip. "Here. Lean on me."

Now her whole body trembled. "Please. You shame me."

"Farida." He moved his hand up her arm as he spoke. "You have nothing to be ashamed of. Why do you hide yourself?" With his free hand, he reached for the dupatta she wore indoors at Face the Future. Once, she had draped it loosely, but lately she wore it low on her forehead and wrapped beneath her chin, so that not a strand of hair showed, a disappointment to Martin. The dupatta fell to Farida's shoulders. She tried to pull it back onto her head as he stroked her hair.

"In our country, an educated woman like you would never be a file clerk. You would hold a high position. You could be my research assistant. You would receive a good salary. It's what your sister wanted." He remembered she'd never seen the letter, and hurried on. "I could arrange for free housing on campus for you. You should come back to Amrika—to America—with us. With me." He untangled his hand from her hair and touched her face, so soft compared to Liv's sun-roughened skin. His fingers came away damp. Tears of gratitude, he thought. "I know you can't say anything. But I'll get you out of here. I promise."

Emboldened by her silence—she would dare not cry out; he knew as well as she that to draw attention to this moment could bring death—he moved closer. She let the dupatta fall and struck at his chest. "Stop! You must not."

He moved closer still, pinning her hands with his own, his body pressing against her belly. He sensed the motion within. It made him feel even more protective. "Your baby, too. I'll take care of it. School, everything it needs. You won't believe how different everything is there." He folded her in his arms and pressed his lips to her cheek, taking care to be gentle so as not to frighten her further. She jerked back. He wrapped one arm tighter still around her. The other moved to her chest.

She started, and at first he thought she was responding to his touch, so he touched his mouth to hers, softly, softly, hardly believing this was finally happening. But she wrenched her head away and looked past him.

"Oh, no," she breathed. "No."

Martin turned, his hand still on the front of Farida's kameez.

Liv and Hamidullah stood in the doorway, each holding a jerry can of gasoline for the generator, Liv pale and gaping, Hamidullah looking at Farida for the first time, his expression both triumphant and knowing, his lips forming a single word:

"Whore."

Thirty-Three

Farida stumbled into the street, arms windmilling, beseeching passing cabs.

Some drove past—a woman alone, it was not proper—but finally one slowed. Farida hesitated when she saw the Hazara driver, but then reminded herself that he had, after all, stopped. The man's face was kind, and a little tired, and she said her thanks as she fell into the car and urged him to drive quickly to Gul's family home. The driver looked surprised as she named the neighborhood whose women surely did not customarily go out alone, but he drove her there without comment and gravely accepted the outrageous tip she offered him.

She nodded to the guard at the gate, trusting in the sort of slow stupidity that, while he noted the strangeness of her arriving alone, would not think—not immediately—to inquire further. She paused outside the house, trying to catch her breath. Inside were the aunties, who would beset her with questions the minute she entered, wondering why she was home so early, and unaccompanied by Gul. She glanced down the street, fearing the sight of Hamidullah. But no, she reminded herself, he would not confront her. That would be the job of the men of the family. She wondered when it would come—soon, she knew—and how they would do it. She knew well the story of Gul's cousin's wife, and she thought, too, of the cooking fire. But the fire was how women killed. Men would most likely use knives, and it would be men who dealt with her transgression.

Or—Farida shuddered at a possibility she had not considered in her panicked flight—what if Hamidullah bypassed the men of the family entirely and went to the courts? There was only one punishment for an adulteress, as she would surely be judged. She imagined herself buried upright to her chest, the dirt banked tight against her, pinning her elbows to her sides, the roar of the crowd dimmed by her own panic. Would the first stone kill her? Or would it take many? She pressed her hand to her stomach and moaned. "Oh, my poor baby."

She looked at the step. There was no customary heap of large sandals. So Nur Muhammed and his group were meeting elsewhere today. A wise precaution, she thought, given that their plan was so near fruition. She eased indoors. Footsteps shuffled nearby, a servant probably, or maybe even one of the aunties. She slipped through the nearest door, into the men's sitting room, pressing herself against the wall until the person passed. For the moment, at least, she was safe.

She drew back her burqa, trying to still her breathing, and glanced around, curiosity driving a tiny wedge into the enormity of her terror. So this was where they planned their big secrets, this ordinary room with its showy sofas of leather and brass upon which no one sat, preferring instead the floor's thick carpet. A few dusty silk flowers sat in vases, but the room was otherwise empty of adornment, save for a large chest.

Her eyes widened. That must be where they kept the device. The baby kicked, hard, demanding attention. Her bookish mujahid, in whom she'd invested such hope. Now he'd never have the chance to defeat his people's enemies with his superior skills.

Unless.

She crossed the room, steps soundless on the carpet, and tested the chest's ornate latch. Locked. She tugged at it in despair, then stood back and studied its simple design, merely a larger version of the tiny tin lock that had inadequately protected the pages of her sister's childhood diary. Farida almost smiled at the memory. She pulled a pin from her hair. She jabbed too hard at first. The pin bent in her trembling hand. She reached for a new one, closed her eyes, and let the remembered movements come back to her. The lock fell open with a metallic click so loud that Farida feared it would alert everyone in the household.

She steeled herself and opened her eyes to see . . . a stack of folded blankets. An audible whimper escaped. She caught her breath, fearing she'd given herself away, but sensed only the normal sounds and aromas of life in the women's quarters: the scent of baking bread, the rhythmic chopping of vegetables being prepared for dinner, the occasional faint laugh at the outrageous gossip of the day. Farida thought of the times she had chafed at the incessant fixation on domestic topics, but now she strained toward the tranquillity of the kitchen, where the women would be helping themselves to a light midday repast. She forced herself to think of the fate that awaited her. Never once had she heard of a woman being shot for infidelity. Nothing so easy would suffice. There was no *if* about her impending death. The only thing she could control was the how.

She plunged her hands into the chest, feeling beneath the blankets. *There.*

Even though she had heard about it for so long, eavesdropping outside the door, the innocuous appearance of the device within was almost disappointing, the row of cylinders, the tangle of wires, all of it tucked into pockets sewn into a simple muslin waistcoat. She studied it, trying to remember what they had said of its operation.

A car slowed outside. Gul, or Hamidullah, or Nur Muhammed, or maybe all three together, would likely arrive at any moment. She flung aside her burqa and lifted the waistcoat—it was heavier than it looked— and shrugged into it, pulling the burqa over it. The cylinders bumped against her belly. Within, the baby shifted in protest. She yanked the tiered earrings from her lobes and tossed them to the carpet, unfastened her necklaces and eased the bangles over her swollen hands. They followed the earrings in a gleaming heap of gold, the bride price that had marked her as a valued commodity.

She pulled a book from her satchel and flung it onto the heap. Then, wriggling two fingers into her shoe, she extracted the roll of Pakistani rupees that Gul had returned to her after she walked into Afghanistan. She sat it atop the book. She thought again, and scooped up some of the money. She cracked the door, looked both ways, and hurried from the home and into the street, walking quickly around the corner, gasping with the unexpected exertion. Now where?

Her breathing eased. She knew. She'd always known where. And whom.

She hailed another cab and settled herself within it. A phrase from *Alice* came to her: "It's no use going back to yesterday because I was a different person then." She thought of the self she was about to become and directed the driver to Face the Future's compound.

For perhaps the final time, she gave thanks for the shield provided by the burqa, as she pressed her hands tight against her stomach to embrace her child. At least no one could see her tears.

Thirty-Four

Gul left the shopkeeper's stall as he always did, in haste and shame.

Daily, he fought the need that drove him back to Khurshid; daily, he found himself lingering longer with her. He felt even worse after the shopkeeper reluctantly accepted his assignment from Nur Muhammed.

"You will be hailed as a martyr. Your son will be taken care of," Nur Muhammed assured the man. Gul assumed an unfortunate accident would be arranged for the son within a few weeks, and that the shopkeeper probably knew as much. But one did not say no to Nur Muhammed. Still, the man naturally wanted to spend as much of his time left as possible with Khurshid, and he could barely bring himself to be civil to Gul, who waited outside the shop in the morning for her to arrive.

Gul consoled himself with the thought that he paid the man handsomely for the privilege of enjoying her first, and that he also paid for her to visit the *hammam* and clean herself before the shopkeeper took his own, abbreviated, turn.

Still, no matter how much he paid the man, not to mention the money he gave Khurshid, he could not cleanse his soul of the stain of consorting with a whore. He became rougher with Khurshid as a result, biting the tender flesh of her buttocks, commanding her to do this thing and that. But as she knelt before him, taking him into her mouth in a perversion he had heard about but never dared imagine, he assured himself that her actions were proof of the depraved nature that deserved the treatment Nur Muhammed had inflicted upon her so many years before.

When he came home from such encounters and glimpsed Farida sitting among the women, placid and heavy with his child, he experienced such confusion that he could not bring himself to spend time in her presence. Farida was everything Khurshid was not, he told himself, a loyal and dutiful wife, and even quite pleasing at night. But he remembered his early doubts about her, the suspicions raised by her ease in dealing with the foreigners. Did his wife, too, harbor a wanton in her soul? Given the right circumstances, could Farida end up kneeling before a near stranger with such apparent enjoyment?

These thoughts tormented him at night and sent him rushing back in the mornings at a too-early hour to the market, where he impatiently awaited Khurshid's arrival. He no longer waited a seemly interval before hurrying into the room behind the shop and pushing her to the floor. He never bothered to unroll the mat or remove his own clothes, although he always insisted that she be naked. Her back soon was a mass of scrapes from the shopkeeper's rough wool carpet, and her arms bore circles of bruises from the fevered intensity of his grasp.

Sometimes he berated her for her choice of occupation. At first, she listened to his comments in silence, but more recently, she had begun to respond with pointed simplicity.

"You are right. I am a harlot. You will return tomorrow, yes? The same time? Perhaps earlier?"

He flung money at her then and fled the place, as eager to leave as he had been to arrive. The time with Khurshid mandated a visit to the hammam on the way home, where he sat sweating away her scent in clouds of steam, resolving to make each day with her his last.

Because this was no time for such frivolity. His father's plans had been approved by whatever faraway puppetmaster had elevated Nur Muhammed and were nearly complete. Staff members from several of the NGOs, along with commanders from ISAF, were to assemble at Face the Future the following day. The device had been prepared and the shopkeeper schooled in how to use it. Heavier weapons secreted away, ready to be trained at the ISAF posts that surely would be abandoned when troops rushed to Face the Future. At the thought of the shopkeeper, it occurred to Gul, not for the first time, that his death would leave Khurshid bereft of her main source of income. The man had suggested as much, his voice tentative and pleading as he raised the issue with Nur Muhammed as they left their last meeting.

"It's not just my son," the man said. "There is a woman."

Nur Muhammed laughed with sympathetic approval. "That kind of woman! You were thankful when I gave her to you, and yet you had no objection when I arranged for my son to have her."

Gul held his face immobile. So his father deliberately had thrown Khurshid into his path. Nur Muhammed must have divined his growing love for his wife, an inconvenient emotion, one that led men to do foolish things, take unnecessary risks. Was there no end to how the man contrived to control him? Cold reality doused his flaring anger. He had thought of keeping Khurshid for himself after the shopkeeper's death, but he knew he would have no way of ensuring that, as soon as he left her company, she would not invite the attentions of other men. As much as it had tormented him to imagine her with the foolish shopkeeper, his brain burned anew at the idea that she might be lying with others as young as he.

So, congratulating himself on his resolve, he told Khurshid—again—that truly he would come to her no more.

But she did not tease him as usual. "Of course. Because tomorrow . . ." She let the word linger, her face somber.

He started. "What do you know about that? Does"—he could not bring himself to name the shopkeeper—"*he* discuss . . . things . . . with you?"

"I am not so stupid as you think." A flash of tolerant amusement in her eyes, a fleeting expression that but for its sardonic overlay reminded him of Khurshid as he'd first met her, still a girl. A girl-turned-woman who'd experienced every conceivable degradation yet shrugged away humiliation as though it were an unworthy, ill-fitting garment.

She took his hand, her voice low, urgent. "You don't have to do it. The Amriki will not rest until they've found you, all of you. You could leave this place. Think of your child. Take your wife—Farida. Yes, I know her name. If you care for her, you will take her today. Go to Pakistan."

"You must not speak of her!" How dare she presume to utter Farida's name?

Gul scrambled to his feet, yet still she clutched at him, nearly wailing. "You must listen to me. I know something of survival."

He flung her away, so hard that she fell.

She lay still and silent then, looking up at him, and he saw himself reflected in the stormy darkness of her eyes, standing over her as Nur Muhammed had done those many years ago, meting out undeserved punishment.

"I am sorry." The apology—to a woman!—slipped out before he could stop it. And again. "I am sorry."

He rushed from the room, even as she shrugged into her burqa, calling after him. Hailed a cab and leapt in, cursing the driver, urging him faster through the maze of slow-moving vehicles and animals, anything to escape the tear-blurred vision of Khurshid in her green burqa.

———

He ordered the cabdriver to let him out some distance from home and walked the final blocks, trying to calm himself.

He was right to extricate himself from the evil charm Khurshid had cast upon him. Farida would have the baby in a few weeks. He reminded himself of the pleasures of her ripe and willing body, one that had known none but him.

At least—he strode faster as fury seethed anew in his brain—none that he knew of. What might she have done in her years among the foreigners? He recalled the reassuring stain on their wedding sheet during the traditional display to relatives, and tried to steady himself. Such confusion was yet more evidence of the darkness that had come of knowing Khurshid. He slowed as he approached the house. Nur Muhammed missed nothing, and even a hint of distraction at this crucial time would displease him mightily.

Gul rounded the corner and stopped. There, as though he had divined Gul's thoughts, stood Nur Muhammed, and beside him, the Talib Hamidullah, their faces dark as the terrible storms that formed over the Hindu Kush. Anguished wails arose from the women's quarters.

Nur Muhammed beckoned him. "Something has happened," he began, "something you must know."

His face swam before Gul's eyes, distorted, although his words were too clear. Gul forced himself to focus instead on the glowering visage of Hamidullah, standing just behind his father. It would not do to show emotion before one so loathsome, necessary though he was. Even as he struggled to grasp the news, Gul caught himself questioning Hamidullah's motives, casting aside his own recent suspicions about Farida, permitting himself the briefest moment of doubt. Blood thrummed in his ears. His breath came short. It was all too much—Khurshid's revelation that she knew of their plan, her plea for him to flee, her near-blasphemous utterance of his wife's name and his own instinctive defense of Farida's honor, and now this apparent proof that there was no honor to defend.

He pounded at his head with his fist to clear it. The sounds of traffic came back to him. Indoors, the women carried on so extravagantly that surely the neighbors would soon know everything.

"I told them to get rid of all of her things," Nur Muhammed said. "Burn her clothing, throw her jewelry into the river. We must not taint anyone by letting them touch something that has belonged to so evil a one."

Gul did not yet trust his voice. Still, he felt his lips form a question: "My son?"

A shadow of pity crossed Nur Muhammed's face. "Yours?" he said, so quietly that even Hamidullah, hovering, could not hear. "She is very large. Is it possible she was pregnant when—" The ugly implication needed no elaboration.

Gul knew then what must be done. In such a situation, no man had a choice. He felt his father's eyes upon him. Gul's next words came unbidden. "Where is the whore and her bastard child?"

The rigidity drained from his father, and Gul knew only then that Nur Muhammed had wondered whether his son was capable of doing the right thing. "No one has seen her. But it won't be long. Come, we must prepare ourselves." Irritation tinged his words. "An unfortunate complication," he muttered, "just a day before our action."

He moved toward the house, Hamidullah following.

Gul stood a minute, thinking. Farida surely knew the consequences of what she had done, knew that among her own people, there would be no escape. But what of her friend, the foreign woman? "Wait," he said as his father and Hamidullah reached the door. "I know where she is. She'll go back to That Place. Those People."

"Then we must hurry," said Nur Muhammed. "We must stop her before she reaches there. Nothing about That Place can attract attention before tomorrow. Come. The knives."

Gul and his father rushed into the men's quarters. There, they stopped so abruptly that Hamidullah nearly stumbled into them. The chest stood open. Nur Muhammed crossed the room in two steps and buried his arms in the chest, feeling beneath the blankets. "It's gone. Who . . . ?"

For the first time in his life, Gul saw fear in his father's eyes.

He pointed to the gold bangles scattered on the floor, as if flung away. Filigreed earrings and heavy gold necklaces, their clasps broken, lay tangled together beneath a small book, its cover bound in worn red leather. Farida kept the book with her always, a keepsake, she had told Gul, of her childhood. He had thought the book sounded silly—something about talking animals and a British girl who got bigger and smaller—but Farida said it reminded her of her own journey from life among the foreigners to her happiness with him. His heart lurched.

Gul imagined his wife, the bomb already wrapped around her pregnant belly, taking a few precious seconds to strip herself of the jewelry his family had given her, to leave behind even the book. He peered more closely at the mess on the floor. Yes, there was the wad of rupees he had replaced for her that day so long ago, after she had stumbled into his country on her bleeding feet.

His father and Hamidullah took wicked Afridi knives with their straight stabbing blades from where they hung on the wall and tucked them discreetly beneath their tunics. Gul grabbed a knife of his own and followed them, fighting the impossible, forbidden desire to save his wife.

Thirty-Five

"Stop here," Farida told the cabdriver when they were still two blocks from Face the Future.

She handed him most of her remaining rupees—far more money than the ride was worth. The man called down the praises of Allah upon her as she stepped from the car. They had halted in front of a restaurant popular with foreigners. A crowd of pitiful widows clustered before it, swarming customers as they entered and left. The restaurant owner burst into their midst, lashing this way and that with a whippy bamboo staff until they scattered, only to regroup as soon as he'd gone back indoors. Farida beckoned to one of the women, in an especially ragged cotton burqa, so filthy its blue had gone gray, and motioned the woman to follow her into an alley.

The woman hesitated when Farida told her what she wanted. "The shoes, too?" Doubt laced her voice.

"Yes, and quickly." Farida stepped out of her own embroidered slippers, tight on her pregnancy-swollen feet, and slid almost gratefully into the woman's cracked rubber sandals. She waited until the woman began peeling off her burqa before doffing her own. The crone's eyes widened at the sight of the apparatus stretched around Farida's waist. Farida threw the foul garment over her body, then advanced on the woman, gripping her throat and putting her face so close she could almost taste the coppery fear on the woman's breath.

"Not a word." She tightened her hand around the woman's throat. "Not one. Do you hear me? If you tell, the people who do this"—she patted at her abdomen, pushing the cloth against her so as to briefly outline the cylinders—"they will come for you and they will find you. Do you understand?" She slipped the rest of her money into the woman's hand. "Stay here. In this alley. Until—you'll know when. It won't be long, *inshallah*."

"Allah!" the woman wailed. Farida whirled and hissed at her before digging her hands into the dust of the alley, grinding her palms together until they bore a convincing layer of grime. The woman keened beside her. Farida fought an urge to stay with her, mourning aloud for lost things. Her gaze fell upon a stone, about the size of her fist, with jagged edges. She imagined it rocketing toward her, bashing against her skull as she stood pinioned to her shoulders within the earth, her baby's kicks slowing as the life leaked from her body. She forced herself to her feet.

"Goodbye, little mother," she whispered to the woman, and stepped back into the street. Farida forced herself to adopt the widows' cringing posture, their sidelong way of creeping along the street. She made her voice high and wheedling as she hunched toward Face the Future, peering through the burqa's screen.

"Please, please, a few afghanis, please. My brave husband, my mujahid, was murdered by the Amriki bombs, oh, help a poor widow, oh, oh, oh," she whined as she inched closer. Her words caught in her throat.

There, as she had feared, was Nur Muhammed's car. Beside it, scrutinizing the few women who passed, stood Hamidullah. Farida cursed the burqa's grille that so badly interfered with her vision. The two people in the car must be Gul and Nur Muhammed. She looked toward Face the Future's gate, mobbed by the usual unruly queue that gathered around any foreign establishment, men and women, futilely begging for jobs and money, begging to be saved.

Farida had hoped that, with Hamidullah gone, the gate would be unguarded, but no, Martin must have pulled someone from the crowd outside, stuck a Kalashnikov in one hand, some afghanis in the other, and appointed him guard for a day. And that man was stopping and turning away every person at the gate.

Someone touched Farida's hand. She flinched. A woman in a burqa of fine blue silk, much like the one Farida had just traded away, offered her some afghanis. The woman stood alone, unaccompanied by a husband or son, likely one of the few women who held a high position in government, hence her confident bearing.

"*Aiiii,* mother." Farida called down blessings upon the woman's head and followed close behind as the woman worked her way through the crowd at the gate, heading toward the presidential palace.

"You! Stop!"

Farida froze at the sound of Hamidullah's voice. Remembering that long-ago day when she walked into Afghanistan, she forced one foot woodenly in front of her, then the next. "One," she counted. "Two." And, between steps, "Afghanis. Please. Afghanis." Her voice quavered. She held out her hand again. It, too, shook. She bent, hoping to hide the telltale bulk of her belly.

"Stop!" Hamidullah yelled again. Someone brushed past her so roughly that she nearly fell.

"Stop!"

Hamidullah's sandals slapped against the concrete sidewalk. He reached out and unforgivably grabbed the woman who had given Farida the money. The woman screamed and whirled to face him, clutching her burqa around her. Farida heard car doors slam and knew without looking that Gul and Nur Muhammed were there.

The crowd at the gate, excited and aroused by this scene of a strange man assaulting a woman apparently of good family—albeit one walking alone—flowed up the street, the guard with them, toward Hamidullah, who shouted to the approaching throng.

"This woman has wronged her husband! She has consorted with other men. With foreigners!" Gul and Nur Muhammed pushed past Farida to follow Hamidullah.

Farida edged toward the gate, now unguarded. She glanced back and saw Gul shaking his head, even as Hamidullah yanked at the woman's burqa, trying to tug it from her head. The woman, silent for long, dangerous moments, regained speech.

"Do not touch me!" she screamed, in a voice emphatically not Farida's. "My husband will kill you. When my brothers are through with you, there will be nothing left!"

Farida gathered the tattered burqa in both hands, lifted it high above her swollen ankles and, gripping her too-big sandals with her toes, trundled through the gate, pulling it nearly closed behind her.

"What were you thinking?" Liv unclenched her fists and slid her hands beneath her thighs, inadequate insurance against the impulse to throw something at Martin, to strike him, to keep hitting him until something broke beneath her blows.

She held herself rigid on one of the rickety chairs. Martin folded into himself on the sofa, his head in his hands. "Oh, God." It was nearly the only thing he had said since she had found him.

Liv was still trying to process that first shock, a series of shocks, really—the sight of her husband kissing Farida, his stricken look as he turned and saw her, and the stark terror on Farida's face before her headlong flight from the building. Liv felt sorrier for Farida than for Martin; sympathy fast followed by a mix of relief and regret at the thought that, this time, they finally would have to go home.

She stood and busied herself preparing tea, slamming the pot onto the burner, trying to calm herself with the familiar ritual. Martin moaned again. "What have I done?"

"Funny. It seems I might be the one to ask that. What have you done?" She came back into the living room, balancing her cup of tea on a tray. She'd made none for him. The tray rattled in her shaking hands, her fury mounting by the moment.

"Nothing, I swear. Oh, God."

"You weren't doing *nothing*, Martin. You were kissing her. She's pregnant, for God's sake. What were you thinking?"

"It's not my fault."

"A pregnant woman threw herself at you?"

He bent his head to his knees and said something into his lap.

"I didn't catch that." She looked at the cup in her hand. Now that she'd made the tea, she couldn't imagine drinking it. Her throat burned with held-in rage.

"She wanted to come to the States."

"Then she would have just asked us to help her. I don't believe you, Martin."

"Oh, God. My career is finished."

My career. There it was. Nothing like the pretty words about being partners, spoken so long ago in their living room in Pennsylvania, when Afghanistan had seemed like an opportunity instead of a graveyard of lost glories. Clayton Williams, she remembered now, had been the one to use the word. Never once had Martin thought of her as a partner.

She put the teacup down—slowly, slowly—resisting the impulse to fling it in his face.

"Your career? That's always your first concern. What about me? When I was attacked, you wouldn't let me report it because of your fucking career. What about our marriage?" As if she didn't already know the answer, hadn't known it all along.

Another groan.

"You'd better pack," she said. "They'll want us out quickly. Even if what you said is true, they won't be able to afford to have you here as the focus of any sort of investigation."

"But tomorrow's meeting. I'm presenting my report."

"Do you really want to be there? By tomorrow, the whole city will know about this."

"Maybe I'll be able to work in Islamabad." He raised his head. Tears streaked his face.

Crying for himself. Oh, Martin. She searched within for sympathy. Found none.

"Maybe," she said, trying for neutrality. Islamabad was crawling with Afghan refugees. By the time the news got to Islamabad, it would likely have been entertainingly embroidered. Liv did the math. Farida had been pregnant, just, when she started working for Face the Future, but no doubt the stories would have Martin siring her child. Just another husband gone native, she could imagine them saying. It wasn't supposed to happen in the Islamic countries, but here was proof that a foreigner could no more control his own nature than a Pashtun could overlook dishonor. The last thought made Liv shiver.

"Martin. Hurry. I don't care if we take separate flights once we get to Islamabad—in fact, I'd prefer it—but we've got to go. We've already missed today's UN shuttle, but I'll book us on the one tomorrow. You do realize, don't you, that we'll be lucky to get out of here alive?"

———

Gul, hurrying with his father toward the growing crowd surrounding Hamidullah and the woman, stopped and inhaled. Surely that was Farida's perfume?

He looked about, focusing on his surroundings for the first time since his father and Hamidullah had described the unthinkable scene with his wife and That Man. But those running past him were, as usual, mostly men, their faces alight to the possibility of excitement. The only woman he saw—other than the one berating Hamidullah with increasing desperation—was a widow who slipped onto the grounds of Face the Future. Gul started to walk away, back toward the car, then looked more closely at the beggar through the gate's narrow opening. The woman moved quickly, but the heaviness of her gait seemed familiar. He glanced back over his shoulder to reassure himself that everyone else was sufficiently distracted farther down the block, then eased through the gate.

"Farida," he called in a low voice.

The woman broke into a lurching trot, heading across the compound toward the house at the far end. He glanced at her feet, swollen in cheap sandals, the toenails painted the same saucy shade of scarlet that Farida had insisted upon even as her pregnancy progressed. "I may look a cow, but I am still a woman," she'd protested when he'd teased her about it.

"Farida, wait. I am alone."

She stopped and stood with her back to him.

"They told me what happened," he ventured.

"No. They told you what they *thought* happened. That Man, that foreigner"—she sounded strangled—"he is the one you should be hunting, for what he did to me."

"But you were alone with him. He touched you. Hamidullah saw it. His hands upon you. You kissed him." Despite himself, his voice rose.

"No. No. Liv—That Woman—left me alone with him. He backed me into a corner. Forced himself upon me. What was I to do?"

Scream, he thought. Fight. Even though he knew better. No one would believe the word of a woman.

She turned to face him. "If I had had *that*"—she pointed to the knife in the hand dangling by his side—"I would have killed him myself for daring to dishonor me, our son. My husband, my love," she said, her voice full of pain, "I never betrayed you."

But he had betrayed her. Still. These things were permitted a man. A mere conversation with a neighbor had brought about the death of his cousin's wife. Decades, centuries of tradition buffeted him, constants in an uncertain world. There was only one way. His hand tightened on the reassuring hilt of the knife. He steeled himself for what must be done.

His gaze fell on Farida's feet, the silly painted toenails so bright and hopeful in their grotesque footgear, and he thought of the day she had walked across the border, bonding herself to him and his people in a way far more consequential than the simple act of marriage. The knife fell from his fingers, and instead of condemning her, he spoke the truth: "I believe you."

Her shoulders slumped. Tears glittered behind the burqa's screen. "Thank you," she whispered.

"I'll tell them. I'll fix this."

Farida straightened and looked past him.

Thirty-Six

Liv stood amid their sad collection of belongings in the living room, including the emergency suitcase she'd packed. So many months in Afghanistan, yet they'd accumulated painfully few things beyond the clothing and the books they'd brought with them, as well as a suitcase packed with trinkets and faux-pashmina shawls. There were a couple of rugs, rolled and bound within sheets tied tight with twine. They'd always meant to buy more, as gifts for relatives, but never got around to it because Martin so hated the mandatory haggling and refused to go to the markets, anyway.

For the first time since she'd seen him with Farida, Liv looked directly at Martin. The beginnings of a potbelly that he'd brought with him to Afghanistan had bloated into a full paunch. The skin of his neck puffed over his collar. His eyes were bloodshot and his hands trembled. Liv tried to remember the confident man on talk shows who delivered opinions on the situation in Afghanistan and inspired such envy among his fellow faculty members. She wondered how he'd spin their time here upon their return.

But at least they'd get to return. Farida, though . . . Liv had heard enough, during those months of talking with women, to know the fate that awaited any woman touched by a man not her husband, let alone a foreigner. Martin hadn't wanted trouble when she herself was attacked, but she'd be damned if she'd let him treat Farida—whose situation was, after all, far more dire—with the same indifference. As soon as she could slip away from Martin, she'd use the satphone to call ISAF, tell them about a woman in danger, downplaying the details, and say that the woman in question was key to their mission.

Martin cleared his throat. "When we get home . . ." he began. He fiddled unnecessarily with the twine circling one of the carpets.

"We? Martin. There is no *we*. When we get home, we'll divorce." As soon as she spoke, she wondered why it had taken her so long to come to this.

Martin gave the twine a final yank. "I'm going over to the office to pack up the files."

The door banged behind him. She'd have to wait to make that phone call. He hadn't responded to her pronouncement about divorce. Liv realized she didn't care.

Martin carried a box to the file cabinet, opened a drawer, and transferred the contents to a carton.

The electricity was still out, the hum of the computers and the drone of fans silenced. The office was deserted. The word had spread, he thought. No doubt his supervisor already was trying to contact him. He disconnected the computers and made sure the satellite phone was turned off. He'd tell the man that the satphone had run down, that the generator that powered the computers during outages was out of gas. Postponing the inevitable. He'd almost certainly be allowed to resign. It was to no one's advantage for word to go out to the wider world. The university job, the book—although maybe with a university press instead of a major publisher—remained within the realm of possibility. And with Liv about to take herself out of the picture, his daydream of bringing Farida to the States remained alive. Maybe he'd bribe Ismail to get her out of the country, at least as far as Islamabad. She could stay with her sister until he could make the necessary arrangements. He'd have to come up with an explanation for Mrs. Khan about why he'd never given Farida her letter, but he'd worry about that later.

On second thought. He crossed to the desk, retrieved the letter from its locked drawer, and without opening the envelope, ripped it in half, then quarters, then again, distributing the scraps among the various trash cans in the office. There. He could say truthfully it had disappeared, adding—again truthfully—that things had a way of going missing from the office.

He returned to the cabinet, dropped an armful of files into the box and leaned against the wall, remembering how Farida had felt against him, fragile despite her bulk. Reality, like a fanged viper, hissed at his foolish notions of rescue. He might never see Farida again.

The sounds of the streets came to him, the usual racket of horns and grinding gears, and over that, a roar that eventually separated itself into shouting male voices. Martin straightened, wiped his eyes, and carried the carton to the window. He started at Farida's husband, standing inside the gate, in animated conversation with one of the beggar widows who were a constant and bothersome presence at Face the Future's entrance. Through the partially open and unguarded gate, he saw a group of men down the street, confronting another woman. Her high, protesting voice reached him, and as he watched, she drew her burqa around her and strode away from the men, who milled about for a few moments before coalescing at some unseen signal. Fists raised, faces contorted, gathering others along the way, the mob surged back up the street toward Face the Future.

Martin dropped the box of files.

───────

Liv, making a final sweep of the bedroom to make sure she hadn't forgotten anything, heard a commotion. She looked out the window and saw a crowd of men up the street, some brandishing Kalashnikovs. She shouted for the servants, even for Martin, damnably out of earshot in the office across the compound. No one answered. From her vantage point, she could see the partially open gate, absent the guard. Maybe the men would rush past on their way to whatever had so agitated them. But what if they didn't? She thought of the men in the market, the way they'd surrounded her, her helplessness against their collective purpose.

Tinny cracks sounded, a few at first, then more, and she belatedly recognized them as shots. She ran down the stairs, grabbed at the flimsy sticks of furniture and jammed them against the door before fleeing back to the bedroom. She pulled the thin mattress from the inadequate springs and hauled it to the window that faced the courtyard. Beneath the shouting of the mob, she heard her own voice.

"Please God, please God, please God," it pleaded through chattering teeth. She leaned the mattress against the window and lay down behind it. She folded her elbows around her ears, her instructor's voice from those long-ago orientation sessions echoing in them: "Above all, protect your head."

One hand opened and closed, wishing for the Beretta on which she'd uselessly trained. She could hear the multiple shots that made one weapon against dozens impractical. She longed for the self-administered escape a gun would have provided against the mob outside. Would she have had the courage to turn the gun on herself? The mob's roar deepened. Yes, Liv thought uselessly, she would have. She squeezed her eyes shut. Her lips moved, but she couldn't hear what she was saying.

"We will find her there! The whore who consorts with foreigners! She shames us all!"

The men, led by Nur Muhammed and Hamidullah, advanced up the street with looks of anticipation. Hands disappeared beneath kameez and emerged with Afridi knives. Men scooped up the heavy chunks of broken concrete that littered the sidewalk and gutters. Those with Kalashnikovs raised them high, occasionally pulling a trigger. They moved as one, mouths open wide in bearded faces, breathing in excited unison.

Gul pulled Farida behind the gate, out of the line of sight of the approaching men. She slumped against the wall. He grasped her arms. "Where is it? The device? We must return it to them."

She felt herself falling through a long, deep darkness. There was no time to make him understand that it was too late; it was enough that he believed her.

He studied her, and then, with a quick movement, pulled the burqa from her body. As she stood frozen in shock, he lifted the device from her shoulders and draped it over his own.

"No. Please, no." She reached for him, but he stepped back, gesturing toward the device. "I will disable it. I know how. Go, now, to That Woman. You'll be safe there." He touched her, a final brush of fingertips against her cheek, then pushed her toward the house. "*Run.*"

The courtyard seemed at least an acre across. Farida stumbled toward the house, shouting and sobbing Liv's name, banging her fists against the locked door. Again she shrieked for Liv. "It's me! Farida!" Unendurable moments passed. Inside, heavy things fell. The door opened a crack. Liv peered over a jumble of furniture, her face chalky. "Dear God, what are you doing here?"

"You must help. Get the police. ISAF. Please. My husband." She turned, just in time to see someone in a ragged burqa pull the compound's gate wide and stand a moment within full view of the mob before turning and racing across the compound toward Face the Future.

———

Martin moved to drop the bar behind Face the Future's metal door. How often had he complained about the building's narrow windows that dimmed the interior, the roughness of its concrete walls? Now he gave thanks for the fortresslike aspect of both.

A widow ran ahead of the mob. Who knows what she had done to provoke their wrath? It didn't matter. He could imagine only too well her fate when they caught her. He turned away from the window so he wouldn't see. A headline flashed through his mind: "American Saves Afghan Widow." A way to erase the unpleasantness with Farida, to redeem himself.

He lifted the bar. Pushed the door open just far enough to admit the beggar. The bar crashed back into place. "You'll be safe here," he said, fishing in his fear-addled brain for the correct Pashto words as he gave the bar a final shove to secure it.

He turned and looked into the face of Farida's husband.

Farida clutched Liv's hands in her own. "You must come, you must come. The soldiers. They will listen to you. We must stop him."

"Who?" Liv dug her feet against the concrete floor. She was taller, but Farida had the strength born of terror and dragged her through the door.

"My husband. He has a bomb. Not his. Those men. But I took it from them. And then he took it from me."

"A *what?*"

"Please. We must get to him before—" Farida pushed the door open and pulled Liv into the courtyard. "Before it kills us all."

The man stood incongruous in the burqa. He pushed the headpiece up above his face but clutched the rest robelike around his body.

Martin edged away from him. *Call ISAF,* he thought. But he'd switched off the satellite phone, and powering it up involved a time-consuming series of steps. He backed against his desk, feeling behind him with one hand for something that could be used as a weapon. A pen rolled to the floor, the sound of its landing swallowed by the din outside. Blows rained upon the door. The bar jumped in its frame.

"What do you want from me?"

"I want nothing." His words were soft, silky. "I have a gift for you."

Martin's gut went liquid as he ran through the possibilities. *A knife? A bullet? The bare hands of the mob?*

"A gift from me," Gul continued. "And especially from my wife, and from our child, and from all of the Afghan people. Something for you Amriki. Something that we gave the Russians before you and the British before them and all the others who came before them."

Farida's husband reached for the bar.

"Don't!" Martin grabbed at his arm but was thrown to the floor.

The door swung open. Nur Muhammed and the others burst through.

Martin tried to crawl away, but Gul grasped his wrist and pulled him to his feet, holding him as he doffed the burqa, then moved his other hand toward his waist. Martin's uncomprehending gaze followed the motion toward what he wore there.

Farida and Liv careened into the courtyard, Liv pulling backward with all her strength, Farida dragging her implacably onward. Shouts rang out around them, and then Liv heard nothing at all.

The ground heaved skyward. Farida's hands fell away. Something slammed Liv down. Flakes brushed her face. She opened her eyes and saw a slow shower of white and thought it was snow, but no, it was summer, even though she felt cold. Bits of debris and paper sifted from the sky, landing in soft heaps atop unmoving bodies. Something was wrong with her ears. They felt as though they'd been stuffed with cotton, sound indistinguishable beyond a muffled hum. She cut her eyes to the right, afraid to move her head. Across the compound, the office was a jumble of rubble and flame. Martin had gone there. *Gone.*

She rolled her eyes to the left. Farida writhed a few feet away, one leg laid open, blood pulsing in scarlet spurts into the gray landscape. Her mouth open and closed, forming the words *my baby, my baby.* Liv forgot about her head and maneuvered onto her side. One of her arms didn't work. She dragged herself to Farida and with her good hand tried to apply pressure above the wound, but the blood leapt mockingly through her fingers. She pulled herself onto Farida and knelt atop her thigh, putting all her weight on it, screaming into the suffocating hush.

Farida!

Farida!

Farida!

Thirty-Seven

KABUL, AUGUST 2002

The man at the desk flipped open a laptop. A second man adjusted a video camera atop a tripod and aimed it at Liv. Each wore a suit and tie in a nod to the U.S. embassy's ostentatious air-conditioning against the outside heat. Despite the corporate mufti, they had economy of motion and the straight-shouldered bearing of military men. The man behind the camera pressed a button. A light glowed red.

"Full name."

"Liv Laurensen Stoellner." Face soft and swollen, a voice scraped over jagged stones.

"Age?"

She turned her face toward her questioner so that she could see him with her good eye. A trail of stitches, coarse black ends poking out like rude hairs, tugged at one side of her mouth. Two days earlier, at a military clinic in Bagram, a medic had spoken to her of luck as he tweezed slivers of glass from her head and dropped them into a bedpan. The shards had sliced through skin, he told her, but stopped short of severing muscle. As he worked, the metallic clatter of the pieces dropping into the pan turned into the tinkle of glass against glass. "I didn't get it all," he said, after a very

305

long time. "Some of these pieces will work themselves out later. Watch yourself doing the huggy-kissy thing. You're liable to cut somebody." He paused. "That was a joke. I'm trying to make you smile." Liv twitched a corner of her mouth. It was the best she could do.

"Mrs. Stoellner?" The laptop quivered as the agent whacked at the keys with knurled hands. Close-cropped hair, the color and texture of steel wool, exposed a cauliflower ear. A boxer, Liv surmised, at least in his youth, maybe even still. His suit jacket strained across shoulders and biceps, and buttoned with ease across a flat stomach.

"Forty." Barely managing a whisper, despite her efforts.

"Just speak as clearly as possible," said the man behind the camera. "Would you prefer to answer the questions in writing?"

Liv held up her right arm, heavy in its cast, by way of reply. Her fingers, fat, purple, and immobile, protruded from the plaster.

"Place of birth?" The man at the desk again.

"Minneapolis."

"Occupation?"

Liv gathered herself for a longer reply. "Until last year, I was a researcher in the library at the college where my husband taught Central Asian studies. We started working for Face the Future after 9/11."

She sank in her seat, sapped by the effort of prolonged speech. The high back of the metal chair pressed a chilly rebuke against her bare neck. She missed the protective weight of her hair gathered at her nape. She fought an impulse to rub her scalp, to trace the cobweb of stitches creeping from beneath the bandages. After so many months in a head scarf, gauze seemed an inadequate covering.

"When, exactly?"

What was the point of asking? They knew everything. "We traveled to Pakistan in February for orientation. Martin left first, and I followed him. We arrived in Kabul in April."

"What does Face the Future do?"

"It purports to provide Afghan women and girls with education and training for jobs."

The studied blankness of the agent's face told Liv he'd registered the sarcasm. He trained his eyes on the screen. "Had you been to Afghanistan before?"

Liv discovered she could speak adequately by moving the corners of the left side of her mouth. "Of course not. But my husband traveled to Pakistan in the 1980s to interview refugees from the Soviet invasion. He wanted to go to Afghanistan when the Russians left, but the civil war and then the Taliban regime made it too dangerous."

"For someone who'd never been, you seem to know a lot about the area." The agent lifted his gaze.

Liv narrowed her good eye, trying to bring him into better focus. The ear, bulbous and crenellated, defied the attempt. "Because of my job, I was able to help my husband with his research over the years."

The agent stretched thin lips and showed a few teeth in something Liv supposed was meant to be a smile. "Will I see your name in the credits of his work?"

"I assume you've examined our records. So you already know that my work is not cited."

"You understand that if we are to apprehend those responsible, we must do a thorough investigation. Sometimes that makes us appear intrusive."

Liv put a hand on the arm of the chair and boosted herself to her feet. She hobbled the two steps to the desk. The man operating the video camera tilted it upward toward her face.

"Intrusiveness," she said, "is hardly an adequate description for what you people do."

Her interrogator leaned across the desk, his hands still on the keyboard, their faces inches apart. She caught scents of soap and shaving cream and well-tended flesh.

"You're upset. That's understandable. Just a few more questions. We're interested, of course, in your friend Farida. If we can find her, she might be able to provide valuable information about the attack that killed your husband. What can you tell us about her?"

"Looks like she's lost a lot of blood," a medic had said to his partner as they strapped Liv to the backboard. His words muted, far away, her hearing only gradually returning. The world tilted as they loaded her onto a gurney.

"That's not my blood. It's hers." Farida still on the ground, a swarm of uniforms around her.

Whose?

Instinct, unbidden. "I don't know. Some woman. A beggar."

Now that same instinct stiffened her spine. She grimaced. Felt a stitch pull free. "She liked *Alice's Adventures in Wonderland*. What does that tell you?"

The camera jerked.

"When did you last see her?"

Liv gave in to the impulse to touch the gauze on her head, as though stemming an ache. Farida had been in her shalwar kameez, no burqa, when she'd come screaming to Liv's door. Had anyone in the compound seen her, recognized her? No, they'd have been drawn to the mob outside. Liv rubbed her forehead. "Earlier that morning, I think. She came by to do some filing. But she went home." Which was true.

"We've been to the family's home. No one has seen her. In fact, they denied knowing her. And her family in Islamabad has heard nothing from her since her wedding. They're in custody now, all of them, and every last one of them proclaiming ignorance. So you see why your assistance is so important."

Liv waited.

"Did you know her husband—what was his name again?" His turn to wait.

Liv's heart walloped against the walls of her chest.

"Gul," he said finally. Of course he already knew it. "Does that ring a bell? One of those people with only one name. So many of them here. Do you remember him?"

Gul. She'd never spoken with him—he'd have deemed it improper—and at first reflexively loathed him, presuming him to be yet another overbearing Afghan husband. But she'd watched from the narrow office window as he awaited Farida each evening, saw his face brighten as she appeared in the doorway, noted how he walked protectively beside her, rather than in front as did most husbands. Liv, seeing his slow smile as he turned toward Farida, had been appalled by the strength of her own envy.

The agent struck a single key. "This incident represents a dangerous escalation in tactics. Any information could be invaluable to our fight against the insurgents."

A single careless word could doom Farida to the new prison of which Martin had spoken. What was it? Something with a musical name. *Guantánamo.* She thought of Farida caged a world away from her baby, that separation as much a torment as whatever she'd encounter during the inevitable interrogations. So often, Farida had protected her. The only way Liv could repay her now was to maintain her silence.

Harsh sounds came from her throat. The agent blanched and reached into his pocket. By the time he'd extracted a handkerchief and held it out, her tears had changed to laughter, ringing clear.

"What does it matter?" Skin so newly rejoined stretched and parted. She touched a fingertip to the spot. It came away red. "People have been trying for two thousand years to subdue Afghanistan, and nobody's done it yet. Do you honestly think that your country will be the one to succeed?"

The agent balled the handkerchief in his fist. "Mrs. Stoellner. It's your country, too."

She put her good hand to the back of his laptop and shoved it shut.

Thirty-Eight

Farida cradled her baby to her chest and made sure to concentrate on the Afghan interpreter and not the Amriki medic. It would not do for anyone to know that she understood English.

"Your leg is free of infection, as is the incision from your C-section. You'll be discharged tomorrow. You will need crutches for a while—we'll send some with you."

Farida looked to the interpreter, narrowing her eyes against the constant glare. Everything in the hospital was either blinding white—the sheets, the walls, the medic's jacket—or shiny, indestructible steel. The bed frames, the trays, the instruments with which they'd ripped her son from her belly.

The interpreter stopped, and the medic spoke directly to him. "How the hell is she supposed to manage on crutches while carrying a baby? And wearing a burqa, too? With no husband, no family? The only reason she's alive at all is that they brought her here instead of one of the local hospitals. Now they'll both starve. It's inhuman."

The interpreter shrugged. Farida knew his thoughts as clearly as though he'd shouted them. *Who cares about yet another maimed Afghan, and a woman, at that?* Kabul was full of broken people.

The medic sighed and turned back to Farida. "All right—what's your name again?" He consulted his chart and addressed her with the name she'd given. "Zainab. You are to take the antibiotic pills we give you. We will discharge you with some formula for your baby, some diapers. Good luck."

Farida stared blankly at the wall until their footsteps faded. Formula. As though her son would need it. Even though her baby was delivered early, unnaturally, her milk had come in almost immediately, her breasts stretched shiny-tight, swollen with rich nourishment. She slid her gown from her shoulder and guided the baby's head. He grunted, flailing with his little fists, until his lips found the nipple. He suckled urgently, forehead wrinkled with concentration.

She bent to breathe in his scent. "My mujahid."

A miracle that he survived, the medics told her via the interpreter for whom she had no need. She'd tilted her chin in defiance. No surprise at all. *This one is a lion.* Which was the name she'd given him: Arsalan, the lion.

Her bravado faded. The medic's words hung in the air. How indeed were they to survive? She'd have to slip into a refugee camp, surround herself with the hopeless. But even so, Kabul was not safe, nor Jalalabad, nor even the place she longed for most, her childhood home, the comfort of her sister's presence. How long before Nur Muhammed's men came looking for her, for her family? She could only hope the Amriki detained her parents and Alia before his men descended upon them. The Amriki had already been sniffing around her bed once, firing questions via the interpreter.

She'd wanted to ask after Liv, but didn't dare. They'd been taken away separately, Liv pulled from her while someone wrapped her leg in a rough tourniquet, and then her water had broken and the voices around her gained a new urgency. After, when the Amriki came with their demands disguised as questions, she'd feigned frailty, had given them only the false name in the barest of whispers. *Zema num Zainab dai.* Adding, her voice gone hoarse—*kondaa.* Widow.

Which was true. She turned her head to the wall.

Now, as Arsalan trained his attention upon her other breast—oh, he was a greedy one, her son!—she fought the lingering grogginess from the drugs they'd given her. It would not take the Amriki long to match the pregnant beggar at the bombing site with Face the Future's pregnant interpreter. They would seek her just as vigilantly as Nur Muhammed's men—especially if Liv had already given her away. Because they'd question Liv, too.

No.

As before, when her thoughts traveled this panicked path, they stopped there, at Farida's recognition of something steely within her friend, something unseen by Martin. Liv would not give her away. But nor could she help her.

Arsalan's mouth slipped from her breast. His eyes closed in contentment. His breathing eased. Farida's arms tightened around him. For this brief moment, her child was safe. But within hours she'd be discharged, loosed defenseless into the world, beyond the hospital's protective walls, a death sentence in one form or another, as the medic had rightly known.

"My poor baby," she murmured. Just as she whispered before she'd stolen the device that was to have provided her escape. But Gul, believing he was saving her, had taken that route instead, and now she was trapped.

Gul. A sob escaped. She turned her head into the pillow with its stiff cotton case smelling of bleach. Her son must never see her cry. Her only hope was that they would let him live. She would face her inevitable death as bravely as Gul had his own.

———

Midnight, and Farida lay awake, clinging to her son, savoring her final hours of safety with him.

The ward lay in near darkness but for the blinking lights of the various machines. Only their faint beeping, and the scraping of a cleaning woman's twiggy broom, disturbed the silence.

Farida saw the woman, bent over her task, her green burqa dragging along the hospital's floor tiles, and thought of her old game—*at least I am not a lowly sweeper*—with bitter regret. What she would give at this moment to trade places with the woman!

The woman stopped beside the bed. The broom fell from her hand.

"*Hssst.* Farida."

Farida cringed. Was it possible that Nur Muhammed's men had sent a woman to steal her back to them? She opened her mouth to scream.

A strong hand clamped over it. "We don't have much time. Give me your baby."

Strength flooded Farida. She twisted away from the woman, clutching Arsalan tighter. This stranger would not take her baby. Never.

"Don't be stupid. I'm going to hold him while you get out of bed."

Farida stilled. The woman removed her hand, slowly, ready to slap it back down again if Farida made a sound.

"Who are you? What are you doing here?"

"We do not have time for this. I knew your husband when he was but a boy, when he was the only person in the world to treat me with kindness at a time when I was surrounded by hatred. And, later, the women of his family—those same women who hated me so—saw to it that I did not die. Now I repay that debt. Take this and give me the baby." She thrust a burqa toward Farida.

Farida pushed herself up. Pain radiated like fire from the cruel incision in her abdomen, the one through which Arsalan had escaped into the world, roaring his displeasure. She inched the burqa down over her head and eased from the bed, her leg now competing with her midsection in intensities of agony.

"Good. Come now. We must leave this hospital, and then go a little farther besides. They will remember a woman with a baby who hailed a cab in front of the hospital. We cannot risk it. Do you think you can walk so far?"

Once, many months before, a lifetime ago, there had been doubts about Farida's ability to walk a great distance, to withstand pain. She had proved them all wrong, those doubters, and won her husband's love and, even more important, his respect.

Now she would do this thing for her son. And, as before, for herself.

She brought her face close to the other woman's to look her in the eye, through the mesh of their respective burqas, blue cloth brushing green.

"I know I can."

She shoved a foot before her. *One.* Then the other. *Two.*

And so Farida counted her steps out of the Amriki hospital, into the unexpected future.

Thirty-Nine

Liv jumped at the sound of knuckles against door.

"Almost ready, Mrs. Stoellner?"

She flattened her hand against her chest, willing her slamming heartbeat into submission. "A few more minutes."

She leaned so close that her breath fogged the mirror in the shiny American bathroom, all gleaming white tile and polished hardware. In her twenty-four hours on U.S. soil, she'd already taken a shower and two baths. She rubbed her good arm against the mirror—the other had gone from a cast to a sling during her remaining time in Afghanistan—and studied the crew-cut woman who stared back. Pale hair, pale skin. Livid scar.

The female agent they'd finally assigned her had brought an assortment of cosmetics. "You'll want to look your best. Not so washed-out. And there's plenty of concealer. I got the medical kind for . . ." She touched her finger to the side of her own mouth and grimaced in something Liv supposed was meant to be empathy, despite the obvious suspicion she and the other agents radiated around Liv. "Nobody will be able to tell."

A container of mousse sat beside the cosmetics. Liv squirted some into her palm and rubbed her hands together and ran them through the lengthening stubble on her head until it stood up in tiny spikes. She located the tube of black eyeliner in the mess on the table. She drew thick lines above and beneath her lashes the way Mrs. Khan had taught her, finishing with a satisfying swoop. And some mascara. Lots. There. Her eyes flashed with new prominence, dark, dangerous. Her lips twitched. Almost a smile. Liv looked for another tube. Found three. The lipsticks the agent had brought were light, tasteful. Liv layered one atop the other, giving her mouth an angry sheen.

The scar tugged one end of her lips down in a new wry look that Liv quite liked. She picked up the concealer. "Total coverage," the label boasted. "Lasts all day." Liv let it fall. She was going to live with the scar the rest of her life. Might as well get used to it.

"Ready."

The door opened. "*Oh.* Oh, my. Maybe some adjustments . . ."

Liv brushed past the agent. "Let's get this over with."

She knew the drill, of course. How many times had she seen it on television, the movies? The victim terrified or resolute or even mutinous, take your pick. Ready, aim, fire. A barrage of shots.

Liv lifted her chin. The cameras flashed, the air alive with the sound of shutters. "Mrs. Stoellner, Mrs. Stoellner!"

She let the scar pull her mouth down, down, until the mob quieted.

"I use my maiden name professionally." A voice scraped over jagged stones. "Laurensen."

And just like that, she was in it, reciting the answers she'd spent hours rehearsing with her handlers. "Shattered," she said. "You know it's always a possibility. But nothing prepares you."

Beside her, the agent pointed to one raised hand, then another.

"How do I feel about the U.S. mission in Afghanistan? I worked for a nonprofit. We had nothing to do with the military mission. We just wanted to help Afghan women. Who need all the help they can get."

Thinking, with each word, of Farida. Her cool, even responses, no matter how nonsensical the question. And these queries *were* inane, on

and on, almost as ridiculous as those during the endless questionings following the attack. Was she getting counseling? Of course. Liv saw no
point in mentioning that she'd terminated the sessions. What would she
do now? Go back to her old job, of course. If they'd have her. A bit of a
joke, as much humor as she could tastefully inject. The college had con-
tacted her almost immediately, panting at the opportunity for such public
magnanimity after the death of one of its own and the grievous injury
of another. Liv would work toward her doctorate while teaching courses
on the lives of women in war zones, a plan arranged after she reminded
Clayton Williams—that idiotic Gray Man, his newly panicked demeanor
at odds with the contrived blandness—that her husband, not she, had
signed the confidentiality agreement.

How did it feel to be back on American soil? The hot showers were
divine. Liv wondered if she'd gone too far. Even though it was the truth.

"Would you go back? To Afghanistan? Would you go?"

The question rose above the shouted incoherence of the others. Liv
searched for its origin. There, in front, stood a woman younger than the
others, hair spiked like her own, eyes that saw through her. The others
had pasted expressions of sympathy on their faces. This woman's whole
demeanor called bullshit. Would she go back? A gauntlet thrown down.

Liv looked over the heads of the crowd. The accordion divider in the
agency conference room blurred. She saw the peaks of the Hindu Kush,
the mud houses in the city below. The people staggering with their loads
of bricks, or of household belongings as they fled yet another conflict,
bent beneath the weight of decades, of whole centuries, of war. Saw the
way they shrugged aside those burdens, stood straight and defiant, secure
in their certainty that although they as individuals might not survive,
their people would. Saw the women. The women.

The room went silent, an alertness mirroring Liv's own. Fingers
twitched above shutter releases. Scent of blood.

"Ms. Laurensen." The woman in the front row knew she'd hit home.
She launched another body blow. "Do you hate her? The woman whose
husband killed yours?"

Liv remembered the way Farida twined their fingers together before a particularly difficult interview. How, that day in the market, she'd pulled Liv to safety, screaming imprecations at the wolf pack of men. The mingled shame and fury on her face when Liv had discovered her in Martin's arms. The same fury Liv herself had felt. But not for Farida. Never for Farida.

"You play a role," Farida had said to her. "You learn to lie. You become stone. You become ice."

Liv let the cold seep into her. "I hate anyone who kills innocent people. Or who stands by while they suffer."

The woman lifted her hand for yet another question. The agent beside Liv stepped forward. "That's all for today. Mrs. Stoellner—ah, Ms. Laurensen—still tires easily. Let's let her heal."

A chorus of shouted "thank-yous" sounded. The veneer of politesse. Not from Liv's interrogator, though. She tipped her head in a nod toward Liv. This round to you, she seemed to say. For now.

Liv turned away. *You are stone. You are ice. This begins now.*

ACKNOWLEDGMENTS

So very many people to thank.

Agent Richard Curtis and Atria editor Loan Le, who saw the book that lay within the pages of my manuscript, and Judy Sternlight of Judy Sternlight Literary Services for helping me get that manuscript to the place that caught their attention.

The team at Simon & Schuster/Atria—publisher Judith Curr, associate publisher Suzanne Donahue, subrights director Lisa Keim, art director Albert Tang, art designer Patti Ratchford, production editor Steve Breslin, copy editor Cynthia Merman, and interior designer Amy Trombat.

The *Denver Post*, whose editors in the terrible days after 9/11 sent teams of reporters and photojournalists to the places that had spawned the attacks. Still can't believe they fell for the memo that aimed to prove I could handle myself in Afghanistan.

Daler Rahkimov and Mirwais Mohmand, whose work as interpreters helped reveal the subtleties in the situations we encountered, and whose friendship eased the stress of those days. Special thanks to Ayaz and Shabab Naqvi and their family, who became dear friends.

Deborah Kruger, whose 360 Xochi Quetzal residency on the shores of Lake Chapala in Jalisco, Mexico, provided a precious month to give this book one last shot.

Two critique groups: the Badass Women's Writers—Theresa Alan,

Andrea Catalano, Orly Konig Lopez, Kate Moretti, Ella Olsen, Jamie Raintree, and Aimie Trumbly Runyan—and Creel: Stephen Paul Dark, Matthew LaPlante, Camilla Mortensen, Bill Oram, and Alex Sakariassen. Each supplied in equal measure suggestions that bettered the book, and support during the days of doubt.

Kathy Best, for key scheduling help for writing.

Tears-in-my-eyes gratitude to Scott, who from the first believed.

And finally and most especially to Razia and her daughters Rahima and Hakima.

ABOUT THE AUTHOR

Gwen Florio grew up in a 250-year-old brick farmhouse on a wildlife refuge in Delaware, with a sweeping view across tide marsh to the waters of the Delaware Bay. The University of Delaware launched her on an award-winning journalism career, with stories ranging from the shooting at Columbine High School to the glitz of the Miss America pageant and the more practical Miss Navajo contest, whose participants slaughter and cook a sheep. She has reported from Afghanistan, Iraq, and Somalia, as well as Lost Springs, Wyoming (population three).

In 2013, she turned to fiction with the publication of *Montana*, which won the High Plains Book Award and the Pinckley Prize for debut crime fiction. Four books in the Lola Wicks mystery series—termed "gutsy" by the *New York Times*—have followed so far.

About Montana—the state, that is. Florio finally rediscovered those long sight lines she fell in love with back in Delaware, the difference being that instead of tide marsh bordered by bay, Montana features prairie edged by mountain and sky. She lives in the university town of Missoula with her partner, Scott, and an exuberant bird dog named Nell, in the shadow of Mount Jumbo, with only the occasional backyard bear.